KU-218-746

Pelican Books
From Woman to Woman

Currently in private practice in her native San
Francisco, Lucienne Lanson graduated in Arts from
the University of California in Berkeley and joined the
United States Army, where she was trained and
served as a physical therapist in the Women's Medical
Specialist Corps. Dr Lanson received her M.D. from
the Medical College of Pennsylvania and completed a
one-year internship before returning to Pennsylvania
to complete a four-year residency in Obstetrics and
Gynaecology. While a resident, she was awarded a
Fellowship by the American Cancer Society and
helped in the establishment of a female pelvic cancer
screening clinic. Before returning to the West Coast
and entering private practice, she was a clinical
instructor for two years at the medical school from
which she graduated and also worked as a visiting
gynaecologist in Ceylon and Ethiopia. Dr Lanson is a
diplomate of the American Board of Obstetrics and
Gynaecology and a Fellow of the American College of
Obstetricians and Gynaecologists.

LUCIENNE LANSON

From Woman to Woman

A Gynaecologist Answers Questions About
You and Your Body

Illustrations by Anita Karl

Penguin Books

Penguin Books Ltd, Harmondsworth,
Middlesex, England
Penguin Books,
625 Madison Avenue, New York, New York 10022, U.S.A.
Penguin Books Australia Ltd, Ringwood,
Victoria, Australia
Penguin Books Canada Ltd, 2801 John Street,
Markham, Ontario, Canada L3R 1B4
Penguin Books (N.Z.) Ltd, 182–190 Wairau Road,
Auckland 10, New Zealand

First published by Alfred A. Knopf 1975
This revised edition published in Pelican Books 1977
Reprinted 1978

Made and printed in Great Britain by
Richard Clay (The Chaucer Press) Ltd
Bungay, Suffolk
Set in Monotype Ehrhardt

Contents

6 Contents

Acknowledgements

Behind every non-fiction work, which by necessity relies heavily on the accumulation of facts and research data from multiple sources, there are many unseen and unsung contributors. And yet for me, there have been a handful of individuals without whose help and encouragement this work would surely have faltered.

I am particularly indebted to Jacqueline Idiart, who with persistence and patience devoted long hours and countless evenings in helping revise and polish the entire manuscript word by word. Moreover, the fact that by profession she is an educator and not medically oriented made her eminently suited to the task. For until every phrase and sentence rang with clarity to her non-medical ears, it had to be revised, and then revised again.

Several friends also were of inestimable value. Peggy Emrey, a nurse–midwife, Dr Marie B. Webster, Dr Martha Biemuller, Dr Anne Pike, and my associate in obstetrics and gynaecology, Dr Beth L. Reimer, were each gracious enough to review the manuscript and offer constructive ideas and objective appraisa regarding the handling of material. But to Dr Beth L. Reimer I owe a special note of gratitude for cheerfully managing our entire practice single-handed during the many long months it took me to complete the book.

My special thanks also go to Nancy Nicholas, my editor at Knopf, for her astute and invaluable suggestions which helped me over some difficult hurdles. I also want to thank Robert J. Donohue, who helped check the manuscript, and Darlene Choy for her assistance with the illustrations.

And lastly, a special tribute to Anna Lanson, the grand lady of the San Francisco French newspaper *Le Californien*, whose spirited support and continuing encouragement made it all possible.

Introduction

From current articles and books, it is apparent that some women are disenchanted with modern medical practices and with gynaecologists in particular. Condescending and judgemental attitudes by doctors and a reluctance to explain, discuss or present possible alternative treatments in plain language are but a few complaints voiced by these women. I can appreciate some of these sentiments, for I too, before I became a medical student, felt the same frustration in being unable to communicate properly with my doctor. Questions that I posed were not always answered to my satisfaction. Attempts to supplement my meagre knowledge of female problems met with little success, for in those days there were no books available for the laywoman.

Moreover, during my thirteen years of college, medical school, and specialist training in obstetrics and gynaecology, the situation remained essentially unchanged. All in-depth information concerning female problems was still securely encased in ponderous volumes of multi-syllabic medical texts and gynaecological journals generally unavailable to the public. Oh yes, there were books for laywomen on pregnancy, childbirth and breast feeding, some of them quite excellent, but what about all the other problems that relate specifically to women?

It became increasingly clear to me as I practised gynaecology that women wanted and needed just this type of information. They also deserved more than a superficial explanation or some mollifying mumbo-jumbo. How can a woman expect to participate in making decisions concerning her health unless she herself is better informed? Without some basic understanding of how her body functions, can she even begin to ask pertinent questions regarding her particular condition, let alone discuss which is the best possible alternative treatment for her?

In many cases doctors are taking the time to explain the reasons for a particular procedure or the need for a specific medication. This is as it should be, for if treatment is to be successful, the close cooperation of an informed patient is essential. But can women reasonably expect their frequently overworked doctors also to assume the sole responsibility for educating them in the complexities of anatomy and physiology?

The more I thought about it, the more I reasoned that among the five hundred or so active women physicians certified by the American Board of Obstetrics and Gynecology, one of us should write an honest and factual book for our sisters – a book that would not consider women or their problems solely from the standpoint of their ability to procreate, but rather a book that would encompass the multiple other physical concerns of women.

This book is written for *all* women regardless of age, social position, educational level or sexual inclination. It is not a substitute for the advice of a trusted physician, nor is it a do-it-yourself text in diagnosis and treatment. Rather, it is a foundation towards a better understanding of yourself and your physical problems as a woman. You will become aware of what's really normal, how and why certain things happen, and when to seek help. Many of the questions posed are taken directly from patients during the privacy of the gynaecological examination. They are important questions that need frank answers. For example, what can be done about an unaccommodating vaginal opening or the opposite problem – just too much room? Can certain pelvic exercises really improve your sex life? How can crash diets or being overweight affect your menstrual cycle? If you think that your problem is unique, you will undoubtedly be consoled to know that it is shared by many other women.

In addition to basic information, I have also tried to include the latest developments in the field of gynaecology as reported in current medical journals and gleaned from specialist meetings. In fact, it may well be years before some of this information finds its way into standard medical texts. The greatest challenge to me, however, was attempting to cover various topics with sufficient depth and clarity so that they would be meaningful to all women irrespective of any previous medical knowledge. Some of you may object to my not including obstetrical care or problems specifically related to childbirth, but there are authoritative, readable works in these areas. Furthermore, to have included these topics with any degree of thoroughness and without immeasurably expanding the book would have been at the expense of other vital issues hitherto overlooked and ignored.

By virtue of the subject matter presented here, certain chapters dealing with relatively minor and benign problems will be written in a lighter vein; others will require more serious contemplation because they include problems that may threaten our very lives. This book is not written to offend or shock any of you. It is written from the heart, for I too am a woman and heir to all the problems of women.

November 1974

Part 1

The Workings of the Inner Woman

1. All is Not Vanity

We know more about sex, sensuality and orgasm than any previous generation; yet, despite this vast array of available information, it is the exceptional woman who is well informed about keeping her female organs functioning with 'all systems go'. Whether she left school at fifteen or has a degree in biochemistry, the average woman consulting her doctor is as enlightened about the workings of her own body as she is about the intricacies of the second-stage rocket blast-off. But is she really to blame for this lack of knowledge when there are almost no readable, authoritative and readily understandable sources to which she can turn for help?

It is little wonder, therefore, that to the average woman the pelvic examination remains a mysterious ritual, her hormones and menstrual irregularities an enigma, and a negative cervical smear obvious proof that she's free of pelvic cancer.

Each year women spend millions of dollars on cosmetics, fad diets and weekly appointments with their favourite hairdresser – for their external beautification. The media are crammed with advice that could be lumped together in one slogan, 'How to succeed in the sex game by making the most of the natural you.' But just how sensuous can you be with an irritated vulva or a distracting vaginal discharge? And how romantic can an older woman feel if she is constantly seized with devastating hot flushes that send her scurrying for the nearest window?

It is the rare woman who will never need counsel regarding some female problem. Whether she be heterosexual, homosexual, bisexual or asexual, no woman can escape or deny the existence of her female organs. No matter what her sexual preference, it is imperative that this portion of her body be kept in optimal health if she is to function effectively as a woman and as an individual.

Psychology has demonstrated the power of the mind over our physical well-being, and the converse is also true. How much peace of mind can a woman have if she suddenly discovers a breast lump and chooses to ignore it? Is it possible for a school-girl to have mental equanimity if her period is two weeks late and she fears a possible pregnancy? What about the oestrogen-deprived woman who, because of vaginal atrophy and in-creasingly painful intercourse, begins to avoid all intimacies with her husband? Can she honestly persuade herself that her be-haviour will not adversely affect their marital relationship? At best, it would be difficult for any of these women to continue functioning effectively when a portion of their mind is con-sumed with fear, uncertainty and worry.

There are those of you who go regularly to a doctor, clinic or private gynaecologist. You are to be commended. Others of you assiduously avoid all medical attention as long as you are feeling well. And still others immediately phone for an emergency appointment for the most fleeting twinge of physical discomfort. But there is another group, and one far larger than I care to con-template. It is you who wait and watch, hoping that time will solve your problem. 'Surely,' you say, 'if that irregular bleeding or that breast lump is nothing serious, there's no reason to be examined.' And as long as you don't know for sure, you needn't worry – but alas, you do worry.

Being a gynaecologist as well as a woman, I can readily empa-thize and understand. I have seen some of my closest friends go through mental agonies with problems that could have been re-solved easily and quickly. Other problems require longer treat-ment and management. But there are few afflictions, diseases or abnormalities of the female organs that do not have satisfactory solutions provided you seek help.

And so this book is written for all of you, whether you are now in perfect or less than perfect health. But regardless of the prob-lem you may now have, or the problems that may arise in the future, there is an answer, there is a solution.

2. What You Have and What It's There For

If you are like many women, your pubic area is a mysterious region exposed to a doctor with understandable reluctance. For lack of a better name, it has been tagged any number of things, but the term 'privates' is by far the most descriptive. In fact, the pubic area is so private that few women really know what's there. Detailed and easily understood descriptions are still not readily available. And probably, if you are now over thirty, sex and genitals were hardly topics for dinner conversation nor part of the school curriculum during your formative years.

So here we are, mature women, still referring to our pubic area and genital organs as though we were talking about some uncharted southern land mass. But all that is going to change – at least, I hope so. No, you are not going to become a specialist in female anatomy, but as long as that 5 per cent of your body is so vitally important (and who can deny that?), why not find out something about it? That's what this chapter is about.

Are you ready to look?

If you have never really examined yourself 'down below', get a large mirror, preferably one that magnifies, and a lamp with a 100-watt bulb. Make sure you are all alone and lock the door.

Ready? For a warm-up exercise, strip from the waist down and stand facing a full-length mirror. You will immediately notice a triangular area covered with hair – the mons veneris (mountain of Venus), or just mons for short. The mons is the pad of fatty tissue covering the pubic bone in women. By pressing against that fat pad you can easily verify the presence of the underlying pubic bone. Since in the mature female the mons is always covered with hair, let's take a closer look at that.

What's pubic hair like?

Through casual observation you may also have noticed that your pubic hair tends to be crisp, coarse and curly. Just how thick and how curly depends not only on your hormones but on your racial and genetic background. Even if you have hair marching up to the navel and creeping around the inside of the thighs, that too can be perfectly normal. In this case, your ancestors may have roamed the shores of the Mediterranean. In contrast, Oriental women tend to have less curly and sparser pubic hair. That also is normal.

Does pubic hair serve any function?

Yes. During sexual excitement, the secretions of certain apocrine (scent) glands located in the pubic as well as axillary (armpit) areas emit a characteristic odour erotically stimulating to the male. Thus, these tufts of hair act as scent traps, thereby permitting the aroma to linger by delaying the evaporation of these glandular secretions.

How do hormones affect pubic hair?

The appearance of pubic hair at the time of puberty depends upon the increased output of two hormones. Oestrogen from the ovaries and androgens from the adrenals are responsible for that almost overnight transformation.

After the menopausal years, as oestrogen levels gradually decrease, there will be other changes, albeit more gradual. In women past the age of sixty, for example, pubic hair frequently thins out and becomes straighter.

Does pubic hair turn grey?

Yes, but unlike scalp hair, pubic hair will usually retain its original colour well past the menopause.

But let's move on to more important matters.

What exactly are the privates?

In order to proceed, get a nice soft rug or mat and sit down. Bend your knees and spread them apart so that you now have an

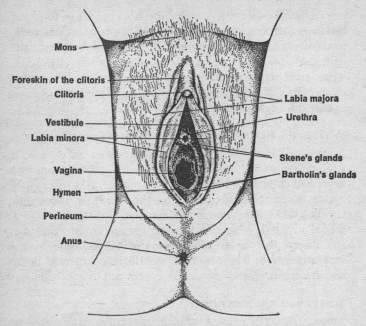

Mons

Foreskin of the clitoris

Clitoris

Vestibule

Labia minora

Vagina

Hymen

Perineum

Anus

Labia majora

Urethra

Skene's glands

Bartholin's glands

1. *Vulva. External genitalia of the female*

unobstructed view of the pubic area. Switch on the 100-watt bulb and focus the mirror.

For practical purposes, the entire area between the legs with the exception of the anus is called the vulva. (See Figure 1.) In other words, the vulva represents your 'privates' or external genitalia, and like your face, the vulva contains certain structures that you are about to identify. By the end of this section you should be able to recognize each part as easily as you can point to your nose, eyes, and mouth.

Did you know that your vulva has lips?

As you track the mons downwards towards the anus, you will notice that the area covered with pubic hair divides and continues on either side for 3–4 inches (7·5–10 centimetres). That hairy area on either side is called the labia majora or the outer lips (or sometimes the big lips). In addition to being somewhat pigmented and well endowed with fatty tissue, sweat glands and hair, the labia majora are also rich in sebaceous (oil) glands. Thus, such common problems as infected hair follicles, sebaceous cysts and other skin troubles can occur there just as easily as they can anywhere else.

What is the function of the labia majora (outer lips)?

Protection – in the form of two plushy pillows cushioning the vital structures and keeping the inner area moist. If you have never had children, your labia majora may actually meet in the middle, forming a soft covering for the area lying underneath. On the other hand, some of you may notice that everything is, indeed, exposed. Whichever the case, spread the outer lips apart and observe that the area in between is hairless, including the inner edges of the labia majora. Why? Because the tissues in this area are highly specialized and do not contain hair follicles.

What about the inner lips?

Running along the inner edge of the labia majora are two elongated ridges or folds of tissue called the labia minora, or the inner or small lips. Not uncommonly, though, the inner lips are not really that small. In fact in some women they can be quite outstanding – even protruding beyond the outer lips. Not only can they vary in size, but the labia minora can also vary widely in colour and texture – from light pink to brownish black, from fairly smooth to downright wrinkled.

What makes the labia minora so different from the labia majora?

In addition to being obviously devoid of hair, the labia minora have no fatty tissue or sweat glands. On the plus side, they are rich in sebaceous (oil) glands, apocrine (scent) glands, blood vessels, and elastic tissue. The presence of this elastic tissue, together with their intimate association with the clitoris, make the labia minora a sexy part of your anatomy.

How sexy?

Very sexy. The labia minora not only fuse together just below the mons, but also surround the clitoris to form its foreskin (prepuce). An extensive network of sensory fibres makes the clitoris and labia minora exquisitely sensitive to stimulation.

To make certain that you have actually identified the labia minora, trace them to the point where they join together and surround the clitoris just below the mons. Although most of the clitoris is actually hidden from view beneath muscle and fibrous tissue, its tip or glans can be seen as a small pink fleshy projection (about the size of an eraser on the end of a pencil).

You still can't find the clitoris? Hmm. Press gently where you think the clitoris might be and you will notice a pleasant sensation. Continue to prod this area gently and you may experience a mounting excitement. That is the clitoris.

Where to now?

Trace the labia minora downward towards and beyond the vaginal introitus (opening). Here you will notice that the labia minora disappear between the vagina and anus.

If you have successfully identified all the above structures, you are now ready to proceed to the inner inner area.

What is the inner area?

An area known as the vestibule, which is lined with mucous membrane and surrounded by the labia minora (inner lips). Within the vestibule are two openings, the vagina and the urethra (the opening through which you urinate).

Are you sure you know where the urethra is?

Easy you say? You may think so – yet how many times when asked to collect a urine specimen have your efforts ended with a wet hand, a puddle on the floor or an empty bottle? Finding the urethra may at times be difficult, unless yours is the obvious pouting type. Just remember that although the urethra lies between the clitoris and the vagina, it is always much closer to the vagina.

To locate the urethra, start again from the clitoris and work your way down toward the vagina very slowly. If you stay dead centre, the first dimpled area that appears is the urethra. But it is very important to stay exactly in the middle, otherwise you might mistake those little niches (Skene's ducts) on either side of the urethra for the real thing. If you still have any doubts about the exact location of the urethra, better run the 'urine test'.

What is the 'urine test'?

This examination is best done in a slightly stooped position in the bath or the shower; be sure to take your mirror with you. Focus the mirror and, while holding it in one hand, spread the labia minora with the other hand and urinate. If you keep a sharp eye, you will learn three things: (1) the exact location of the urethra, (2) one of the functions of the labia is to help direct urine in a steady stream, for you may have noticed that with the lips apart you were spraying, and (3) urine does not harm mirrors.

Now that you have satisfactorily identified the urethral opening, let's examine the entrance to the vaginal canal, also known as the vaginal introitus.

What's at the vaginal introitus?

This may come as a surprise, but all of you, regardless of whether or not you are virgins, still have a hymen. The hymen is nothing more than a semicircular strip of mucous-membrane tissue lying across the lower portion of the vaginal opening. It is either quite obvious or hardly apparent, and if you cannot identify it, don't worry. The presence of an intact hymen is *not* equated with virginity, nor is its absence definite proof that you have been sexually initiated. Some women, especially those who have had children, may notice delicate little irregular fringes of tissue across the lower portion of the vagina. These tattered remains of the hymenal ring are of no importance, but on occasion some women may mistake them for small growths.

Can the hymen ever interfere with intercourse?

Since the hymen usually stretches easily and normally covers only a small part of the vaginal opening, it seldom interferes with sexual intercourse even the first time. On very rare occasions, however, the hymen may block the entire vaginal opening; this is called an imperforate hymen. Under these circumstances, normal intercourse would not be possible. But because an imperforate hymen would also trap menstrual blood within the vaginal canal, the apparent lack of menstruation in an otherwise well-developed girl would invariably lead to early diagnosis. This condition is corrected by minor surgery: removal of the hymen (hymenectomy) or opening it by cutting (hymenotomy).

Are you ready for the vaginal plunge?

If you have never examined your vagina, now is the time to become familiar with this truly amazing structure. There is nothing perverted or dangerous about exploring the inner vaginal area.

Like the other genital organs, the vagina develops and ripens under the influence of oestrogen hormones. From a small, thin-walled, fragile structure in childhood, the vagina becomes transformed into a succulent, stretchable passageway some 3–5 inches (7·5–12·5 centimetres) long and wide enough to accommodate three or more fingers. During sexual excitement, it can extend an additional 2 inches (5 centimetres) in length and measure up to 2 inches (5 centimetres) in diameter. And, at the time of delivery, it can dilate to a full 5 inches (12·5 centimetres) across to accommodate the passage of the baby.

As you can see, inserting two fingers into the vagina for this examination should not cause any discomfort. Nor is it necessary for you to wear a rubber glove. If you are right-handed, the examination can be made easier by placing your left foot on a small stool or step; if you are left-handed, just reverse the position. If you need lubrication, almost anything will do – baby oil, petroleum jelly (Vaseline), cold cream or even water.

So lubricate the index and middle fingers and gently insert

them through the vaginal opening. Or if you prefer, just one finger will suffice.

How does the inside of the vagina feel?

If this is the first time you are exploring your vagina, your initial impression may well be that everything feels 'squishy'. Perfectly normal; carry on. Sweep your fingers around the walls and feel how pliant and stretchable they are. Continue to probe as far back into the vagina as you can. You will notice that for all practical purposes the far end seems to be closed. This means that it is impossible for such items as tampons, diaphragms, and the like to get lost 'up inside'. In other words, with no place to go, all such items will remain in the vagina until removed or expelled.

If you press upward against the roof of the vagina, you may feel the urge to urinate. Some of you may have already experienced this temporary sensation while inserting a fresh tampon.

Why does pressure against the roof of the vagina make you want to urinate?

Because you are also exerting pressure on the bladder. Think of the vagina as occupying the middle floor of a three-storey building, with the bladder occupying the top floor and the rectum occupying the ground floor. Thus, the floor of the bladder lies against the ceiling of the vagina, and the floor of the vagina lies against the ceiling of the rectum. (See Figure 2.) Since the tissues separating the vagina and the bladder are only a fraction of an inch thick, any pressure exerted against the ceiling of the vagina will be automatically transmitted to the nearby bladder.

What is located at the far end of the vagina?

The cervix. Projecting an inch or so (2–3 centimetres) into the far end of the vagina is the lower portion of the womb, which is called the cervix, or sometimes the mouth or neck of the womb. Those of you who have had a complete hysterectomy (removal of the entire womb) will notice, of course, that the cervix is

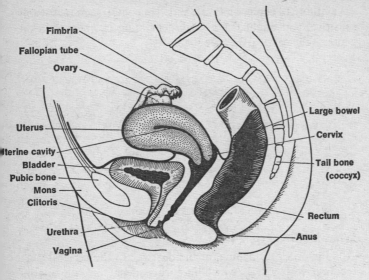

2. *Side view of the female pelvis with organs in their normal anatomical position*

missing. In this case the upper end of the vagina is simply sealed and closed.

Otherwise the easiest way to feel the cervix is to bend slightly forward and insert your fingers as far back as possible. If your fingers are somewhat short, straining or bearing down as during defecation will make the cervix more readily accessible by displacing it slightly downward.

What does the cervix feel like?

Somewhat similar to a rounded cabinet knob about 1–2 inches (2·5–5 centimetres) across and about as firm as the end of your nose. If you have located the cervix, push it around a bit. You will notice that instead of being a rigid immovable object, the cervix actually has some give to it. That is as it should be, because the body of the uterus and its cervix are partially supported and suspended by ligaments, or bands, that stretch.

Continue to explore its surface. If your fingers are reasonably sensitive, you might feel a small depression or opening in the centre – the cervical os. (See Figure 3.)

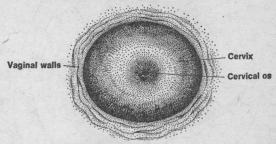

Vaginal walls

Cervix

Cervical os

3. *Normal cervix as viewed during a pelvic examination*

What is the cervical os?

It is the cervical opening, or the doorway to the cervical canal (endocervical canal), which in turn widens into the uterine cavity. The cervical os is as big around as the head of a kitchen match, but through this portal the world's greatest people have passed. If you have ever given birth, it is that little cervical os, that matchhead opening together with its canal, that stretches and dilates to let the baby out. When the doctor or midwife announces, '4 fingers' or, 'you can push now', this means that the os and its canal are completely dilated, that is, open to their maximum capacity.

In the nonpregnant woman, the cervical canal is the route for sperm as they swim upward from the vagina to meet the egg, as well as the passageway for menstrual discharge as it trickles down from the cavity of the womb into the vagina.

But enough self-exploration. You have done well to come along this far, so relax and settle back as we proceed upward and take a closer look at the womb (uterus).

What about the uterus?

Although the fertile valley between the Tigris and Euphrates is regarded by some historians as the cradle of civilization, we women know better. The real cradle is the uterus. Just how far do you think civilization would have come without the uterine cradle? (See Figure 4.)

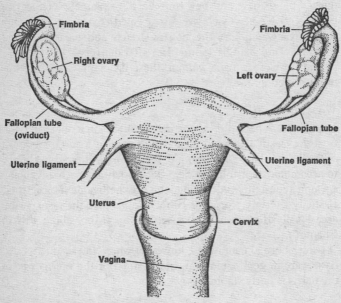

4. *Front view of the womb*

What makes the uterus such a remarkable cradle?

S-T-R-E-T-C-H-A-B-I-L-I-T-Y to accommodate pregnancy. Without a doubt the uterus is one of the most fantastic organs in the body. Doctors can transplant kidneys, hearts, and even lungs, but have they ever transplanted a uterus successfully? Not yet, but they are working on it.

From the size of a small pear, the uterus can blow up to bigger than a water melon and then revert to the size of a respectable pear in short order. In the nonpregnant state the uterine cavity would barely hold a teaspoon of water, and yet nine months later, it can accommodate a 9-pound (4-kilogram) baby, a 1-pound (0·45-kilogram) placenta (afterbirth) and some 3 pints (1·8 litres) of amniotic fluid.

Not only do the muscle fibres of the uterus stretch and thicken during pregnancy but new muscle fibres, elastic connective tissue, and blood vessels are also formed. Even the ligaments that partially support the uterus stretch and enlarge during pregnancy and snap back into place after delivery.

And, in nonpregnant women, those ligaments serve another useful function.

What function?

In addition to partially supporting the uterus in its normal position, the elastic ligaments also give the uterus a certain amount of flexibility. Thus, for example, the uterus will bend backward to accommodate a full bladder. But sometimes with advancing age and repeated childbearing, the uterine ligaments lose their elasticity the way worn-out rubber bands lose their snap, and occasionally the uterus may start to sag. (More about this in Chapter 13.)

Under normal conditions, however, where the ligaments and tissues are in good condition, the position of the uterus within the pelvis is fairly stable.

What is the normal position of the uterus?

Most women have what is called an anteflexed uterus. This means that the uterus is tilted forward forming a right angle to the vagina. In this position the uterus normally rests on top of the bladder. (See Figure 5.) To visualize this, imagine that the inside of your forearm is the vagina and the palm of your hand is the front of the uterus. Now flex your wrist forward ninety degrees. Your palm will be at right angles to your forearm just the way the uterus is at right angles to the vagina.

In some women the reverse is true. The uterus is retroflexed, or tilted backward. (See Figure 6.) Using the same example, extend your wrist back. There will be an angle between the uterus and vagina, but now the uterus is bent in the opposite direction, or towards the rectum. That retroflexed position occurs in about one out of five women. Rarely does a normal retroflexed uterus cause backaches or decrease a woman's chances of becoming pregnant. Therefore, if you have been relying on that tipped uterus to keep you from getting pregnant, better read Chapter 16 immediately!

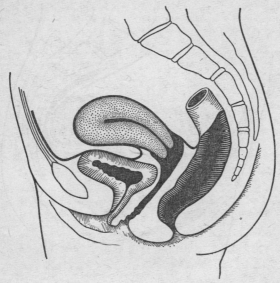

5. *Anteflexed womb. Notice how the body of the womb overlies the bladder*

How large is the uterine cavity?

In the nonpregnant woman, the uterine cavity is hardly more than a triangular slit, with its widest point no bigger than a thumbnail. It is continuous with the cervical canal below and with the two minute openings of the Fallopian tubes above. (See Figure 7.) When you menstruate, it is the lining of this small cavity that is shed to produce the bloody discharge. During the intervening three to four weeks, the lining is rebuilt and the whole process repeats itself. The menstrual flow, which consists of blood, cellular debris and mucus, comes entirely from the breakdown of the tissue lining the uterine cavity. Contrary to what some people think, no blood comes down from either the tubes or the ovaries.

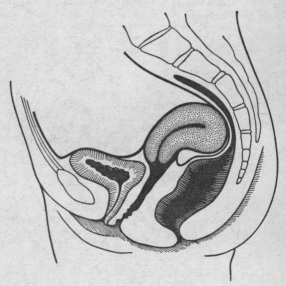

6. *Retroflexed womb. Notice how the womb is tilted back towards the rectum*

What makes the uterus as big as a pear if the cavity is so small?
Muscles, thick heavily muscled walls, comprise about 90 per cent of the uterus. And attached to either side of the uterus near the top are the delicate Fallopian tubes.

What purpose do the Fallopian tubes serve?
It is the place where the egg and the sperm meet.

How big are the Fallopian tubes?

Each of the inner tubal passageways is only slightly bigger than a bristle on a hairbrush. Outwardly, however, muscular elastic walls make each tube as thick around as a drinking straw. These relatively thick elastic walls are necessary to maintain the flexibility of the tubes, as well as to protect the delicate inner passageways. The length of each tube is about 4–5 inches (10–12·5 centimetres).

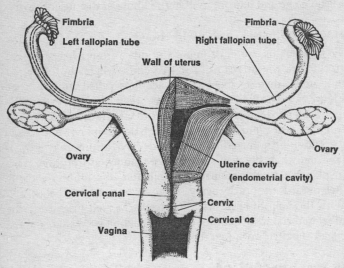

Fimbria — Left fallopian tube — Fimbria — Right fallopian tube — Wall of uterus — Ovary — Ovary — Uterine cavity (endometrial cavity) — Cervical canal — Cervix — Cervical os — Vagina

7. *Back view of the womb showing the uterine cavity. Notice how it is continuous with the cervical canal below and with the two minute openings of the Fallopian tubes above*

What other function do the tubes serve?

In addition to being the meeting place for the sperm and the egg, the tubes are actually responsible for the survival and maintenance of the fertilized egg during the three days it takes it to reach the uterine cavity.

Why are the tubes so vital for the survival of the fertilized egg?

Would you be able to drive from Glasgow to London without stopping for a bite to eat? Of course not, and neither can the fertilized egg travel the 4 inches (10 centimetres) of tube in three days without nourishment. This makes the highly specialized cells along the tubal passageway essential for the survival and growth of the fertilized egg. For when the fertilized egg arrives at its destination, it must be sufficiently mature and robust to dig a little niche and implant itself in the lining of the uterine cavity.

How does the egg get into the tube?

To answer this, we must follow the tubes from where they are attached to the uterus to their free ends, where they flare out into small, delicate fingerlike projections called fimbria. (See Figure 7.) The fimbria, though less than an inch (2·5 centimetres) long, are absolutely vital to the safe transport of the egg from the ovary into the tube. Through some unknown mechanism, these little fingerlike projections have an uncanny way of knowing when the egg is about to be launched from the ovary (ovulation). At the moment of ovulation, the fimbria actually inch towards the nearby ovary and hover over it like a helicopter. With the help of specialized hair cells (located just inside the tubal fimbria) which beat in unison, a suction is created, and the egg is literally drawn into the tube.

In what part of the tube is the egg fertilized?

If conditions are favourable, as soon as the egg enters the tube, it finds itself surrounded by those long-distance swimmers, the sperm. It is here in the last 2 inches (5 centimetres) of one of the Fallopian tubes, near the fimbria, that fertilization most commonly occurs.

What if you have your tubes tied?

To put it simply, each tubal passageway is cut and the ends are tied shut. The sperm can't swim up and the egg can't come down, and never the twain shall meet. No fertilization, no pregnancy. But you will still have your periods and your hormonal function just as before. (See Chapter 17.)

Women who may have had one tube surgically removed can still, of course, become pregnant as long as the remaining tube is normal.

For now, however, let's turn our attention to those stimulating and life-creating organs, the ovaries.

What about the ovaries?

As for their general size and shape, the ovaries resemble two large stewed prunes. Their colour is greyish white. They are attached to either side of the uterus by a special ligament 1–2 inches (2·5–5 centimetres) long, and actually nestle within the shadow of the tubal fimbria. The ovaries are further supported by other ligaments and surrounding tissues. Because they are suspended by these somewhat elastic ligaments, the ovaries also enjoy a certain freedom of movement. Thus at times they can shift position and lie behind rather than alongside the uterus.

What is the function of the ovaries?

Like two chemical factories they pour the ovarian hormones oestrogen and progesterone into the bloodstream, letting the rest of your body and the world know that you are, indeed, a woman. Oestrogen is the hormone responsible for giving your breasts that fullness, your hips those contours, and for changing your vagina from a fragile structure into that stretchable, succulent, moist, throbbing receptacle of love. It accounts too for the growth and nourishment of the clitoris and labia.

Some investigators also believe that oestrogen may be instrumental in the prevention or retardation of osteoporosis (softening of the bony skeleton) and hardening of the arteries. The fact that few women, compared to men of comparable age, are stricken with coronary artery disease supports the idea that oestrogen may afford built-in protection in delaying some of these degenerative processes.

Progesterone prepares the uterus for possible pregnancy by

stimulating the growth of the lining of the uterus (endometrium) so that the egg – if fertilized – may have a rich tissue bed to implant itself in securely.

What else do ovaries do?

Ovaries also make eggs (ova). How does ovulation occur? Do the ovaries take turns making eggs? How well can you function with only part of an ovary? All this and more in Chapters 5 and 6.

3. The Internal Pelvic Examination

Running a close second in popularity to the dental appointment is the gynaecological check-up. Even if you can stoically tolerate having your molars ground to a nub by the dentist, it is only the pelvic that universally evokes the cry, 'I hate this examination!' Rarely does a session pass without at least one woman expressing this sentiment. And regardless of whether she has had several pregnancies and innumerable pelvics, it is always with a deep sigh of resigned martyrdom that she gets on to the examining table and inches her hips to the edge.

What makes women dislike this examination?

Modesty for one thing. We don't usually mind exposing other parts of our anatomy for a physical examination, but when it comes to our 'private parts', that is a different story. And especially when that area is being scrutinized under a glaring 150-watt bulb – that is indeed dropping the seventh veil.

What makes some women so modest?

Conditioning during the early formative years. By virtue of our unique anatomy, we were not built to stand over public urinals and gawk at each other's genitalia, nor did we, as young girls, ever play the game: 'How big is yours?' Even in the most disreputable public facilities there is the sanctuary of a toilet complete with door.

As a result many women are modest. But it is more than modesty that makes some women cringe when the term pelvic, internal or female examination is mentioned.

What, for instance?

The possibility of offending. Regardless of how fastidious some of us are in our personal hygiene, many women would prefer taking time off from work to bathe or shower before a scheduled appointment. Although this is seldom necessary, the desire to be clean is as natural as brushing one's teeth before going to the dentist. Just make a point of not douching before a pelvic examination. More about this shortly.

Are there other disquieting things about a pelvic examination?

Yes, indeed. Whether or not we think we are in good health, there is always the concern that the doctor might find something wrong. But this somewhat uneasy feeling is a perfectly natural emotion associated with any physical examination.

For those of you who have never had a pelvic examination, there is also the fear of the unknown. What is going to happen to me? Will it hurt? Will I bleed afterward? Will I still be a virgin? If you have listened to the stories of some of your well-meaning friends, you may have built up a solid wall of resistance. Allow me to allay your fears and uncertainties as to what really takes place and why.

Will knowing more about the pelvic examination make you like it more?

Of course not. But at least it might help you to relax. You may even react like one girl after her first pelvic: 'Gee, that wasn't so bad after all.'

So who needs a pelvic?

We do, you and I. Since we were fortunate enough to have been born women, let us give ourselves every chance to live as confident, healthy women.

At what age should you have your first pelvic?

That, of course, depends on you and whether you have any problems. By the age of eighteen, however, many women may have had an examination. This can reassure most of you that you are, indeed, perfectly normal. It may also be a good opportunity to air problems (sexual or otherwise) that you may have been reluctant to discuss.

For those of you contemplating intercourse (regardless of your age or status) it can be comforting to know that you are free of any physical problems, such as a hymenal ring just a little too snug to permit easy penetration.

Is a girl ever too young to be examined?

No. There is no age limit on a thorough gynaecological examination provided that the symptoms warrant it. Although most doctors are competent in dealing with prepuberal problems, they may on occasion refer a case to a specialist adept at handling and examining young female children anywhere from infancy to early adolescence.

Specially adapted instruments make these examinations as easy as checking your child's ears or nose. So if you think that your daughter really does have a problem, do not hesitate. She is not too young.

Do you need to prepare yourself for a pelvic examination?

Not really, but knowing what to expect can certainly be helpful. For those of you making an appointment for your first gynaecological examination, a few preliminaries are in order.

When should you plan your appointment?

If you feel your problem is not urgent, arrange your appointment for between periods. Although examination is possible during menstruation, certain smear tests are less accurate when mixed with menstrual blood. However, if your problem is one of constant bleeding or spotting, do not wait for it to stop. And, if you cannot remember or do not know when your period is due, make an appointment anyway. You can always cancel if necessary.

What about douching before a pelvic examination?

Don't douche for at least twenty-four hours before a pelvic examination. And if you have an unpleasant discharge, it is especially important *not* to douche. Douching in this case would be like wiping away the fingerprints at the scene of the crime. Flushing the offending organisms down the drain would make it more difficult for your doctor to identify the culprits responsible. Bath or shower if you like, but leave the inside vaginal area undisturbed.

How about intercourse before a pelvic exam?

Perfectly all right, but make certain that you don't use any vaginal cream or lubricating jelly. These chemical substances can also interfere with certain smear tests.

How else should you prepare yourself?

If you are still having menstrual cycles, know the date of your last period. Invariably you will be asked this question. If you have trouble remembering, start now by keeping track of your periods. If your menses are completely irregular, or if you have had any unexpected spotting or bleeding, no matter how insignificant, make a note of it and bring this information with you. With regard to other health problems that may trouble you, making a list beforehand will help you to have all your questions answered.

If you are taking any prescribed medicine the doctor will surely want to know. This will prevent any possible duplication and may even alter the treatment chosen for you. If you do not know the name of the drug, bring it with you. It can usually be readily identified. For those of you taking oral-contraceptive pills, do not answer 'No', when asked if you are taking any medication. It is surprising how many women do not consider them a drug.

What is a thorough gynaecological examination?

The fact that the female organs influence other organ systems, and vice versa, makes it impossible to isolate them from the rest of the body. Whenever a problem exists in one area, it follows that other areas, as a consequence, may also be affected. So it is the responsibility of your doctor to find out if you are functioning as a total woman. Don't be surprised, therefore, if your appointment for a routine pelvic becomes a thorough physical, complete with a detailed medical history. And be prepared to answer some questions.

What kind of questions?

If yours is a routine appointment, most of the questions will seem fairly general. Really they are quite specific. In addition to the usual questions regarding menstrual cycles, pregnancies, the presence or absence of discharge, etc., your doctor may also ask for information about possible problems in other areas – bladder, bowels, heart, lungs, etc. You may wonder what all these questions have to do with a simple pelvic check, but be reassured; this shows a real interest in your well-being.

Those of you with a specific complaint may be unaware that about 85 per cent of the time, your doctor can make a fairly accurate diagnosis on history alone.

What about the physical examination?

Since you can anticipate a fairly thorough physical, you will usually be given an examining gown. You will have to remove all your clothes with the exception of your shoes, so dress simply. It is also best to empty your bladder just before a pelvic examination. But make a point of asking beforehand whether a urine specimen will be wanted. This will help avoid the frustration of trying to coax urine out of an empty bladder. Just as in any complete physical, you will be weighed and your blood pressure will be taken. In addition, a good gynaecological examination should include listening to your heart and lungs, peering down your throat, and even checking your neck for any enlarged or tender lymph nodes. If you wonder why your doctor is gently pushing against your windpipe, he is just examining your thyroid gland.

What does the thyroid do?

Think of the thyroid as your body's pace setter. If it is tuned up high, your motor will run fast; if it is sluggish, you may lack pep, energy, and may even gain weight. You are gaining weight? You think your thyroid is to blame? Probably not, but disturbances in the thyroid gland can occasionally be responsible for menstrual irregularities, which will be discussed later. (See Chapter 9.)

What about the breasts?

Since this is a unique and important area of your anatomy, the whole of Chapter 22 is devoted to breast problems. Suffice it to say for the moment, no physical is ever complete without a careful examination of both breasts.

Does your doctor examine your stomach?

Not specifically. But let us clarify the term stomach. Unless you have studied anatomy, what you commonly refer to as your stomach is in actuality your abdomen. The entire area lying between the lower ribs and the groin is known as the abdomen, of which the stomach itself constitutes only a very small part.

So what can your doctor tell by examining your abdomen?

Plenty. By just looking at the skin, for example, your doctor can usually tell if you have ever been pregnant. Most of you know about stretch marks, but even in their absence, there is frequently a faintly pigmented or darker line extending from just above the pubic hair to the navel. This darkening of the skin is caused by hormonal changes during pregnancy, and although this line will fade to a great extent, it will still be discernible to an astute observer.

More important than skin changes, however, is the presence of any enlarged organ, tumours or areas of tenderness. All these findings may be valuable clues in helping to diagnose your particular problem, if you have one. In the normal nonpregnant woman, it is virtually impossible to feel either the uterus or ovaries on abdominal examination alone. That requires a pelvic.

What happens now?

We are finally ready to lower the seventh veil for the mysteries of the pelvic examination.

In addition to the examining gown, you may be given a sheet to cover your lower abdomen and thighs. Its purpose is to preserve whatever modesty may still remain. It is not, as some of you may think, to hide what the doctor is doing.

What is the position for a pelvic?

Proper positioning and relaxation are vital for a good pelvic examination. Help yourself as well as your doctor by relaxing as you lie on your back. Let those knees spread apart comfortably and focus your thoughts on something pleasant. If your mind is at ease, tension will drain from your body. And it will be over before you know it.

What is next?

Before examining the female internal organs, your doctor will visually inspect the external genitalia, or vulva. (See Chapter 2.) All the structures from the mons to the anus are scrutinized and a general evaluation of the vulva is made.

What is the doctor looking for?

Hormonal disturbances for one thing. Is the clitoris larger than normal? Are the labia majora (outer lips) plump, plush cushions or are they thin and flattened as a result of oestrogen deficiency? And what about the pubic hair? Is it sparse and straggly or thick and luxuriant?

Anaemia, too, can sometimes be detected. In some countries the colour of the tongue is used as a rough barometer of anaemia, but frequently the vulva can serve the same purpose. Are the tissues around the vaginal opening a nice healthy pink or are they somewhat pale?

What about signs of chronic and current infection? Are the labia red, swollen, and irritated? Has the skin become thick and leatherlike from persistent scratching as a result of chronic irritation?

Are there any warts, pimples, sores, or unusual swellings? Does the vaginal opening seem well supported, or does it appear large and relaxed?

From this partial list you can appreciate the importance of simple visual inspection.

Can the doctor tell if you have ever been pregnant?

If the only pregnancy you ever had terminated in an early abortion, either spontaneous or induced, it would be almost impossible to tell for sure. The nipples may have become slightly more pigmented, but in all probability an early pregnancy loss would have left neither the stretch marks nor the dark line between the pubic hair and the navel. In addition, there would be no evidence at the perineum of stretching, tearing or an episiotomy. (See Chapter 13.) Even the cervical os, on further examination, would probably fail to show convincing proof of ever having been dilated.

Suppose you had a full-term pregnancy?

In about 95 per cent of women, that fact can usually be verified by physical examination alone.

Can the doctor tell if you are really a virgin?

Sometimes. The presence of an intact hymen does not prove or disprove virginity. With the increased use of tampons, a girl's hyman can be stretched and yet, by definition, she is still a virgin – that is, she has never had sexual intercourse.

A girl whose vaginal opening will barely admit one slender finger is in all probability a virgin, i.e. successful penetration by a penis has not been accomplished. On the other hand, there are some women who can be examined easily but who are, indeed, virgins.

The presence of an intact hymen is also no guarantee that a girl is leading a celibate life. Some girls have found themselves surprisingly pregnant in spite of a snug vaginal opening and an intact hymen. But more about these misadventures in Chapter 15.

Can the doctor tell if you masturbate?

If you are asking whether persistent stimulation causes telltale signs in the form of a more prominent clitoris and labia minora, the answer is probably yes, at least with regard to the labia minora. However, if you want to know whether your doctor can tell if you masturbate, the answer is no.

Why is the answer no?

As was mentioned in Chapter 2 the labia minora normally come in a variety of colours and textures, not to mention size. Even if you have masturbated frequently over a long period of time, unless you are a participant in a research project in which minute, exact measurements of your labial dimensions are recorded over a period of years, you can breathe easily. In fact, you should breathe easily anyway, for there is nothing perverted or abnormal about masturbation.

Is masturbation really normal?

With few exceptions, almost every individual, both male and female, has masturbated at one time or another. Masturbation will not harm you and at times may even be beneficial by allowing you to release pent-up sexual tension if the proper partner is not available. For some women, it has also been helpful in enabling them later to achieve orgasm more readily during sexual relations.

And since we are discussing sexual matters, let's bury another fairly common misconception.

Is your doctor thinking about sex because he is examining your sexual organs?

Emphatically no. And this information comes from those in the know. According to my male colleagues, the pelvic examination is as sexually exciting for them as clipping toenails is to a chiropodist. Ho hum. But let's get on with the examination.

What happens now?

After a thorough inspection of the vulva, your doctor will now focus on the vaginal entrance, or the 'vaginal introitus' as it is frequently called. In women who have had children there may be some relaxation of the vagina as well as a shortening of the distance between the vagina and anus. This area, also known as the perineum or the perineal body, is where an episiotomy (see Chapter 13) can be done just prior to delivery. Before proceeding to the inner vagina, the doctor will usually check your Bartholin's glands.

What are Bartholin's glands?

Two small mucus-producing glands located on either side of the vaginal introitus. No previous mention of them was made because under normal conditions they can neither be seen nor felt. However, by gently rolling this area between his fingers, the doctor can detect any swelling or tenderness. On occasion one of these glands can fill with mucus and form an obvious non-tender swelling known as a Bartholin's cyst. At other times a Bartholin's gland may become infected and form a painful abscess. Although they are not serious, recurrent cysts or abscesses of this type may require minor surgery to prevent future flare-ups.

What is the function of Bartholin's glands?

The mucus secretions from these glands help keep the vaginal entrance moist. It was once thought that they were solely responsible for the increased lubrication around the introitus at the time of sexual arousal. It has now been well documented that the vaginal walls are the main contributors of this lubrication. Nonfunction or removal of both Bartholin's glands, therefore, would not appreciably decrease the amount of moisture and secretion during sexual stimulation.

How is the inner vagina examined?

If this is indeed your first pelvic examination, you may well wonder at the array of cold, gleaming metal instruments. They are vaginal speculums – but don't be alarmed, they are not all intended for you. Before using a speculum to examine the inner vagina, your doctor will estimate the size of your vaginal introitus. Just as vaginal openings come in different sizes, so also do speculums – from the peanut size to the giant jumbo variety. With few exceptions there is one speculum just right for you. (See Figure 8.) No competent doctor will insert a speculum that

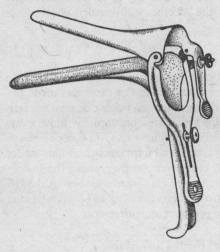

8. *Vaginal speculum*

may be uncomfortably large, and a kind-hearted doctor will usually moisten that cold metal instrument with warm water, thus making its insertion more comfortable.

What happens if your vagina is unusually small?

If there is no speculum that can be inserted without causing discomfort (a rare occurrence), then no speculum will be used. Any necessary smears or cultures can usually be taken, if absolutely necessary, by inserting a cotton-tipped applicator (similar to a Q-Tip) through the vaginal opening.

Why is the speculum usually necessary?

Because the walls of the vagina normally rest against each other, the speculum, by gently dilating the vaginal canal, allows your doctor to examine not only the vaginal walls but also the cervix.

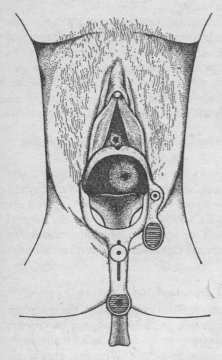

9. *Cervix and vaginal walls exposed by use of the speculum*

(See Figure 9.) Thus, the presence of any discharge, cervical infection or irritation can be readily seen.

If there is an unusual discharge, your doctor may simply examine the secretion under a microscope. If, however, you are concerned about the possibility of a gonorrheal infection, a culture will probably be taken. How this is done will be explained in Chapter 10.

What other tests is he likely to do?

A cervical smear or cancer-screening test. (See Chapter 4 for complete details.) For the time being, be reassured that the cervical smear as well as the taking of any other vaginal smear or culture is a painless procedure.

A few doctors when examining the cervix may also use a colposcope, a telescope-like instrument which magnifies the surface of the cervix. Using the colposcope allows the doctor to see the cervix in great detail and perhaps detect suspicious tissue changes. (See Chapter 23.) But this type of examination is neither routine nor generally done by most doctors. Screening for an early cancer of the cervix still relies primarily on a cervical smear.

What else can be seen besides the vaginal walls and the cervix?

If you explored your own vagina as described in Chapter 2, you know that nothing else can be seen. Not infrequently, however, a patient will ask, 'How do my fibroids look?' or 'How do my ovaries look?' It would be helpful if we could see the internal pelvic organs by means of the speculum, but unfortunately we have to rely on the bimanual examination for further information.

What is the bimanual examination?

After the necessary smears and cultures are taken, the speculum is removed and the doctor will gently insert one or two fingers into the vagina. For this purpose, he or she will usually apply lubricating jelly on the examining glove. With the other hand, the doctor will then press along the lower portion of the abdomen.

Why are two hands necessary?

The vaginal hand (one or two fingers, that is) pushes up against the cervix and stabilizes it while the abdominal hand presses downward. Thus, the womb is literally being held and examined between your doctor's two hands. The same technique is applied in feeling the ovaries. (See Figure 10.)

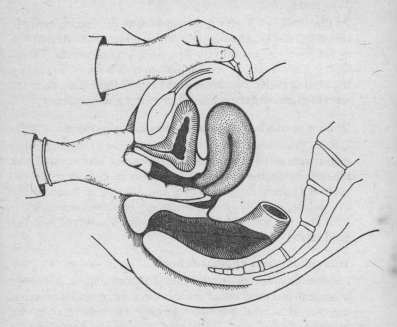

10. *Bimanual examination of the womb*

What can the doctor tell by this examination?

All about the womb for one thing. Is it normal in size and shape? Is it as movable as it should be, or is it fixed in one position because of possible scar tissue from a previous pelvic infection or some other problems?

The more at ease you are, the easier the examination and the more informative. So give your doctor a fair chance by relaxing those abdominal muscles and let your knees spread apart comfortably. The proper evaluation of the uterus also depends on your having an empty bladder. Even if you are not reminded to empty your bladder, be sure to do so before the examination.

However, the interior of the uterus (the uterine cavity) cannot be examined bimanually.

Why not?

As discussed in Chapter 2, the entrance to the uterine cavity is through the cervical opening (os), which under normal conditions is not much bigger than the head of a kitchen match. Therefore, it is not humanly possible for anybody's fingers to explore the uterine cavity. Nonetheless, as you will learn later, there are ways of examining the inside of the uterus when necessary.

What else can be felt on bimanual examination?

Usually the ovaries. They are checked for any enlargement that might represent a cyst or tumour. In women who are well past the menopause, the ovaries will frequently be difficult to feel because of a natural decrease in size. And, if a woman is excessively overweight, feeling normal ovaries may be almost impossible – somewhat like feeling for a walnut through a mattress. Another good reason for staying slim!

What about the Fallopian tubes?

Because the tubes are such soft and pliable structures, it is rarely possible to feel them under ordinary circumstances. However, in the case of a tubal pregnancy (ectopic pregnancy) or in the presence of tubal infection, the tube or tubes may be sufficiently thickened and enlarged to be palpable (capable of being felt).

So what's that finger doing in your rectum?

Since the innovation of the rubber glove, rectal examination has soared in popularity – at least for your doctor. Without a doubt, this examination is the least understood and the least appreciated judging by such common remarks as 'Is this really necessary?' or 'What on earth can you tell from that?' Although not uncomfortable, a rectal examination may give you a temporary sense of insecurity in your back passage. But no pelvic examination is really complete without a rectovaginal.

What is a rectovaginal examination?

As you learned in Chapter 2, the ovaries are fairly movable and at times may actually hide behind the uterus. When your doctor

doctor inserts his middle finger into the rectum and his index finger into the vagina, he is able to reach higher and further than by the vaginal route alone. Since the rectum is continuous with the large bowel, it is not limited in length as is the vagina. Ovaries, therefore, that may have escaped detection by the vaginal route may now be within easy reach.

Suppose the ovaries were felt by the vaginal examination, why do a rectovaginal examination?

Doing a rectovaginal examination also enables your doctor to get a better feel of the back wall of the uterus. It is also important to check the space between the vagina and rectum for any tenderness, nodules, etc.

What about the rectum itself?

In addition to the obvious presence of haemorrhoids, other growths within the rectum, such as polyps, can be readily felt. In older woman this examination is particularly important because a large number of early colon cancers first appear within 5–6 inches (12·5–15 centimetres) of the anus.

Is a vaginal examination always done?

No. In young girls or women whose vaginal opening is too small to accommodate even one finger, the digital vaginal would be bypassed in favour of a simple rectal and abdominal evaluation. Having a gynaecological examination should not cause pain or hymenal injury.

How often should you have a pelvic examination?

That depends on you and what your doctor may advise. Otherwise, it is a good idea to get yourself checked every year or so. This is especially important for those of you over forty (no matter how well you are feeling). A regular physical examination can help you to stay in top-notch shape.

4. The Cervical Smear or Cytotest

Extensive publicity may have alerted you to the importance of routine cervical smears (cytotests); other than that, little additional information has been made available to the average woman. For this reason it is not surprising that you, like so many others, know very little about the cytotest or cervical smear beyond the fact that it has something to do with early cancer detection.

About two million women are tested each year in Britain, compared with the potential seventeen million or thereabouts (women over twenty) who may be at risk from cervical cancer.

What is being done to improve these statistics?

Some general practitioners make a point of suggesting the test to women patients every two years or so, but many find the pressure of work too great to offer this kind of preventive care. In any case, your doctor would be able to tell you where you can be tested – sometimes it means going to a clinic at the hospital. Local health authorities are now establishing 'well woman' clinics where the cytotest is just part of a complete physical check-up.

Women are also being screened at family planning and antenatal clinics. Mobile cytotest clinics with a 'please walk in, no appointment needed' approach have been very successful in bringing the test to busy women at home or at work.

But well over half the tests done are on women under thirty-five, and medical authorities are all the more concerned as it is women *over* thirty-five who are more at risk.

What's so important about the cervical smear?

The cervical smear is by far the best method of detecting an early cervical malignancy. The fact that *there are absolutely no symptoms whatsoever in an early cancer of the cervix* makes this important procedure an integral part of a thorough gynaecological check-up.

What exactly is the cervical smear?

The cervical smear is a method whereby cells that are normally shed from the cervix and the uterine cavity are collected, smeared onto a glass slide, and examined under a microscope. All of you know what dry, peeling skin or dandruff is. Well, essentially the same process of shedding and regeneration of cells occurs in the vagina, cervix and lining of the uterine cavity.

What does the cervical smear really show?

Whether or not there are any abnormal or atypical changes within the cells themselves. In contrast to normal cells shed from the vaginal walls, cervix and uterine lining, malignant or cancer cells have a totally different appearance. Their nucleus or central core is frequently larger and stains a much darker colour when exposed to certain laboratory dyes. Then too, the tissue source of any suspicious cells can at times also be identified. In other words, a malignant cell shed from the cervix looks different from a malignant cell shed from the uterine lining. Needless to say, this valuable information can be of great help in pinpointing the possible location of an early cancer.

Examination of the vaginal cells in particular can also give some indication of a woman's oestrogen level. More about this shortly.

Is the smear test ever used on men?

Yes, very definitely. In fact the smear is also used for tracking down abnormal cells elsewhere in the body – for example, in the lungs and stomach. But by far its greatest clinical application is the early detection of pelvic cancer in women.

How is the cervical smear actually taken?

Studies have shown that the most accurate method of detecting early pelvic cancer depends on the sampling of cells from three areas: the secretions normally found in the upper vagina, the surface of the cervix, and the area just inside the cervical os (endocervical canal). In collecting cells from the cervix proper, most doctors will scrape the surface of the cervix with a small wooden or metal spatula. With respect to the collecting of samples from vaginal secretions and the endocervical canal, the technique may vary from doctor to doctor – a cotton-tipped applicator, a small pipette or a spatula may be used. All three samples thus collected are then separately smeared onto a glass slide. The slide is immediately sprayed with a fixative or else immersed in a solution containing a preservative. In other instances the slide is allowed to dry naturally.

Is it painful to have a cervical smear?

Emphatically no. Although your toes may curl at the thought of having your cervix scraped, the surface of the cervix is remarkably insensitive. Unless you are told that samples are being taken for a cancer test, most of you will be completely unaware of any sensation.

What happens to your cervical smear after it's been taken?

Few appreciate the intricacies involved in the processing of a single cervical smear. Along every step of the way there must be rigid and specific handling of the slide to assure maximum accuracy in its interpretation. Its accuracy depends not only upon how well the smear was taken, but also upon the proper fixation, staining and interpretation of the material.

With rare exception your smear will be sent to the cytology (cell-screening) department of a pathology laboratory. Unlike the other departments that analyse blood and urine specimens, the cytology department is devoted exclusively to the processing and microscopic examination of cellular material.

All slides after proper staining with specific dyes will be assiduously scrutinized by specially trained technicians. In addition many cytology departments employ a second team to double-check randomly selected slides that initially were labelled as normal. Any slide that is the least bit suspicious is always referred to a cytopathologist for final interpretation.

What is a cytopathologist?

A doctor who specializes in the microscopic interpretation of abnormalities in cellular material. Thus, any slide that is not completely normal is always checked by a cytopathologist. It is his or her responsibility to evaluate and classify all suspicious smears and to report the findings to your doctor. Not infrequently the cytopathologist may request a follow-up smear within three to six months for further evaluation. If for any reason a slide is technically poor and difficult to interpret, your doctor will be notified and another smear asked for.

How reliable is a cervical smear in detecting early cancer of the cervix?

If you have an early cervical cancer, you have a 95- to 100-per cent chance of having it detected by the smear test.

What about the 1 to 5 per cent that may go undetected?

In almost all such cases, studies have shown that the next smear will reveal the abnormality. Equally important and far more comforting is the fact that even if there is a one- or two-year interval between smears, the cancer, with rare exception, will still be early enough to be completely curable.

If there is an early cervical cancer, why can't your doctor see it?

Because at this stage there is nothing to see. In other words, your cervix may look completely normal and yet when those superficial cells are scraped off and examined under a microscope, they may show beginning malignant changes. That is the beauty of the smear – it arouses suspicion where there is none.

How reliable is the cervical smear in detecting other female cancers?

Although the smear is helpful in detecting cancer in other female organs, its accuracy in these instances is far less. With regard to cancer involving the lining of the uterine cavity (endometrial cancer), the accuracy of the smear can range anywhere from 40 to 85 per cent. Unlike cancer of the cervix, a malignancy involving the lining of the uterine cavity usually gives early symptoms that will alert your doctor. In these cases, therefore, other procedures will be necessary to establish a diagnosis. More about that in Chapter 23.

With regard to cancer of the Fallopian tubes or ovaries, the smear test, with rare exception, is not reliable.

Can the cervical smear be used for anything else besides cancer detection?

Yes. As you may or may not know, the cells of the vaginal walls undergo cyclic changes in response to hormone fluctuations. The examinations of smears taken from the vaginal walls may at times be helpful in assessing your oestrogen hormone level.

Because of these cyclic cellular changes, it is also important to submit with each smear such pertinent information as the woman's age, date of her last menstrual period, and current hormone therapy including the use of any birth control pill. All these factors must be considered in the proper interpretation of the smear.

If you have had a hysterectomy (removal of the uterus and cervix) is it still necessary to have a routine cervical smear?

That depends on several factors. If the reason for the hysterectomy was a malignancy involving either the cervix or the uterine cavity, then repeat smears of the upper vaginal area are necessary. In these cases the test should probably be repeated once every three months during the first year following the operation. This close follow-up with smears and periodic pelvic examinations would make for early recognition of any recurrence. Thus, appropriate therapy could be promptly instituted, if necessary.

If your hysterectomy was done because of a benign condition (noncancerous) – for example, fibroid tumours – the taking of a smear would not be essential unless your doctor were specifically interested in evaluating your oestrogen level.

For those of you who have had a partial hysterectomy (removal of the upper portion of the uterus but not the cervix), a routine smear is called for just as for other women.

How often should other women have a cervical smear?

A cervical smear every two or three years is accepted as sufficient under ordinary circumstances in Britain but I, and most other American gynaecologists, would recommend routine smears at least once a year. In the postmenopausal woman on hormone therapy, or in the woman who has a strong family history of cancer, it may be advisable to repeat smears more frequently. But here again there are no set rules. Each woman must be evaluated individually.

How is the cervical smear graded?

Before answering that question, it is important to understand that the *smear, of and by itself, does not prove or disprove the presence of cancer.* For that diagnosis, other studies are necessary. The smear, however, can alert your doctor to the fact that additional tests may be needed.

For practical purposes your smear will usually be reported as belonging to one of five classes. By and large, most smears will be reported as Class I negative. This means that all the cells surveyed were normal in every respect.

Class II is also considered negative, but in this case some of the cells showed minimal or atypical changes probably as the result of a vaginal or cervical infection – rarely because of malignancy. A Class II smear is not uncommon, and in the majority of cases it will revert to Class I on simple treatment of your particular vaginal or cervical infection. A Class II smear is therefore no cause for alarm, but it does require a follow-up smear usually within three months after completion of local therapy.

A Class III smear is questionable. It is frequently reported by the cytopathologist as being suspicious.

A Class IV smear is interpreted as positive – possible malignancy; a Class V smear is reported as positive – probable malignancy.

Cervical smears reported as positive, that is, either Class IV or Class V, always demand further diagnostic studies.

What other studies are necessary for a diagnosis of pelvic cancer?

Because this is an important subject, the discussion of how a cancer is diagnosed and treated is covered in Chapter 23.

With regard to Class III cervical smears, it is still best to proceed with the same diagnostic studies.

What percentage of women with a Class III cervical smear do have an early cervical cancer?

In most surveys, less than 20 per cent of women with a Class III smear will actually have a malignancy. However, in those women whose studies prove negative for cancer, more frequent smears would usually be advisable as an added precaution.

Is it ever possible to have a positive cervical smear and not have cancer?

It is possible, but the presence of any positive smear (Class IV or V) the burden of proof that you do not have cancer lies heavily on your doctor. He or she must be able to show beyond any doubt that you are indeed free of pelvic malignancy. All diagnostic studies would have to be completely normal and subsequent serial smears would have to revert to Class I negative. Short of this, no competent doctor would dismiss the original positive smear as being incorrect.

5. The Menstrual Cycle

Man has sounded the depths of the ocean floor and soared into outer space, and yet some of what we now accept as fact regarding the menstrual cycle is still woefully enigmatic. Even today certain aspects of the menstrual cycle are among the most controversial subjects in endocrinology. What you probably take for granted is in reality one of the most complex biochemical and psycho-physiological processes in the human body, male or female. Part of the explanation lies in man's inability, as yet, to unscramble all the infinite and wondrous workings of the human brain and mind.

What does the brain have to do with the menstrual cycle?

Everything – or almost everything. Some twenty years ago, it was generally accepted that the pituitary gland was *the* brain centre in control of ovarian function. More recent studies have shown that the pituitary gland is actually under the control of a higher brain centre, the hypothalamus. But we can't stop there. For if the truth be known, the hypothalamus is also affected by and responsive to our mental and emotional state.

Women have been known to stop menstruating spontaneously under great physical and emotional stress. Other women exposed to similar situations can run the opposite course. They can bleed continuously. And a stalwart few seem to carry on with regular periods in spite of all calamities. It is little wonder that in the whole realm of human physiology, probably no other bodily function has been the centre of such passionate oratory, violent debates, and wild theories as our monthly flow.

What wild theories?

Incredible as it may seem, menstruation in the human female was equated with the oestrus cycle of lower animals as recently as the turn of this century. In other words, most scientists at that time assumed that women, like the female dog, went into heat – except that women did it monthly instead of twice a year. There were other scientists who were equally confused. Were women like the domestic hen, capable of laying an egg every day? Or did they respond like the female rabbit, ovulating every time they had intercourse?

Fortunately for us, the work of Walter Heape early in the 1900s did much to advance the frontiers of science. Through his inspired research and liberal attitude, woman was at last elevated to the status of the monkey. It was Heape's contention that perhaps the human female, like the monkey, actually ovulated before the appearance of any menstrual discharge. Once this striking similarity between monkey and woman was confirmed, the poor rhesus monkey never knew another moment's peace. From that time on, the rhesus monkey has been one of the few mammals extensively used for studies involving the female reproductive system. Other animals also have contributed to our cause.

What other animals?

Would you believe sows and mice? In the early 1920s, while many of his less dedicated peers were dancing the Charleston, a young dynamic anatomist, Dr Edgar Allen, in conjunction with a biochemist, Edward Doisey, was on the verge of making a momentous discovery – the hormone oestrogen.

It was already a confirmed fact that each ovum (egg) within the ovary was enveloped in a small saclike structure called a follicle. However, the fluid within each follicle surrounding the ovum was not known to have any hormonal function. It was Dr Allen's theory that the follicular fluid contained a specific substance that was somehow important to the reproductive cycle. As far as he was concerned, all he had to do was to prove it. But how? His monetary resources were pathetically meagre and, besides, it was going to take hundreds of ovaries to extract even a measurable amount of this fluid. Fortunately, at long last the answer came. He would ask the Swift Packing Company to salvage ovaries from slaughtered sows. And as the story goes, on many a cold night Allen and Doisey, their arms straining from the weight of buckets brimming with pig ovaries, trudged home, grateful and triumphant.

Night after night with the help of their wives, they aspirated and collected the precious follicular fluid, later to be injected into female mice whose ovaries had previously been removed. After countless experiments, there was no longer any doubt in Allen's mind. The injection of this fluid caused specific cellular changes in the vaginal smear of the mice – changes that had previously been observed only in mature mice with two good ovaries.

But Allen's struggles were just beginning. Scientists scoffed when he presented his findings at the annual American Anatomists' meeting. Scepticism rippled through that august body, and only the few who believed that this fluid could contain a hormonal substance nodded in admiration. Others violently challenged the idea that the studies done on mice could be applied to the human female.

There was only one recourse open to Allen; he had to prove his theory by successfully repeating his experiments on – the monkey. And thus, all doubt was forever removed. Now, everyone believed.

By virtue of the work done by Allen and Doisey, as well as notable experiments by such eminent pioneers as Corner, Bartelmez, Hartman, and Markee, many of the intricacies of the menstrual cycle have gradually been revealed and understood.

What follows in the next few pages is based on the contributions of these men and our friend, the rhesus monkey. But the final story of menstrual physiology is not yet written. It is for this reason that only the most basic concepts can be presented with any degree of reliability.

Are the basic concepts regarding the menstrual cycle important to you as a woman?

More than you may now realize. Many female bleeding problems (apart from tumours or other growths) are the result of disturbances in the menstrual cycle. Until you can appreciate the delicate balance of various hormones necessary for the maintenance of regular periods, many of these worrisome problems will not make sense to you. Only by knowing what is normal will you begin to understand the causes of such common disorders as irregular periods, skipped periods, premenstrual spotting and the like.

Again, it must be stressed that you would be doing yourself a great injustice by using this chapter or any other chapter in the book as a guide to self-diagnosis. You as a woman are infinitely too complex to be bound between the covers of any book.

What is menstruation?

Ask any woman and you will probably get an inadequate answer. Chances are that you equate menstruation with your monthly periods, and in a sense you are right. But menstruation is more than a periodic bloody discharge from the uterine cavity. True menstruation implies the occurrence of two elaborate and precisely timed events prior to actual bleeding: (*a*) ovulation (release of an egg) by the ovary, and (*b*) specific changes in the tissue lining the uterine cavity as a result of that ovulation.

Where do the eggs come from?

Before a young girl matures sexually, the ovaries must be transformed from small nubs of inactive tissue into glorious plump organs capable of producing oestrogen and forming eggs on a cyclic basis.

When a girl is born, each ovary already contains anywhere from 40 000 to 400 000 immature eggs (ova). By means of simple arithmetic, you can calculate that if a woman has regular, uninterrupted periods for some thirty years, she will have actually released only 360 of these eggs.

What happens to the rest of the eggs?

Many are called, few are chosen. For every egg that completely matures, untold numbers are lost in the attempt and become mere microscopic specks of scar tissue forever embedded in the substance of the ovary. But before even one egg can be released and even one drop of oestrogen can be produced, certain profound changes must occur.

What kind of changes and when do they start?

During the first seven to eight years of every woman's life, the immature eggs lie buried deep within the ovaries awaiting that magic touch from up above. What actually triggers certain cells in the pituitary gland to begin functioning remains obscure. It is known, however, that by the time most girls reach the age of seven or eight, the pituitary gland begins bombarding the ovaries with a special hormone, the follicle-stimulating hormone, better known as FSH.

What does FSH do?

As the name implies, the follicle-stimulating hormone stimulates the follicles. A follicle is a microscopic ovarian entity consisting of a small ring of cells forming a saclike structure within which an immature ovum, or egg, is contained. On a selective basis, certain follicles began to enlarge and mature under the effect of this hormone.

After sufficient stimulation by FSH, specialized cells within each follicle begin to produce oestrogen, which in turn is gradually released into the bloodstream. As more and more follicles ripen, greater amounts of oestrogen are subsequently secreted and before too long, that marvellous oestrogen makes its presence known.

What does oestrogen do?

The very first sign of oestrogen stimulation is the development of breast buds. Changes in both the nipple and breast tissue may begin as early as eight or nine years of age. Once the breasts start to develop, menstruation will usually begin within two or three years. Interestingly enough, the younger a girl is at the time of recognizable breast development, the shorter the waiting period until her first period. Thus, a girl who has breast buds at nine may be menstruating by the time she reaches ten. On the other hand, some girls can remain as flat as ironing boards until much older. But regardless of how little or how much young girls have in the bosom department, *some breast development always precedes the onset of their first period.*

If vaginal bleeding should occur without any evidence of breast or nipple development, something other than normal menstruation is probably responsible. If this should happen, the girl should be seen by a doctor.

What follows breast development?

Once the breasts have started to bloom, other changes both subtle and not so subtle begin to appear. Among the more obvious physical changes are those in body contour and a definite pre-adolescent growth spurt.

Oestrogen with the help of androgen hormones (secreted by the adrenal glands) also stimulates the growth of pubic hair and axillary (underarm) hair. In the usual sequence of events, pubic hair appears several months before the onset of menstruation. Axillary hair, however, may be quite sparse or even absent until much later.

What about the less visible changes?

As the ovarian follicles continue to secrete oestrogen, mass preparation for the first menstrual period is well under way. Unbeknownst to that young girl who may now be proudly sporting her first bra, size 32 AAA with padding, the uterus, cervix, vagina and vulva are also being transformed.

How does oestrogen affect the uterus?

Before the first menstrual period can ever take place, there is a marked increase in the size of the uterus, accompanied by dramatic changes in the endometrium. The word 'endometrium' means within the womb. Therefore, 'endometrium', or 'endometrial tissue', as it is sometimes called, refers to the tissue lining the uterine cavity. The term 'endometrial cavity' is another way of saying the uterine cavity.

How does oestrogen affect the endometrium?

As more and more oestrogen stimulates the endometrium, it begins to thicken as new cells grow and develop. Because there is such a marked increase in cellular growth, the term *proliferative endometrium* is used to describe this normal thickening of the uterine lining. With sexual maturation, these same proliferative tissue changes normally occur on a monthly basis as a direct result of oestrogen stimulation *prior to ovulation* in every mature menstruating female.

As long as the level of oestrogen reaching the endometrium is maintained above a certain critical level, the tissue lining the uterine cavity will continue to grow and thicken. In other words, there will be no shedding and no bleeding. But when the oestrogen level drops, the endometrium whose growth and support depended upon oestrogen begins to disintegrate. Thus, the uterine lining sloughs and bleeding occurs.

What causes the oestrogen level to drop?

Cyclic fluctuations of FSH and other pituitary hormones. As FSH increases, the oestrogen level decreases and vice versa, as if they were on a seesaw. Like the pounding of the waves upon a shore or the beating of your heart – everything has a rhythm of its own. Nothing in nature is static. And so it is with oestrogen production.

Thus, a young girl may have matured only sufficiently to experience the effects of oestrogen, such as breast development, changes in body contour, uterine growth and so on. She may also have experienced her first periods as a result of drops in the oestrogen level on the endometrium. But without the final step in sexual maturity – *ovulation* – reproductive capacity is not possible.

What is ovulation?

It is the moment of truth: the rupture of a chosen follicle with the release of the egg it contained – the egg carrying half of the genetic inheritance of a potential human being.

How does ovulation come about?

A young girl may look physically developed, but before she can claim to be sexually mature, other hormones in addition to FSH and oestrogen must come into being.

Once again it is the brain via the pituitary gland that brings forth yet another hormone, the luteinizing hormone, or LH for short.

What does LH do?

It 'springs' the egg from the chosen follicle. FSH by itself stimulates the follicles to grow and secrete oestrogen. FSH can also cause the chosen follicle to migrate towards the surface of the ovary; but something else is needed before the egg can break out of its follicular prison.

If you were actually able to observe an ovary just prior to ovulation, you would see the chosen follicle bulging on the surface of the ovary like a small blister, not much bigger than a quarter of an inch (0·6 centimetres) across – waiting. For what? For LH. It is that final surge of LH, the master stroke from up above, that ruptures the follicle and releases the egg. How this actually happens remains unclear, but somehow LH together with FSH makes it possible.

Has the moment of ovulation ever been observed?

Innumerable times in our friend the rhesus monkey, but seldom have scientists witnessed ovulation in the human female. The egg itself is just barely visible to the naked eye. Nonetheless, the residual evidence that ovulation has occurred can be seen in the remains of the ruptured follicle. In most cases there would probably be a trace of blood-tinged fluid oozing from the site of rupture on the surface of the ovary.

What happens to the ruptured follicle after the egg is released?

Everything in nature has a purpose – even the remnants of the ruptured follicle that stay behind in the ovary. Up to the time of ovulation, that follicle was primarily concerned with the production of oestrogen. After ovulation the ruptured follicle continues to produced oestrogen, but in addition it now secretes a second and exceedingly important hormone, *progesterone*.

Because of its new function – the production of progesterone – the ruptured follicle also acquires a new name, the 'corpus luteum'. 'Corpus luteum' literally means yellow body. Why yellow body? Because certain chemical changes associated with the production of progesterone cause the remnants of the ruptured follicle to turn a bright canary yellow.

What does progesterone do?

It prepares the tissue of the uterine lining (endometrium) to receive the fertilized egg. If you have ever had the wonderful experience of growing a prize flower from seed, you can appreciate the importance of careful preparation of the soil. The fertilized human egg is like an exalted seed. If it is to implant properly and continue to grow normally, progesterone must transform the proliferative endometrium into an even thicker, richer, more luxuriant tissue bed known as *secretory endometrium*. Thus, progesterone causes the growth of specialized cells that secrete certain nutrients (hence the name 'secretory endometrium') necessary for the support of the fertilized egg. Without these postovulatory changes in the endometrium, no respectable egg could survive. In fact, many early spontaneous abortions may be the result of poor preparation of the endometrium because of inadequate progesterone levels.

Regardless of whether or not the egg is fertilized, the transformation of the uterine lining into secretory endometrium invariably occurs after ovulation. Therefore, it is very easy for your doctor to determine whether or not you have ovulated.

How is that possible?

By simply taking a small shred of tissue from the uterine lining just before your period and examining it under a microscope (endometrial biopsy). Ovulation results in the production of progesterone, and progesterone is responsible for changing the uterine lining to secretory endometrium. Therefore, the finding of secretory endometrium by means of an endometrial biopsy would be *indirect* proof that you had, indeed, ovulated.

What would be direct proof of ovulation?

Short of actually recovering the egg, pregnancy would be irrefutable proof that ovulation had occurred.

What happens if the egg is not fertilized?

Through some mechanism, as yet not known, the corpus luteum gets the word that its offspring, the egg, did not make it. Without fertilization there is no further need for the elaborate preparation of the endometrium. As a consequence the corpus luteum begins to shrink and the levels of oestrogen and progesterone gradually decrease. The endometrium, whose support depended upon these two ovarian hormones, starts to disintegrate, resulting in menstruation. In time the corpus luteum becomes a residual speck of nonfunctioning grey scar tissue within the ovary.

Suppose the corpus luteum doesn't shrink?

Then you may have what is known as a persistent corpus-luteum cyst of the ovary. (See Chapter 19.)

What else happens?

The drop in oestrogen and progesterone levels signals to the pituitary gland that the project was cancelled. The pituitary gland responds by increasing the output of FSH. Thus, another fresh crop of follicles is stimulated and the whole process repeats itself.

What happens if the egg is fertilized?

Then all systems are 'go' for the corpus luteum. For the first two or three months following implantation of the fertilized egg, the continuing growth of the pregnancy depends upon a functioning corpus luteum. Rather than regressing, it continues to pour out those marvellous hormones, oestrogen and progesterone, so vital for the growth of the fertilized egg now embedded within the uterine lining. By the end of this critical period (sixty to ninety days after conception) the placenta (afterbirth) is sufficiently mature to sustain all the needs of the growing foetus; the function of the corpus luteum then ceases.

What happens to the ovaries during pregnancy?

With the subsequent regression of the corpus luteum, there is no further activity within the ovaries for the duration of the pregnancy. They are literally in a state of suspended animation – no stimulation of follicles, no ovulation and no hormone production. Oestrogen and progesterone, as well as other hormones associated with pregnancy, are derived exclusively from foetal and placental sources.

How soon after the end of pregnancy does menstruation resume?

Approximately 85 to 90 per cent of women will menstruate within the first three months following the termination of a pregnancy, whether the pregnancy ended as an abortion or a full-term baby.

For the remaining 10 to 15 per cent, the first period may be delayed as long as four to six months.

What happens if you are breast feeding?

In this case the resumption of normal menstrual cycles may be even more delayed. Although some 30 per cent of nursing mothers may have their first period within twelve weeks of delivery, the majority of lactating women may not menstruate for several months.

Can you become pregnant even though you are breast feeding and have not had a period?

Yes, indeed. Breast feeding will inhibit ovulation to a certain extent, but it is a highly unreliable method of birth control. There have been many nursing mothers who were completely oblivious to a superimposed pregnancy until they felt the foetus kicking. Therefore, if you do not want another pregnancy, take precautions. Otherwise, you may be like the woman who did not see a period for four years – but was blessed with three beautiful tax deductions.

6. More about Periods and Launching Eggs

Dating back to the first clay tablets, historical records are full of misconceptions and myths regarding menstruation. Not only has the menstruating woman been ostracized, segregated, isolated and labelled as unfit to touch, but she has also been reputed to have powers that would do credit to any nuclear detonation. To quote from a translation of Pliny's *Natural History*, written at the beginning of the Christian era,

The touch of a menstrous woman turned wine to vinegar, blighted crops, killed seedlings, blasted gardens, brought down the fruit from trees, dimmed mirrors, blunted razors, rusted iron and brass (especially at the waning of the moon), killed bees, or at least drove them from their hives, caused mares to miscarry . . . [and so forth].

Fortunately for girls who are about to experience their first period, some progress has been made in the dissemination of more accurate information. But there is still a long way to go.

Many parents today fail miserably in preparing their daughters for menstruation. What should be greeted as a perfectly natural and welcome event can become a traumatic experience. This is especially true for the girl ahead of her peers in sexual maturation. How emotionally prepared can a nine-year-old girl be for her first period unless she has been counselled by a wise mother?

It is no longer sufficient to expect that your daughter will learn all about it in time. The time is now, because the average age at which menstruation first occurs is gradually getting lower.

At what age do most girls start menstruating?

Some girls will start menstruating at the same age as their mothers did. According to statistics, however, the average age for starting menstruation has fallen over the last 150 years. In 1860 the average age was seventeen years; today the average age in Britain is thirteen years.

But statistics do not take into account the fact that every girl operates according to her own biological timetable. Anywhere from ten to sixteen years is within the normal range. And for some girls, their first menstruation will occur between the ages of sixteen and eighteen, sometimes even later.

How about the girl who menstruates before the age of ten: is there something wrong?

Not necessarily. There are many instances of true precocious puberty. These girls for some unknown reason experience a premature activation of hypothalamic, pituitary and ovarian functions. In other words, sexual maturation starts young – but in all other respects, these girls are completely normal.

On rare occasion such girls may menstruate at four, ovulate at five and make the headlines at six by having a baby. And if you think that's young, there have been documented cases of true precocious puberty occurring before the age of two.

Is very early 'menstruation' always a sign of precocious puberty?

Unfortunately no. Early breast development and cyclic vaginal bleeding in a very young girl may actually be a sign of organic disease. The differentiation between premature–normal development and premature–abnormal development can be at times difficult to establish. This is especially true if the girl is fairly close to what might be considered a normal age for her first period. One is less likely to suspect an endocrine (glandular) problem in a girl of nine than in a five-year-old.

Suffice it to say that if any question or doubt exists about whether bleeding is normal, the child should be seen by a doctor.

What about the late bloomer?

Nothing causes more furrowing of maternal brows than a teen-age daughter who is obviously lagging behind her contemporaries. By fifteen her mother is convinced that menstruation should have started. Her anxiety may even drive her to wonder – could her daughter be pregnant?

In situations like this, professional reassurance can do much for both daughter and mother. A thorough examination by a sympathetic doctor will, in the majority of cases, show that the girl is developing normally, albeit at a slower rate. By sixteen or seventeen there should be some breast development and other signs of oestrogen stimulation. It is also important to determine whether the vaginal canal is open. Nothing can impede the flow of menstrual blood as effectively as an imperforate hymen (see Chapter 2).

What else should be done?

In most cases, nothing. Time will accomplish wonders – like bringing on a period. Providing that the physical examination is otherwise normal, many doctors will prefer waiting until the girl reaches her eighteenth birthday before recommending an extensive hormonal evaluation. By that time, it will indeed be the rare girl who has not menstruated.

Would it be wrong to induce periods in a late bloomer?

Not necessarily wrong, but why accelerate the girl's biological timetable? Sometimes more harm can be done both psychologically and physiologically by unwarranted meddling. In those unusual cases where there is an endocrine (glandular) disturbance, inducing periods by hormones may obscure and delay recognition of the true problem.

What other factors can delay the onset of menstruation?

Any number of things. Nutrition, for example, is one of the most important factors in normal development. Girls who suffered from chronic malnutrition in Europe during the Second World War showed dramatic sexual retardation. In this country, emotional problems, nervous disorders and various chronic illnesses have all been influential in delaying the onset of menstruation.

Is there any relationship between the age at which you first menstruate and the subsequent onset of the menopause?

No. Here again you may follow your mother's pattern, but more and more women are going through the menopause later and later. At the present time, the average age at which all menstruation ceases is about fifty.

How often should you menstruate?

Although most women menstruate every twenty-five to thirty days, anywhere from twenty-one to thirty-five days is considered within normal limits. But whether you have a period every twenty-one days or tend to have longer cycles, the time interval between periods is not as important as the establishment of a predictable pattern. For most women this pattern is usually determined by the third year after the onset of the first menses. Thus, any consistent departure from your regular cycle length, particularly if it falls outside the normal twenty-one-to thirty-five-day interval, may indicate a menstrual disorder.

How do you calculate the length of your menstrual cycle?

This may seem like a simple matter to many of you – but oh, what confusion exists!

The length of your cycle is calculated from the first day of one period up to but not including the first day of the following period. For example, if your period starts October 1 and your next period begins October 28, your cycle length is twenty-seven days. Day one of your menstrual cycle is the first day you see even the barest trace of blood. In other words, any spotting or staining that may immediately precede the real flow must be taken into account when calculating the length of your menstrual cycle.

Is it ever normal to have two periods in one month?

It can be. For those of you averaging twenty-eight-day cycles, it stands to reason that if your period began March 2, then your next period should begin March 30: two periods in one calendar month – perfectly normal in this case.

How long should your period last?

Anywhere from three days to five days is average, but there are many women who consistently flow as long as eight days, while others stop completely after only two days. And even from one month to the next it can be normal for the length of your period to fluctuate slightly.

How much blood is actually lost?

Much less than you probably think. In one study a group of women salvaged every drop of menstrual blood over several months. After each period they submitted all of their used tampons and towels to a gallant research team for chemical analysis of the iron content. The results? Most women lost between 50 and 175 cubic centimetres (approximately 2–6 fluid ounces or 3–9 tablespoons) of blood per period and the average women lost less than 4 fluid ounces. So if you are really convinced that your bleeding exceeds 8 fluid ounces per period, then you had better go to your doctor. There can be many reasons for increased menstrual blood loss (more about that in Chapter 9).

Why are some periods heavier than others?

Contrary to what some women believe, the uterine cavity does not 'store up' blood between periods. How much you do bleed, aside from such factors as emotional influences or organic disorders, is in part determined by the amount of endometrial tissue to be shed. As a general rule, the thicker the endometrial tissue, the heavier and longer the menstrual blood flow. Thus, just as the length of your cycle can occasionally vary, so too can the amount of bleeding. At the other extreme, women on oral-contraceptive pills may experience very scanty periods. With this medication, the endometrial lining tends to be considerably thinner.

Why doesn't menstrual blood clot?

Because it has already clotted in the endometrial cavity, and the same blood can clot only once. Before that clotted blood can pass through the cervical canal and into the vagina, certain enzymes within the uterine cavity dissolve the clots and reliquefy the blood. Therefore the blood that flows into the vagina and onto your tampon or towel is in reality serum, the reliquefied portion of blood that can no longer clot.

Why, then, do you sometimes pass clots?

This is one of the areas currently under clinical and laboratory investigation. Part of the explanation may have to do with the amount of bleeding. The heavier the flow, the greater your chances of passing clots. It is reasonable to assume that if your flow is unusually profuse, some blood may escape so rapidly that it passes intact into the vagina where it can now clot. In other words, this blood does not linger in the uterine cavity long enough to go through the slower process of clotting and then being reliquefied.

The passage of clots therefore is not necessarily abnormal. Some of you may have experienced a sudden warm gush of blood and clots. Others may pass the biggest clots after a sudden change of position. This phenomenon can readily occur if you have been lying down and then suddenly stand. As you were lying down, the blood that failed to clot in the endometrial cavity subsequently pooled and clotted in the upper vagina. So what happens? When you stand up – out comes the clot!

What does the menstrual flow consist of?

Primarily a mixture of blood, degenerated cells and mucus. The blood that you actually pass (with the exception of a few clots) is almost entirely serum. The degenerated cells are fragments of the sloughed (shed) lining of the endometrial cavity, and the mucus (the sticky stuff) is an outpouring from the glands of the cervical canal.

What causes the characteristic menstrual odour?

If you were able to reach inside the uterine cavity and remove the menstrual debris before it trickled down into the vagina, there would be no odour. That characteristic menstrual odour is caused by the action of vaginal bacteria on the blood elements. Therefore, regardless of how diligent a woman is in her personal hygiene, it is impossible to eliminate this odour completely; at best it can only be minimized. (For more on odour, see Chapter 12.)

Just because your period comes every month, does that mean that you are ovulating?

Not necessarily. Even if you are perfectly normal it is not un- common to have an anovulatory (no-egg) cycle. Your period may still come at the expected time, and yet you may not have ovulated. How often this happens is difficult to say, but once or even twice a year is not outside the realm of normality.

Are some women prone to anovulatory (no-egg) cycles?

Very definitely. In fact, anovulatory cycles are very common among young girls just starting to menstruate and among older women beginning the menopausal years. At one extreme the immaturity of both the ovary and the brain centres controlling ovarian function is responsible for the lack of ovulation. In older women the gradual waning of ovarian function results in the ovary's inability to eject an egg on a monthly schedule. In both instances the mechanisms are in a sense protective.

How is that?

Anovulatory cycles in a young girl protect her from conceiving until her body and bone structure are sufficiently mature to handle a pregnancy. The fact that anovulatory cycles are common in early adolescence has been documented by studies among ethnic groups where marriage at the time of puberty is a tribal custom. Rarely will these child brides conceive for at least two to three years despite extensive sexual activity. Fortunately for them, ovulation is initially sporadic.

On the other hand, if you are approaching the menopause – how many of you in your late forties or early fifties would welcome a pregnancy? This does not mean, of course, that you cannot get pregnant, but your chances are considerably lessened.

Does ovulation ever cause abdominal pain?

Seldom. Although a few women will insist that they can pinpoint the exact moment of ovulation by the sudden onset of lower abdominal pain at mid cycle, the majority of women are completely unaware of any physical sensation. Furthermore, any reliance placed on this pain phenomenon either as proof of ovulation or as a signal to abstain from intercourse for the rhythm method of contraception demands a word of caution.

Pain arising from an ovary can easily be confused with pain from other abdominal organs and vice versa. Bowel spasms, for example, can readily mimic ovulatory pain. You can appreciate, therefore, how common practices such as overindulging in rich food or eating incompatible foods can easily confuse the issue. The pain you may interpret as ovulation might in reality be due to gas.

Is it ever possible to bleed at the time of ovulation?

Yes. Associated spotting or bleeding lasting anywhere from a few hours to two or three days may occur, but the presence of ovulatory bleeding is less common than ovulatory pain. The term *Mittelschmerz* (middle pain) has been used to describe this midcycle ovulatory pain with or without uterine bleeding.

Why does ovulation sometimes cause uterine bleeding?

At the time of ovulation, when the mature follicle ruptures and releases its contained egg, the ruptured follicle can literally be so shaken up that its oestrogen output temporarily decreases. As you may recall from Chapter 5, the integrity of the endometrium (lining of the uterus) depends on the maintenance of a certain oestrogen level: therefore, the temporary drop in oestrogen may be sufficient to cause shedding of some endometrial cells with resultant bleeding in between regular periods.

It should be stressed that uterine bleeding during ovulation is relatively uncommon. Any and all bleeding between periods should be properly evaluated by your doctor.

How can you tell if you are really ovulating?

Short of becoming pregnant, you can't, yet there is an indirect method of determining this event – the *basal-body-temperature* (*BBT*) *chart*. The only equipment needed is a thermometer, a pencil, a piece of paper and perseverance. If you can read a thermometer and are faithful in recording your temperature every morning before getting out of bed, you will have indirect proof of whether or not you are ovulating. But, it is very important that you take your temperature *immediately* upon awakening. No getting out of bed for a quick trip to the toilet. No smoking, eating, drinking, talking or brushing of teeth allowed. The term 'basal body temperature' refers to the temperature of the body at complete rest.

What does your temperature have to do with ovulation?

At the time of ovulation there is a small but definite elevation of your basal body temperature. As you may recall, the ovum is launched from the mature follicle; the remnants of that follicle (corpus luteum) then begins producing a second hormone, progesterone, which in turn further prepares the uterine tissue bed to receive the fertilized egg. (See Chapter 5.) The hormone progesterone is responsible for the rise in basal body temperature, which is subsequently sustained until shortly before the onset of menstruation. In other words, unless ovulation occurs there can be no production of progesterone, and hence no elevation in basal body temperature. Although the rise in temperature averages only 0·4–1·0° Fahrenheit (0·2–0·5° Centigrade), it is nonetheless significant.

Under ordinary conditions your normal body temperature, taken orally, is usually 98·6° F (37·0° C). During sleep, however, your temperature dips as a result of decreased muscular and metabolic activity. How low it dips can depend upon both the length and the depth of sleep. Not uncommonly, your basal body temperature may register as low as 97·2° F (36·2° C). With subsequent activity as you wake up, it will quickly return to its usual 98·6° F (37·0° C).

How exactly do you keep a basal-body-temperature (BBT) chart?

If you do not have any graph paper, just take a sheet of ordinary paper and number from one to thirty-five across the top of the page, leaving a small margin above the numbers. These numbers represent the days of your cycle. If your period comes every twenty-eight days, then you will use only twenty-eight numbers. If your periods are further apart than thirty-five days, make room for the additional days needed.

Along the side of the paper, starting at the top, write the degrees of temperature ranging from 99·0 down to 97·0° F

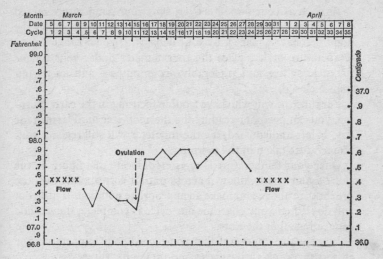

11. *Basal-body-temperature chart : ovulatory cycle. Notice the drop and sharp rise in temperature at the time of ovulation*

(37·2°–36·1° C). Make the first number appearing at the top 99·0° F (37·2° C). (See Figure 11.)

To avoid eye strain, as well as to ensure that you record each day's temperature in the right place, divide the paper in squares. Opposite each temperature figure draw a line across the paper. From the top of the paper to the bottom, draw a line separating each day of the cycle. You are now ready to start your chart – or almost.

What comes next?

Now you have to wait for your period to start. Day one is the first day of your menstrual flow. Above number one on your chart write down the date that your period begins. Above each subsequent day of your cycle write down the corresponding date.

It is not necessary to record your temperature during the menstrual flow, but it is important to begin *immediately* thereafter. For purposes of keeping a complete record, put an X under each day of your period.

As soon as your period is over, start your temperature record the next morning. Be sure to shake down the thermometer the night before and place it by your bedside. If you are taking your temperature orally, place the thermometer under your tongue for at least five and preferably six minutes – and keep your mouth closed.

For those of you who have trouble focusing in the early morning, you can postpone reading the thermometer until later in the day. If left undisturbed, the thermometer will still register your temperature taken in the morning.

Once your temperature is registered, locate that figure on the side of your chart, follow it across until it corresponds with the proper date above and make an appropriate notation. A little dot will do. When your chart for one cycle is complete, draw a line connecting all of the dots.

It is equally important that you record your temperature for at least two consecutive cycles and preferably three.

What's wrong with keeping a BBT chart for just one month?

It is apt to be misleading. You may, for example, just hit the one cycle wherein you failed to ovulate. Then too, how many times have you felt a cold or sore throat coming on? Any slight infection, by elevating your temperature, will completely invalidate your basal-body-temperature chart for that month.

When are you most likely to ovulate?

That depends on the length of your cycle. Ovulation usually occurs fourteen days (plus or minus two days) before your next anticipated period. If you are running a twenty-eight-day cycle, then your most fertile time, the moment of ovulation, will occur around mid cycle or just fourteen days before your next period. If you menstruate every twenty-five days, you are more apt to ovulate around the eleventh day of your cycle, or fourteen days prior to your next period. Similarly, if your periods come every thirty-five days, you may ovulate around day twenty-one, again fourteen days prior to your next period. As you can see, the time interval prior to ovulation (although there are many exceptions) tends to be the most variable portion of your menstrual cycle. Once ovulation has occurred, the subsequent period will usually follow two weeks later.

For practical purposes, however, ovulation can occur either two days earlier or two days later than that fourteen-day time limit. For the woman who consistently runs twenty-eight-day cycles, ovulation can occur anywhere from day twelve to day sixteen. But even that can vary. (See Chapter 16.)

Is it important to keep a BBT chart?

Only if you are really interested in knowing whether or not you are ovulating. In fact, whenever a woman has failed to conceive, a doctor will almost invariably request that she keep a record for at least three months.

For those of you eager to avoid pregnancy, it might be advantageous to know whether you are ovulating – and if so, when. This application of the BBT chart is, however, more limited. In Chapter 16 you will find out why.

How can you tell by your BBT chart whether you are ovulating?

During the first few days following your period, you will notice that under normal circumstances your temperature is fairly stable, not varying more than 0.2° F (0.1° C) in most cases. At the time of ovulation, your temperature will drop to a point lower than the one recorded on the previous day. Following that low reading, there will be a steep rise in temperature the very next morning. If the difference between the low and the high reading in temperature on these two successive days registers between 0.4 and 1.0° F (0.2–0.5° C), this would indicate that ovulation may have occurred. Additional evidence of ovulation would require that the temperature elevation be sustained (within the 0.2° F – (0.1° C) of the high reading) until two or three days prior to your next period. At this time, as a result of a decrease in progesterone output, your temperature would return to preovulatory levels.

What if you do not ovulate?

Without ovulation there is no corpus luteum (see Chapter 5) to produce progesterone, and without progesterone there is no change in basal body temperature. Your chart would therefore fail to show that characteristic temperture elevation associated with ovulation. To point out the differences between an ovulatory and no-egg (anovulatory) cycle, Figures 11 and 12 may be helpful.

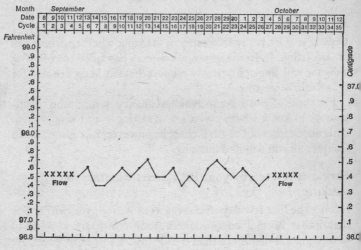

12.   *Basal-body-temperature chart : anovulatory (no-egg) cycle. Notice the flat curve*

What happens if the temperature does not return to preovulatory levels?

You might be pregnant. In fact, a sustained temperature level after ovulation which continues beyond the time when you would expect your period is probably one of the earliest methods of detecting a possible pregnancy. Remember, if the egg does get fertilized, the corpus luteum continues to pour forth oestrogen and progesterone. And where there is progesterone, there is heat. (See Figure 13.)

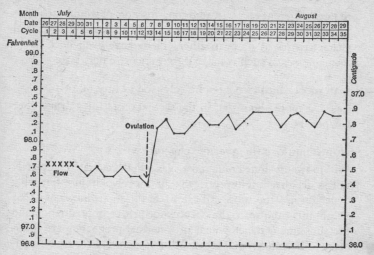

13. *Basal-body-temperature chart : pregnancy. Persistent elevation of temperature and no menstrual period suggest pregnancy*

Can you ovulate more than one egg at a time?

Very definitely. All fraternal twins (non-identical) are living proof that this does occur. They are the product of two separate eggs fertilized by two separate sperm. This double ovulation can occur either from one ovary or from both ovaries (one egg from each ovary). In either case, the tendency toward double ovulation seems to be an inherited trait.

On the other hand, identical twins seem to occur by chance only. They are the product of a single egg fertilized by a single sperm. The fertilized egg, after certain modifications, splits into two equal parts.

If two eggs can be released at about the same time, is it ever possible to have these eggs fertilized by two separate acts of intercourse?

Yes. But the only way to verify this phenomenon would be for a woman of one race to have intercourse (in fairly rapid succession) with two men of two other races – in short, three individuals of three different races. In addition, this woman would then have to give birth to fraternal twins, each twin showing the racial characteristics of its own father. There have even been documented cases of such twins, but they are extremely rare.

Can more than two eggs be released at any one time?

Yes, but more about that in the section on fertility drugs. (See Chapter 15.)

How long does the average egg survive?

Within twenty-four hours most eggs will degenerate completely unless fertilized. However, the first twelve hours following ovulation are the most critical. If fertilization does not occur within this time span, the chances for proper impregnation and the subsequent development of a normal pregnancy are diminished. This may be another factor responsible for early spontaneous abortions – some eggs are just too old to make the grade.

Do the ovaries take turns making the eggs?

According to studies on our friend the rhesus monkey, ovulation does seem to alternate on a monthly basis between the two ovaries. However, this ping-pong effect is by no means constant or absolute.

In women who have had one ovary surgically removed, ovulation will usually continue on a monthly basis provided that the remaining ovary is normal. In other words, losing one ovary will not necessarily make you any less fertile. Some women have even become pregnant with only a portion of one ovary remaining.

Can a female be born without ovaries?

Yes. Although this condition is fortunately rare, it does occur with sufficient frequency to be recognized as a definite entity – Turner's syndrome.

How is Turner's syndrome diagnosed?

Because the absence of ovaries is a genetic defect, other physical malformations occasionally accompany this condition. For example, a female infant born with this syndrome may show an obvious neck deformity. In extreme cases the neck can be markedly shortened and broadened by a fold of skin extending from the base of the ears to almost the tip of the shoulders.

In less severe cases, the neck changes may be very subtle or almost non-existent, thus making an early diagnosis of Turner's syndrome less likely.

How else can this condition be diagnosed in a preadolescent girl?

Interestingly enough, this girl, almost without exception, will never grow beyond 4 feet 7 inches (1·4 metres) in height. An astute mother will probably notice that her daughter is not growing as tall as she should, but if the whole family tends to be on the short side, this too may go unnoticed until later.

How much later?

Without ovaries there will be no breast development, no feminine contours and no menstruation. By the time this girl is in her early teens, she may be wondering why she isn't developing like her other girl friends.

What happens now?

Sooner or later the total lack of sexual development will drive this girl and her mother to see a doctor. The obvious absence of any oestrogen effect, in addition to her short stature, will almost cinch the diagnosis. It is exceedingly important, however, that the diagnosis be verified by appropriate hormonal and laboratory studies.

At best, it is difficult for any doctor to tell a young girl that she was born without ovarian tissue. For this means that she'll never be able to have children. It also implies that she will need female hormone therapy for at least the next thirty to forty years.

Why does she need hormone therapy?

It is truly amazing what oestrogen therapy can accomplish. Almost overnight this girl will begin to develop sexually. In addition, the cyclic use of oestrogen and progesterone will establish monthly uterine bleeding, much like a normal menstrual period. In this particular situation oestrogen is also vital in preventing premature ageing that would otherwise occur if the condition remained untreated. With the exception of being unable to have children, the girl can function like any other woman.

Will oestrogen make her grow any taller?

In this case no amount of any hormone, including the growth hormone given at any age, will make her grow one bit taller than 4 feet 7 inches (1·4 metres).

How about ovarian transplants?

Recently there have been several successful ovarian transplants reported in young women whose two ovaries were previously removed because of extensive disease. Not only do these women menstruate regularly, but they are also capable of becoming pregnant. As proof of this, the year 1973 ushered in the first ovarian-transplant baby. In the future, young girls with Turner's syndrome may perhaps be candidates for this operation.

Part 2

The Unpredictability of Woman

7. Premenstrual Tension

Does your personality change for the worse seven to ten days before your period comes? Do you become tense, irritable and nervous? Can you suddenly explode over the least irritation and then, in the next moment, dissolve into uncontrollable weeping? Or do you become sullen, withdrawn and morose, defying anyone to make you smile? Then perhaps you are a victim of premenstrual tension.

The extent to which each woman reacts during this phase of her cycle depends in part upon her basic personality. For the average woman, these emotional upheavals tend to remain mild and well under control most of the time. But a few women have premenstrual tension of such serious proportions that they can be blasted right out of orbit.

How far out of orbit?

In extreme cases, way out. In court records, acts of aggression and hostility during the premenstrual phase abound. Most of the crimes of violence committed by women are perpetrated during that time. The very disturbed woman who directs her hostility inward stands a greater risk of committing suicide or having a fatal accident premenstrually than at any other time in her cycle.

Fortunately, such severely afflicted women are in the minority. Most women compensate remarkably well. However, even a stable, well-adjusted woman may on occasion suffer symptoms related to premenstrual tension.

What kind of symptoms?

That heavy, bloated, puffy feeling for one thing. And just about any part of your anatomy can be affected. In fact, during the week prior to menstruation, some women may carry as much as 3–5 pounds (1·4–2·3 kilograms) of extra fluid, and in extreme cases may tip the scales 10 pounds (4·5 kilograms) heavier. Don't be too surprised, therefore, if you can't squeeze into your shoes or if your breasts feel as if they have been treated with silicone.

Extra fluid can also cause your stomach to stick out and your waist to expand overnight. Until fairly recently this premenstrual abdominal bloating was believed to be caused by gas, but studies have shown that the walls of the intestine temporarily store excess fluid and actually become waterlogged. Furthermore, there is also a shift of fluid from the bowel passageway to the walls of the intestine. As a result your faeces may become somewhat harder. Thus, constipation can be another strain during the premenstrual phase. Fortunately this shift of fluid is only temporary, so don't reach too quickly for your favourite laxative. As soon as your period gets under way and the body fluid readjusts itself, you are likely to have the reverse situation for a day or two – loose bowel movements. That too can be normal.

So where does all this extra water come from?

Blame it on your hormones. Part of the explanation may have to do with oestrogen. In addition to all those glorious effects on your body, oestrogen also influences another physiological function – salt and water exchange. The more oestrogen in your system, the less salt and water pass through the kidneys. Thus, the higher the oestrogen level the greater will be the salt and water retention. Therefore, just after ovulation, when the oestrogen level is high, the kidneys will filter less water. Result? You will pass less urine. Consequently the water that bypassed the kidneys is redistributed back into your tissues.

What other symptoms can fluid retention cause?

Headaches, terrible pounding headaches that would be a challenge for any aspirin commercial on television. Only in this case, even aspirin with or without those extra ingredients would probably not help much. Surprisingly enough, the culprit responsible for true premenstrual headaches may well be water retention within the brain tissues. In fact, many of those emotional upheavals – irritability, nervous tension, insomnia, depression and so on – have been attributed to 'water on the brain'. And you thought you were just hard to get along with.

How long can these symptoms sometimes last?

Until the oestrogen level dips to its lowest point just prior to the onset of menstruation. When this happens, there is a subsequent decrease in salt and water retention. Consequently, you will pass more urine and as your body rids itself of excess fluids, all those unpleasant premenstrual symptoms (bloating, constipation, headaches and so on) will disappear.

Can all these premenstrual symptoms be blamed on oestrogen and water retention?

To a certain extent, but there are still many unanswered questions. Even though oestrogen can cause fluid retention, there are some investigators who feel that the real basis for premenstrual tension is an imbalance between oestrogen and progesterone. But whether all that distress is brought about by too much oestrogen, too little progesterone, or from some other mechanism (adrenal gland factors, for example) – nobody knows for sure.

There is even clinical evidence that certain women may be allergic to their own hormones – especially progesterone. Such bizarre symptoms as giant hives, running noses and painful mouth sores experienced premenstrually by some women can certainly make one wonder.

But regardless of what causes premenstrual tension, this phenomenon does not seem to occur in the absence of ovulation. For example, women who are taking birth-control pills (with suppression of ovulation) do not experience true premenstrual tension. They may be bothered with minor bloating or weight gain, but their symptoms tend to be milder and without cyclic regularity.

Can premenstrual fluid retention affect your sex drive?

Given the right partner, the proper setting and the inclination, any woman can be sexually aroused regardless of what her ovaries are doing. For some women, however, there may be an increased sex drive during the week prior to menstruation. Some authorities relate the greater need for orgasmic release to a heightened physical awareness of the clitoris and labia minora as a result of premenstrual fluid retention within these tissues. But whether an increase in sex drive at this time is solely attributable to fluid retention is a debatable point.

Not uncommonly, these same women may be the ones who experience sudden surges of energy prior to menstruation. Windows get washed, furniture gets rearranged and household projects abandoned the week before are completed in a flurry of activity. And in addition to doing all that *plus* playing a smashing set of tennis, and chairing a committee meeting, they may still be eager for sex.

How about the woman who complains of being excessively tired?

Contrary to those old advertisements, all women do not drag around because of iron-poor blood. That listless, knocked-out, shaky feeling may well be related to premenstrual changes in carbohydrate metabolism, and more specifically to a lower blood sugar level. So if you find yourself irresistibly drawn to a sweet shop or making tracks for the nearest baker, that craving for sweets may actually be a physiological need to raise your blood sugar level.

Do all women suffer from premenstrual tension?

Of course not, but if you ovulate regularly and are between the ages of twenty and forty-five, you may be a candidate.

No one can predict how you as an individual woman will be affected during your premenstrual phase. On-the-job efficiency studies have shown that women during the premenstrual phase do function just as effectively as during any other time of their cycle. Tests measuring mental ability, muscular coordination, strength and speed show that these activities are essentially unchanged when compared to previously established performance levels.

Needless to say, however, if you are among the 15 per cent of women who really suffer, the time has come to seek relief. Gone are the days of putting up with unnecessary discomfort (not to mention making everyone else miserable) just because you think it is part of being a woman. Although your grandmother probably received a condescending pat on the shoulder from the doctor and was told, 'Learn to live with it', the chances are that yours may be more attuned to your premenstrual blues.

So what can be done about it?

Even though some investigators deny the importance of water retention as a cause of premenstrual tension, many women do experience relief by eliminating some of that excess tissue fluid.

For those of you with only minor discomfort, the simple expedient of restricting your salt intake seven to ten days before your period can work a small miracle.

What does salt have to do with water retention?

Salt (sodium chloride) plays an important role in proper water balance. Whenever you consume more salt than you need or excrete less salt than usual, your body responds by mobilizing the necessary fluid to dilute the excess salt in your system. To get an idea of how this works, think of what would happen if you drank only sea water. Your body, in an attempt to handle the excess salt, would respond by conserving fluid ordinarily lost through such channels as urine, faeces, perspiration, saliva, etc. Result? With all that extra fluid ordinarily excreted now being retained and poured back to neutralize those salt-laden tissues, you would blow up like a balloon in no time at all.

To a much lesser extent, the same mechanisms operate when you excrete less sodium during the premenstrual phase of your cycle. If you remember, oestrogen causes a decrease in the amount of sodium filtered through the kidneys. Therefore, during your premenstrual phase your body is forced to handle more salt and water because of the oestrogen effect. Reducing your own salt intake can certainly help that waterlogged feeling. But hiding the salt shaker to avoid *adding* salt to food is not enough. You must also be aware of what foods are normally high in salt and sodium compounds.

Like what for instance?

Such common items on your shopping list as kippers, ham, bacon, sausages, cooked meats (e.g., bologna, salami and frankfurters) are particularly high in sodium. The same goes for baking soda, various food seasonings containing monosodium glutamate, packaged or canned soups, stock cubes, most salad dressings, sandwich spreads, yeast extracts and all those snack foods that crackle and crunch – potato crisps, Ritz crackers, savoury biscuits and nuts of all varieties. Cheeses, too, with the possible exception of cottage cheese, are another big source of sodium. And oh, Mexican cooking and Chinese food with a dash of soy sauce – delicious – but not for you, if you collect water like a rain barrel.

In addition to a low-salt diet, the use of diuretics may also be indicated.

What about diuretics?

Among the wide range of diuretics available, the ones most commonly used in the treatment of premenstrual tension belong to the thiazide group. These preparations are not only effective in flushing away excess fluid, but are also sufficiently mild so that side effects are seldom a problem. However, you should follow the instructions of your doctor. A course of tablets just before your period is usually enough to give relief.

You may also be prescribed tablets to supplement your potassium intake.

Why a potassium supplement?

Potassium is one of the body's most important minerals. With increased salt and water loss as a direct result of the diuretic, there may also be an increased output of potassium in the urine. And excessive loss of potassium could lead to muscle weakness, intestinal distension, constipation and so on, just what you don't need. With the dosage of diuretic you would be taking, this potassium loss is not severe, but you can help ensure against it by eating lots of fruit, especially oranges, figs and bananas, which are naturally rich in potassium. You could, for instance, take your diuretic pill with a glass of pure orange juice. Women who require larger doses or more prolonged diuretic therapy (for conditions other than premenstrual fluid retention) may be prescribed a potassium supplement in the form of a liquid.

Will taking diuretics improve your premenstrual disposition?

Maybe – particularly if diuretics can help eliminate puffy eyelids, tight skin, a bloated stomach and swollen hands, feet and ankles. Diuretics can also help flush away some of that extra 'water on the brain'. This in itself can make you easier to get along with by decreasing some of your nervous tension and anxiety. But women whose main premenstrual problem is emotional instability find that diuretics are rarely the whole answer.

What else can help?

If your trouble is emotional then the best way to tackle it is by accepting that it is so. If you are depressed and moody or irritable and liable to fly off the handle, then just knowing that you are like that makes it easier to feel less at the whim of your emotions. You can then try to protect yourself from demanding situations – like caring for the neighbours' toddlers or an important interview at work – by avoiding them during your premenstrual days.

If your circumstances make this impossible, your doctor may suggest a mild tranquillizer. Here, again, the medication would be started a week to ten days before your anticipated period. Needless to say, tolerance to any tranquillizer varies from woman to woman. What would be just the right dosage for one woman might make you feel like a zombie. If you are taking tranquillizers for the relief of premenstrual tension, do not hesitate to decrease the dose prescribed if you feel over-sedated. But make a point of informing your doctor.

A word of warning: tranquillizers, alcohol and sleeping pills are all central-nervous-system depressants. If you take any of them together the effect is hazardous and can be fatal. Choose one only – have either the Valium or the whisky but not both.

Suppose diuretics and tranquillizers don't work?

There is still hope. For the very few women who fail to be relieved of their premenstrual tension even by the use of diuretics and tranquillizers, some doctors may recommend hormone therapy as a last resort.

As mentioned earlier, true premenstrual tension does not occur in the absence of ovulation. Since some authorities believe that premenstrual tension is a result of the subnormal production of progesterone, therapy aims at supplementing that sagging progesterone output with a synthetic form (called progestogen) taken from about day eighteen to day twenty-five of the menstrual cycle. In the event that progesterone alone fails to bring the desired relief, complete suppression of ovulation by the appropriate preparation of oestrogen–progestogen (combined pill) may be the ultimate answer for premenstrual tension.

8. All about Period Pains and Other Miseries

If you have been blissfully spared from premenstrual tension, there may be other problems just prior to and during your period.

What problems?

Black-and-blues that seem to come from nowhere. Have you ever discovered an unsightly bruise on your leg or arm without any recollection of having tripped over the coffee table? That spontaneous bruising may be related to a decreased oestrogen level just prior to menstruation.

What does a drop in oestrogen have to do with bruises?

Ordinarily any blow severe enough to rupture capillary walls and allow blood to escape into the surrounding tissue will result in a bruise. Oestrogen, in its own unique way, increases the strength and resilience of capillary walls so that a normal decrease of this hormone around the time of your period makes those delicate blood vessels more vulnerable. In a few women lower oestrogen levels have even been implicated in those unusual instances of bleeding from the nose, rectum or bladder during menstruation. A much more common complaint, however, is the annoying recurrence of premenstrual complexion problems.

Can a drop in oestrogen also cause skin blemishes?

Teenagers aren't the only ones plagued with complexion problems. Prior to menstruation there is a normal increase in sebaceous-(oil)gland activity partially kept in check by oestrogen. In women with oily skin especially, excessive production of sebum (oil) together with a cyclic drop in oestrogen output can result in recurrent small outbreaks of premenstrual pimples.

What can be done about it?

Aside from local cleansing and diet restrictions that may or may not be helpful, more severe complexion problems are occasionally treated by suppressing sebaceous-gland activity with oestrogen. To be effective, this treatment usually requires high doses of oestrogen, sufficient in many instances also to inhibit ovulation. For this reason birth-control pills are sometimes prescribed in selected cases. For other women, decreasing the skin bacterial count by small daily doses of the antibiotic tetracycline or similar medication is sometimes equally effective in eliminating the pimple problem.

If by now you are beginning to appreciate how changing hormonal levels can affect you, it is time to broach the subject of dysmenorrhoea (pronounced: *diss*-men-or-ree-a).

What is dysmenorrhoea?

Painful menstrual cramps, or what are generally called period pains. Although most of the cramps are probably contractions of the uterus, some of the discomfort may be caused by spasms of tiny arteries within the wall of the uterus. In any event, dysmenorrhoea is one of the most common gynaecological complaints among teenagers and women in their early twenties. As distressing as severe dysmenorrhoea can sometimes be, young women are not the only victims.

Who else suffers from period pains?

Employers. Millions of work-hours are lost each year because of period pains. Typewriters stand idle, drawing boards are deserted, manuscripts to be edited accumulate and unpunched time cards gather dust.

In schools and colleges 10 per cent of all female students are conspicuously absent from one to three days every month. Many of these girls may have already tried over-the-counter chemists' remedies with little success. For others, prior consultation with a physician may have been less than satisfactory.

Why unsatisfactory?

Women's menstrual discomforts are not always given full consideration. Therapy is limited to aspirin, and if that proves unsuccessful the usual advice, 'Wait until you have a baby', frequently serves as a substitute for proper evaluation and treatment.

Radical approaches in cases of severe dysmenorrhoea are fortunately rare, but they do occur, as indicated by the following comment sent by a reader to the doctor's column of an American newspaper: 'When I try to talk to my family physician about it, his only answer is hysterectomy. At the age of nineteen, this seems to be a pretty drastic step.'

While a hysterectomy would permanently cure this girl of her dysmenorrhoea, the solution would be similar to treating a recurrent ache of the big toe by an above-the-knee amputation.

At the other extreme from those who would propose drastic surgical measures, we find a handful of psychiatrists who are equally radical in their own way. For them the universal solution to severe cramps is psychiatric help. Since most of these experts have never experienced the pain, as far as they are concerned the majority of girls suffering from severe dysmenorrhoea are undoubtedly maladjusted and neurotic. In short, these physicians feel that dysmenorrhoea is all in a woman's head.

Are those period pains all in your head?

Some may be, but most menstrual pains are located much further down. In fact, a good case of dysmenorrhoea installs itself in the middle of the lower abdomen and is frequently accompanied by a heavy aching sensation localized in the lower back and radiating down both legs. It is not uncommon either to experience an acutely uncomfortable feeling of intense vulvar fullness and pressure. In even more serious cases, nausea, vomiting, diarrhoea and headaches can be superimposed physical distresses.

When do the pains usually start and how long can they last?

Menstrual pains can start any time around your period – either before or during the flow. Dysmenorrhoea may even precede menstruation by two days, and although the pains can persist for another three to four days, the most severe pain rarely lasts longer than four to twelve hours.

At times this pain can be of such intensity that nothing short of an examination by a physician can differentiate between severe dysmenorrhoea and a serious abdominal problem. In such a situation and especially if the girl is vomiting, she may well be whisked to hospital in the middle of the night by distraught parents.

What causes period pains?

Nobody knows for sure, but one factor that definitely plays a role is ovulation. Without ovulation and the subsequent formation of a lush uterine lining (secretory endometrium) prior to menstruation, dysmenorrhoea rarely occurs in a young woman. Recent evidence seems to indicate that the shedding of a secretory endometrium can cause longer and harder uterine contractions. Some of you may even have noticed that when you do have a particularly severe cramp, it may be accompanied by the distinct sensation that 'something' has been discharged from the uterine cavity. A sustained spasm of the uterine muscles may also aggravate existing pain by damming up menstrual debris within the uterine cavity.

Can using tampons block the flow of menstrual blood from the uterine cavity?

Highly unlikely. Even if you should use two tampons (side by side for heavy flow), it is most improbable that they could block the cervical opening. Therefore, the use of tampons would in no way aggravate menstrual discomfort by damming up drainage from the uterus.

Why are initial periods in an adolescent girl usually painless?

Lack of ovulation. With rare exception initial periods for approximately one to two years in a young girl are usually anovulatory (no egg – ovum – is released). If ovulatory cycles are responsible for menstrual cramps, then it is entirely possible for a girl to begin menstruating at twelve and not experience painful periods for perhaps another two or three years – or until she begins to ovulate on a monthly basis.

Does not having painful periods mean that you did not ovulate?

Not necessarily. Periods can be painless in women who ovulate regularly. During the menstrual flow the intermittent uterine contractions that normally occur during all menstrual bleeding may be so mild as to remain below the level of conscious awareness.

What about the older woman whose periods become increasingly painful?

Painful periods after years of relative comfort, especially in women over twenty-five, are usually due to secondary dysmenorrhoea, which simply means that the menstrual discomfort is the result of some specific pelvic problem, for example, an old tuban infection or endometriosis. (Endometriosis is one of the more common causes of pelvic distress in women; see Chapter 20 for further information on this pertinent topic.)

Can your doctor always tell what is causing your pains?

Despite the fact that dysmenorrhoea in most young women is probably related to ovulation, an attempt should be made to exclude other possible causes. Here again there is no substitute for a detailed history and a thorough physical examination. Almost without exception the majority of young women who suffer from moderate or even severe pains will have upon examination completely normal pelvic organs. For this reason the term primary dysmenorrhoea is used to describe the occurrence of period pains in the absence of any pelvic abnormality.

Before the relationship between dysmenorrhoea and ovulation was firmly established, various theories were advanced in an effort to explain those awful pains. Since some of these theories are still in circulation and may contain an element of truth, let's examine them briefly.

What were those theories about period pains?

One of the old favourites involved the so-called 'infantile uterus'. In a few women the body of the uterus is somewhat small in relation to the size of the cervix. Doctors reasoned that such an underdeveloped uterus would probably have difficulty in expelling menstrual debris without cramping and significant pain. The theory, although reasonable, was largely discredited by the finding that women with an 'infantile uterus' who suffered from pains could be made comfortable by the suppression of ovulation.

Another popular concept put the blame on poor posture.

Slouching teenage girls suffering from dysmenorrhoea were instructed to throw back their shoulders, tuck in their hips and flatten their tummy – a sure cure for period pains. Those with more severe posture problems were fitted with shoulder straps; despite a possible improvement in general appearance, the pains still won out.

But of all the theories, the most generally accepted explanation for period pains was the presence of a cervical stenosis, or a narrowing of the cervical canal. It was logical to assume that if the cervical canal were partially blocked, the uterus would respond by contracting harder in order to rid its cavity of menstrual debris and blood. Treatment was therefore directed towards relieving the obstruction. For years doctors assiduously dilated the cervical canal of dysmenorrhoeic girls. In the few *bona fide* cases of cervical stenosis, temporary relief was obtained.

Although cervical dilatation may still be necessary in the treatment of other conditions today, its use in relieving period pains has largely been supplanted by more effective therapy.

What can you do about relieving your period pains?

Giving birth to that first child can definitely relieve period pains and discomfort in some women. Why this should be still eludes researchers. The relative painlessness of menstruation following delivery cannot wholly be attributed to the stretching and opening of the cervical canal during childbirth: women who have had Caesarean sections without benefit of cervical dilatation can also experience considerable relief during subsequent menstruation.

So although that often repeated advice, 'Wait until you have your first child', may be partly true, there are other home remedies short of pregnancy that can give relief in less severe cases of dysmenorrhoea. Among the more popular do-it-yourself treatments are the following: heat, nonprescription analgesics, exercise routines, alcoholic beverages and sex.

What about heat?

Ah, wonderful, soothing, relaxing, tension-releasing heat for the cramped pelvic and low-back area and aching legs. Without a doubt heat is one of the oldest and most effective ways of decreasing pain. But whether you luxuriate in a warm bath or snuggle into bed with a cosy hot-water-bottle on your tummy, thirty minutes at any one time will usually give you maximum benefit. Just make certain that the temperature is not too high. And, if you tend to fall asleep while using an electric heating pad, turn it to a medium setting. Prolonged exposure at high temperatures can injure the skin. That temporary red-and-white splotchy look is a sure sign that you overdid it.

Since you can't take your bath, hot-water-bottle or heating pad to work without being too conspicuous, many women will need more help.

What kind of help?

Nonprescription analgesics (pain killers) such as aspirin, salicylamide, paracetamol and combinations of these drugs with a few other things, such as caffeine, thrown in. The wide range of brand names includes Disprin, Phensic, PR Tablets, Anadin, Panadol, Hedex and so on. Analgesic preparations containing codeine and its compounds – for example, Veganin, Panadeine Co., Codis and Paracodol – can only be obtained from pharmacists. Although all of these preparations have been formulated for the broad range of aches and pains, they can also provide occasional relief from period pains. As far as dosage is concerned, follow the directions.

In order to gain the maximum benefit from any of these preparations, start the medication at the first twinge of discomfort. Pain is much easier to control if it is dealt with promptly. You will get faster relief and need less medication in the long run.

Nonprescription analgesic drugs currently marketed as specifically for period pains include EP Tablets (which contain coedine) and Feminax (which contain codeine and a drug to reduce spasms of the uterus). For the woman who finds them effective, the additional cost may be worth it. In any event, the same principle applies – take the medication promptly for maximum benefit.

How about the woman who has trouble swallowing pills?

Since this is not an uncommon problem, a small suggestion might be in order. For those of you who down three glasses of water in rapid succession and still find that pill or tablet obstinately clinging to the roof of your mouth or, worse yet, half dissolved and burning the back of your throat, there is a solution. Take the medication with food and everything will go down without a struggle. Apple sauce, a piece of banana, or soft bread will do. Put the food in your mouth and just before you are ready to swallow, slip the pill or capsule in, mix thoroughly, then swallow. It really works.

Can exercise help relieve period pains?

If you dislike taking medication and want to stay in shape, daily exercises may be the answer to your period pains. Among hundreds of dysmenorrhoeic teenagers who faithfully followed a prescribed exercise routine, almost 70 per cent of them noted definite improvement in menstrual discomfort. If exercises are going to help, relief probably won't be noticed for at least three or four months. Just keep at it every day. Patience and perseverance may triumph in the end.

What are some of these exercises?

Although any daily exercise routine can minimize period pains, the following two exercises have proved effective in helping dysmenorrhoeic girls:

Exercise one. Stand with your feet together and the left side of your body 18–24 inches (50–65 centimetres) away from the wall. Place your left forearm against the wall at shoulder height and your right hand against the hollow of your hip. Strongly contract the abdominal muscles and tighten the buttock muscles at the same time. If you do this properly your pelvis should be tilted forward – somewhat like doing the bumps. Keep those muscles contracted and move your pelvis sideways towards the wall. Hold this position for approximately three to four seconds and then relax. At no time should your heels leave the floor or your hips touch the wall. After doing this routine three times, change positions and repeat three times on the other side.

Exercise two. Standing with feet together, raise your arms out to the sides to shoulder height. Twist your trunk to one side and try to touch the outside of your left foot with your right hand. This should be repeated ten times on each side.

Remember, if you want results, these exercises should be done every day. Who knows, you may win a double bonus – no monthly pains and a better figure.

What about alcoholic beverages?

Alcohol, taken either straight or mixed in a hot drink with boiling water, sugar and lemon juice, stands high on the list of favourite home remedies for period pains. The mechanism of pain relief, although not completely understood, may in part be due to the dilatation of pelvic blood vessels combined with an increased pain tolerance as a result of alcohol's numbing effect on the brain. Indeed, for many adult women, there is nothing quite so effective in relieving menstrual misery as two or three doubles of their favourite tipple followed by a nice warm bath.

Undoubtedly after that much therapy many of us would be ready for bed – if we could find it – but job and family responsibilities rarely allow us such abandon, especially on weekdays. Nevertheless, if the pains should strike after hours and you are fresh out of your favourite medication, alcohol may serve as a temporary soothing measure.

Can having sex help period pains?

Just plain sexual intercourse, no – but having an orgasm, yes. Since some of you may avoid intercourse during your period, masturbation to the point of orgasm can be beneficial. In fact, many women say that orgasmic release can minimize menstrual pains as well as associated low-back or other pelvic discomfort.

Some of the relief obtained from cramping is again probably due to dilatation of pelvic blood vessels. However, you should be aware that following orgasm, there will usually be a temporary increase in the rate of menstrual flow, but the total amount of blood lost during your period will remain essentially the same. For those of you who prefer obtaining orgasmic relief with a partner, the use of a diaphragm during intercourse will help contain any excessive flow.

Suppose all those home remedies fail, then what?

If you've been through the heat and aspirin routine, have drunk yourself into a stupor, exercised for three months and also masturbated – all for naught – the time has probably come to ask your doctor for help.

What can your doctor do for your period pains?

Besides offering a sympathetic ear, your doctor can also provide relief from those awful pains. Any number of effective remedies are available, and one of them is bound to solve your problem.

Ideally, relief should be obtained with as little medication as possible. Although hormone therapy does alleviate pain in almost all cases of dysmenorrhoea, it is usually chosen only for the most extreme cases which haven't responded to other forms of treatment. Sixty per cent of women with moderately severe pains can be made completely comfortable simply by the use of prescription analgesics. For this reason, most doctors prefer to try treatment with nonhormonal drugs for two or three cycles. If, at the end of that time, results have been less than satisfactory, then hormone therapy would be considered.

What medications would initially be tried?

Pharmaceutical companies have not been lax in dealing with dysmenorrhoea. Scores of prescription drugs variously described as analgesics, antispasmodics, sedatives, tranquillizers, vasodilators, etc., are listed for the treatment of menstrual cramps. Most of the vast array of proprietary drugs commonly prescribed for dysmenorrhoea contain aspirin, phenacetin, paracetamol and codeine in various combinations. However the regular use of codeine, even when combined with other ingredients, can have disadvantages.

What can be the disadvantages of taking codeine for period pains?

Because codeine is a narcotic, sedation (that heavy, drugged feeling) and occasional dizziness are common side effects. What is more, for some women it's like drinking three double gins on an empty stomach. They feel really 'woozy'. Since the ideal treatment should also allow you to stay mentally alert, codeine may not be the best answer. Narcotics also have a tendency to make you more sensitive to pain after their effect wears off.

What about the use of hormones?

If all else has failed, hormone therapy can undoubtedly relieve your period pains. The two most practical approaches would be either suppression of ovulation by an oestrogen–progestogen combination (for example, birth-control pills) or hormone therapy that does not interfere with ovulation. The choice of treatment would, of course, depend upon certain factors.

What factors?

Whether or not you want to become pregnant. Until very recently the only effective hormone therapy for menstrual cramps depended upon the suppression of ovulation. With the advent of a new synthetic progestogen (dydrogesterone), relief from severe primary dysmenorrhoea can now be achieved without interfering with ovulation.

In other words, whether you do or don't want to get pregnant, or even if you are not currently concerned with that problem, there is now a perfect solution for you. But your doctor should be made aware of any contraceptive needs you might have because this will definitely influence his choice of treatment for your cramps.

What medication is available if you do want to avoid pregnancy?

If there are no reasons against using oestrogen therapy, the most straightforward solution to your pains would be oral-contraceptive pills or some other oestrogen–progestogen combination. Ovulation would then be suppressed, pregnancy would be prevented and your period would be gloriously painless.

However, if the pill is not for you, those cramps can still be relieved by the use of dydrogesterone. But if you use dydrogesterone, some form of contraception would be necessary if you are sexually active and want to avoid conception. Dydrogesterone does not suppress ovulation.

What is dydrogesterone?

Marketed under the trade name Duphaston, this synthetic progestogen – usually prescribed for days five to twenty-five of the cycle – relieves dysmenorrhoea by decreasing the intensity of uterine contractions during menstruation.

Can any woman take dydrogesterone?

Unlike some hormone preparations, dydrogesterone has to date proved remarkably free of unpleasant side effects. Furthermore, since it doesn't interfere with ovulation, it is ideal for relieving period pains in adolescent girls, in women who may not need a contraceptive, or in women hoping to conceive. Among women who have become pregnant while taking dydrogesterone, there have been no reported adverse effects on the foetus.

The one disadvantage of dydrogesterone may be economic, as this hormone preparation is more expensive than birth-control pills.

Are there any cases of primary dysmenorrhoea beyond help?

Emphatically no. We've come a long way since your grandmother's day in alleviating period pains. No one is beyond help. So, if you are consistently losing time from work, school or, worse yet, missing important social engagements, it is worth going to your doctor. Even if the pains can't be banished completely, you can at least get relief. You certainly don't *have* to go through your reproductive life laid out for two days every month.

9. Irregular Periods and Common Bleeding Problems

And a certain woman, which had an issue of blood
twelve years, and had suffered many things of many
physicians and had spent all that she had, and was
nothing bettered, but rather grew worse. When she
had heard of Jesus, came in the press behind, and
touched his garment. For she said, if I may touch but
his clothes, I shall be whole.
And straightway the fountain of her blood was
dried up . . .

MARK 5, 25–9

Two thousand years have passed since this woman was healed
by the Great Physician, and yet we too live in an age of miracles.
Today, as a result of tremendous advances in endocrinology,
hormone therapy and diagnostic and surgical techniques, bleeding problems previously considered insoluble can be treated and
corrected.

Almost every woman at some time in her life will experience
irregular bleeding. Rather than being a disease in itself, however,
irregular bleeding is merely a symptom of some underlying disturbance. Hormonal imbalances, local tissue trauma, organic
lesions (polyps, tumours and so on) and even medical conditions
not related to pelvic problems are some of the many reasons for
menstrual irregularities and abnormal bleeding.

Hormonal disturbances resulting in lack of ovulation, for
example, can be responsible for scanty and infrequent periods.
By the same token, persistent lack of ovulation in an otherwise
healthy woman can also mimic benign and malignant pelvic conditions by causing profuse, prolonged and frequent bleeding.
Curiously enough, lack of ovulation in some women will not
interefere with their having regular periods. Needless to say, the
diagnosis of female bleeding problems can be challenging at
times.

Since irregular bleeding in women is a very complex subject, only the most frequently encountered problems will be reviewed. The first part of this chapter will discuss hormonal bleeding problems caused by lack of ovulation. Other causes of irregular bleeding, such as tissue trauma, infections and organic lesions, will then be surveyed.

What is really meant by irregular periods?

By the time most girls reach seventeen or have been menstruating for at least three years, a fairly predictable menstrual pattern establishes itself. A significant menstrual irregularity persisting for at least three or more months would be an obvious departure from the established pattern. This irregularity could manifest itself in any number of ways: heavy bleeding, prolonged bleeding, more frequent bleeding, scanty bleeding, skipped periods or even unexpected cessation of all bleeding.

Considering the complexities of hormonal interplay necessary for maintaining regular menstrual cycles, it is not surprising that this intricately balanced system gets out of whack from time to time.

Regular menstrual cycles depend on complete hormonal harmony and optimal physical health combined with mental and emotional equilibrium. Should you fall short in any of these rigorous requirements, you too might join the vast company of women intermittently plagued with bleeding problems. Nonetheless, there are times when even menstrual irregularities can be considered normal.

When is that?

At the two extremes of the reproductive years – in the young girl just beginning her periods and in the older woman approaching the menopause. In both instances lack of ovulation can result in menstrual irregularity.

How can lack of ovulation cause menstrual irregularity in the adolescent?

Until a girl matures sexually and ovulates regularly, menstruation may remain completely unpredictable. Periods of light to heavy bleeding may be followed by absence of menstruation for two or more months at a time, depending on the level of circulating oestrogen. For many girls such menstrual irregularities may continue from one to three years. Bleeding in the sexually immature female is caused by a relative decrease in the output of oestrogen, the only hormone produced by the ovaries until they are sufficiently mature to begin ovulating. With further sexual development, a second ovarian hormone, progesterone, comes into play as a direct result of ovulation. It is the production of progesterone that is largely responsible for the regulation of menstrual cycles. The gradual decrease of the progesterone level towards the end of the cycle (as the corpus luteum degenerates) is what causes the uterine lining (endometrium) to shed *on time*. (See Chapter 5.) So once ovulation is established as a monthly event, the shedding of the uterine lining becomes controlled and predictable.

What about menstrual irregularity in the older woman?

In contrast to the adolescent girl whose periods become regular as the ovaries mature, the older woman approaching the menopause runs the opposite course: the ovaries begin slowing down, ovulation becomes more sporadic, periods become increasingly scanty and infrequent, until finally all menstruation ceases. For some menopausal women, however, persistent lack of ovulation for months at a time can lead to a different type of menstrual irregularity – heavy, flooding periods.

Why the heavy, flooding periods in some older women?

Even in the absence of ovulation, the ovaries of a menopausal woman continue to produce oestrogen, which in turn stimulates the growth of the endometrium. But, and this is an important *but*, without ovulation there is no progesterone to control and regulate the shedding of the endometrium at predictable intervals. Since there may be a span of four to five years between the start of anovulatory (no-egg) cycles and the cessation of all menstruation, this means that the menopausal woman is particularly subject to small but continuous oestrogen stimulation of the endometrium.

Since oestrogen is responsible for the growth and support of endometrial tissue within the uterine cavity, the maintenance of the oestrogen output above a certain critical level allows the growing endometrial tissue to remain intact – no bleeding. Thus, several weeks and even months may pass without any menstrual period.

However, this situation cannot go on indefinitely. Eventually there is an overgrowth or a superabundance of this tissue. Although oestrogen production may continue essentially at the same rate, it is now unable to support the *surplus* of endometrial tissue. As a result the lining of the uterine cavity begins to disintegrate and shed, thereby producing a heavy and frequently prolonged bleeding episode. A woman who may not have menstruated for three or four months may suddenly find herself soaking four or five sanitary towels. Another woman may bleed intermittently for several days or even weeks. Although many menopausal women will have menstrual irregularities as their ovaries slow down (see Chapter 21), this particular type of heavy, flooding period may in some cases be the result of endometrial hyperplasia.

Endometrial hyperplasia – what's that?

Endometrial hyperplasia is an exuberant overgrowth of normal endometrial tissue (uterine lining) caused by long, continuous oestrogen stimulation. Without ovulation and thus without progesterone to regulate the shedding of the endometrium, continuous hormone stimulation of the endometrial tissue by oestrogen *alone* can lead to endometrial hyperplasia. Moreover, this condition is so frequently responsible for abnormal bleeding in the menopausal woman as to be considered almost commonplace.

Endometrial hyperplasia is not malignant. It is a benign condition. Furthermore, it is not limited to older women. Any woman, even a teenager, who has long, persistent oestrogen stimulation of the uterine lining without regular ovulation, can have grossly irregular periods as a result of endometrial hyper-plasia.

As an aside, birth-control pills (although they do suppress ovulation) do not cause endometrial hyperplasia even if taken continuously. On the contrary, the combination of oestrogen and progestogen in the pill in most cases causes the uterine lining to become quite thin.

What can be done about endometrial hyperplasia?

Treatment will depend primarily upon age, the findings on pelvic examination, and duration and severity of the bleeding. In a young woman, cyclic hormonal therapy for three or four months may be all that is needed to correct the situation.

In older women, however, since organic lesions (both benign and malignant) occur more frequently in this age group, any abnormal or irregular bleeding must be approached more cau-tiously. When dealing with grossly irregular bleeding in older women, many doctors prefer to establish a definite diagnosis before proceeding with any specific therapy. This usually implies at the very least an endometrial biopsy or more likely a 'D and C' (dilatation and curettage). The latter procedure essentially involves the scraping of the uterine lining under anaesthesia. The endometrial tissue is thereby removed and microscopically examined for any abnormality or malignancy.

If the diagnosis of endometrial hyperplasia is verified, a D and C would effectively stop the bleeding as well as resolving the problem permanently for a number of women. In others, how-ever, there could be a recurrence of the condition, particularly if the ovaries still produce a fair amount of oestrogen. Under these circumstances, appropriate hormonal therapy could help to keep the condition in check.

Can endometrial hyperplasia ever lead to more serious problems?

In a few instances, it can ultimately develop into a pre-malignant or pre-cancerous lesion necessitating a hysterectomy (removal of the womb). For this reason it is important that women, and

especially older women, with an initial diagnosis of endometrial
hyperplasia be followed closely with regular pelvic examinations,
as well as endometrial biopsies or similar studies when indicated.

What about the young woman whose periods never become regular?

Although most menstrual irregularities in teenage girls tend to
correct themselves in time, a persistent lack of ovulation in
younger women for months and even years is usually indicative
of a definite hormonal disturbance. One such hormonal disorder,
known as the polycystic ovarian syndrome (Stein–Levinthal syndrome), can be responsible for irregular periods and ultimately
cause cystic enlargement of both ovaries. During adolescence,
girls thus affected may initially have heavy erratic bleeding interspersed with fairly regular periods. With continuous lack of
ovulation, however, periods gradually become more scanty, less
frequent, and in many cases cease altogether (amenorrhoea).
Under these circumstances, persistent lack of ovulation not only
results in infertility but can also cause the ovaries to become enlarged as the result of being peppered with multiple small cysts
(thus the name, polycystic ovarian syndrome). Since the polycystic ovarian syndrome is an important cause of infertility, as
well as being responsible for gross menstrual irregularities in
younger women, let's find out more about it.

How does the polycystic ovarian syndrome develop, and what are those cysts?

Normally, during each menstrual cycle many ovarian follicles
begin to grow and develop under the influence of the pituitary
hormone FSH. Ultimately only one of these follicles will mature
fully, migrate to the surface of the ovary and release the egg it
contains. (See Chapter 5.)

In the polycystic ovarian syndrome, this orderly progression
of events is disturbed. The chosen follicle does not rupture and
release its egg, but instead continues to sit, just below the surface
of the ovary – literally stuck. When this happens the pituitary
continues to pour out its hormones in a frustrated attempt to

trigger the release of the egg. As a consequence more and more follicles are stimulated but they too become entrapped in the ovary just below the surface.

Eventually, over a period of many months, both ovaries become studded with multiple follicular cysts, each cyst measuring only a fraction of an inch, but by virtue of their numbers, sufficient to cause an obvious enlargement of the ovaries – up to two or three times normal size.

Why does this ovarian disturbance happen?

Nobody knows for sure. There is evidence to implicate an internal biochemical disturbance in the ovaries themselves, or else a mix-up in central control, possibly at the hypothalamic level. More recent evidence seems to favour the latter possibility.

Why is amenorrhoea so frequently associated with the polycystic ovarian syndrome?

Amenorrhoea, or absence of menstruation for months at a time, may be the result of a relative decrease in oestrogen output. Some women with this syndrome may initially go through a stage of endometrial hyperplasia because of persistent lack of ovulation and continuous oestrogen stimulation. But in time it is also possible for the ovaries to become so disturbed that they are incapable of releasing enough oestrogen to stimulate even a normal build-up of endometrial tissue. As a consequence, the endometrial lining becomes quite thin and, on rare occasions, even atrophic. Thus, all menstruation may cease for lack of sufficient tissue to shed.

The polycystic ovarian syndrome is one of the major causes, other than pregnancy, of prolonged cessation of menstruation in younger women.

Are there any other problems associated with the polycystic ovarian syndrome?

Excessive weight gain may affect up to 40 per cent of women with this condition. Moreover, 70 per cent of women so afflicted are plagued with the growth of superfluous facial and body hair.

What accounts for the unwanted hair growth?

Hirsutism, or the abnormal appearance of dark, coarse facial and body hair, caused by this syndrome is definitely related to increased levels of testosterone in the blood. If you wonder how the male sex hormone, testosterone, got mixed up with this syndrome, you must realize that even *normal* female adrenal glands and ovaries produce small amounts of androgens that are ultimately converted into testosterone. In the polycystic ovarian condition, it is usually the affected ovaries that simply produce more than their normal share of testosterone. Fortunately, however, the extra testosterone manufactured by the deranged ovaries is not usually enough to produce other masculinizing effects, such as a decrease in breast size, temporal balding or clitoral enlargement.

For those of you who want to rush right out and get your doctor to have your testosterone level checked because of a little fuzz on your upper lip, two additional comments are necessary. Unless the facial hair has just recently appeared, or the amount suddenly increased, chances are that it is the result of racial and genetic factors. Secondly, you probably won't be able to get the test done unless you are being extensively evaluated by a specialist in endocrinology for a specific problem.

Can anything be done for women with the polycystic ovarian syndrome?

Very definitely. Even though the ultimate and ideal solution to this hormonal disorder lies in the establishment of regular ovulatory cycles, the selection of appropriate therapy depends in part on a woman's tentative family plans, as well as on clinical evaluation and the results of extensive hormonal studies.

In women who do want to become pregnant, ovulation can frequently be induced by the use of fertility drugs or, occasionally, by surgery on the ovaries. (See Chapter 15.) However, in the teenager or the woman not currently interested in becoming pregnant, attempts at induction of ovulation may be postponed in favour of temporary hormonal therapy.

In what way can hormonal therapy help?

Even without triggering ovulation, proper hormonal therapy can do much to straighten out the distressed ovaries. The use of an oestrogen–progestogen combination would halt continuous stimulation and growth of ovarian follicles by suppressing pituitary hormone output. Thus, further cystic enlargement of the ovaries would be held in check. And the cyclic use (three weeks on, one week off) of hormonal therapy would further assure the regular monthly shedding of the uterine lining.

As an extra bonus, testosterone output by the ovaries would also decrease, thus preventing further abnormal hair growth. In time this could mean the possible thinning and lightening of excess facial hair in a few cases. But in most women, superfluous facial and body hair present prior to therapy would not be affected.

Can emotional disturbances ever cause hormonal bleeding problems?

Absolutely. Adverse mental and emotional stresses can readily shake up the delicate hypothalamic–pituitary–ovarian system. Psychologically traumatic situations, such as a blighted romance, marital separation, or the death of a loved one have all been implicated in upsetting previously normal periods.

However, all emotional upheavals affecting ovulation and menstruation need not be cataclysmic in intensity. A less dramatic but nonetheless common example is that of the young woman who leaves home for the first time. She may be only five miles down the road and yet the abrupt physical separation from her family is sufficiently distressing to disturb normal hormonal interplay. For many such women this could temporarily mean skipped or scanty periods. Less commonly, severe emotional or psychic stress can bring about the reverse problem – psychogenic bleeding.

What is psychogenic bleeding?

Few conditions so dramatically illustrate the power of the mind over the body as that typified by psychogenic or spontaneous bleeding under stress. One such case involved a young over-wrought student who virtually went to pieces at the thought of having to take an oral or written examination.

Invariably this girl would begin bleeding during every quiz, weekly or mid-term examination. As the term progressed, the bleeding became so increasingly predictable and heavy that it was necessary for her to put on a sanitary towel prior to entering an examination. Needless to say, after weeks of frustration on the part of the university physicians to diagnose and solve her problem, psychotherapy and the abandonment of her degree course effected a solution.

Emotional factors aren't the only ones that can cause trouble. Any long-standing chronic illness or acute physical ailment, if serious enough, can disrupt hormonal balance. Medications, particularly tranquillizers, have also been directly responsible for upsetting normal periods in some women. Along similar lines, crash diets, when carried too far, are notorious in creating general havoc in the hypothalamic–pituitary system.

How can crash diets affect your periods?

If you plan to limit your weight-loss to a mere 5–10 pounds (2·3–4·5 kilograms), then the following need not concern you. But if you suddenly decide that those 40–50 pounds (18–22 kilograms) of excess baggage must vanish instantly, you may be asking for trouble. Crash diets that transcend the boundaries of sanity can bring your menstrual periods to a screeching halt. Long before achieving your desired silhouette, a too rapid weight-loss or continuous poor nutrition can adversely inhibit the hypothalamic and pituitary centres – and then, good-bye periods, hello amenorrhoea.

Even with a return of sensible eating habits, it may be months before hormonal balance and menstruation are re-established. If you have just changed your mind about going on a radical reducing diet, you should also know that being obese is another potential threat to regular menstruation.

How can overweight affect your periods?

Lack of ovulation and irregular bleeding in some women have been linked to excess body fat. Since small amounts of oestrogen are normally stored in body fat, the more fatty tissue you have, the more oestrogen is likely to be removed from your bloodstream and retained in these areas. Being extremely overweight also means that the body needs an increased blood plasma volume to nourish the excess adipose tissue. A larger plasma volume further dilutes the concentration of circulating oestrogen. In short, your ovaries may be perfectly normal and produce ample amounts of oestrogen, but if too much oestrogen is being stored in body fat, you may actually have too little oestrogen circulating in your bloodstream. This can mean a relative oestrogen deficiency, sufficiently severe to disrupt the normal hormonal balance necessary for ovulation and regular periods. For some women, just losing that extra weight can restore ovulation and normal menstruation.

As mentioned earlier, women with the polycystic ovarian syndrome may tend toward obesity. In this situation, however, a simple weight-loss will unfortunately not restore ovulatory cycles because the hormonal disturbance is too profound.

Is your thyroid ever to blame for menstrual irregularities?

It can be, but less often than commonly supposed. An overactive thyroid can indirectly cause scanty and infrequent periods. At the other extreme, and in teenagers especially, a sluggish, underactive gland can be responsible for heavy and frequent periods. But unless there is a *bona fide* need substantiated by clinical evaluation and thyroid-function studies, treatment to supplement the thyroid hormones is usually of little value in correcting menstrual irregularities.

If you ovulate regularly, can you still have normal bleeding problems?

Yes. Although the majority of hormonal bleeding problems are the result of anovulation (lack of ovulation), such is not always the case. Even in the absence of organic disease, irregular uterine bleeding can occur during ovulatory cycles.

Midcycle bleeding or spotting at the time of ovulation has already been described in Chapter 6. Slight imbalance in hormonal interplay during an ovulatory cycle can also account for other irregularities such as more frequent periods, prolonged periods, heavier periods and one of the most common complaints, premenstrual staining.

What about premenstrual staining?

In order for your flow to start normally, the cyclic decrease of oestrogen and progesterone levels just prior to menstruation must be perfectly synchronized. If your menstrual flow is invariably ushered in by a brown, gunky discharge or a continuous pink-tan staining lasting three to four days or even longer, your problem may be due to teetering levels of progesterone resulting in scanty premature shedding of the uterine lining. If the spotting becomes prolonged or a source of concern to the woman, hormone treatment to 'top up' progesterone during the last few days of the cycle will usually resolve the problem.

Besides hormonal disturbances, what else can cause irregular bleeding?

Even if your hormones have managed to stay in perfect balance despite all adversities, there are many other conditions that can cause irregular bleeding. To mention just a few in passing, iron-deficiency anaemia can provoke heavier periods, as can a deficiency in blood platelets, an important factor necessary for proper blood clotting. In fact, a decrease in blood platelets (thrombocytopenia) is occasionally the only explanation for profuse menses in a young woman.

Other causes of abnormal bleeding can be brought about by tissue trauma, polyps and adenomyosis (more about these shortly), certain fibroid tumours (see Chapter 19), endometriosis (see Chapter 20) and malignant changes (see Chapter 23).

Surprisingly enough, one of the most common causes of

abnormal bleeding can occur during the first few weeks of pregnancy.

Abnormal bleeding in early pregnancy?

Whenever a woman of reproductive age complains of irregular bleeding or spotting, most doctors will automatically consider pregnancy as a possible diagnosis. Complications involving an early pregnancy constitute the number-one reason for abnormal bleeding in this age group.

Although missing a period is usually the first indication of pregnancy, not all women keep close track of their periods, nor do all women have consistently regular cycles. Therefore, it is not unusual for a woman to have bleeding as the result of a pregnancy of which she is unaware. A threatened loss in early pregnancy may cause intermittent spotting at the time of the expected period and can be easily mistaken for a scanty or unusual flow. Or a heavy, gushing late period may in reality be a miscarriage (spontaneous abortion).

Is bleeding and tissue trauma following first intercourse common?

Despite the popular use of tampons and the ease with which most hymens can be stretched, there are some women who at the time of first intercourse still have a relatively snug vaginal opening. If this is the case, persistent penile thrusts by an over-eager and generally inexperienced partner can cause pain and hymenal lacerations. Fortunately, most of these hymenal tears are not serious. Bleeding is minimal and healing occurs rapidly.

Aside from possible psychological trauma and making the area tender and off-limits for a few days, there are times when hymenal bleeding and tissue trauma can be sufficiently distressing to necessitate professional help.

Casualty officers see their share of bruised and bleeding hymens. For young teenagers especially, this can be a particularly frightening and embarrassing predicament. Frightening because they don't know how to stop the bleeding and embarrassing because, once the girl has been treated, her family will usually be contacted so that someone can come to take her home. If the girl is obviously young (sixteen is the legal age of consent to sexual intercourse), or if she is distressed or shows signs of forced intercourse, the hospital authorities will also want to be satisfied that hers is not a case of illegal intercourse, rape or indecent assault.

Many of these scenes can be avoided if the young couple involved are a little more knowledgeable.

Is there any way of avoiding hymenal injury during first intercourse?

Any woman contemplating sexual intercourse should have some awareness regarding the size of her vaginal opening. Being able to slip in a tampon is no assurance that penile penetration will be readily accomplished. Even super tampons do not approach the diameter of the average penis in full erection.

Perhaps the most practical method of determining the adequacy of the vaginal opening is the digital technique, or the two-finger estimate.

How can you be sure you have an accommodating vagina?

If you can insert the tips of your middle and index fingers into the vagina and then separate them at least one quarter of an inch or more, your vaginal opening is probably adequate. If your dimensions are such that this manoeuvre causes slight discomfort, the impetus of sexual excitement and increased vaginal lubrication may be sufficient to overcome any difficulty. However, if you do experience pain, gentle dilating exercises are probably in order.

What kind of dilating exercises can enlarge a small vaginal opening?

Lubricate the vaginal entrance with K-Y lubricating jelly (non-prescription), Vaseline or a similar product and slip into a warm bath. Sometimes the added heat makes the tissues stretch more easily.

Insert the middle finger about halfway and gently press downward toward the rectum until you can feel the vaginal opening stretching. When you reach the point of mild discomfort, hold your finger there for a few moments and then relax. By alternately sustaining and releasing the pressure for three or four seconds at a time, the tissues will gradually give – but stop before it becomes painful.

If your vagina can initially accommodate the tips of both fingers, so much the better. In this case, just spreading the fingers apart intermittently will be sufficient. Exercising about five minutes a day should bring noticeable improvement in about two or three weeks.

If perchance you cannot even insert one finger into the vagina and are contemplating intercourse, the best advice is to have yourself examined. You may need a minor surgical procedure (hymenectomy or hymenotomy) to enlarge the vaginal opening.

But since advice sometimes comes too late, let's go back to the first problem – bleeding after first intercourse.

What can you do if hymenal bleeding does not stop?

If you have just experienced first intercourse and there is hymenal bleeding that seems reluctant to stop, there may be a solution short of seeing a doctor.

But don't handle the problem by lying down and elevating your hips and legs. This method only serves to hide bleeding temporarily by allowing blood to pool in the upper vagina.

In many instances the source of the bleeding can readily be seen by simply examining yourself with a mirror. Therefore, unless the hymenal tear involves a fair-sized blood vessel or the injury lies further up the vagina, continuous firm pressure against the bleeding point will usually resolve the problem. A sanitary pad rolled into a tight ball makes a handy, efficient pressure bandage. Place the rolled pad tightly against the vaginal opening and sit on a firm, flat surface for at least ten to fifteen minutes. This position should effectively compress the pad against the hymenal area. Avoid the temptation to check on the bleeding until the allotted time is over. If, however, bleeding still continues at a worrisome rate, you probably do need help. Better call your doctor or go to the nearest hospital emergency room.

Can bleeding ever occur after intercourse in a woman who has an accommodating vagina?

Yes. Postcoital bleeding, that is, spotting or bleeding after intercourse, can frequently be caused by benign cervical problems. The cervix, because of its location at the far end of the vagina, is particularly vulnerable to deep penile thrusts during intercourse. Thus, the impact of the penis against a raw, chronically irritated cervix (cervicitis) or a dangling cervical polyp can account for the unexpected and painless appearance of postcoital bleeding.

Cervical problems such as the above can also be responsible for intermenstrual bleeding (bleeding between periods) and bleeding after douching.

What causes these cervical problems in the first place?

Cervicitis and cervical polyps (which originate in the endo-cervical canal) are usually the result of a persistent, mild cervical infection. Since the vagina provides a warm, dark, moist environment, it is not surprising that the presence of organisms both normal and abnormal, menstrual blood or tissue trauma resulting from childbirth can all contribute to making the cervix a frequent site of chronic irritation and infection.

What can be done about chronic cervicitis?

If the possibility of a malignancy has been eliminated as the source of the cervical bleeding (negative cancer smear), most cases of chronic cervicitis can be treated effectively in outpatients by simple cauterization – that is, destruction of the infected tissue by the application of heat, cold or chemicals. (See Chapter 19.) Following cauterization and subsequent healing, a red, raw and irritated cervix will revert to its normal pink and healthy state.

What about cervical polyps?

Since cervical polyps are small, fragile, tear-shaped growths that usually dangle on a stalk and protrude through the cervical os, they can sometimes be easily and painlessly removed in out-patients. On the other hand, the successful removal of polyps located well within the cervical canal may necessitate a stay in hospital. With rare exceptions, cervical polyps are always benign. Nevertheless, for diagnosis and verification, cervical polyps are routinely submitted to a pathologist for microscopic examination.

Not all polyps are cervical, however, nor are they all so easily dispensed with. Endometrial polyps are another common source of abnormal bleeding.

What's so different about endometrial polyps?

Unlike cervical polyps, endometrial polyps sprout from the endometrial lining. They are not the result of infection, but rather represent discrete and usually benign overgrowths of normal endometrial tissue in response to continuous oestrogen stimulation. They are frequently multiple and can either spread out within the uterine cavity as broad, flat projections of tissue or dangle from small stalks. On rare occasions, if one of these stalks is long enough, an endometrial polyp can make an appearance through the cervical os just like a cervical polyp. Under ordinary circumstances, however, endometrial polyps can neither be felt nor seen on routine pelvic examination. Unless they cause symptoms – bleeding between periods, prolonged postmenstrual spotting or staining or occasional heavy and prolonged periods – their presence may be completely unsuspected.

Diagnosis as well as the correction of the condition usually depends upon scraping out the uterine lining under anaesthesia (D and C: dilatation and curettage).

Can anything else cause prolonged, heavy periods?

Adenomyosis. In this unique situation, which most commonly affects women between the ages of thirty-five and fifty, misplaced fragments of endometrial tissue from the uterine lining actually become embedded within the muscular walls of the uterus. How or why this happens remains unclear, but the end result is an enlarged, soft and boggy uterus. Periods can become increasingly long, profuse and frequently associated with a sense of pelvic pressure and discomfort. Unfortunately, adenomyosis does not respond readily to hormonal therapy, nor can the symptoms be alleviated by a dilatation and curettage. Therefore, where pelvic discomfort does exist and bleeding is excessive, removal of the uterus (hysterectomy) is sometimes the best solution.

Similarly, the presence of misplaced fragments of endometrial tissue on the ovaries or elsewhere in the pelvic cavity (endometriosis) can also be a source of menstrual irregularity and pelvic distress. (See Chapter 20.)

Does cancer of the female pelvic organs usually cause irregular bleeding?

Not necessarily. Much depends upon the location of the malignancy and the extent of the disease. Although cancer of the female organs is reviewed in Chapter 23, a few pertinent comments are in order here.

Bleeding is never present with early cancer of the cervix. Detection of an early curable cervical cancer relies almost exclusively on routine cervical smears. In endometrial carcinoma (cancer involving the lining of the uterine cavity) spotting may be the very first indication that all is not well. Fortunately, if these early symptoms are reported and properly investigated, chances are really excellent for a complete cure of endometrial cancer. As for a malignancy of the ovaries, irregular bleeding is rarely present as an early symptom.

Is it ever possible to bleed after straining or lifting a heavy object?

It is surprising how many women, particularly postmenopausal women, will attribute an unexpected episode of bleeding or spotting to some unusual physical exertion. Although abnormal uterine bleeding may on rare occasions coincide with strenuous physical activity, there is usually some other explanation for it.

What about postmenopausal bleeding?

Any bleeding or spotting that occurs six months or longer after the last period should be investigated. Oestrogen supplemental therapy in the postmenopausal woman, for example, can and does cause uterine bleeding on occasion. But if there is any abnormal bleeding, the possibility that an early malignant or premalignant lesion may be the cause must always be considered. *Hormones of and by themselves do not cause pelvic cancer*. Moreover, staining that lasts only a day or so does not mean that the problem is of no consequence. Conversely, heavy or prolonged bleeding does not necessarily indicate a more serious condition. In other words, any postmenopausal bleeding should be reported promptly – regardless of whether it's profuse or nothing more than an occasional pink stain. The important fact is not the amount of bleeding but the presence of blood itself.

Why is it important to report any unusual bleeding promptly?

As you may appreciate from this brief survey of the more common bleeding problems, there are any number of reasons for irregular periods and abnormal bleeding, some quite simple and others profoundly complex. The proper management of abnormal or irregular bleeding, regardless of your age, begins with you. Unless you make a point of presenting your complaints without undue delay, you will be doing a disservice both to yourself and to your doctor. It goes without saying that any problem causing abnormal bleeding or menstrual irregularity has a good chance of being effectively resolved when treated promptly.

Part 3

The Vulnerability of Woman

10. Vaginal Infestations, Infections and Irritations

Living a celibate existence, steadfastly refusing to sit on a public toilet seat, and being fastidious in your personal hygiene is no assurance that you will be spared a visit from one of the 'unwelcome three'. If you are currently bothered with a vaginal discharge, a vulvar irritation, or itching of the external genitalia, you might find consolation in knowing that 25 per cent of the women who go to a gynaecologist seek help expressly for one or all of these problems.

Do you realize that crabs are staging a comeback?

Whatever you call them – pubic lice or pediculosis pubis – crabs are back. Unlike body and scalp lice, these creatures are irresistibly drawn to pubic hair. With the apparent increase in sexual permissiveness, infestation of the hair-bearing area of the vulva by this six-legged louse is now a potential threat to many women.

How can you get crabs?

Easily. Although sexual intercourse with an infested person is the simplest, just an intimate hug will suffice if you are both unclothed. And beware of close physical contact with articles that may be contaminated, such as sheets, blankets, sleeping bags, clothing, etc. They too can invite an invasion.

What are the symptoms?

A maddening pubic itch, particularly devastating in the middle of the night. The itching is apparently caused by a noxious substance excreted into the skin by this mini-vampire. Once it latches on, the crab louse, which requires human blood for survival, pierces the skin and buries its head inside a pubic hair follicle.

How can you be sure you have crabs?

By looking carefully. Even though an average infestation may have six or seven adult crabs, spotting one readily may not be that easy. Each crab louse measures only about 1·2 mm in diameter and may require a magnifying glass for identification. Other telltale signs are the eggs or nits, tiny (0·5 mm) oval white specks usually deposited near the junction of the hair and skin.

What should you do about those awful crabs?

First of all, don't panic. As loathsome as crabs may be, they don't carry any horrible disease.

Do not shave your pubic hair or use any questionable local medication. Injudicious self-treatment may add to your misery by superimposing a severe skin irritation while the crabs, undaunted, merrily carry on.

It is best to see your doctor or to visit a special clinic. For all you or anybody else knows, perhaps you picked up the crabs while trying on that new bikini at one of the more fashionable shops. So don't let embarrassment delay your seeking help.

What is the best treatment?

Your doctor will prescribe treatment with a shampoo, a lotion or cream. A four-minute pubic-hair shampoo followed by a thorough drying will usually eradicate most infestations. The crabs will succumb and any remaining nits can be easily removed by a fine-tooth comb. Occasionally a repeat shampoo treatment in twenty-four hours may be necessary.

If cream or lotion is prescribed, it should be liberally applied over the infested area and left on for twenty-four hours. The cream and lotion have the added advantage of being able to kill the lice on clothing. If a repeat treatment is necessary, a delay of four days is recommended before reapplying.

In addition to getting rid of your personal hangers-on, you should also know how to avoid reinfestation.

How can you prevent a crab comeback?

All clothing, sheets, blankets, sleeping bags, mattresses and anything with which you have been in close contact should be
laundered (boiling water) or dry-cleaned. Moreover, make sure
that your partner, if any, gets and uses his own course of
treatment.

If your budget can ill afford such a cleaning bill and as your
mattress can't squeeze into your washing machine, there is
another solution. The crab louse once deprived of the blood of a
human host will die within twenty-four hours. And since the
tiny nits take about a week or ten days to hatch, all articles can
actually be self-sterilized and made crab-free if left undisturbed
and away from human contact for at least two weeks.

What about other vulvar afflictions?

Contact dermatitis of the vulva – an inflammatory reaction of the
vulvar skin – is also definitely on the upswing. Slight reddening
of the vulvar skin followed by an itching sensation may be the
only symptoms. More severe reactions can progress to labial
swelling and an eruption of clear, bubble-like blisters that
eventually drain and crust over.

If you happen to have sensitive skin, or if you are allergic, any
number of unsuspected agents may be responsible for a localized
vulvar irritation. Just using a new bath soap or laundry detergent
can cause trouble. Bubble-bath products in particular have been
blamed for acute vulvitis (inflammation of the vulva) in young
girls. Sprucing up your bathroom with a flashy new coloured
toilet paper has been a source of allergic reactions in women
sensitive to the dye. Condoms, douche ingredients, vaginal
foams for contraception, sanitary towels, new synthetic fabrics
in undergarments, tights, girdles and feminine spray deodorants
have all been implicated in making sensitive women absolutely
miserable.

Allergic reactions from drugs can also cause vulvar distress.
Medications such as aspirin, phenacetin, sulphur drugs and
phenolphthalein, an ingredient in many laxative preparations

(for example, Ex-lax and Feen-a-mint), have on occasion been responsible for vulvar inflammation.

What can be done about contact or allergic vulvitis?

The cure depends upon identifying and eliminating the offending agent. Soap and hot water should definitely be avoided. For temporary relief, cool compresses of boric acid (one tablespoon in 1½ pints – about 0·9 litres – of water) or else soaking in a tepid cornflour bath (two cups of cornflour in half a tub of water) twice a day may hold you over until you get help. Furthermore, be sure to pat yourself gently dry (no rubbing) and avoid nylon underwear, tights or tight-fitting undergarments that, by trapping moisture, could aggravate the skin irritation. Loose-fitting cotton underwear is definitely preferable.

If additional relief is necessary, your doctor would probably prescribe a soothing cortisone lotion or ointment to be applied locally. In extremely severe cases, antihistamines as well as cortisone by mouth for a few days may be indicated to reduce the inflammatory and allergic tissue response.

What else can cause vulvar irritation?

Vaginal problems. Without a doubt vaginal infections and abnormal discharges are definitely one of the most common causes of vulvar inflammation.

Is it normal to have a vaginal discharge?

Yes, indeed. Vaginal secretions are both normal and necessary. Without secretions from the cervix, vaginal walls and Bartholin's glands, the inside of the vagina would feel like a roll of dried parchment. Your vagina needs moisture and lubrication just as your mouth needs saliva.

Under normal and healthy conditions, endocervical glands produce a clear mucus secretion. As this mucus drains downward and mixes with discarded vaginal cells, normal bacteria and Bartholin's gland secretions, it assumes a whitish colour. Moreover, when this normal white vaginal secretion comes into contact with underwear, it gradually changes in colour to pale yellow as the result of oxidation (exposure to air). As long as the discharge is not excessive, does not cause itching, irritation, swelling or an unpleasant odour, it is probably normal.

In certain situations, however, normal vaginal secretions increase temporarily.

What changes can account for increased vaginal secretions?

Several factors – oestrogen level, emotional stress and sexual excitement.

During ovulation (midcycle), higher oestrogen levels increase cervical secretions and that may account for your noticing a clear mucus drainage at this time. In the same way, higher oestrogen levels in women taking oral contraceptives can also cause a definite increase in vaginal secretions.

Emotional stress and sexual excitement in particular are also commonly associated with a more obvious but temporary discharge. During sexual arousal, the profuse, clear secretion that bathes the entire vagina and introitus actually comes from the vaginal walls as an indirect result of dilatation and engorgement of vaginal blood vessels. Even in women over sixty the vagina can still exude considerable lubrication when properly stimulated. Thus, factors such as age, relative lack of oestrogen, or previous hysterectomy do not materially diminish the vaginal 'sweating' phenomenon under conditions of sexual excitement.

Nonetheless, age alone can definitely alter other normal vaginal secretions.

How does age influence vaginal secretions?

With gradual oestrogen withdrawal in the postmenopausal woman, the thick, succulent, corrugated vaginal walls gradually become relatively thin, dry and smooth. Cervical secretions diminish and normal bacteria indirectly responsible for maintaining normal vaginal acidity become scarce. As a result, vaginal secretions become scanty and relatively alkaline.

Why are normal vaginal secretions acid in the younger woman?

Protection. Maintenance of a relatively acid vaginal environment discourages the growth of some organisms responsible for distressing vaginal discharges.

In women during the reproductive years, for example, cyclic, normal decreases in vaginal acidity just before and after menstruation may be sufficient to give lurking culprits a foothold or even aggravate an existing abnormal discharge. Menstrual blood can also provide a delectable environment for the propagation of unwanted outsiders.

What outsiders?

Excluding gonorrhoea (see Chapter 11), the top contenders currently responsible for plaguing many adult women with vaginal infections and abnormal discharges are *Trichomonas vaginalis* (protozoon), *Candida albicans* (fungus) and *Haemophilus vaginalis* (bacterium).

Although their impressive names will probably slip from your memory in short order, a personal encounter with any of them will undoubtedly leave a more lasting impression.

What about *Trichomonas vaginalis*?

This one-celled microscopic protozoan organism produces a copious, watery, malodorous, yellowish or greenish-white discharge. In severe infections the discharge can be so excessive as to cause marked vulvar irritation and chafing of the upper inner thighs and rectal area.

The associated itching, soreness and inflammation of the vaginal opening and vulva can dampen any woman's enthusiasm for sex. Coitus, if attempted during an acute infection, can be painful.

Where does it come from?

No one really knows. Although about one woman out of five harbours this protozoan organism without any telltale signs or symptoms, *Trichomonas vaginalis* is not a normal inhabitant of the vagina or anywhere else in the human body. Moreover, this vaginal infection is not acquired either by faecal contamination of the vagina or by oral genital sex (cunnilingus). Even if the trouble-causing protozoa are introduced into the mouth or transferred to the rectum in certain varieties of sexual play, they do not survive long enough in these two areas to end up as a source of vaginal reinfection.

How, then, do women become infected?

Since 60 to 80 per cent of male partners of infected women unknowingly harbour this organism in their urinary tract, the vast majority of *Trichomonas vaginalis* infections are acquired through contact of sexual organs or coitus with an infected partner. Almost without exception this specifically implies either penis-to-vagina or close vulva-to-vulva contact. The fact that the organism does not survive in the mouth or the rectum makes the transmission of *Trichomonas vaginalis* among homosexual men virtually impossible. Men thus acquire the organism only through coitus with an infected woman. Furthermore, once contracted, *Trichomonas vaginalis* can readily ping-pong back and forth between sexual partners.

Occasional cases have been attributed to inter-changing moist washcloths, wet bathing suits, or to sitting on that infamous and perennially contaminated toilet seat, but these are really unusual sources of infection. Similarly, sharing a swimming pool with a group of carriers is also a highly unlikely mode of transmission. Most *Trichomonas vaginalis* organisms rapidly succumb when exposed to chlorinated water.

Do men ever suffer from *Trichomonas vaginalis*?

Rarely. Even when the organisms are present within the male urethra, only a few men will notice slight burning after ejaculation. Thus, many men can be carriers and unknowingly infect and reinfect their female sexual partners.

Are there any special tests to detect a *Trichomonas vaginalis* infection?

Other than the copious and malodorous discharge so charac-teristic of an acute vaginal infection, definite diagnosis depends on microscopic identification of the protozoa.

Nonetheless, since some women can harbour this organism without obvious signs of vaginal infection, many doctors make routine checks of vaginal secretions. The presence of *Trichomonas vaginalis* can also be detected by a cervical smear and is frequently reported as an incidental finding.

Can *Trichomonas vaginalis* ever cause other problems?

Acute vaginal or cervical infections can be a cause of atypical or slightly abnormal cervical-smear reports. In this respect, the *Trichomonas vaginalis* protozoon is the culprit most frequently responsible.

Appropriate treatment of the infection will allow the vaginal and cervical cells to return to normal and the cervical smear to revert to Class I negative. (See Chapter 4.)

What can be done about *Trichomonas vaginalis* infections?

Even if there are no symptoms, the presence of *Trichomonas vaginalis* still warrants treatment to prevent a possible flare-up of the organism. Currently the most effective medication is the prescription drug metronidazole (Flagyl). In about 95 per cent of affected women, a single course of treatment with metroni-dazole (by mouth) will eradicate the infection if the sexual partner is also treated simultaneously.

A decrease in discharge and vulvovaginal irritation will fre-quently be noticed within two or three days. However, improve-ment or disappearance of the symptoms is not an indication to stop taking the tablets before the end of the course. Premature discontinuation of your metronidazole or failure to treat your sexual partner may be responsible for treatment failure or recurrences necessitating repeat treatment.

Isn't local vaginal treatment just as effective against *Trichomonas vaginalis*?

Not really. Because the organisms can also set up headquarters in the female urinary tract (urethra or bladder), sometimes causing a burning sensation on urination, treatment limited to the vagina in the form of medicated creams and suppositories, etc. will rarely provide a complete cure. At best, local therapy only brings temporary relief by decreasing the vaginal population without affecting possible urinary-tract culprits. Thus, the organisms located outside the vagina would escape treatment and remain potential sources of self-reinfection.

On occasion, however, local vaginal therapy in a few women may initially hasten comfort by reducing excessive discharge.

What about the fungus among us?

Whether your doctor calls it moniliasis, vaginal thrush, candidiasis, or just plain yeast, vulvovaginal infections caused by the fungus *Candida albicans* are currently the most prevalent and the most stubborn to treat.

Unlike *Trichomonas vaginalis*, with its copious and offensive discharge, *Candida* excels in provoking intolerable vaginal and vulvar itching sufficient in many instances to drive the most placid woman frantic. Itching is invariably followed by scratching and, of course, the more persistent the itch–scratch cycle, the greater the irritation, inflammation and swelling of the labial structures. Breaks in the skin from excessive scratching can also invite a secondary bacterial infection. Frequently, just urinating will cause a burning sensation as the urine comes into contact with the raw and irritated tissues.

The type of discharge produced by this fungus can vary from woman to woman. Some women may only notice a slight, watery, white drainage. Others might complain that the vagina actually feels dry. More commonly, thick curdlike chunks of a white cheesey substance mixed with a water discharge may be seen at the vaginal opening. If it is profuse, the discharge can cause an intensely itchy rash on the entire vulva, from the mons to well beyond the rectum and along the upper inner thighs.

Where does this fungus come from?

Many places. In many women, *Candida albicans* is a normal vaginal inhabitant. It is also frequently harboured in the mouth and intestines of both sexes. Even in healthy individuals without any apparent signs or symptoms, this fungus has been recovered from urine, seminal fluid and between folds of opposing skin surfaces (for example, under the foreskin, between the buttocks, etc.). All of these areas can be potential sources of vaginal infection or reinfection. But unless certain conditions favourable for its growth and propagation occur, the fungus when present ordinarily remains quite unobtrusive.

In women who do not have *Candida albicans* as a normal vaginal inhabitant, the fungus can readily be introduced by faecal contamination of the vagina or, less commonly, by cunnilingus or coitus with a partner who harbours the organism. On the other hand, the chance of developing a fungus (monilia) infection of the mouth is extremely remote. (See Chapter 14.)

But regardless of whether the fungus is a normal vaginal inhabitant or is introduced into the vagina, the same principle applies – as long as conditions remain unfavourable for its growth, nothing will happen.

What can cause a fungal flare-up?

Many things, including pregnancy, oral contraceptives, an increased blood sugar level, antibiotics and various unknown factors.

How can pregnancy or birth-control pills cause a fungal infection?

By creating just the right vaginal environment for the growth of this fungus. The explanation is indirectly related to the higher oestrogen levels found both in pregnant women and in women taking oral contraceptives. Because oestrogen normally causes glycogen (a carbohydrate) to be deposited within the vaginal cells, a higher level of oestrogen will therefore result in an increased amount of vaginal cellular glycogen and thus a 'sweeter' vaginal environment.

What does glycogen have to do with this fungus?

This fungus grows, multiplies and thrives in a glycogen-rich environment. Under these circumstances, a woman whose vagina was previously unreceptive to the growth of the fungus may experience her first real vaginal infection. Just starting on birth-control pills, for example, can precipitate a sudden and acute vaginal fungus infection in some women, sufficiently distressing to discourage sexual intercourse. At times, a persistent vaginal fungus infection may even be aggravated by excessive intake of sweets and cakes and, less commonly, by an undiagnosed mild diabetic condition.

During pregnancy, vaginal fungus infections are exceedingly common and invariably affect 15 to 25 per cent of all pregnant women. Until delivery and the re-establishment of a less 'sugary' environment, treatment is seldom successful. In many pregnant women the infection spontaneously disappears after delivery, thereby requiring no additional treatment.

Can a vaginal fungus infection during pregnancy affect the baby?

Infrequently, and only during delivery, if then. As the infant passes through the vaginal canal, it may pick up the organism. Most fungus infections (thrush) in the newborn that are acquired this way are limited primarily to the mouth and throat. They are rarely serious and can be readily treated and cured.

Can anything else precipitate a vaginal fungus infection?

Antibiotics (particularly tetracycline – less commonly penicillin and others) prescribed for unrelated problems such as strep throat or urinary infections may also result in a vaginal fungus infection in susceptible women. Although the explanation for this phenomenon has been attributed to the suppression by the antibiotic of normal protective vaginal bacteria, which exert an

anti-fungal effect, the exact mechanism is not completely understood.

How can a vaginal fungus infection be diagnosed?

Frequently by simple inspection or microscopic examination of
vaginal secretions. Otherwise a culture can be taken.

What is a culture?

Whenever proper and definitive treatment of an infection depends on the accurate identification of the responsible organism
(whether bacterium or fungus), the secretion, discharge or
material suspected of containing the organism is smeared onto a
special medium capable of nourishing the offender in question
and causing it to proliferate. Within twenty-four to forty-eight
hours, sufficient growth of the organism will have occurred to
make a specific laboratory identification.

In regard to gonorrhoea in women, for example, a culture is
virtually indispensable in making the diagnosis. (See Chapter
11.)

What about treatment for vaginal fungus infections?

Since there is no magic pill that will effectively eliminate *Candida
albicans*, treatment depends on anti-fungal vaginal creams or
suppositories (pessaries).

To be really effective, treatment should be continued for at
least two and, in stubborn cases, as long as five weeks. This
usually means inserting a vaginal cream or suppository – for
example, nystatin – twice a day, continuing for one week after
symptoms have gone. For some women, the gunky drainage from
dissolving suppositories or creams frequently causes them to use
the medication sporadically or even discontinue therapy at the
first sign of improvement in symptoms. Needless to say, inadequate treatment invariably accounts for another flare-up.

In severe or persistent infections, the vagina can be treated
with a gentian-violet solution (a messy purple medication). This
really does help, but watch out for stubborn stains on underwear
that will challenge any enzyme detergent.

For the woman on birth-control pills who is plagued with repeated vaginal fungus infections, sometimes nothing short of temporarily stopping oral contraceptives will effect a cure.

If the symptoms aren't too distressing, there is no reason to abstain from intercourse during treatment. But under these circumstances, it is advisable for the man to wear a condom to avoid possible penile irritation from the fungus.

Is there any other treatment for recurrent and stubborn vaginal fungus infections?

When vaginal reinfections have been persistent, the use of drugs by mouth can be helpful. The purpose of taking anti-fungal medication by mouth is to suppress the growth of bowel fungi that could conceivably be the cause of repeated vaginal infections by faecal contamination. Curiously enough, eating yoghurt can also be helpful by indirectly diminishing the number of intestinal *Candida* organisms. Other than keeping bowel fungi in check, yoghurt and oral anti-fungal medications have no direct effect on *Candida* organisms already located in the vagina. These can only be eliminated by local treatment.

One of the newer and more promising medications for the local treatment of acute and recurrent fungus infections is the vaginal cream Monistat. Odourless and relatively greaseless, this preparation seems to effect a high rate of cure with the use of only one intravaginal application at bedtime for two weeks.

What about vaginal bacterial infections with *Haemophilis vaginalis*?

Happily for all concerned, *Haemophilis vaginalis* is the least obnoxious of the vaginal offenders. Symptoms are frequently mild and may amount to nothing more than a slight greyish white, somewhat malodorous discharge.

The affected woman is usually cured by treatment with oral antibiotics for five or six days. However, since transmission of these bacteria can occur through sexual intercourse, it is usually best that the male partner also be treated with oral antibiotics.

Other vaginal bacterial infections (*E. coli*, etc.) will usually respond to the same type of systemic medication. At times, local vaginal anti-bacterial creams can also be used.

Is it ever possible to be infected with more than one organism?

Not only possible but not that uncommon. *Trichomonas vaginalis* and *Candida albicans* in particular like to go steady, but any combination is possible – including all three together.

Is there any way to protect yourself against any of these vaginal infections?

Although avoiding oral contraceptives, pregnancy or just giving up sex would certainly eliminate many potential problems, short of these drastic measures, there are a few precautions that might help in making you less vulnerable to vaginal infections.

Both bacterial and fungus infections can come from the anus. Thus, most faecal vaginal contamination may be avoided by always wiping backwards, away from the vagina. Sanitary towels, because of their failure to stay securely in place, can also inadvertently spread unwanted bacteria from the back passage to the vagina. Tampons, for this reason, are more hygienic and have the added advantage of minimizing menstrual odours.

If you have been plagued with repeated fungus infections, you should investigate your diet. Sometimes by cutting down your carbohydrate and sugar intake (and that includes alcohol) fungus recurrences may be discouraged. If tetracycline or other broad-spectrum antibiotics are prescribed for an unrelated problem and you are prone to fungus infections, the simultaneous use of an anti-fungal vaginal preparation may be advisable.

In order to avoid *Trichomonas vaginalis* infections, no single measure is really effective unless you become celibate or have an uninfected partner. Otherwise, talking your partner into wearing a condom will prevent infection. Other measures that will afford partial protection are contraceptive creams, jellies or foams if used prior to intercourse. Most of these preparations have some anti-trich ingredients.

What can be done if you are stricken while away on vacation?

If you have a devastating and unexpected encounter with one of these vaginal visitors when you are miles away from home, the following measures may temporarily lessen distressing itching and vulvar irritation: (1) Avoid hot water and soap as they can aggravate an acutely inflamed vulva. (2) Use plain water, either cool or tepid, for cleansing purposes, and pat yourself dry, no rubbing. (3) If the itching is really bothersome, try spreading a thin layer of calamine lotion over the area two or three times a day. (4) Cool witch-hazel compresses or else just soaking in plain, tepid water three or four times a day for ten to fifteen minutes may bring additional relief. (5) Avoid tights, nylon underwear and garments that have a snug crotch. Increased moisture retention from poor air cirulation around the vulva can aggravate any symptoms you may have. Either substitute loose-fitting cotton panties or go without.

These are merely stop-gap measures, however, and should not be substituted for your seeking professional help as soon as possible. Your symptoms may be temporarily alleviated, but permanent relief depends on the identification of the organism and its elimination by appropriate treatment.

11. Venereal Diseases

Second only to the common cold, gonorrhoea ranks as the most prevalent communicable disease in the United States, with syphilis in fourth place. In the United Kingdom the incidence of venereal diseases declined from the end of the Second World War till the 1960s, but since then has increased steadily. So – on statistics alone – a woman is more at risk than her mother was. Therefore you cannot any longer assume that venereal disease is reserved for the sexually promiscuous or limited to the economically disadvantaged. Regardless of social background or age, more and more women, including those who limit their sexual activity to one partner, are no longer safe from possible infection.

But equally don't assume that a vaginal discharge or a sore vulva means you necessarily have VD: of every four women who go to VD clinics in Britain two only require treatment for, e.g., thrush or trichomoniasis (see Chapter 10), and one needs no treatment at all. But because in a woman VD can show no symptoms at all for some time, it makes sense to know what VD is if you are at risk.

What are venereal diseases?

Infections which are caught by means of sexual contact with an infected person. The commonest venereal disease is gonorrhoea; syphilis is the next most common, but more destructive, and genital herpes is sometimes seen. Others are rare in the United Kingdom as they are tropical venereal diseases.

We'll start with gonorrhoea, because it's the most common.

What is gonorrhoea and what causes it?

Whether you are more familiar with the terms GC, clap, strain or dose, gonorrhoea is an extremely contagious disease caused by the Gram-negative gonococcus bacteria *Neisseria gonorrhoeae*. The gonococcus requires a moist mucosal surface for survival. Loss of moisture or exposure to air causes the organism to die rapidly. The disease, therefore, is almost exclusively transmitted either by sexual intercourse or by intimate contact with the genital organs of an infected person. Nonetheless, there may be exceedingly rare instances wherein the infection was possibly acquired by other means, such as contact with a freshly contaminated towel or sheets.

Can gonorrhoea be acquired by oral genital sex?

Yes. Gonorrhoea of the mouth and pharynx (throat) can be acquired by fellatio (mouth to penis) or by cunnilingus (mouth to vulva) with an infected partner. Although many of the gonorrhoeal mouth and throat infections acquired by oral genital sex can be present without symptoms, there have been reported cases of multiple ulcerations of the tongue, lining of the mouth, and lips following such exposure. It is also possible to have gonorrhoea limited to the mouth and throat without genital involvement. In such a case, an individual with oral gonorrhoea could theoretically transmit the infection to the mouth or genital organs of another person.

What is the incubation period for gonorrhoea?

Usually three to seven days following sexual contact with an infected person. However, some men may harbour the gonococcus organisms for as long as six weeks before symptoms appear. In women, the incubation period may vary even more – from one week to twelve months. In other words, it is possible for a woman to be infected by the gonococcus for a year before any symptoms develop.

Does gonorrhoea eventually produce symptoms in all infected women?

Emphatically no. Eighty per cent of all women with gonorrhoea may never develop any obvious symptoms. For the most part these women will remain asymptomatic carriers. This means that although they may themselves never experience the pelvic problems associated with gonorrhoea, they will unknowingly be a source of gonorrhoeal infection to all their sexual contacts.

Do men always develop symptoms?

No. As many as 10 per cent may remain free of or completely oblivious to all symptoms. For the remaining 90 per cent, pain on urination and/or erection drives them to seek prompt medical attention. The majority of gonorrhoeal infections are therefore probably transmitted by asymptomatic individuals both male and female.

What are the early symptoms of gonorrhoea in women?

For the 20 per cent of women who *do* develop symptoms, an early gonorrhoeal infection initially tends to remain localized.

Early symptoms are most commonly the result of gonorrhoeal involvement of the urethra, cervix, rectum and, less frequently, a Bartholin's gland.

The urethra (urinary channel), because of its vulnerable position near the vaginal opening, is usually the first site attacked by the gonococcus. Inflammation of the urethral lining produces a purulent discharge associated with burning and frequent urination. Since these symptoms may be temporary and even mild, many women simply mistake them for a passing bladder irritation.

Subsequent involvement of the cervix and, specifically, invasion of the cervical (endocervical) glands by the gonococcus usually provokes a purulent, copious, yellow discharge. However, distinguishing between a cervix infected by gonorrhoea or by some other organism is not possible without specific tests (more about this shortly).

The involvement of the rectum is usually the result of contamination of the anal orifice from a copious vaginal discharge or from anal intercourse with an infected partner. (See Chapter 14.) In rare instances there may be swelling of the rectal mucosa, pain, bleeding and even pus formation, but in the vast majority of rectal gonorrhoeal infections *there are no symptoms whatsoever*. However, if gonorrhoea is limited to the rectum (as it is in approximately 10 per cent of infected women), it means that the infection could ultimately find its way to the vagina and hence to the cervix. Equally important, a woman with such a condition could unknowingly continue to infect and reinfect her sexual partners.

How long can gonorrhoea remain localized?

Nobody really knows. In some women invasion by the gonococcus may never extend beyond the cervix. Moreover, on occasion a localized gonorrhoeal infection has been known to clear without treatment.

In other women, a relatively silent invasion of the inner passageways of the Fallopian tubes can occur. But even here the body's natural defence mechanisms tend to destroy the gonococcus organisms, leaving scarred and sealed tubes as mute testimony to a probable old and unsuspected gonorrhoeal infection.

However, 10 to 15 per cent of all infected women ultimately develop obvious symptoms as the infection spreads beyond the cervix. Although the time interval is variable and often unpredictable, upward extension of the gonorrhoeal infection most frequently occurs during the first menstrual period following exposure to gonococcus.

How does menstruation encourage the spread of gonorrhoea in the pelvis?

Having a period is somewhat like rolling out the red carpet: the cervix softens, the canal dilates slightly, and the cervical mucus plug dissolves. Moreover, menstrual blood and cellular debris from the uterine cavity are the perfect media for the gonococcus to feed on and thrive.

From the cervix the gonococcus organisms pass into the uterine cavity, but involvement of the uterine lining is transient and mild. The real trouble begins when the gonococci invade the Fallopian tubes, causing inflammation and the development of pus within the tubal passageways.

If earlier symptoms were minimal, ignored, or event absent, a gonococcus infection of the upper genital organs usually produces pelvic distress. Postmenstrual lower abdominal tenderness, a more obvious discharge, fever, chills and the aggravation of pelvic pain by sexual intercourse or physical exertion are among the common complaints.

What can be done about tubal infection (salpingitis)?

Infection of the Fallopian tubes by gonococcus demands proper and immediate attention. A delay of as little as twenty-four to thirty-six hours from the onset of abdominal pain and other symptoms may well make the difference between complete recovery and permanent tubal damage. According to one report, 15 per cent of women subsequently became sterile as the result of tubal scarring and blockage precipitated by a single episode of gonorrhoeal tubal infection.

Although a stay in hospital is frequently necessary, an early and mild tubal infection can occasionally be treated on an out-patient basis with antibiotics, analgesics for pain relief and bed rest – plus strict abstinence from all sexual intercourse for a minimum of at least six and preferably eight weeks.

Why no sex for so long?

Following prompt treatment of an early tubal infection, pain and discharge may be minimal within a week or ten days. Yet, despite a remarkable improvement in these obvious symptoms, much more time is needed before all inflammation subsides.

Premature resumption of sexual activity can be responsible for spreading other unwanted bacteria into the healing but still inflamed tissues. It is a well-known fact that recurrences or flare-ups of tubal infections are commonly caused by bacteria other than gonorrhoea. Gonococcus may do the initial damage, but other bacteria (for example, *E. coli*, strep, etc.) can really finish the job in a devastating manner.

Women who foolishly resume sexual activity too soon, who delay seeking prompt treatment, or who otherwise have a history of repeated tubal infections may subsequently develop more serious complications.

What kind of complications?

Although blood-borne infections from gonorrhoea can be responsible for arthritis, heart lesions and even meningitis, to mention just a few problems seen in both sexes, these complications are fortunately not that common. In women, however, a severe gonorrhoeal infection can have other tragic results – permanent sterility being the least of them.

From the Fallopian tubes, the infection can spread to the nearby ovaries, forming massive tubo-ovarian abscesses that can literally fill the entire lower abdomen. More critical and life-threatening complications ensue when one of these abscesses ruptures, releasing pus into the pelvic and abdominal cavity (peritonitis). In these situations – despite all those wonderful antibiotics, miracle drugs and the intensive-care units of the best hospitals – sometimes nothing short of complete removal of all the female pelvic organs (womb, tubes and ovaries) will save a woman's life.

Among women who recover without the intervention of major surgery, many frequently require repeated stays in hospital for recurrent pelvic inflammatory disease (PID): tubal and ovarian infections, intractable pelvic pain, abnormal bleeding and incapacitating dysmenorrhoea. Temporary relief can be obtained from appropriate medical treatment. But here again, permanent relief from pain and recurrent infections usually requires the ultimate removal of the female pelvic organs.

This aspect of gonorrhoea, so conspicuously absent from most lay publications on venereal disease, is not included here to alarm you but rather to help overcome the apathetic and complacent attitude of some women who regard a gonorrhoeal infection as only a minor and temporary inconvenience.

Early and uncomplicated gonorrhoea can be readily treated and cured, but the ravages of extensive gonorrhoeal infections with superimposed invasion by other bacteria on these already compromised tissues can make a woman a pelvic cripple, if not threaten her very life.

What can happen if a pregnant woman gets gonorrhoea?

If gonorrhoea is acquired during the first few weeks of pregnancy, there is the possibility of a spontaneous abortion or direct extension of the infection to involve the Fallopian tubes.

Contraction of the disease after the third month of gestation tends to confine the gonococcus to the lower genital tract. The development during pregnancy of the cervical plug, a thick tenacious mucus blob within the endocervical canal, seems to afford protection against the upward extension of the organism. Symptoms, if present, are thereby restricted to the lower genital tract until after delivery, when further spread of the infection can occur. If the gonorrhoeal infection is unrecognized and untreated, there is always the added danger that the infant may become infected during delivery.

How does gonorrhoea affect the newborn?

The eyes of the newborn are particularly vulnerable to the ravages of the gonococcus. Contamination of the delicate ocular tissues by GC causes a violent inflammatory reaction that can rapidly progress to corneal ulceration, scarring and blindness.

Because gonorrhoea was once a common cause of blindness in the newborn, hospitals require that the eyes of every newborn be treated with a prophylactic instillation of either a silver nitrate or penicillin solution immediately after delivery.

Do birth-control pills have any effect on gonorrhoeal infections?

Apparently so. Oral contraceptives enhance a woman's chances of acquiring gonorrhoea. Increased vaginal alkalinity, as well as increased moisture and secretions attributable to the hormonal content of birth-control pills, makes for a perfect environment in which the gonococcus can flourish. According to some experts, a woman on the pill who experiences penile entry by an infected partner has almost a 100 per cent chance of acquiring gonorrhoea. The risk of acquiring gonorrhoea decreases to 40 per cent in women similarly exposed who are not on the pill.

How is gonorrhoea diagnosed?

Since there are currently no reliable blood tests for gonorrhoea, detection of gonococcus infection still depends on the identification of the organism by either a smear or a culture.

In the smear method, the discharge is spread onto a glass slide, stained with a special dye, and examined microscopically for the gonococcus. Smear tests in men can be highly accurate; in women, however, smear tests are notoriously unreliable in detecting gonorrhoeal infection. For this reason most clinics depend on the culture method. (See Chapter 10.)

An accuracy of almost 95 per cent in diagnosing gonococcus in women is obtained if cultures are taken from each of three areas: the endocervical canal, urethral opening and anus. Interestingly enough, in about 10 per cent of infected women, cultures from the anal area were the only ones reported as positive for gonorrhoea. Moreover, 60 per cent of the women who have a positive cervical culture for gonococcus will also have a positive rectal culture.

In women harbouring the gonococcus without apparent symptoms, the external genitalia, vagina and cervix may look completely normal. In these instances, gonorrhoea may well be discovered when a routine culture is being screened or if a woman finds out she has recently been exposed.

What if a woman has recently been exposed to gonorrhoea?

If your partner suddenly admits that he has just been treated for the clap, get yourself checked immediately.

Your doctor may take a smear or culture for you, but if it is positive he or she may want to refer you to a special VD clinic anyway. It could be simpler to go straight to a VD clinic to get yourself tested.

There are NHS clinics throughout the United Kingdom which give a confidential service to diagnose and treat venereal diseases. You don't need to be referred by your doctor to go to one and for some clinics you don't even have to make an appointment.

What is the treatment for gonorrhoea?

Despite the increasing resistance to penicillin by many strains of gonococcus, penicillin is still the drug most favoured for treating a gonorrhoeal infection.

When penicillin was first introduced, a single injection of 300 000 units completely eradicated an early gonococcus infection. Today the recommended dose in uncomplicated gonorrhoea (for both men and women) is 4·8 million units of aqueous procaine penicillin, given at one time in two deep intramuscular injections (buttocks). At these dosage levels, penicillin, unlike other antibiotics, has the unique advantage of being able to abort incubating (that is, beginning) syphilis should it also be present. In addition, many doctors routinely give 1 gram of probenecid (Benemid) by mouth before the penicillin injection. This drug allows the penicillin to remain at higher and more effective concentrations in the body for a longer period of time.

For individuals who may be allergic to penicillin, the second drug of choice is tetracycline: 1·5 grams by mouth followed by 0·5 gram every six hours for four days. Premature interruption of therapy or the occasional practice of sharing the tetracycline capsules with sexual acquaintances accounts for frequent treatment failures. Of necessity, if the infection is to be eradicated, the entire prescribed dose must be taken by the individual patient. New evidence also indicates that the tolerance of the gonococcus to tetracycline is increasing at an even faster rate than its tolerance to penicillin.

To help overcome the disadvantages of oral tetracycline, a new antibiotic, spectinomycin (Trobicin), is beginning to replace tetracycline as the second drug of choice. Given in an intramuscular injection, spectinomycin is an antibiotic intended exclusively for the treatment of gonorrhoea. It has not yet been established whether spectinomycin can abort incubating syphilis.

How can a woman know whether her gonococcus infection is cured?

Proof of having been cured depends on two and preferably three negative cultures taken usually at one-week intervals following treatment. Needless to say, staying free of a recurrent gonorrhoeal infection implies adequate and prompt treatment of all sexual partners. Having had gonorrhoea does not immunize a woman against subsequent infection.

Can a woman ever develop a natural immunity against gonorrhoea?

Some researchers believe that the absence of symptoms in eight out of ten women may represent some form of an immune response. In other words, these women may be manufacturing specific antibodies in their genital tract that make them symptom-free carriers of the gonococcus.

If this antibody premise is proved true, two marvellous possibilities may be realized: the eventual development of a reliable and specific blood test to detect gonococcus even in the absence of symptoms, and the perfection of a vaccine against gonorrhoea.

Is there any way a woman can protect herself against getting gonorrhoea?

It stands to reason that the more sexual contacts a woman and her partners have, the greater her chances of acquiring gonorrhoea or syphilis. Although the condom (sheath, rubber, Durex, French letter) is the most effective protection against a potential gonococcus invasion, its use of necessity depends on partner cooperation. Using contraceptive creams, jellies or foams prior to coitus may discourage the growth of gonococcus organisms, as can douching immediately after intercourse. But except for the condom, no precaution is really dependable in protecting a woman against gonorrhoea.

However, if you really think that you may have contracted the clap, the best advice is to see your doctor promptly or visit a clinic. A gonorrhoeal infection in many women is not clinically apparent. Therefore, unless you specifically go to a VD clinic, don't assume that your doctor will detect or even check for gonorrhoea unless you advise him of your concern.

What about syphilis?

Syphilis is by far the most awesome of the sexually transmitted infections. Slowly and insidiously this disease, following spontaneous clearing of early symptoms, gradually reappears years later with devastating consequences in 30 per cent of all untreated cases.

What causes syphilis?

Syphilis (also known as the pox or 'bad blood') is caused by the spirochete, a corkscrew-shaped organism (*Treponema pallidum*) that twists and burrows its way through tiny breaks in the skin and mucosal tissue. Even the smallest scratch on any skin surface or mucous membrane can provide a way in for the organism. Although the chancre, or primary lesion (site of entry of the spirochete) can occur on the lips, tongue, tonsils, fingers, etc., most primary lesions occur on the penis or vulva.

How long is the incubation period?

Anywhere from ten to ninety days following exposure, with three weeks being the average. The length of the incubation period depends on the total number of active spirochetes that enter the body at the time of contact with the infected partner: generally, the greater the number of spirochetes, the shorter the incubation period.

What is meant by the different stages of syphilis?

The disease progresses as follows: early syphilis (primary and secondary stages), latent syphilis (no obvious sign of the disease – detectable only by a blood test) and late syphilis, formerly called tertiary syphilis.

In the primary stage, the first detectable lesion is the chancre, a painless hard sore that heals by itself within six to ten weeks. Commonly associated with the primary lesion is a painless hard swelling of local lymph nodes that drain the area around the lesion (for example, inguinal or groin nodes in a genital chancre).

With the subsequent widespread dissemination of the spirochetes through the bloodstream, the disease moves into the secondary stage of early syphilis. The appearance of secondary skin lesions may occur during or shortly after the healing of the chancre or may be delayed for months. Most typically, the skin lesions appear as a generalized non-itchy rash or as multiple skin and/or mucous-membrane eruptions – anywhere from the scalp down to and including the soles of the feet. Occasionally the rash is so transient and indistinct that it goes virtually unnoticed. Other symptoms associated with secondary syphilis may include sore throat with hoarseness, occasional pain in bones and joints, and at times even a patchy loss of scalp hair.

Individuals with signs of early syphilis, that is, either the chancre or the generalized skin eruptions of the secondary stage, are highly infectious. Because all these skin lesions are teeming with spirochetes, it is during these stages of early syphilis that an infected individual can easily transmit the disease to a close contact.

If untreated, the disease evolves into latent syphilis. During this stage there is no clinical evidence of the disease, nor can it be transmitted to another individual. The one exception is the pregnant woman with latent syphilis whose unborn child can readily be infected. The diagnosis of latent syphilis can only be made with a special blood test.

For the one out of three untreated individuals who will progress from latent syphilis to the final stage, late syphilis, symptoms may not appear for an additional ten to fifteen years. Because the spirochete can affect any organ, prediction of the final outcome in any individual is not possible. Destructive lesions of the heart, blood vessels, brain, spinal cord, bone, skin, etc., are all possibilities.

It will be seen from these descriptions that the recognition of early syphilis is a matter of vital concern.

What does the chancre or primary lesion of syphilis look like?

In a typical case of early syphilis, the chancre first appears as a painless red swelling about the size of a small pea. Within a week's time it rapidly enlarges to the size of a marble, ulcerates, and forms an open or crusted hard painless sore with a central depression somewhat like a small crater.

Can a chancre sometimes go unnoticed?

Yes. In men, although the lesion is usually apparent, a chancre of the glans penis may initially go unnoticed in an uncircumcised male if it is under the foreskin. In women the chancre is most commonly present on the vulva or around the vaginal opening, but on occasion it may be located on the cervix or even along the inside vaginal wall. When the chancre appears in these latter locations its presence is frequently unsuspected by the woman.

How early can syphilis be accurately diagnosed?

Until the blood test registers positive for syphilis (usually within two to four weeks *following* the first appearance of the chancre), a definite diagnosis of syphilis during the primary stage can only be obtained by scraping the chancre and checking for the presence of spirochetes under a special dark-field microscope.

Because a chancre can sometimes be overlooked and missed, any woman who may be worried about a possible recent contact should have an initial blood test for syphilis. If negative, the blood test should be repeated in six weeks and again at three months (ninety days). If the blood tests are still negative for syphilis ninety days after possible exposure, this would virtually assure the individual that there had been no contact with the disease.

What kinds of blood test can detect syphilis?

A Wasserman test or straightforward blood serology can detect syphilis. Routine testing for this disease is standard procedure for all hospital admissions, donations of blood and in ante-natal clinics. So you may well have been tested for syphilis without knowing what the test was for. Of course, if *any* test is positive, the subject is notified and treatment given.

What is the treatment for syphilis?

Once the diagnosis is confirmed, the drug of choice is again penicillin. Blood tests following treatment should revert to normal and register negative. This means that if you have been successfully treated for early syphilis, subsequent blood tests for the disease would show no evidence of previous contact with the infection.

If, however, the infection is diagnosed and treated at a later stage (for example, during latent syphilis), the blood test may on occasion remain weakly positive despite successful treatment and eradication of the disease.

If you have been treated for early syphilis, can you get reinfected?

Yes. Prompt and adequate treatment of early syphilis affords no protection against future reinfection.

What about congenital syphilis (syphilis acquired before birth)?

Early diagnosis and treatment of syphilis in the pregnant woman is vital if the foetus is to be spared. Since maternal spirochetes do not pass the placental barrier until after the fourth month of pregnancy, treatment before the sixteenth week will completely prevent syphilitic infection of the unborn child. Once the foetus becomes infected, however, every month that passes without treatment increases the chances of serious involvement and possible death for the foetus. An undiagnosed, severe infection during pregnancy may end in spontaneous abortion, a still-born baby at term or a live infant with syphilis. Since the spirochetes invade the bloodstream of the foetus directly, there is no primary or chancre stage in congenital syphilis.

How does syphilis affect the newborn?

If the infant is born alive, it is fairly likely to have multiple skin or mucous-membrane lesions in addition to bone, liver and spleen involvement. Treatment at this stage may or may not save the child's life.

In other affected infants, the disease may be latent and unsuspected for at least two years and frequently asymptomatic until just prior to puberty. Early diagnosis in these children depends on a blood test. Treatment given immediately will prevent damage: untreated, the nerves and bones of the child may be attacked. The results are blindness, deafness, destruction of the bones of the nose and of the permanent teeth. The brain and spinal cord may also be affected. Treatment given after these symptoms have developed cannot put right damage which has already been done, though it will prevent further deformations.

Are there other venereal diseases besides gonorrhoea and syphilis?

Since by definition a venereal disease is one that is transmitted almost exclusively by sexual intercourse, three other diseases currently fit into this classification: lymphogranuloma venereum, chancroid and granuloma inguinale. Infection with any one of them can cause destructive genital lesions, but fortunately their over-all incidence is low – less than one affected individual per 100 000 population.

Nonetheless, there is a fourth entity, genital herpes, which is being seen with increasing frequency. Although this infection can be transmitted by a single act of coitus with one infected partner, it is more apt to occur in women with multiple partners and especially among those previously treated for other venereal diseases.

What about genital herpes infections?

Most of you are probably familiar with the common fever blister or cold sore caused by the herpes simplex virus type I, but a closely related virus, herpes simplex virus type II can affect the vulva, cervix and upper vagina. The fact that it may be a precursor to cancer of the cervix or in some way linked to its development has recently put herpesvirus type II in the medical spotlight.

Most genital herpes infections are caused by contact with the type II virus during sexual intercourse; however, recent studies indicate the individuals who harbour the type I virus around the lips and mouth can transmit the virus to their partner's genital organs during cunnilingus or fellatio. In fact, some 10 per cent of all genital herpes infections may be caused by the type I virus because of an apparent increase in oral genital play. Since type I virus is not implicated in the possible development of cervical cancer, the infection is potentially less serious than exposure to type II, but the physical symptoms can be just as distressing.

What are the symptoms of a genital herpes infection?

Fever, general malaise, swollen and tender lymph nodes, intense itching and painful blisters or blisterlike eruptions (vesicles) along the vulva and genital mucous membrane are among the primary complaints. Moreover, inflammation and swelling around the urethral area can make urination extremely painful and at times virtually impossible, thus necessitating catheterization. In infections with herpesvirus type II, the cervix is also apt to be red, irritated and ulcerated, often leading to discharge and even vaginal spotting.

Symptoms may vary depending on whether it is a woman's initial exposure to the virus or a recurrent infection. If a woman has had no previous encounter with any of the other herpesviruses (for example, cold sores, shingles, etc.) and thus has no antibodies against this group of viruses, running into herpesvirus type II for the first time can be downright distressing. Fortunately, however, most symptoms usually disappear within two to three weeks.

Are recurrent infections as distressing as the initial exposure?

Although recurrent infections of genital herpes may be milder with only tiny, blisterlike eruptions along the vulva, such is not always the case. Furthermore, repeat infections are usually re-activations of the virus rather than the result of re-exposure. In other words, once infected, a woman continues to harbour the virus, which under certain circumstances can precipitate recurrent active infection. Just what factors can trigger viral re-activation are not known. Nonetheless, repeat infections have occurred following trauma to mucous membranes during intercourse, hormonal disturbances and even as the result of emotional stress.

Should an active infection occur during the last few weeks of a pregnancy, most doctors advise delivery by Caesarean section. A herpesvirus type II infection of the genitalia can cause serious and even fatal infection to the baby if it is allowed to pass through the birth canal. In contrast, a genital herpes type I virus infection has not been implicated as a potential threat to the newborn.

How can a woman know if she has contracted the virus?

During active infection, cell studies from vulvar lesion scrapings can indicate exposure to the virus, as can smears from the cervix in women with no symptoms. Apart from these studies, special blood tests (although not as yet generally available) can detect past infection with type II herpesvirus by the presence of antibodies. The fact that women with high antibody levels to type II herpesvirus have a greater incidence of cervical cancer as compared to other women is the basis for the current medical interest in this genital infection.

Is there any specific treatment for genital herpesvirus infections?

At the moment there is no known treatment that will permanently eradicate the virus. Therapy is still confined to relief of symptoms. Applications of cold milk compresses four to six times a day for five to ten minutes as well as a local anaesthetic ointment such as lignocaine may be helpful. Where pain during urination is extreme, spraying cold water onto the vulvar area while voiding can minimize discomfort. For this purpose a small plastic bottle filled with cold water and equipped with a spray top can be extremely useful. Otherwise, sitting in a pan of cold water while urinating also helps.

More recently, a new technique using special dyes applied locally to the lesions in conjunction with fluorescent lighting is providing marked relief from painful vulvar blisters in a few limited studies. Whether this technique will prove to be entirely safe and free from serious side effects is currently under intensive investigation.

What about follow-up care for women with genital herpes?

All women who contract herpesvirus type II should have a cervical smear more frequently. Although proof to substantiate a cause-and-effect relationship between herpesvirus type II and cervical cancer is still lacking, there is sufficient incriminating evidence to warrant frequent check-ups.

What is being done about the problem of venereal disease?

Both gonorrhoea and syphilis are 'notifiable' diseases, like, for example, diphtheria and typhoid. This means that every case has to be notified to the Chief Medical Officer of Health. What is more, every doctor's contract prescribes that his or her duties include 'any necessary action at his/her discretion for the follow-up of any person suspected of suffering from a venereal disease'.

The special VD clinics are better placed than general practitioners to curtail the spread of venereal diseases, both in terms of skill and resources, and because they are available to the whole community. Each clinic aims to trace the sexual contacts of any infected person, and invite them to come for tests, so that they can be given treatment if necessary. All information is handled in the strictest confidence, so the contacts are not even told who has named them. If a contact is named by many infected people, the clinic will try to back up their letters with a visit from a social worker in order to persuade him or her to come for tests and treatment. (This kind of follow-up depends on the social workers' work load. It is hardest to achieve in the big city areas where it is most needed.) Often persuasion or self-interest – if not public duty – brings the culprit forward, yet VD specialists are still concerned at the numbers of infected people without symptoms. As we've seen, most of them are women.

Mass awareness of any health menace begins with individual awareness. With the incidence of venereal disease increasing, every sexually active non-monogamous person runs a higher risk of infection. If your sex life is not confined to a mutually faithful relationship with a single partner, you may have reason to be concerned. Until researchers develop effective vaccines against gonorrhoea, syphilis, genital herpes and other venereal diseases, you must assume responsibility for yourself. So don't let possible feelings of guilt or embarrassment delay you. After all, only you can evaluate your own situation, nor is it only you who may suffer if you delay.

12. Vaginal Odour

No longer content with making the American public super-conscious about halitosis, bromidrosis, armpitosis and question-able household odours, Madison Avenue has also intimated for several years that if the truth be known, all women need a feminine hygiene spray deodorant.

From the climbing sales figures reported for feminine hygiene deodorants, now in excess of $58 million annually, there is no denying that many American women are seeking a gyno-cosmetic product comparable in effectiveness to underarm deodorants. Despite the biological differences between the sexes that make potential odours more of a problem for women, it is also true that American women as a group are the most aseptic, germ-free, scrupulously impeccable and odour-conscious Homo sapiens ever to walk the earth.

It is therefore time to analyse this provocative and hush-hush subject of odours from a more objective viewpoint.

Is it normal to have a biological scent?

Yes. Since it was nature's intent to make the human female the more sexually attractive of the species, woman is endowed with 75 per cent more apocrine (scent) glands than her male counterpart. These glands, which normally develop during puberty, are particularly concentrated in the labia minora, circumanal region, underarm area and around the nipples and umbilicus. Unlike ordinary sweat (endocrine) glands that excrete primarily an odourless combination of water, salt and lactic acid, the apocrine glands intermittently exude a somewhat milky, organic material that emits a characteristic but inoffensive odour.

Just as fingerprints are individually specific, each person has a distinct olfactory signature resulting from differences in glandular activity of the skin, hormone levels and emotional tension. These individual differences account for the common observation that the same perfume does not have the same fragrance when worn by different women.

Yet, although each woman is unique, there are certain factors common to all women that can adversely alter the normal biological scent.

What factors?

Because of the vulva's anatomical configuration, perspiration, for example, is frequently combined with decreased absorption of moisture. In overweight women, further deepening of the normal vulvar folds along with close contact of the upper inner thighs tends to increase normally retained moisture. Similarly, tights or tight-fitting underwear, particularly if made of nylon, also work to trap moisture and prevent its evaporation. Since offensive body odours are caused by bacteria acting upon perspiration as well as upon other normal secretions from sebaceous and apocrine glands, the more bacteria interacting with normal or increased vulvar skin secretions the greater the possibility of an unpleasant odour.

What can decrease odour formation?

Nothing has yet challenged the effectiveness of plain soap and water in reducing the number of skin bacteria, in addition to eliminating any accumulated skin secretions. But unless one gently but thoroughly washes between the vulvar folds, bacteria and skin secretions may be untouched by even the soap and water routine. Plush, luxurious washcloths are usually too bulky to be effective. Much more efficient is the use of either a lightweight washcloth or a well-soaped finger, particularly between the inner and outer lips and junction of the labia minora and the clitoris. This latter area especially tends to accumulate bacteria and cellular debris (smegma) that might be a factor in the formation of clitoral adhesions. (See Chapter 14.)

To douche or not to douche – is that the question?

Whether you do or don't douche is a personal matter. If douching makes you feel secure, confident, dainty, or whatever else you want to call it, your freedom of choice in this matter should be tempered by knowing what douching can and cannot accomplish.

Since normal vaginal secretions are odourless, and a healthy vagina maintains a certain acidity and cleanses itself through the action of normal bacteria and mucus drainage, douching is not necessary.

Are there any times when douching may be advisable?

As mentioned in earlier chapters, douching immediately after intercourse can afford some protection against possible infection with *Trichomonas vaginalis* (TV) and even against gonorrhoea. But as for keeping you from getting pregnant, douching after intercourse (see Chapter 16) is doomed to failure. By the time you run to the bathroom (a real mood-breaker), many of the sperm will already have passed the point of no return. Moreover, if you are using a contraceptive cream or jelly, douching may well wash away your protection.

Aside from these practical considerations, some women douche purely for aesthetic reasons. The desire to be impeccable in intimate situations and especially in oral genital sex is only natural. For most women, however, such precautions are rarely necessary. Simple vulvar cleansing beforehand is usually sufficient to ensure one's being free of any unpleasant odour.

How often can one douche?

Although the normal vaginal bacteria return within a few hours after douching, no one really knows how long a normal vagina can maintain its natural protective mechanisms when exposed to repeated irrigations over a long period of time. Some women admit to douching every day and have never experienced any particular problem. On the other hand, too frequent and improper douching (particularly with strong solutions) can, by altering the normal vaginal environment, create irritation and discharge.

Therefore, to be on the safe side, twice a week is a good limit

if you must douche, unless specifically advised otherwise by
your doctor.

Are prepackaged vaginal douche products safe to use regularly?

Yes, provided of course you aren't allergic or sensitive to one of
the ingredients. With the advent of prepackaged and pre-
measured vaginal douche powders, most of which are properly
buffered to maintain normal vaginal acidity, vulvovaginal irritations from improper douching now seem less common. For those
of you who can resist such tempters as raspberry or orange
sherbert flavoured douches, the old-fashioned two tablespoons of
plain white vinegar in a quart of warm water, although not as
enticing, is just as good and a lot cheaper. Douching daily with
plain tap water, however, can in a few women create problems
by upsetting vaginal acidity.

When shouldn't you douche?

During pregnancy and for at least four weeks following delivery.
Since the cervical os and canal may be slightly open especially
during late pregnancy, douching may inadvertently cause either
premature rupture of the membranes (bag of waters) or the
introduction of fluid within the uterine cavity. In either case the
development of an intrauterine infection could potentially
jeopardize the foetus. Similarly, douching too soon after delivery,
before the uterine lining has a chance to heal completely, could
also lead to an intrauterine infection. In this case, bacteria from
the vagina could be flushed against the cervix and thus work
their way into the uterine cavity.

Is douching harmful during menstruation?

No. By the same token, douching during menstruation accomplishes very little other than momentarily flushing out the
blood and cellular debris from the vagina. Nonetheless, some
women who have intercourse during menstruation will douche at
this time and insert a diaphragm before coitus solely for aesthetic
reasons.

Is there a right and wrong way to douche?

Most women douche while sitting on the toilet. At best, even with the douche bag sufficiently elevated, douching in the sitting or squatting position rarely accomplishes more than a token flush of the vagina. If you still prefer this method because it's faster, more convenient and seems to do the job, that's fine. However, if you have been given a special douche prescription to treat a vaginal infection and can rely on being undisturbed in the bathroom, why not get the greatest benefit from that medication by douching properly?

What is the proper way to douche?

In the bath lying down. If you are using a bag and hose (preferable to a syringe), mix the douche ingredients with warm water as instructed and place the bag so that it will hang about two feet above your hips while you douche. In many baths, attaching the bag to the tap will be just about the right height. For added comfort, heat the bath by rinsing it with warm water before stepping in. You are now ready to proceed.

Gently insert the douche nozzle into the vagina as far as it will go and lie back. Allow the solution to begin flowing and at the same time (using both hands) close the vaginal opening against the nozzle so that the vagina literally becomes flooded. If this is done correctly, you will notice a slight pressure sensation as the vagina expands to accommodate the fluid. At this time clamp off the hose, release your hold, and allow the vagina to drain. If sufficient fluid was retained for proper douching, it will be rapidly expelled with a swoosh. Repeat the same process until the bag hangs empty.

What about the presence of an unpleasant odour despite douching?

Normal vaginal secretions from a healthy vagina do not have any odour. If an unpleasant odour or obvious discharge persists or returns fairly promptly after douching, it may indicate a vaginal or cervical infection and should be checked out.

In the absence of any discharge or irritation of the vagina or vulva, the presence of a particularly fetid odour may be the result of a forgotten tampon.

How can a woman forget a tampon in the vagina?

Easily. Changing tampons is done so automatically by regular users that often one cannot remember having removed the used tampon before inserting a fresh replacement. Even checking for the telltale string can at times be deceptive. Occasionally that little string adheres so snugly to the vulva that unless you probe the vaginal entrance or examine yourself with a mirror, you too might inadvertently insert a fresh tampon without removing the old one.

What happens now?

Because a forgotten tampon encourages the growth of un-desirable bacteria, you will invariably notice an increasingly unpleasant odour within a few days – usually after your period is over. Despite the odour, however, forgotten tampons do not cause vaginal problems. Equally consoling is the fact that a tampon lost in the vagina remains in the vagina until removed or spontaneously expelled. There's just no other place for it to go. Therefore, if you suspect that a lost or retained tampon might be the problem, don't be alarmed. Just check it out.

How can you remove a lost tampon?

If your vagina can accommodate two fingers, recovering a lost tampon can be quite easy. Either squat or bend forward from a standing position and insert the index and middle fingers into the vagina as far as you can reach. Prior lubrication of your fingers with cold cream or Vaseline also helps. Since the tampon is probably lying next to the cervix, you may have to strain or bear down as if you were having a bowel movement in order to bring it within reach. Once located, the tampon can usually be grasped and removed by your fingers, chopstick style. Douching afterwards in such a case would definitely be advisable.

What about feminine hygiene deodorants?

Presumably able to cover up odours and to inhibit the growth of bacteria, feminine hygiene deodorants come in either spray or spray powder form. All of them contain a propellant, but information about other substances that they might contain is not readily available. The fact that feminine hygiene deodorants are currently listed as cosmetics exempts the manufacturers from having to list the ingredients or to demonstrate the effectiveness or safety of these products.

Do feminine hygiene sprays really eliminate odours?

The answer is elusive. Further studies may clarify this point, but already questions are being raised about whether the pretesting of these products adequately substantiates their deodorizing claims.

Be that as it may, feminine hygiene deodorants have found a ready market despite questionable pretesting and potential hazards to some women.

What potential hazards?

Acute and diffuse inflammation of the vulva for one thing. Other complaints attributable to the use of feminine hygiene deodorants range from itching and burning of the vulva to severe local allergic reactions requiring hospitalization.

Some women will be sensitive or allergic to any product even when properly used and proved safe. However, the point to be made is this: when a product is known to be so chemically irritating to the vaginal mucous membranes that even the manufacturers warn against its vaginal use, how really safe are feminine spray deodorants when by their very intent they must be sprayed near and around the area that is to be avoided? In women with relaxed vaginal openings, for example, even spraying at the recommended distance of six to twelve inches can in no way avoid contact with exposed vaginal mucous membranes.

The restrictions banning their use on tampons and prior to

sexual intercourse because of potential vaginal and penile irritation raise another provocative question.

Of what real value are feminine hygiene deodorants?

Since odour-conscious women are probably most concerned with the possibility of offending during menstruation and at the time of sexual intercourse, limitations prohibiting the use of spray deodorants on tampons and prior to coitus seem to greatly detract from their value.

So although feminine hygiene deodorants presumably can be used after intercourse or for those in-between times, so can other and more effective products such as soap and water.

In all fairness to the cosmetic manufacturers of feminine hygiene deodorants, for some women they are no doubt on the right track. At the present time, however, the available products seem to fall short in both efficacy and safety.

Will a new and better deodorant spray be produced?

In view of the inherent sensitivity of vulvar mucous-membrane tissue, plus the occurrence of menstrual bleeding and sometimes abnormal vaginal discharges, it is very debatable whether even concerted research efforts will eventually produce a spray so magical that a single squirt or two will eradicate any or all objectionable odours for x number of hours.

So while the search goes on for the ideal product, the use of soap and water is still the best way to maintain an odour-free and hygienic external genital area.

13. Bladder Infections and Sagging Supports

If you have recurrent bladder infections, lose control of your urine, or have the sensation that your vagina is way too big for your partner, there is an answer – and the solution can begin with you. This does not mean that you can ignore your prescription for bladder medication or circumvent vaginal plastic surgery where truly indicated. But it does imply that distressing urinary disturbances and problems related to sagging pelvic supports can frequently be improved and at times even prevented by the knowledgeable and motivated woman.

Sexual intercourse, pregnancy, childbirth and the law of gravity all work to stretch and strain the vaginal tissues and pelvic supports. Ageing and gradual oestrogen depletion also cause those supports to weaken, thin and lose their snap. Moreover, the unique anatomy of the female genital urinary system further predisposes women to a variety of bladder disturbances. As you will soon see, this can sometimes mean intermittent loss of urinary control. For others, bladder irritations and bladder infections seem to recur with annoying regularity.

Are women really more susceptible to bladder infections than men?

Bladder infections are three times more prevalent among women under forty as compared to men in the same age group. And the precipitating factor in some acute and recurrent bladder infections in the female can be sexual intercourse. In fact, for the young woman just beginning an active sex life, 'honeymoon cystitis' may be her very first encounter with a urinary problem.

Are you a candidate for 'honeymoon cystitis'?

Whether or not you are on your honeymoon, sexual intercourse can set the stage for cystitis, that is, a bladder infection.

Why this should be is readily explained. A lot has to do with the female's shorter urethra. The male urethra averages 7–8 inches (17–20 centimetres) from the tip of the penis to the bladder, whereas the female urethra measures a scant 1·6 inches (4 centimetres) in length. Furthermore, the presence of bacteria around the vulvar mucosa and the closeness of the urethral opening to the vagina also help set the stage for a potential bacterial invasion of the bladder.

Now, if you add one more factor, penile vaginal intercourse, the curtain rises on act one of acute honeymoon cystitis. Although any woman is vulnerable, the young bride whose vaginal opening is relatively snug is most susceptible. Intercourse for her in the conventional male-on-top position will automatically direct the penis along the roof of the vagina – or, from another point of view, against the floor of the urethra and bladder. The pumping action of the penis in this position not only irritates those structures above the vaginal wall but also pushes bacteria from the outside vulvar area into the woman's urethra and bladder.

Since invading bacteria normally take a day or so to establish themselves, acute cystitis usually strikes about thirty-six hours following the initial precipitating intercourse. Don't blame last night's love making for this morning's problem. Symptoms won't begin until the morning after the night before *last*.

Honeymoon cystitis is no joke. It is a real bladder infection that requires treatment and supportive care.

Are all sexually active women more vulnerable to cystitis?
They may all be more vulnerable, but interestingly enough, many women seem strangely resistant to any bladder infection. Just why this should be is currently being investigated.

Some experts attribute the lack of infection in some women to a highly developed local immune mechanism in the bladder wall. Other evidence indicates that women with recurrent cystitis have substantially more bacteria around the urethral and vaginal areas than women who remain uninfected. The fact that personal hygiene plays no significant role in this phenomenon has lent support to the idea that perhaps there may be a subtle biological difference among women in regard to the prevalence of vulvar mucosal bacteria.

In a few isolated instances, uncircumcised males harbouring bacteria beneath the foreskin have been a source of recurrent urinary infections in their sexual partners. Even less common, but nonetheless a potent method of introducing bacteria, is the practice of having anal intercourse and then reinserting the penis into the vagina without taking the precaution of washing or cleansing the male organ.

But regardless of the possible causes, for those of you who suffer from recurrent bladder infections, or for those of you taking off on your honeymoon, a few helpful suggestions, if followed, may well prevent a bout with cystitis.

Can you really avoid acute cystitis?

Often, yes, providing you know a few basic facts and are willing to take precautions.

To begin with, an empty bladder is not so readily infected. Despite the fact that bacteria may be 'milked' into the bladder during sexual intercourse, an infection is unlikely to occur unless sufficient urine is present to stimulate the growth of the bacteria. Secondly, should urine be present in the bladder at the time of intercourse, the more dilute it is the better your chances of avoiding a possible infection. Dilute urine definitely lowers the bacterial count. This means making sure that your intake of water and fluids is more than adequate. For you June honeymooners or others exposed to hot weather, excessive loss of body fluids through perspiration will normally result in the excretion of a more concentrated urine. To maintain a dilute urine under these circumstances it is especially important to increase your intake of fluids to the point where your urine may actually be colourless.

Thus, to avoid cystitis: (1) Make sure you empty your bladder before intercourse. (2) Empty your bladder after intercourse. (3) In addition – and this is extremely important for women who have recurrent flare-ups of cystitis – drink two to four glasses of water after intercourse. This will ensure an adequate volume of urine to effect proper voiding, as well as the presence of a dilute urine. You will undoubtedly have to get up during the night to urinate, but that's what it's all about – flushing out the bacteria before they can cause trouble.

Women who follow this regimen have enthusiastically endorsed it as being very effective. Some urologists suggest that as an extra precaution showers be substituted for bathing to reduce further the incidence of bladder infections among susceptible women.

How can you tell if you have a bladder infection?

In contrast to some acute kidney infections with resultant shaking chills, high fever, flank pain and general malaise, the symptoms of most bladder infections are tame. Women with cystitis complain primarily of frequent urination, a burning, stinging pain along the urethra during and immediately after voiding, and occasional mild cramping discomfort over the pubic area. Fever, if any, rarely causes the temperature to exceed 99° F (37° C). When the cystitis is particularly severe with marked irritation and inflammation of the bladder lining, an otherwise healthy woman may even pass bloody urine.

Symptoms, however, can be misleading. Not all painful urination can be blamed on an actual bladder infection. Any irritation or inflammation of the tissues around the urethra or bladder can produce similar complaints. Vaginal infections, vulvar irritations and gonorrhoeal involvement of the urethra in particular (see Chapter 11) can readily mimic acute cystitis.

What else can cause pain on urination in the absence of infection?

Painful urination occurring *shortly after intercourse* is most commonly the result of trauma to the urethra during coitus. Penile friction against the floor of the urethra and bladder in a woman with insufficient vaginal lubrication and/or a snug vaginal opening can be contributing factors.

In the postmenopausal woman, for example, the vaginal walls are relatively thin and have a diminished capacity to expand and dilate during coitus: this makes the overlying urinary structures even more vulnerable to injury and inflammation.

But sexual intercourse is not always the precipitating factor. Urethral pain, burning on urination and at times slight urethral bleeding noticed after voiding in postmenopausal women can be the result of an oestrogen deficiency. An oestrogen deficiency by itself can cause chronic low-grade inflammation of the urethral mucosa as well as vaginal and vulvar atrophy. Fortunately, most of these urological complaints in older women can be markedly improved by either oral oestrogen or local oestrogen therapy in the form of vaginal creams or suppositories. (See Chapter 21.)

How, then, is a bladder infection diagnosed?

Most commonly by the microscopic examination of urine for the presence of bacteria and pus cells. Since the majority of bladder infections are caused by Gram-negative bacteria (bacteria that will stain pink when subjected to certain dyes for identification purposes, specifically *E. coli*) that respond to most bladder medications, your doctor will probably order a simple urine test to confirm the presence of bacteria and pus cells.

If, however, following treatment, your urine still shows a significant number of bacteria and pus cells, or if you have had recurrent flare-ups of cystitis, a urine culture and sensitivity test may be necessary. As explained in Chapter 10, a culture has the advantage of identifying the bacteria responsible for the infection. A urine culture can also gauge the severity of the infection by specifying the number of bacteria present per cubic centimetre of urine.

A urine sensitivity test goes one step further by actually testing the bacteria's resistance or sensitivity to the more commonly used antibiotics and bladder medications. In other words, a urine culture and sensitivity test will tell your doctor what bacteria are causing your infection, how severe the infection is, and what medicine will work best against it.

Needless to say, if the diagnosis and treatment of your case of acute cystitis depends upon an examination of your urine, you should know how to collect a specimen properly.

What is the best way to collect a urine specimen?

Under normal and healthy conditions, urine is sterile (it has no bacteria). It is therefore important that you not confuse the issue by allowing your urine specimen to be contaminated with bacteria from the outside of your urethral or vaginal area. Short of using tubes to your bladder, the only reliable way of collecting a clean, uncontaminated urine specimen is with the mid-stream clean-catch method:

(1) Gently but thoroughly cleanse the outside of the urethral and vaginal area. If you happen to be menstruating at the time, plug the vaginal opening with a tissue or tampon to avoid contaminating the urine with blood. (2) Since proper collection of the specimen is best done while standing, either step into a bath or shower or, if you prefer, straddle a toilet facing the tank. (3) While holding the urine receptacle in one hand, spread the inner lips apart with the other hand and begin urinating. If you are having just a routine urine test, a clean, dry jar with a screw top is adequate. (Specimens for urine cultures require special sterile containers that either your doctor or the laboratory will provide.) (4) As soon as you are certain that your urine stream is not deflecting off any vulvar surface, simply catch the urine in the container. Just make sure that the container does not come into contact with your vulva.

If there is going to be any delay in submitting the specimen to the laboratory, better refrigerate it. Urine culture results require at least forty-eight hours. A routine test can take only a few minutes. In any event, most doctors will start treatment while awaiting laboratory confirmation.

What is the usual treatment for acute cystitis?

Other than drinking six to eight glasses of water a day to keep the urine diluted and the bacteria flushed out, treatment can never be generalized. Currently there are any number of effective drugs that can be used. The sulphonamides are an old and reliable group (Gantrisin, Gantanol, etc.). Antibiotics such as nitrofurantoin (Furadantin, Macrodantin), ampicillin and tetracycline are also highly effective. And there are many others.

Regardless of what medication your doctor prescribes, *follow the instructions*. Symptoms may disappear within one to three days, but continue taking the medication as prescribed. This is particularly important in dealing with urinary infections. Depending upon the drug used, most bladder infections require a minimum of ten to fourteen days and sometimes as long as three to five weeks to eradicate. Some infections may even need months of continuous treatment.

The all-too-common practice of stopping the medication as soon as the symptoms subside should be avoided. You may be comfortable, but the infection is still there. Premature interruption of treatment only invites another flare-up, and in short order. Worse yet, you may run the risk of having the infection ascend into the kidneys. Kidney infections can be very serious, and a serious kidney infection can also be silent – no symptoms. It is therefore important that your urine be checked after treatment too. Only then can you and your doctor be sure that the infection has been eradicated.

Besides bladder infections, women are also more vulnerable to other urological problems.

Ever laugh so hard that you actually wet yourself?

At times this can be perfectly normal if you happen to be sitting on a full bladder. For some women, however, incontinence can be a real problem and they don't laugh about it.

So-called *stress incontinence*, or the sudden and involuntary expulsion of a few drops of urine as the result of increased intra-abdominal pressure, is probably (apart from bladder infections) one of the most prevalent and distressing urological complaints among women. For women with this problem any strain, bearing-down effort, or even a sneeze, cough, or laugh can cause a sudden, small loss of urine. And although urinary control is immediately resumed, the problem is embarrassing and unpleasant.

What is required for good urinary control?

Assuming that there are no disorders of the central nervous system or severe psychiatric disturbances to cause primary incontinence, the ability to control one's urine depends primarily upon the integrity of pelvic muscles and connective fibrous tissue. These structures in turn support the bladder and urethra in their normal anatomical position. (See Figure 2, Chapter 2.) Furthermore, the angle at which the urethra joins the bladder is of critical importance in urinary control. Therefore, any weakness in these vital pelvic supports that allows the urethra to sag, thus changing its normal position in relation to the bladder, can set the stage for stress incontinence. The fact that women with this problem rarely have incontinence while lying down (even if they sneeze) is further evidence that stress incontinence is primarily a problem of inadequate pelvic support.

What can be done about stress incontinence?

The problem can be corrected. Since marked stress incontinence is most commonly associated with inadequate urethral support (see urethrocele, Figure 15), the solution depends upon getting the urethra back up where it belongs.

Vaginal plastic surgery and/or certain urethral suspension operations done through a cut in the lower abdomen can successfully reposition the urethra. Short of surgery, however, many women can be relieved of *mild* stress incontinence by the simple expedient of exercising and strengthening their pubococcygeus muscle.

What exactly is the pubococcygeus?

One of the most important muscles you have as a woman – a broad band of muscular tissue that stretches like a taut hammock from the pubic bone in front to the coccyx, or tail bone, behind. Try visualizing this muscle as an internal sling or G-string stretching between the legs from front to back. The pubococcygeus (pronounced pu-bo-cocks-uh-gee-us) forms the floor of the pelvic cavity and supports the pelvic organs. In a normal and healthy state, this muscle encircles the urethra close to where it joins the bladder, surrounds and supports the middle third of the vagina, and encompasses the rectum just above the anal opening. (See Figure 14.) A good toned-up pubococcygeus is also necessary for normal bladder and bowel control.

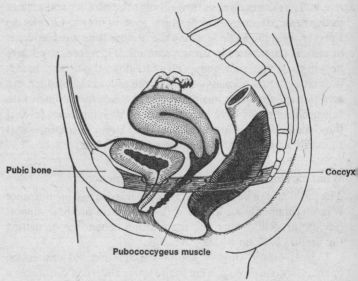

Pubic bone —

Coccyx

Pubococcygeus muscle

14. *Pubococcygeus muscle. Muscular sling between the pelvic bone and the coccyx (tail bone) which helps support the female pelvic organs in their normal anatomical position*

Exercising this muscle regularly can definitely minimize and even overcome any tendency toward sagging organs and vaginal relaxation, whether the result of childbirth or ageing. On the other hand, a flabby or overstretched pubococcygeus can ultimately result in stress incontinence, widening and shortening of the vagina, and sagging of the urethra, bladder, womb and rectum. Since the pubococcygeus at the time of birth is weak and underdeveloped, observing the vulva of a newborn female infant may further convince you of the importance of this muscular support.

What does the vulva of a newborn female infant look like?

Much like the vulva of a woman with marked inadequate pelvic support. The entire external genitalia sags and protrudes to such an extent that all orifices gap open – the urethra, vagina and rectum.

Not until the infant begins to assume an upright position does the pubococcygeus begin to strengthen, tighten, and gradually draw up the pelvic organs into their proper anatomical positions. As the muscle further strengthens, all that previously bagged and sagged becomes tucked up inside. And lo and behold, the toned-up pubococcygeus muscle now makes urine and faeces control possible.

How can you exercise the pubococcygeus muscle?

If you have never consciously used or contracted this muscle, doing these exercises may initially be difficult – but stay with it, you will soon learn.

First and most important, you must know beyond any doubt that you are indeed contracting the pubococcygeus. Since this muscle surrounds the urethra, vagina and rectum and extends from the pubic bone to the tail bone, contracting this muscle will produced a tightening sensation from the urethra to the rectum. Some women describe the sensation as a 'pulling up' or a 'drawing together' of the external genitalia.

Contracting the pubococcygeus muscle can be done in any position – lying down, sitting, standing, walking, or even while standing on your head. You should not have to contract any other muscle. All too often women will hold their breath, make terrible facial grimaces, tighten their stomach muscles, squeeze their buttocks together, or worse yet, push down. *Pushing down as if you were having a bowel movement is to be avoided.* Contraction of this muscle does just the opposite. It draws the anus closer to the urethra, tightens up the rectal sphincter, and prevents the inadvertent passage of flatus (gas).

If you are still not sure whether you are contracting the correct muscle, the next time you go to the toilet check yourself by alternately stopping and starting your urine stream until your bladder is empty. Being able to stop voiding on command involves contraction of this muscle. Relaxing it will allow you to resume voiding. For additional confirmation, you might try inserting one finger into your vagina. As you contract the muscle your vagina will tighten and squeeze your finger.

Now that you have identified the muscle and know how to contract it, let's proceed with the exercise programme.

What exercise programme will strengthen the pubococcygeus muscle?

If you expect results, you are going to have to be conscientious. Muscles don't increase in bulk and strength overnight. But those of you with mild stress incontinence should start to notice definite improvement within two months.

An effective exercise programme should include at least two hundred or more contractions every day. Each contraction should be as forceful as possible and held for a full three seconds. Relax in between for the same amount of time. Some experts suggest spacing the exercises over several hours, or perhaps doing eight to ten per half hour. Since you can do them anywhere, in any position, and without anybody being the wiser, there are really no excuses. It's up to you.

How else can you benefit from exercising this muscle?

Regular exercise of this muscle will also promote healthier and firmer tissues by increasing the blood flow through the pelvis. With better circulation your female organs will look better, feel better and function better. Even haemorrhoid problems may become a thing of the past.

Last but not least, exercising the pubococcygeus can help to keep the vagina the way it was meant to be – snug, sensuous and responsive.

Will exercising the pubococcygeus improve your love life?

Perhaps not your love life, but surely your sex life.

If you will recall, the pubococcygeus normally encircles and supports the middle third of the vagina. Slackness or loss of tone in this middle area, whether the result of childbirth, ageing or lack of exercise, will gradually cause the vagina to become shorter and wider. Such a vagina is no longer able to contract or expand properly, nor to ensheath the penis effectively during coitus.

Women with this problem frequently complain of a lack of vaginal sensation during sexual intercourse. Men complain that their organ seems literally lost inside the woman. When sensation decreases for both partners, sexual satisfaction is obviously lessened.

Proper exercises done conscientiously not only maintain a normal, functioning vagina in optimal condition but also help restore any loss of shape and tone to the important middle third of the vaginal canal. Instead of being loose and flabby, the vagina can once again become snug and cylindrical. Keep working and within a couple of months both you and your mate will begin to notice a difference. In fact, try contracting the pubococcygeus while having intercourse. Your partner will enjoy being nipped, and your own sexual pleasure will also be enhanced.

Will this exercise programme benefit all types of problems resulting from pelvic organ relaxation?

That depends on how much relaxation there is and how far the problem has progressed. Even in those cases where vaginal plastic surgery may be indicated, exercise will still help by promoting better blood circulation and healthier tissues.

As previously mentioned, women with mild stress incontinence and perhaps a bit of urethral sag can be materially helped by strengthening the pubococcygeus muscle. Thus, in some cases surgery can be avoided. In other women, however, pelvic organ relaxation may present a more serious problem.

How serious?

What originally may have started as a weakness in the pubococcygeus muscle and connective tissue support can become an actual defect. In essence, the weakened muscle may have become so stretched and thin that its fibres literally begin to separate and tear. With more and more separation between muscle fibres, a hole or defect is eventually created – somewhat like wearing a hole through the heel of a sock.

So what happens?

Without proper support maintaining the pelvic organs in their normal anatomical position, they gradually prolapse or herniate through the defect and in time bulge down and into the vaginal canal. The urethra, instead of being nicely tucked against the pubic bone, visibly sags downward; this condition is called a urethrocele. (See Figure 15.) In a similar manner the bladder or the rectum can herniate through the muscle and connective tissue defect and bulge into the vaginal canal. (See cystocele, Figure 16; rectocele, Figure 17.) In women with marked loss of pelvic support, the womb may also start to prolapse and inch its way down the vaginal canal. Exercises under these circumstances

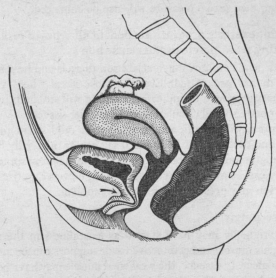

15.   *Urethrocele. Notice how the urethra bulges into the vaginal canal*

will obviously not repair the defects or tuck those organs back in place.

Does that mean that surgery is necessary?

Not always. The need for surgery really depends on how much trouble this causes. Surprisingly enough, some women with marked pelvic organ relaxation have very few complaints. Others may have minimal relaxation and yet experience great distress.

What kind of problems can you expect with pelvic organ relaxation?

Everything is relative. Symptoms will vary depending on the extent of the defect, the degree of relaxation and the particular organ involved. Thus, for example, a woman may complain primarily of stress incontinence because of a sagging urethra, whereas her bladder and rectum may still be fairly well supported. Another woman with good urethral and bladder support may only be bothered by increasing constipation attributable to an enlarging rectocele. Any combination of symptoms is possible. Symptoms, when present, are primarily related to the organ involved.

What about a prolapsed bladder (cystocele)?

Most women with a large cystocele complain of a lump or bulge just inside the vaginal introitus. Other women, particularly after prolonged standing, will be bothered with a heavy, dragging sensation in the pelvic area. On occasion the bladder may be sufficiently prolapsed to appear at the vaginal opening as a ball or swelling. Not uncommonly a woman will mistake this swelling for a dropped uterus or even a tumour.

In any event the woman with a large cystocele may have difficulty in emptying her bladder completely. As you can see from Figure 16, marked prolapse of the bladder can actually cause a large portion of the bladder to sag below the level of the urethral outlet. Therefore, trying to empty the bladder completely when this has happened would be somewhat like trying

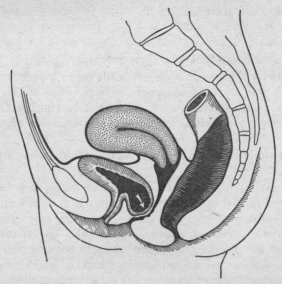

16. *Cystocele. Notice how the bladder wall bulges into the vaginal canal*

to urinate uphill. For this reason a woman with a large cystocele will still have the sensation of 'having to go' after she has just been, or the feeling that her bladder is not quite empty, which of course it isn't. This sort of distress may become particularly severe at bedtime. Although the woman may just have been to the toilet, as soon as she lies down, she feels the need to go again.

One solution, of course, is corrective surgery to eliminate the problem.

Some women have discovered that simply by inserting a finger into the vagina and elevating the 'bulge', they can empty their bladder. As expedient as this manoeuvre may be for the moment, it does not resolve the problem for long.

Why not?

The tendency for some urine to be retained in the bladder at all times (residual urine) makes the stagnant urine a perfect breeding place for any lurking bacteria. Thus, women with cystoceles are much more susceptible to chronic and recurrent bladder infections with all the attendant distressing symptoms, such as frequent and painful urination. Chronic irritation of the bladder floor almost invariably leads to urinary incontinence – not stress incontinence but another type, *urge incontinence*, or the sudden loss of a few drops of urine whenever the all too frequent, strong desire to urinate hits unexpectedly.

It should be emphasized, however, that not all cystoceles provoke such problems. Many women function surprisingly well despite an obvious bladder prolapse.

What about a rectocele?

Even when quite large, rectoceles, unlike urethroceles or cystoceles, do not usually cause too many problems. (See Figure 17.) The possible exception may be the woman who has always been

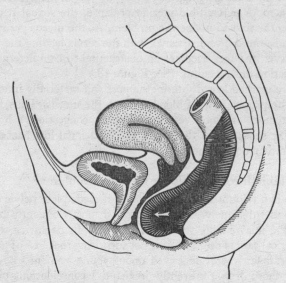

17. *Rectocele. Notice how the rectal wall bulges into the vaginal canal*

troubled with constipation. Occasionally a woman with a large rectocele may suffer with intermittent faecal impaction unless bowel movements are regular and the faeces kept reasonably soft. What can happen is that material may collect and subsequently harden in the pouched-out rectal wall just above the anus. As more and more faeces accumulate in the rectal passage, it becomes increasingly difficult to have a bowel movement. Here again, some women have resorted to using a finger to exert vaginal pressure against the bulging rectal wall, thereby facilitating evacuation.

What kind of symptoms does a prolapsed uterus cause?

Although special ligaments help maintain the normal position of the uterus, its support also depends on the integrity of the pubococcygeus and pelvic connective tissue. Any subsequent weakening of these supports can result in a prolapse, or descent, of the uterus into the vaginal canal (dropped uterus).

With minimal sagging, there may be few or no symptoms. With a more perceptible uterine prolapse, the sexual partner may be the first to notice the problem. As the uterus gradually descends into the vaginal canal, with the cervix leading the way, the cervix in effect becomes an obstruction to complete penile penetration during coitus. (See Figure 18.)

More marked loss of uterine support will materially interfere with the proper flow of blood through the uterus. Thus, with engorgement of blood vessels and pelvic congestion, a heavy, dragging sensation in the pelvis plus occasional low backaches are common complaints.

Is childbirth responsible for all these problems?

There is no doubt that the problems of inadequate pelvic support and subsequent vaginal relaxation most frequently begin with the unavoidable stress of childbirth. In countries where obstetrical care is minimal, it is not surprising that loss of pelvic support is fairly prevalent even among young women.

For those of you currently pregnant, a conscientious pubococcygeus exercise programme may well minimize tissue trauma during labour and delivery. As the baby's head descends through the vaginal canal, a pubococcygeus with good tone and elasticity will give to allow the baby's head to pass and, following delivery, will contract back to its normal position around the middle third of the vagina. Exercising in the weeks after delivery will further help the inner vagina resume its original shape and tone much sooner and perhaps even improve on what was there before.

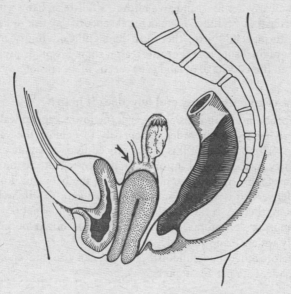

18. *Marked prolapse of the womb (dropped womb). In this particular example,
     the cervix has descended all the way to the vaginal opening*

On the other hand, a flabby pubococcygeus muscle can easily be overstretched, and some of its fibres can actually be torn and pushed downward by the pressure of the baby's head. In such a case the muscle may never recover completely.

Even with a good pubococcygeus muscle, other unrecognized tissue damage can also occur during childbirth.

Tissue damage – where?

To the lower vagina and introitus when, just prior to delivery, the baby's head begins to appear at the vulva (crowning). Unnecessary prolongation of this stage of labour, with repeated bearing-down efforts, invariably causes thinning and disruption of the underlying muscle and fibrous supports of the vaginal introitus.

It is the rare woman who can go through an unaided delivery (particularly her first) and give birth to a full-term baby without suffering tissue trauma. Even in the absence of any tear or laceration during childbirth, there can be significant injury to the lower vaginal supports. For this reason some hospitals prefer to shorten the end stage of labour by means of an episiotomy.

What is an episiotomy and how does it help?

An episiotomy is an incision through the lower vaginal wall and underlying tissues in order temporarily to enlarge the vaginal outlet. The purpose of this minor procedure is to maintain the integrity of the vaginal introitus by preventing the tissue from overstretching, thinning and tearing to let the baby out. Following delivery, it is a simple matter for the doctor to stitch up the incision, thereby returning the tissues to their normal position. Without an episiotomy the vaginal introitus might be permanently widened and relaxed.

Factors other than childbirth, though, can also be responsible for inadequate pelvic support.

What other factors?

Some women just seem naturally predisposed to weakness of the muscles and connective tissues. Marked uterine prolapse has been reported in fairly young women who have never been pregnant.

Being overweight can also place strain on those supports, as can excessive coughing from a chronic lung condition and persistent straining during defecation. But a more common cause, and one that none of us can avoid, is advancing age. If the pelvic

supports are already compromised, gradual oestrogen withdrawal and time may aggravate the problem further. For
example, a small cystocele causing no symptoms at forty-five
years can become large and uncomfortable by the age of sixty-
five.

What can be done about inadequate pelvic support?

Though (as we've seen) a certain amount can be done by
exercises, if you have persistent backache/urinary complaints/
constipation, if life is a misery of dragging pelvic organs, the
answer is normally surgery, sooner or later. The timing and kind
of surgery will vary depending on your age, your desire to have
more children, your physical condition, the presence of any other
associated pelvic problem and the extent of your discomfort.

For the younger woman whose pelvic muscles have relaxed
but who desires another pregnancy, surgery will usually be postponed until she has completed her family. Surgical repairs can
be rapidly undone by another vaginal delivery.

What kind of surgery is usually done?

True stress incontinence can be corrected by either vaginal or
special low abdominal surgery in selected women. Problems
attributable to poor pelvic support can be handled most effectively by vaginal plastic surgery. Various surgical techniques are
used to re-suspend the pelvic organs in their normal anatomical
positions and repair the defects in the internal muscles and connective tissue supports. This kind of operation usually involves
about ten days' stay in hospital.

Will a severely prolapsed uterus be removed?

Not necessarily. Much will depend on the age of the woman and
the degree of prolapse. Some gynaecologists may advise the
removal of the prolapsed uterus of an older woman if they want
to achieve a permanent vaginal repair. A hysterectomy (removal
of the uterus) would also eliminate the possibility of the uterus
developing problems in later years.

There are no hard and fast rules, however. Treatment must always be individual.

Can anything else be done for those sagging organs besides surgery?

If symptoms are present and sufficiently distressing, corrective surgery is by far the best answer. Nevertheless, there are instances in which an associated disabling medical problem may increase the risk of any operation. Elderly women with severe

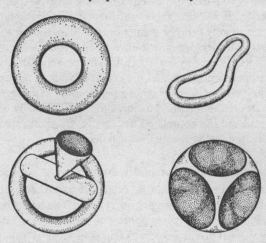

19. *Vaginal pessaries*

cardiac conditions or respiratory insufficiency generally make poor candidates for surgery. Thus, symptomatic relief in a few women may necessitate their being fitted with a vaginal pessary to keep those sagging organs tucked up.

A vaginal pessary – what's that?

A simple appliance usually made of hard rubber or plastic. In contrast to contraceptive diaphragms worn solely for birth-control purposes, vaginal pessaries are not designed to cover the cervical opening. Their sole purpose is to help support the uterus and vaginal walls in their normal position. Since pessaries come in various shapes and sizes (see Figure 19), the selection of the most appropriate device depends on the extent of vaginal relaxation and the degree of prolapse.

Vaginal pessaries are no panacea. They have many inherent drawbacks.

What's wrong with vaginal pessaries?

For the woman who does obtain symptomatic relief, a vaginal pessary is undoubtedly a real blessing. However, any device left in the vagina tends to create an irritating and malodorous discharge. Regular douching and vaginal creams are used to decrease discharge and odour formation. Moreover, the pessary must be removed, cleaned and replaced periodically. Since this must be done professionally, it requires a visit to the doctor at least every six to eight weeks.

Even when properly fitted (see Figure 20), a vaginal pessary

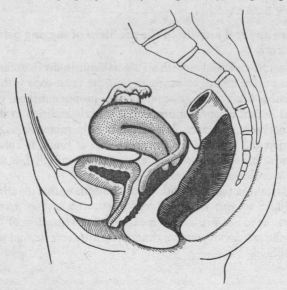

20. *Vaginal pessary in place*

can abrade vaginal tissues with subsequent discomfort and spotting. This is especially so among elderly women, whose thin vaginal mucosa is very susceptible to any irritation. On the other hand, a pessary that fits too loosely may be readily expelled during defecation or straining down.

But the biggest disadvantage of the pessary for women who are sexually active is its interference with normal intercourse. Although the extent of interference during coitus will vary depending on the type of pessary used, any such device tends to limit the depth of penile penetration.

To say the least, vaginal pessaries are rarely the first-choice, ideal solution even for the elderly. Fortunately, with improved anaesthesia, women who were previously resigned to a pessary are now safely undergoing surgery. Women in their seventies and even in their eighties are now having their prolapse problems surgically corrected. In fact, many of these women bounce back faster and are in better physical shape than many younger women.

Is there any real answer to the problem of sagging pelvic supports?

Since nature endowed us with a vulnerable anatomy in exchange for our unique ability to bear children, we must cope with the situation as best we can. Factors such as proper nutrition, good general health, competent obstetrical care, in addition to those pubococcygeus exercises, can certainly help minimize vaginal relaxation and loss of pelvic support. Yet at times, in spite of good medical and personal care, a few women will still face some of these unpleasant problems.

Today, the notion that nothing can be done or that it's all part of being a woman is completely unwarranted. You may be beyond the aid of preventive measures, but regardless of your age or the severity of your condition, you are never beyond some kind of help.

Part 4

The Sexuality of Woman

14. Intercourse and Other Sexual Activities

If visitors from outer space suddenly popped into one of our bookshops, they would soon be convinced that earth people, unlike other creatures of the universe, are equipped with only two bodily functions – eating and sex. Next to cookbooks and diet guides sex books have been boom best-sellers over the past twenty-five years. Ever since Kinsey dared to ask intimate questions, and then had the audacity to publish his results, the world hasn't been the same. Before that time, sex was strictly a private matter, for better or for worse. Today, because of Kinsey and the myriad publications on sex that followed in the wake of his original work in 1948, topics previously considered by some as taboo are now discussed with disarming candour. As a result, women are becoming increasingly aware of their own sexuality and what it means in terms of their total expression as individuals. Women are expecting more from sex and are willing to give more. They are also exploring new dimensions in sensuality and physical gratification.

This chapter does not pretend to have the answer on how to make every sexual encounter a memorable moment of rapturous ecstasy. Rather, its purpose is to provide the individual woman with an insight into seldom discussed factors that can affect her total sexual response. Attention is also focused on changes, both temporary and permanent, involving the female organs which can influence sexual gratification. Furthermore, this chapter is about how the act of sex and other expressions of physical intimacy can work to the good or to the detriment of a woman's mental and physical well-being.

Ideally, what happens to a woman's body during the act of sex?

All women vary in their sensory awareness and response to love making, depending upon a number of factors – age, general health, oestrogen level, mood, type and intensity of stimulation, etc. And yet there are basic physiological and anatomical changes common to all women who do reach climax during the act of sex. For practical purposes, the physiology of the female sexual response is divided into four phases: the excitement phase, the plateau phase, the orgasmic phase and the phase of resolution. Failure to reach orgasm implies that the woman's sexual response was arrested either at the excitement or the plateau phase.

What about the excitement phase?

The first response to sexual stimulation is vaginal lubrication, whether it be psychologically induced (for example, by reading a sexy story) or initiated by direct physical contact. Within ten to thirty seconds of effective erotic stimulation, the vaginal walls and introitus become moistened and bathed with lubricating fluid. Vaginal lubrication, the female equivalent of penile erection, is not a secretion from any gland or organ. Rather, it is a thin, mucoidlike fluid that seeps through the vaginal walls when there is vascular engorgement of vaginal blood vessels. The production of vaginal lubrication does not therefore depend upon the presence of an intact cervix, uterus, ovaries, or even functioning Bartholin's glands. In women past sixty, for example, atrophic vaginal tissue-changes resulting from age and oestrogen deficiency do not materially interfere with the production of this lubricating material. And although two or three minutes of effective sexual stimulation may be required to achieve an adequately lubricated vagina, the older woman nonetheless still reacts in the same basic manner as does a woman forty years younger.

As sexual stimulation continues and more and more blood is pumped into the pelvic region, there is a gradual venous congestion of all the sexual organs; the labia minora (inner lips) thicken and enlarge noticeably and the diameter and length of the clitoris increase. The labia majora (outer lips) of women who have never had children tend to thin out, flatten and elevate outward and upward, thus exposing the vaginal opening. In women who have given birth at least twice, the labia majora also flare away from the vaginal opening in preparation for penile penetration, but in this instance there is marked enlargement of the lips, sometimes to as much as two or three times normal size. At the same time, and common to all women, the inner two thirds of the vagina (the area closest to the cervix) begin to widen and lengthen. As the plateau phase approaches, the cervix and the body of the uterus, now markedly engorged, are gradually elevated and pulled higher into the pelvic cavity, thus further ballooning and expanding the innermost third of the vagina.

But sexual response is not limited to the pelvic organs. It is a total body response as indicated by a rise in blood pressure, an elevated pulse rate, more rapid breathing and an increase in muscular tension throughout the body. The nipples become erect and the breasts may noticeably increase in size by as much as 25 per cent during the latter stages of the excitement phase. Seventy-five per cent of women on occasion also develop a fine rash or skin flush involving the chest, back and abdomen.

How does the plateau phase differ from the excitement phase?

The plateau phase is essentially a continuation and an accentuation of all the changes that occurred during the excitement phase. However, there are three notable differences involving the outer third of the vagina, the clitoris and the labia minora.

As tension mounts, the outermost third of the vagina (the area closest to the outside) actually decreases in diameter as a result of marked vasocongestion of the lower vaginal tissues. This constriction of the lower vagina allows the vaginal walls to grip the shaft of the penis more firmly. The clitoris, which previously had been relatively enlarged, retracts and disappears beneath its hood or foreskin, and decreases some 50 per cent in length. And the labia minora (sometimes referred to as sex skin) change colour from light pink to bright red to a deep burgundy hue. (Interestingly enough, once these marked colour changes of the labia minora occur, orgasm invariably follows.) Pupils dilate, breathing accelerates, nostrils flare and the cords of the neck stand out.

And then comes orgasm?

Yes – an almost seizurelike, tension-releasing, exquisitely pleasurable response which is the acme of physical gratification in sexual activity. The lower vagina and surrounding tissues, as well as the womb and at times even the rectal sphincter, contract rhythmically. A few women at the time of orgasm may have a compelling urge to urinate, which can be accompanied by a small involuntary loss of urine. The more intense the orgasm, the more intense the total body reaction and the more numerous the contractions. Most orgasms rarely last longer than ten to fifteen seconds, and yet a really good strong orgasm can have as many as twelve to fifteen distinct pelvic contractions that gradually become weaker and spaced further apart as the climax ebbs.

What about the phase of resolution?

The phase of resolution begins when the last vaginal contraction fades, and continues until all the pelvic organs have returned to their pre-excitement state. The involuntary muscular contractions that are experienced primarily as vaginal contractions allow the pooled and stagnant blood in the pelvic organs to dissipate rapidly. Thus, within thirty minutes, the uterus, vagina, labia and clitoris return to their normal state. In fact, the clitoris resumes its usual size and position within ten to twenty seconds after orgasm. In contrast, the uterus, which can enlarge as much as twice normal size, may take anywhere from ten to thirty minutes to become decongested following orgasm. Needless to say, without orgasm there can be no rapid decongestion of the pelvic organs such as that experienced during the phase of resolution. (More about this shortly.)

What percentage of women actually experience orgasm during coitus?

That depends on whose statistics are quoted. According to various surveys conducted on married women, anywhere from 22 to 75 per cent usually or almost always experience orgasm during coitus; 30 to 45 per cent experience it sometimes or occasionally; and 5 to 22 per cent have never once achieved orgasm during intercourse.

Orgasm during coitus for women as contrasted to orgasm for the vast majority of men is not a 'one, two, three, push the button' affair. It is a complex process that can be affected by a multitude of factors, some obvious and some obscure.

Does coital position or length of foreplay affect a woman's ability to achieve orgasm?

Coital position is apparently not a crucial factor in a woman's ability to experience orgasm. And yet many women do find that the superior position (face to face and on top of the male partner) may succeed where other positions have failed. In the superior position, a woman is essentially in control: she can change the angle, depth and tempo of penile thrusting, and she can ma- noeuvre her body so as to provide close clitoral contact depend- ing on her erotic needs. Because the male partner experiences less physical strain while reclining on his back, this position may allow him to delay his orgasm more easily.

On the other hand, the length of time devoted to foreplay and the actual duration of penile vaginal intercourse seem to play a greater role in enhancing a woman's ability to reach orgasm. According to some experts, foreplay prolonged for at least twenty minutes and penile vaginal intercourse sustained for fifteen minutes (quite a feat for many men) allow nearly 98 per cent of women ultimately to reach orgasm.

In addition to the above factors, however, it is even more important to be spontaneous and to experience each moment for its own pleasure. Assessing or monitoring one's sexual perform- ance or lack of it on the basis of achieving the one big goal –

orgasm – can be distracting. When orgasm becomes the sole objective, sometimes the harder one tries the more difficult and elusive it becomes. Sexual arousal and desire are emotions. A mere act of will will not induce vaginal lubrication or achieve orgasm.

Can the size of the penis play a role in a woman's sexual satisfaction?

Some women are sexually aroused at the sight of a well-endowed man. But in actuality the size of the erect penis bears very little relationship to a man's ability to satisfy a woman sexually. There is also no truth to the prevalent belief that the bigger the penis, the greater the man's virility or prowess as a sexual partner. Therefore, unless a woman is psychologically conditioned to believe differently, penile size as such should have no effect on her ability to respond sexually or to obtain satisfaction from intercourse. However, two rare exceptions should be noted: where the penis is so large as to cause actual physical discomfort despite adequate lubrication and a normally accommodating vagina; and when the penis is so abnormally small that effective coital contact cannot be maintained.

Can vaginal size affect a woman's enjoyment of intercourse?

Although there are a few women who do have an exceptionally small or large vagina, they are just that – exceptions. Since the vaginal walls normally lie against each other, most healthy average vaginas effectively ensheath the penis during intercourse. This close contact between the penis and the vaginal walls enhances physical enjoyment for both partners. With continued stimulation and arousal, the normal vagina will dilate and expand to accommodate deep thrusting by almost any size penis.

However, difficulties during first intercourse can be encountered if the woman has too snug a vaginal opening. This is occasionally seen in women who have never used tampons or have never engaged in sexual play wherein the vaginal opening was dilated manually. For such women, pain at the vaginal opening during penetration or, less commonly, complete inability to permit penile entry can definitely be a detriment to sexual enjoyment. Fortunately, however, a hymen rarely offers much resistance to firm but gentle stretching. In fact, if the woman is sufficiently aroused and lubricated, penile penetration even the first time can frequently be accomplished with little difficulty. The idea that all first intercourse must be accompanied by pain and obvious hymenal bleeding just isn't so. Nonetheless, if you are concerned about the adequacy of your vaginal opening, see Chapter 9 for details on how to determine its size and what you can do if it doesn't seem to measure up.

The opposite problem, a too relaxed vagina, is not only a common complaint of many women but may also be a source of sexual dissatisfaction for some. Most women who express concern about a too relaxed or over-stretched vagina are usually in their late thirties or forties and have had at least two children. Even with the best obstetrical care, the unavoidable strain and stress of childbearing can weaken and disrupt the normally firm muscle and connective tissue supports of the vaginal walls and introitus. The vaginas of these women tend to become wider, shorter and less capable of making tight contact with the penetrating penis. Women who have this problem will notice that the penis no longer seems to fill the vagina. And their partners will complain that their organ feels lost inside. For some couples, this relative disproportion between penis and vagina, although a source of decreased sensory awareness, does not detract from their enjoyment of the sexual act.

For other women, a too relaxed *vaginal opening* may also interfere with clitoral stimulation during coitus. In these instances effective *indirect* clitoral stimulation, which normally occurs when downward traction is exerted on the labia and clitoral hood during active penile thrusting, is greatly impaired.

Can anything be done for the vagina and introitus that seem too large?

Very definitely. Where an over-stretched vagina seems to be interfering with the full enjoyment of sexual intercourse, a change in coital position may be helpful. Since the object is to tighten the vaginal canal as well as the vaginal opening, some women find that bringing their legs together once the penis has been introduced allows for closer contact. This manoeuvre is easily accomplished if the woman lies on her back while the male partner, on top, places his legs outside hers.

If a too relaxed vaginal opening prevents adequate indirect clitoral stimulation during coitus, the woman-on-top position or the side-by-side position can help resolve the problem. In either of these positions, direct clitoral stimulation can occur during deep penile penetration.

For women, however, whose main concern is a too wide or relaxed vaginal canal, a more satisfactory solution (other than changing coital position) would be the firming and strengthening of certain pelvic muscles essential for the maintenance of normal vaginal tone. Exercising the pubococcygeus muscle (Kegel's exercises) can significantly improve a too relaxed vagina. (In Chapter 13 these exercises as well as the benefits derived therefrom are extensively discussed.)

If vaginal relaxation or stretching has progressed beyond the help of corrective exercises, vaginal plastic surgery can be used to restore the vagina to more normal dimensions. Although most vaginal plastic surgery is done to alleviate the symptoms associated with the prolapse of pelvic organs, such as the bladder (see Chapter 13), some gynaecologists now accept that tightening the vaginal canal and introitus to enhance sexual enjoyment is a warranted operation.

If a woman has never had children, can an active sex life lead to pelvic relaxation and an over-stretched vagina?

Not really. Even if a woman has frequent intercourse with multiple and physically well-endowed partners, the vagina will maintain its tone and elasticity to a remarkable extent. Pelvic organ relaxation or a vagina that lacks tone and firmness is primarily the result of childbearing. Advancing age, however, can further aggravate or even initiate such a condition.

Can a hysterectomy (removal of the uterus) shorten the vagina and thus interfere with deep penile penetration?

No. A carefully performed abdominal hysterectomy (through an abdominal incision) should not shorten the vagina in any way. According to a recent report, two thirds of the women who had this operation showed an average increase in vaginal depth of 0·39 inch (1 centimetre). Of the remainder, about two thirds showed no change in vaginal depth and the others (about an eighth of the whole group) showed some shortening. Even in these instances, the decrease in vaginal canal length was less than 0·2 inch (0·5 centimetre). Perhaps of greater interest is the fact that although a hysterectomy seals and closes the vaginal canal at the top (where the cervix used to be), there is no impairment to the vagina's ability to dilate and expand during sexual intercourse.

What about the woman who has a vaginal hysterectomy?

Most vaginal hysterectomies (removal of the uterus through the vagina), unless done for the express purpose of sterilization, are frequently combined with vaginal plastic surgery. Since this type of surgery, as opposed to what is done in an abdominal hysterectomy, does involve re-suspending sagging pelvic organs, there is a slightly increased chance of shortening the vaginal canal. But here again the shortening, if any, is minimal and occurs in only a minority of women. Even when vaginal plastic surgery is performed on women past seventy, most surgeons make it a point to preserve a sexually functional vagina.

Does removal of the uterus lessen a woman's ability to enjoy sex?

There is no denying that a few women will attribute their lack of sexual interest or ability to be aroused to their hysterectomy. These women almost without exception have a history of some sexual maladjustment, often the result of pre-existing psychological factors. Apart from mental and emotional variables that can adversely affect sensuality, there is no scientific basis to support the idea that the removal of the uterus has an effect on sexual response.

Meticulously documented studies have repeatedly shown that vaginal lubrication during sexual excitement can be just as copious without as with a uterus. Also, the inner vagina can expand and dilate whether or not the uterus is present. And equally important, orgasm as a physical and emotional experience can be of the same intensity as before a hysterectomy. In fact, women who have had a hysterectomy still report feeling pleasurable *uterine* contractions along with the vaginal contractions and other pelvic throbbing at the time of orgasm. The explanation for this interesting phenomenon, although not completely understood, may be the result of a conditioned response. In other words, if a woman was previously aware of uterine contractions during orgasm, the same physical sensation may occur even in the absence of the uterus.

What about sexual enjoyment for the woman whose ovaries are removed?

If a woman's ovaries are removed prior to the menopause, her sexual response will ultimately resemble that of a postmenopausal woman. (See Chapter 21.) Without normal oestrogen stimulation to help maintain the tone and vascularity of pelvic tissues, there is a gradual thinning of the vaginal and vulvar tissues. As described elsewhere, this usually means a delay in the onset of vaginal lubrication and a decreased ability of the vaginal walls to expand and dilate. And although orgasm can be just as emotionally and psychologically gratifying, its physical intensity is apt to be diminished.

Wouldn't oestrogen replacement therapy in such a woman prevent these physical changes?

To a remarkable extent, yes, and for several years. But advancing age does eventually slow and decrease sexual response with or without oestrogen therapy. And yet, if regular and effective sexual stimulation is maintained throughout the years, there is no reason why the older woman can't continue to enjoy sex all the days of her life. Sixty per cent of all women over sixty are still sexually active.

Can other physical problems contribute to a woman's inability to reach orgasm?

According to some experts, clitoral adhesions may be a possible cause for lack of orgasm and even painful coitus. During infancy the prepuce or foreskin of the clitoris normally adheres tightly to the glans, thus acting as a sheath encasing the clitoris. With maturity the clitoris becomes free, but on rare occasion, the prepuce of an adult woman may still adhere firmly to the glans. Moreover, the accumulation of smegma between the glans and the prepuce may also contribute to the formation of clitoral adhesions. In a few women, such adhesions, by preventing adequate exposure of the clitoris during the excitement phase of sexual stimulation, might be a factor in their being nonorgasmic. In a limited study involving nonorgasmic women where clitoral adhesions did exist and were removed, a small percentage subsequently did become orgasmic.

And yet, there can be so many reasons for lack of orgasm as well as painful intercourse in women, that to attribute clitoral adhesions (even if they should be present) as a possible cause demands further evaluation.

Does pain during coitus usually interfere with a woman's ability to experience orgasm?

Not necessarily. It all depends on where the pain is located, its intensity, and how sexually aroused the woman may be. Moreover, if a woman has previously enjoyed coitus on a regular basis, the excitement as well as the anticipation of the moment may, to a great extent, allow her to disregard any subjective discomfort. On the other hand, pain during intercourse can be a real detriment to a satisfying sexual encounter for some women.

What are some of the physical reasons for pain during intercourse?

The location of the pain during intercourse and the type of discomfort experienced are frequently important clues to the possible cause. For example, pain that is localized around the vaginal opening or lower vagina can usually be attributed to one of three causes: a too snug vaginal opening, insufficient vaginal lubrication and irritation or inflammation from a vaginal or vulvar infection.

Pain from a too snug vaginal opening is not necessarily limited to the woman with no previous sexual experience. It can also occur in the postmenopausal woman because of vaginal atrophic changes and particularly if sexual intercourse is infrequent. If a woman has recently been delivered, the over-enthusiastic repair of an episiotomy can temporarily tighten the vaginal opening just a little too much. Fortunately, however, all of these causes of pain related to a snug vaginal opening can usually be remedied by appropriate measures which, of necessity, must be individualized.

Insufficient vaginal lubrication at the time of penile penetration is perhaps one of the most common causes of dyspareunia, or painful intercourse. Friction of the penis against relatively dry vaginal walls can irritate and traumatize the nearby urethra and bladder. As mentioned in Chapter 13, intercourse without sufficient lubrication can result in bladder spasm and painful urination immediately following coitus. Without adequate lubrication to bathe the vaginal opening and labia minora, even clitoral stimulation can be unpleasant. Although the use of lubricating jellies applied around the introitus prior to intercourse can be helpful, a persistent lack of effective lubrication does reflect inadequate sexual arousal.

In contrast to the above, the sudden development of a stinging, burning discomfort around the introitus (vaginal opening) and lower vagina during intercourse can usually be traced to tissue irritation. Acute inflammation of the vulva resulting from contact with an irritating substance or perhaps an individual allergy is being seen with increasing frequency. Similarly, any of the vaginal infections can also be a source of acute discomfort in an otherwise sexually well-adjusted woman. (See Chapter 10.)

Curiously enough, a few women (even in the absence of infection) have complained of a vaginal burning sensation immediately following ejaculation by their partner. But if a condom was worn, or the penis withdrawn prior to the release of semen, the distress was completely avoided. In these unusual instances, the problem was eventually traced either to a prostate infection in the male or to a rare allergic reaction of the woman to her partner's semen.

What about pain on deep penile penetration?

Pain that is felt deep inside the vagina during active penile thrusting can be caused by a variety of factors. Endometriosis, or the condition wherein fragments of displaced endometrial tissue become implanted and grow along pelvic structures, is one of the most notable examples. As discussed in Chapter 20, endometriosis is notorious for creating a sharp, stabbing pain during deep penile penetration. Then too, the impact of the penis against a tipped (retroverted or retroflexed) uterus and especially if the uterus tends to be somewhat enlarged, boggy and congested can be another source of pain. Actually, penile impact against any inflamed pelvic tissue, such as that which develops during an acute tubal infection (see Chapter 11), can also be a source of distress. Less commonly, excessive scar tissue formation along the upper vagina as a result of extensive surgery or radiotherapy can be a cause of recurring pain on deep penile penetration.

When the pain is persistent and unamenable to corrective therapy (as in the case of the scar tissue), changing coital position so as to limit the depth of penile penetration can bring relief. Employing the rear-entry position, that is, with the woman lying on her side or her stomach with her buttocks facing her partner's abdomen, can help. Or if the woman prefers lying on her back with her partner on top, she can still limit the depth of penile penetration by bringing her legs together after the introduction of the penis.

Is forcible sexual intercourse, or rape, invariably painful?

Rape or forcible sexual intercourse without consent is a subject that is receiving increasing publicity. In the United States over 46 000 cases of rape were reported in 1972, and it is further estimated that closer to 230 000 rapes were actually perpetrated. Figures for the United Kingdom are difficult to estimate, as many cases are not reported to the police and many of the sexual assaults reported are not classified as rape. However, rape is a potential threat to all women, so let's discuss it more fully.

For the woman who is sexually assaulted, there is no question that such an experience is emotionally and physically devastating. Even the sexually active woman who otherwise is not physically abused during an attack can experience vaginal tissue trauma and pain. Yet, in America it is believed that as many as three out of four women who are sexually assaulted never report the incident or seek medical attention. The necessity of having to relive the experience by giving minute details to the police, and the need to be further questioned and examined by a doctor who may or may not be sympathetic, are among the reasons why women are reluctant to report sexual attack.

But the trauma doesn't end there. If the rapist can be identified and apprehended, legal proceedings are frequently weighed in favour of the accused. To obtain a rape conviction, a woman must be able to prove that she was sexually assaulted and that the act occurred without provocation or consent on her part. All too often this puts the woman's character on trial. In addition, it must be proved that there was *penile* entry and that the victim resisted the attack. Is it any wonder, then, that very few of those rapes cases that *are* reported ever end with a conviction?

Today, interested groups are trying to amend the laws to protect the rights of women. Particular attention is being given to the man's possible defence that it was reasonable for him to assume that the woman consented. But apart from legal matters and the need for emotional support, any woman who is sexually assaulted should receive medical attention. For even if she was fortunate enough to have escaped obvious physical injury, the possibility of venereal disease and pregnancy should also be considered.

What exactly is the medical procedure in cases of alleged rape?

Since rape is not a medical diagnosis but rather a decision to be reached by a court of law, examining doctors are not permitted to draw conclusions regardless of the physical findings. This means that the general appearance of the woman as well as any obvious physical injury and, more specifically, evidence of trauma to the genitalia should be noted in detail and recorded in writing. If a woman is planning to prosecute the offender, it is especially important that she not bathe or change her clothing prior to the medical examination. The fact that even in *bona fide* rape cases a careful medical examination cannot always corroborate *forcible* penile entry makes it imperative that evidence such as torn or bloody clothing that could substantiate a woman's testimony be presented for proper inspection.

In addition to a careful physical examination, it is also necessary that certain laboratory tests be performed.

What kinds of laboratory tests?

Although ejaculation at the time of penile penetration is not a necessary requisite to obtain a conviction of rape, the finding of semen in or around the vagina can be extremely helpful. For this reason swabs from the vagina and vulva are taken and examined for the presence of acid phosphatase, an enzyme found in semen. Moreover, it is also possible by subjecting the semen to certain tests to establish the blood group of the attacker. Material taken from the upper vagina and vulva is also examined immediately for the presence of motile sperm. And equally important, smears as well as cultures from the vagina, cervix and rectum for gonorrhoea are also an integral part of any examination in a case of suspected rape.

What is done to protect the rape victim from venereal disease?

First, any sexually assaulted woman should receive prophylactic antibiotic therapy for protection against venereal disease. An injection of 2·4 million units of benzathine penicillin G (Dibencil, Penidural) given intramuscularly will usually protect the woman against the development of gonorrhoea and probably syphilis. Where there is a history of an allergic reaction to penicillin, other appropriate antibiotics would be substituted. (See Chapter 11.) If the smears and/or cultures taken for gonorrhoea prove to be positive, follow-up visits for repeat cultures are in order. It would also be advisable to do a blood test for syphilis. A positive blood test for syphilis immediately following the attack would mean that the woman already harboured the disease, as the incubation period of the spirochetes runs anywhere from ten to ninety days. A positive blood test would, of course, require immediate treatment. A negative blood test would call for repeat testing at six and twelve weeks following the attack. If the blood test for syphilis was still negative after ninety days subsequent to the assault, a woman could be virtually certain that she had not contracted the disease.

What precautions are taken against pregnancy in a woman who has been raped?

Some doctors will recommend a course of the synthetic oestrogen diethylstilboestrol as a precaution against pregnancy. (See Chapter 16.) If started within seventy-two hours of intercourse, high doses of oestrogen make the lining of the womb unreceptive to the implantation of a fertilized egg. On the other hand, taking this drug is often unpleasant – it frequently induces nausea and vomiting – and many doctors consider this treatment too extreme, even for a rape victim. (A second disadvantage is the risk that diethylstilboestrol taken early in pregnancy may harm the fertilized egg if it *is* implanted.)

It is important that a woman also be advised against having sexual intercourse without contraception during the remainder of that particular menstrual cycle. Otherwise if she does become pregnant, she won't know who is the father.

Should a period fail to come (up to four weeks after diethyl-stilboestrol treatment), most doctors would readily support a request for an early abortion.

Other than the precautions against pregnancy just mentioned, resumption of normal intercourse in a sexually assaulted woman will of course depend upon the extent of her physical injuries, if any, and how emotionally traumatized the incident has left her.

Can there be psychological reasons for pain during normal intercourse?

Pain during intercourse in a physically normal and healthy woman is more common than generally supposed. Even today, despite changing moral values and greater permissiveness about sexual activity, with or without the sanction of marriage, many women still feel guilty, fearful and apprehensive about their own sexual needs and drives. Many of these psychosexual maladjust-ments can be traced to early childhood influences stemming from over-rigid parents with condemning attitudes towards all sexual expression. More often than not, the problem is further com-pounded by gross ignorance and misleading information about sex. It is therefore not surprising that intercourse for some women, rather than being a pleasurable experience, is frequently a painful ordeal to which they reluctantly submit.

Of all the possible mechanisms that can account for painful intercourse because of deep-seated psychosexual conflicts, the most outstanding example is vaginismus.

What exactly is vaginismus?

An involuntary and usually painful contraction of the muscles surrounding the lower vagina. If a woman anticipates pain or subconsciously resists the entire idea of intercourse, this muscular tightening can be so extreme as to prevent penetration of the penis. In such instances, consummation of the sexual act is virtually impossible despite a normal vagina and pelvic organs.

These same women frequently make it impossible for themselves to be examined pelvically. For as soon as they are approached (and prior to any physical contact), they automatically clamp their knees together, arch their back off the examining table and effectively squeeze their vagina shut, making the insertion of an examining finger an exercise in futility. Needless to say, for a doctor to persist under these circumstances would not only aggravate the patient's pain but could also adversely affect any future attempts at corrective therapy.

Where vaginismus is extreme, successful resolution of the problem may necessitate long sessions of intensive psychotherapy with an understanding and enlightened counsellor. And yet, if the woman, and the man concerned, express a genuine desire to correct the situation and to save their relationship, the outlook for resolving the problem is considerably more favourable. In such instances, a patient, gentle, yet firm and knowledgeable partner is frequently the important determining factor in success. All too often, however, even if such women eventually overcome their fear and reluctance, they are seldom able to really enjoy sex.

For them, as well as for other women who rarely or never experience orgasm for a variety of other reasons, lack of sexual gratification despite regular intercourse may lead to other problems.

What sort of problems can persistent lack of orgasm during sexual intercourse cause?

Regular sexual stimulation up to but not including orgasm can, over a period of weeks and months, ultimately be detrimental to a woman's sense of well-being. During sexual arousal the pelvic organs become flooded with arterial blood. Objectively, this can be noted in the woman's initial response to stimulation by the production of vaginal lubrication. Along with this vaginal sweating phenomenon, further stimulation causes the cervix, uterus, vulva and clitoris to become congested, swollen and enlarged as more blood is shunted to the genital area. If, however, the stimulation is only transient or quickly withdrawn, the pelvic tissues become rapidly decongested as the blood vessels promptly return to their normal (non-engorged) state. But if the stimulation is prolonged, more intense and carried up to but short of orgasm, upon cessation of stimulation the pelvic blood vessels do not empty rapidly. Instead, the genital tissues remain congested and engorged with stagnant blood for varying amounts of time. The uterus itself, which can frequently enlarge in size by two or three times during prolonged sexual excitation, may take hours to return to its former size.

Therefore, in women who are consistently aroused sexually and yet fail to reach orgasm, persistent engorgement of the pelvic blood vessels (chronic pelvic congestion) can ultimately cause a variety of symptoms.

How does consistent lack of orgasm affect these women?

In many ways. Vague abdominal discomfort, backaches and a sense of pelvic fullness are among the most common complaints. If congestion of the cervix and vaginal walls is particularly marked, a constant vaginal discharge in the absence of any infection may be the most notable symptom. For other women, chronic pelvic congestion (because of consistent lack of orgasm) may ultimately make them tense and irritable and interfere with normal sleep.

Can anything relieve the symptoms of chronic pelvic congestion?

The answer is simple – orgasm by whatever means are available. But for some women, that answer isn't so simple.

Why isn't orgasm a simple solution to chronic pelvic congestion?

A few women are truly their own worst enemies. Although consistently ungratified sexually, they are still reluctant to express this fact to their partners. Some women even compound the problem by feigning orgasm regularly. For others, if orgasm isn't achieved during intercourse, the idea of obtaining sexual release by masturbation (whether by their partners or by themselves) is totally unacceptable and an obvious sign of their own sexual inadequacy – at least to their way of thinking.

The fact that the sex drive, in contrast to other bodily functions, can be suppressed indefinitely by sheer will-power makes the entire realm of sexuality and, particularly, the desire to be sexually gratified an area frequently loaded with guilt feelings and self-deprecation. Sex is a natural bodily function. Being sexually stimulated up to but not including orgasm is not the way nature intended it to be. Eating is also a natural function, but how much nourishment and satisfaction could we derive from food if we simply chewed and never swallowed?

This does not mean that for the woman every act of sexual intercourse must be accompanied by orgasm in order to be emotionally and physically satisfying. Sometimes just being held closely or knowing that you are giving pleasure to someone you love can be intensely gratifying. Rather, what it does imply is that regular sexual stimulation without orgasm over weeks and months can be an important factor in many seemingly unrelated pelvic and other physical complaints.

For when it comes to avoiding or even relieving chronic pelvic congestion, a small orgasm is better than no orgasm.

How does orgasm or reaching a climax solve pelvic congestion?

During orgasm, involuntary muscular contractions (involving the vagina, uterus and other pelvic structures) not only block further arterial blood from entering the pelvis but also rapidly drain off all the pooled and stagnant blood. Thus, within minutes, all the congested and swollen tissues are back to normal. Subjectively, this rapid emptying of pelvic blood vessels after orgasm is experienced as a warm, pleasant, flushing, glowing sensation in the pelvis.

Although orgasms do differ in intensity depending on a variety of factors – mood, length and type of stimulation, etc. – even having a less intense or a less physically satisfying orgasm can still resolve the problem of pelvic congestion. Under these circumstances, it just may take a little longer for the pelvic organs to return to their normal pre-excitement state.

But penile vaginal intercourse or manual masturbation aren't the only ways to experience orgasm and thus avoid chronic pelvic congestion. Oral genital sex is another variety of sexual activity that can lead to the same pleasurable end result.

What is meant by oral genital sex?

Stimulation of the penis or vulva by the mouth, lips or tongue for purposes of sexual gratification. Fellatio is oral stimulation of the penis; cunnilingus is oral stimulation of the vulva. There is nothing new or different about oral genital sex. Records of this type of sexual activity date back to the first clay tablets. Nor is oral genital sex practised exclusively by homosexuals. According to various surveys the higher the educational level and economic status, the more likely heterosexual couples are to include oral genital sex as a regular part of their normal sexual activity.

There is nothing perverted or abnormal about this type of sexual play. Moreover, the idea that oral genital sex is dirty because it involves mouth contact with organs associated with excretory functions is really without foundation. There is no reason why the genitals can't be as clean as any other part of the anatomy. All it takes is the simple hygienic expedient of a little soap and water. Needless to say, without proper cleansing of the body, oral genital sex can be less than exciting. By the same token, having regular intercourse with a partner who never bathes, changes his underwear or who doesn't bother to brush his teeth can also be a turn-off.

Whether you do or don't engage in oral genital sex is a matter of personal choice and preference. But for many couples this type of love making remains one of the most pleasurable and exciting forms of sexual activity. So whether fellatio and cunnilingus are performed simultaneously or alternately as a preliminary to intercourse, or whether mouth to genital stimulation is carried all the way to orgasm, oral genital sex is here to stay.

Can infections of the mouth or throat ever be acquired by oral genital sex?

Yes, indeed. Avoiding infection during love making really boils down to choosing your partner with care. Nonetheless, when it comes to transmitting or acquiring infections, oral genital sex is much less hazardous than penile vaginal intercourse. *Trichomonas vaginalis*, for example, a protozoan organism that commonly inhabits the male urethra as well as the female vagina, can never be transmitted to the mouth. This organism is unable to survive outside the confines of the genital urinary tract.

Fungus or yeast infections of the mouth acquired by oral genital sex with an infected partner are exceedingly rare. In the first place, the partner in question would have to have a roaring fungus infection of the vagina or penis. Moreover, the partner performing either cunnilingus or fellatio would have to be physically debilitated and suffering from chronic malnutrition. Fungus infections of the mouth are virtually never seen in relatively healthy and sexually active adults.

Venereal diseases, on the other hand, can be transmitted during oral genital sex. Gonorrhoea of the mouth and pharynx (throat) can be acquired during fellatio with an infected man or during cunnilingus with a woman who has the infection. Similarly, a syphilitic chancre of the lips, tongue, palate or tonsils can develop if the sexual partner has a syphilitic lesion of the genital organs.

With regard to the transmission of viral infections from the genital organs to the mouth (such as genital warts and herpes simplex virus type II), although conceivable, there have to date been no reported cases. In contrast, virus infections of the mouth or lips and specifically herpesvirus type I (responsible for the common cold sore or fever blister) can be transmitted to the genital organs of the sexual partner during cunnilingus or fellatio. (See Chapter 11.)

What infections can be transferred from the mouth to the genital organs during oral genital sex?

The three principal organisms that could be transferred from the mouth and ultimately be a source of genital infection are the gonococcus (gonorrhoea), the spirochete (syphilis) and *Candida albicans* (a fungus). Although remote, it is possible that an individual with either a syphilitic chancre or gonorrhoea of the mouth and pharynx could infect the genital organs of his or her partner during oral genital sex.

Similarly, a few cases of vaginal fungus infection may originally have been acquired during cunnilingus. But the fact that the fungus *Candida albicans* is frequently a harmless inhabitant of the mouth and intestinal tract of both sexes, as well as the vagina of many healthy women, makes its possible transmission during oral genital sex a matter of little concern. Unless conditions are favourable for its growth, the fungus, even when introduced into the vagina, will remain quietly unobtrusive. (See Chapter 10.)

Other than infection, can oral genital sex ever be hazardous to a woman?

Only if air is blown into the vagina of a pregnant woman. As mentioned in Chapter 18, this type of sexual activity could lead to a fatal air embolism of the *mother's* brain by forcing air into the blood vessels lining the pregnant uterine cavity. (As an aside, douching with a *bulb syringe* during pregnancy could also inadvertently force air into the uterine cavity and thus result in a similar maternal catastrophe.)

Don't some couples also engage in anal sex?

Anal intercourse is in a class by itself. Although some couples will experiment with this form of intercourse just to satisfy their curiosity, the incorporation of anal intercourse as a regular part of sexual activity can lead to problems. To begin with, the anus was not biologically or anatomically designed to accommodate the erect penis. Therefore, if anal intercourse is to be tried at all, it is essential that the woman be receptive to the idea; that the introduction of the penis be done extremely gently; and that the organ be well lubricated with Vaseline, K-Y lubricating jelly, or a similar product. Saliva just won't do. Moreover, once the penis is introduced into the rectum, it should never be reinserted into the vagina or permitted to contact the vulva without careful cleansing of the organ. Failure to take this simple precaution allows the contaminated penis to introduce unwanted rectal bacteria and other organisms into a woman's urethra and vagina, thus leading to urinary and/or genital tract infections. (See Chapter 13.)

What about the possibility of acquiring other infections through anal intercourse?

Some men have acquired penile urethral infections from rectal organisms during anal intercourse. But here again, gonorrhoea is by far the most common infection acquired through such sexual play. In men, gonorrhoea of the rectum can usually be traced to anal coitus with a homosexual contact. In women, rectal gonorrhoea is probably acquired through anal intercourse with an infected partner or through contamination of the anus from a copious gonorrhoeal discharge emanating from the cervix. Or, a woman with gonorrhoea of the cervix can have her infection transferred to the rectum by engaging in anal coitus following vaginal intercourse. (See Chapter 11.)

Besides possible infection, anal intercourse, even when performed gently and with the necessary precautions, can be injurious and a cause of local anal and rectal problems.

What kind of rectal problems can anal intercourse provoke?

The most common injury, and one that can occur the very first time, is a crack or split in the mucous membrane of the anal canal due to the disproportion in size between the penis and the anus. Such injuries can cause pain and bleeding that can be further aggravated during normal bowel evacuation. Subsequent attempts at anal intercourse under these circumstances can compound the problem by deepening and widening the split (anal fissure). Anal fissures are notoriously slow to heal and frequently become infected. Needless to say, existing problems such as haemorrhoids can also flare up as a result of this type of sexual activity.

But anal intercourse, if practised regularly and over a long period of time, can result in an even more serious problem – relaxation and dilatation of the anal sphincter. This means that excessive stretching of the important muscle fibres surrounding the anal opening could eventually make it difficult for an individual to control the passage of flatus (gas). In extreme cases (and a few have been reported), control of faecal material, especially if the stools were loose, could be further impaired.

Why, then, do a few couples include anal intercourse as part of their sexual activity?

The anus can be exquisitely sensitive to sexual stimulation. Furthermore, anal intercourse can evoke the same erotic sensations as those experienced during vaginal intercourse. In women who perhaps have a relaxed or overly stretched vagina, the tightness of the anal sphincter may create for both them and their partners an added dimension in sexual excitement. Since anal intercourse is also done most commonly in the rear-entry position, this further frees the male partner to stimulate simultaneously the breasts, clitoris or labia minora. For some women, orgasm under these circumstances can be more intense than that experienced otherwise.

Can orgasm per se ever be detrimental to a woman?

Orgasm in a pregnant woman with a ripe cervix (a cervix that is already partially thinned and dilated), particularly if she is several weeks from term, can bring about the onset of premature labour. Orgasm causes rhythmic contractions of the uterus. Therefore, orgasm in women with a ripe cervix could, by precipitating uterine contractions, provoke the onset of labour. Although of no consequence to the woman already close to term and with a mature baby, there have been reported cases of premature labour and delivery apparently precipitated by orgasm. For this reason, any woman whose cervix begins to dilate and thin eight or more weeks before term should be cautioned against any type of sexual activity that could induce orgasm.

What type of sexual activity produces the most intense orgasm?

According to carefully documented studies, masturbation in women not only includes the most physically intense orgasm but also evokes the greatest number of pelvic contractions. It can also bring the average woman to orgasm faster than any other type of sexual stimulation. Why this should be can probably be explained by an old French saying, 'On n'est jamais aussi bien servi que par soi-même,' – which means, one is never so well served as by one's self. Despite the fact that masturbation, at least for women, can elicit a really great orgasm, there's nothing like sharing sex with a compatible partner to make the experience emotionally rewarding.

What then, is really good sex?

Good sex is more than technique, timing, position or even experiencing orgasm. It is also more than an accelerated heart rate, increased blood pressure and vascular engorgement of the genital organs. Really good sex involves total physical, emotional and psychological satisfaction. But it can seldom attain that peak unless there is a strong, continuing relationship between two sensitive and responsible individuals who mutually love and respect each other.

Sex, like any other form of human expression and interaction, cannot remain static. A good sexual relationship needs to grow and to be nurtured if it is to become the physical expression of love between two people. It means feeling good about your body and having an open attitude towards the needs of both you and your partner. Equally important, spontaneity and feeling free to communicate are essential.

No individual responds exactly the same way every time to the same sexual stimulation. Moods change from day to day and from moment to moment. What might have been terribly exciting last night may be undesired this morning. So why not open up to your mate about what really pleases you and when. You may happily discover that what you secretly dreamed in your fantasy world coincides with what your loved one has also wanted to share with you, but never dared.

Part 5

The Prerogatives of Being a Woman

15. How to Become Pregnant

With the current emphasis on family planning and birth control, the subject of how to become pregnant might seem irrelevant or of minor concern. Yet about 10 per cent of marriages today are involuntarily barren.

For the couple unable to conceive and anxious to have children, the decreasing availability of babies for adoption has made their infertility problem even more of a concern and challenge. It is, therefore, important that all factors in the barren couple that could contribute to infertility be investigated and evaluated.

The last decade has seen remarkable advances in the field of reproductive medicine. Today 60 to 70 per cent of 'infertile' couples can *eventually* achieve their desired goal of conception, but many of the treatments described in this chapter are practised in Britain only at specialized infertility clinics, or in gynaecology departments of teaching hospitals. (Recent work in the field of immunology, antigens and sperm antibodies may in the near future offer hope for others.)

How can you become pregnant?

A sperm must get together with an egg. Exactly how this happens may seem obvious, but misunderstandings still abound.

How does a sperm get together with an egg?

With the exception of artificial insemination, there is only one way. The male partner must have an erection and deposit sperm in or around the vagina. Penile penetration into the vagina is not absolutely necessary. Sperm deposited around the outside of the vaginal opening can result in pregnancy. On occasion sperm can also be present at the tip of an erect penis *prior to ejaculation*. The practice of coitus interruptus, or the withdrawal of the penis from the vagina before ejaculation, has at times been responsible for impregnating an unwary woman.

Once deposited, those seedy sperm move at an incredibly fast rate. From the vagina they swarm into the cervical canal, swim through the uterine cavity, and ascend into the Fallopian tubes. If all conditions are favourable, total travel time from the cervix to the rendezvous with the egg in the outer third of the Fallopian tube has been clocked at less than five minutes.

Can you become pregnant the first time you have intercourse?

Yes, the very first time can do it. However, for the young couple having sexual intercourse at least every other day, 25 per cent of the women will be pregnant within one month. At the end of six months 60 per cent will have conceived, by the end of one year 80 per cent, and after eighteen months 90 per cent. If after trying for eighteen months you still haven't conceived, then regardless of your age or the frequency of intercourse, your chances of becoming pregnant rapidly decline.

At what age are women most fertile?

Between twenty and twenty-four, with twenty-four probably being the time of maximum fertility. From twenty-five to thirty there is a slight decline followed by a steady drop-off during the thirties. After forty there is a marked drop, and after forty-five your chances of becoming pregnant are rather slim.

What about fertility in men?

Here again, twenty-four seems to be a very good year. Unlike women, men maintain a fairly high rate of fertility throughout a longer period of their life. The ability to have an erection, ejaculate and discharge healthy sperm may continue into the sixties, seventies and beyond. Nevertheless, by forty-five there tends to be a slight decline in male fertility.

How old is too old?

For some men no age is too old. In women, however, the ovaries do retire eventually. But even if you are over forty-five, as long as your periods are regular, don't despair. Ovulation and conception can occur up to the age of fifty and beyond. You might just beat the world's record – pregnant at fifty-seven.

However, there are disadvantages to starting your family after thirty or thirty-five.

What's wrong with having that first baby after thirty or thirty-five?

By the time a woman is thirty her fertility is already slowly declining. This means that if you are waiting to be financially secure or to have just the right home and surroundings in which to raise children, you might find that becoming pregnant may not be that easy. Furthermore, since such common female problems as endometriosis, fibroid tumours and other pelvic conditions manifest themselves in the late twenties and thirties, here again you may have passed the optimal reproductive years in which to start your family.

Statistics have also shown that women past thirty-five in particular tend to have a higher rate of complications during pregnancy and delivery. There is also a small but decided risk of giving birth to a congenitally abnormal infant. Mongolism, for example, among the general population occurs in about one out of 700 live births. There is a marked variability of its incidence depending upon maternal age: for women under thirty the incidence of mongolism runs about one out of 2,000 live births, whereas in women over forty, their chances of giving birth to a mongoloid child can be as high as 1–2 per cent.

But for those of you who are anxious to conceive regardless of your age . . .

228 From Woman to Woman

How often should you have intercourse if you want to become pregnant?

More often than you probably think. Most sperm quickly lose their ability to impregnate after forty-eight hours, while the ovum is most receptive to fertilization during the first twelve hours of its twenty-four-hour existence. Possible conception, therefore, in any one menstrual cycle is primarily limited to a scant forty-eight- to sixty-hour period. This means having sexual intercourse at least four times a week, or at least every other day. Less frequent intercourse decreases your chances for speedy conception.

Does having more sex improve your chances of becoming pregnant?

If four times a week is ideal, then five times or more should be even better. Not necessarily so. Too much sex can actually work against you especially if your partner is somewhat sub-fertile. On an average most men discharge anywhere from 3·5 centimetres to 5 centimetres (half to one teaspoon) of semen at any one time. Ejaculations in excess of four times weekly decrease the volume of semen. And less semen means less sperm being deposited. So unless your partner is superfertile, slack off.

Can position during sexual intercourse influence conception?

Yes, indeed. Varying your position may add zest to your sex life, but if your aim is pregnancy, let's be practical. Nothing is quite so successful in keeping the sperm in close contact with the cervix than the conventional position of male on top and woman on her back with hips flexed and buttocks elevated on a small pillow.

Following ejaculation the man should not withdraw his penis from the vagina until it has resumed its normal flaccid state. Pulling out too soon will allow some of the semen to fall away.

And by all means don't jump out of bed immediately

afterwards. Gravity can be your enemy. It is better to lie on your back for at least half an hour or longer.

Does having a tipped uterus make any difference?

Despite the fact that there may be less contact between the cervix and pool of semen, a tipped or retroverted uterus (contrary to what many believe) does not decrease your chances for conception. All other things being equal, if the sperm are anywhere near the cervix, they'll make it.

What about the use of lubricating jellies or Vaseline before intercourse?

Not if you want to get pregnant. In exchange for allowing the penis to penetrate more easily in the women with a snug vaginal opening or insufficient lubrication, Vaseline or lubricating jellies inhibit effective sperm movement. On the other hand, saliva will not interfere with sperm movement. In fact many women resort to using good healthy spit around the vaginal opening when natural lubrication may be less than adequate. Douching before intercourse will also not interfere with sperm mobility.

Will having an orgasm improve your chances of becoming pregnant?

If orgasm in a woman was necessary for conception, there would be a prompt and precipitous drop in world population. Nevertheless, having an orgasm may aid migration of the sperm through the cervical canal by causing a slight protrusion of the alkaline cervical mucus (more about this soon). Aside from this minor factor, orgasm in the woman is not a prerequisite to conception.

When are you most fertile?

During the ovulatory phase of your cycle, or approximately two weeks before your next period. If your periods tend to be irregular, keeping track of your basal body temperature as described in Chapter 6 may help pinpoint the moment of ovulation. But don't despair if your chart doesn't look like the example. Temperature charts sometimes need professional interpretation.

If you can pinpoint the moment of ovulation, when's the best time to have intercourse?

Usually twenty-four to thirty-six hours before the actual moment of ovulation as evidenced by the rise in your basal body temperature. If you hit it just right, impregnation is much more likely to occur if the sperm are eagerly assembled on the tubal runway and awaiting the arrival of the freshly launched egg.

Moreover, by avoiding the inadvertent impregnation of an abnormally late, and so over-ripe, egg, you have a smaller chance of a miscarriage (spontaneous abortion) or a congenitally abnormal baby.

However, if you want to try to influence the sex of your child, you might want to change your timing somewhat.

How can timing intercourse influence the sex of the unborn child?

The closer you can time intercourse with the moment of ovulation, the better your chances of having a male child. On the other hand, having intercourse after ovulation or two to three days before anticipated ovulation will much more likely result in a female.

Other factors can also play a role in sex determination.

What factors?

Since the sex of the child is predetermined by the sperm (X sperm for female, Y sperm for male), factors such as vaginal acidity, depth of penile penetration at the time of ejaculation, and orgasm in the woman can favour impregnation by either an X sperm or a Y sperm. However, *results cannot be guaranteed.*

According to several clinical studies, by manipulating these various factors your chances of achieving the desired sex of the child may run close to 80 or 85 per cent.

How can you increase your chances of having a boy?

To speed the Y sperm on their way, the following routine is suggested: (1) The most important factor is, of course, timing. Plan intercourse at the time of ovulation or just a few hours before you ovulate. Be sure that you abstain three or four days beforehand. (2) Prior to intercourse take an alkaline vaginal douche by dissolving one tablespoon of baking soda per pint (two tablespoons per litre) of warm water. The increased vaginal alkalinity will further enhance the passage of Y sperm. (3) There should be penile penetration at the moment of ejaculation to assure the deposition of Y sperm close to the cervix. (4) Plan to have an orgasm yourself. The protrusion of the alkaline cervical mucus at the time of climax will also aid Y sperm migration.

In essence, the easier it is to conceive (fresh Y sperm meeting fresh egg) and the more you enjoy it, the greater the chances of having a boy baby.

Suppose you want a baby girl?

Then you must give the X sperm the edge by making it more difficult for the Y sperm to get through: (1) Have your *last* intercourse about two to three days before your anticipated ovulation. (2) Prior to intercourse take a vinegar douche of one tablespoon of white vinegar per pint (two tablespoons per litre) of warm water. (3) At the moment of emission, penile penetration should be fairly shallow. (4) Bypass the orgasm this time.

As you might guess, conception under these circumstances will certainly be more difficult. Should impregnation occur, however, the chances of having a female offspring are definitely increased. In this instance the winning combination is the result of an old X sperm meeting a fresh, young egg.

To what extent should you rely on a BBT chart?

For those of you anxious to conceive regardless of the baby's sex, don't get carried away or compulsive about this type of record keeping. Three or four months of temperature taking is plenty. If at the end of three cycles you have a fairly good indication of when you ovulate, the time of subsequent ovulation can be projected with some degree of accuracy. Obsessive timing of intercourse around the exact day of ovulation is both unnecessary and a potential source of friction. The best advice is to just go ahead and enjoy intercourse every other day or so during your most fertile week. At that frequency of coitus, your chances of conception are probably just as good as adhering to a meticulous time schedule.

If you haven't been able to conceive, when should you consult a doctor?

Many gynaecologists will advise trying for at least a full year. However, for the older, childless couple, it might be foolish to postpone evaluation for that length of time. Age, general health and specific medical problems, past or present, may make an earlier evaluation desirable.

Is the female partner usually to blame?

The female partner is accountable for only slightly more than half of the infertility problems. In approximately 35 per cent of all barren marriages, the husband is solely responsible for lack of conception, and in an additional 10 per cent, the husband is partly responsible. For this reason, many doctors prefer to evaluate the male partner first before proceeding with the more involved studies necessary to determine any female infertility factor.

If the man can perform sexually, does that mean he's fertile?

Not at all. Being able to have an erection and ejaculate semen inside the vaginal canal is no guarantee of fertility. You may be sleeping with the world's greatest lover, but unless he can deliver vigorous sperm, he'll never make you a mother.

Fertility in the male or the ability to impregnate an egg requires the following: (1) the testicles must produce normal sperm; (2) the sperm must then pass through the male genital tract (vas deferens) and mix with secretions (seminal fluid) from the prostate and seminal vesicles; and (3) the semen (seminal fluid plus sperm) must be ejaculated from the penile urethra and delivered preferably against the cervix.

How is fertility in the male evaluated?

By the simple expedient of examining the semen – if you can get a specimen. Unfortunately few men will willingly accept the inference that they may be subfertile. Many infertility investigations have ground to a halt because of a recalcitrant male with a sensitive ego. Nevertheless, if your parter does cooperate, part of the battle is won. Should he pass the test with a high score, he will be more inclined to discuss 'your' infertility problem with the doctor.

How is semen collected?

Usually by masturbation or coitus interruptus following four or five days of sexual abstinence. Best results are obtained if the entire ejaculate is deposited in a clean glass jar (not necessarily sterile), tightly capped and delivered to the laboratory within a few hours.

When it comes to semen specimens, how fertile is fertile?

According to recent studies it takes at least 20 million sperm per centimetre for the fertilization of a single ovum. Thus, with the average ejaculate measuring 3–4 centimetres, this means that a *minimally* fertile man should release at least 60–80 million sperm during a single act of coitus to effect conception. But, apart from the total number of sperm ejaculated, the most important factor affecting male fertility is sperm motility; at least 60 per cent of all sperm must be motile and normal in shape if impregnation is to occur.

What happens if your partner fails the semen test?

He should be given another chance. The quality and number of sperm can be adversely affected by emotions, physical stress, febrile illnesses, as well as too frequent intercourse and even prolonged sexual abstinence. Don't give up hope yet. His second or third performance may dazzle everyone.

What about the man who still doesn't pass?

A doctor specializing in infertility may be able to help him. Even assuming that your partner is hormonally and genetically normal, other conditions can readily account for a poor sperm count. Having had mumps complicated by orchitis (inflammation of the testes) as a child is frequently a cause of zero sperm production (azoospermia). Similarly, any past infection (gonorrhoea, for example), scrotal injury or obstruction to the proper blood supply of the testicles can contribute to a decreased sperm count.

Subfertility may also stem from less obvious and unsuspected reasons.

Is your partner's job too hot for his own good?

Have you ever wondered why those priceless testicles dangle in such a precarious location? The reason is literally a matter of degrees. To be functional, the testicles must hang in the cool of the scrotum. An undescended testicle (one retained within the warmth of the abdominal cavity) just can't manufacture sperm. Too much body heat eventually destroys the special cells that produce sperm.

Similarly, men exposed to excessive heat around the genital area, such as truck drivers who spend long hours in hot engine cabs or men employed as stockers on blast furnaces, have notoriously low sperm counts.

On the less dramatic side is the low-sperm man who further compromises his fertility by being a hot bath devotee. A fast shower would be preferable if he is really eager to get you pregnant.

Men's pants can also be a detriment in cases of borderline infertility.

Does your partner need to change his underwear?

As improbable as this may seem, many a subfertile husband has finally impregnated his wife by the simple expedient of changing his underwear. Tight pants, jock straps and trousers with snug crotches can raise the testicular temperature by hugging the scrotum closer to the body.

Switching to breezy boxer pants has made more than one man a father.

Can anything else help a low sperm count?

No specific treatment, including vitamin and hormone therapy, has been universally effective. However, since sperm counts can be adversely affected by physical and emotional factors, general health measures such as proper diet, regular exercise, adequate rest and cutting back on alcohol and tobacco consumption, along with avoidance of unnecessary tension, may be beneficial.

Otherwise, if none of these measures proves helpful, perhaps your partner should consider having his sperm frozen.

How would freezing his sperm help?

If one ejaculation doesn't have enough sperm to impregnate you, pooling several emissions might do the trick. Semen specimens from low-sperm husbands can be frozen, stored and subsequently used to inseminate their wives artificially. Some doctors specializing in infertility problems will arrange this for you.

With the technique of three to four repeated inseminations during the ovulatory phase, approximately half the women will become pregnant within two to four months. In unusual cases where the husband has no sperm, the couple may elect artificial insemination with a donor's sperm. Under these circumstances, the pregnancy success rate can be as high as 60 to 80 per cent.

If your partner is fertile, what's your trouble?

Most young and apparently healthy women fail to conceive for one of the following reasons: their cervix is working against them, the tubal passageways are blocked or they simply do not ovulate regularly.

Do you have a friendly cervix?

You will never get pregnant unless the sperm can squirm through the cervical canal and reach the tubes in time to meet the incoming egg. A friendly cervix implies both a healthy cervix free from chronic infection and an unobstructed cervical canal whose glands secrete the right kind of mucus at the proper time.

What's so important about cervical mucus?

Without a certain quality of cervical mucus, most sperm will be entrapped and die before they can pass through the cervical canal.

Under normal conditions, both the quality and the quantity of the cervical mucus changes during the menstrual cycle. Right after your period, the cervical canal normally contains a thick plug of tenacious mucus – a sure trap to ensnare those sperm, thus keeping them from swimming up through the canal. As oestrogen levels increase and ovulation approaches, miraculous things happen. The small cervical os gapes slightly and the mucus now becomes profuse, watery and stringy. You may notice an increased amount of clear discharge during the ovulatory, or fertile, phase of your cycle. It is only during these few days at mid cycle that sperm can successfully penetrate the cervical mucus in any great number.

Following ovulation the cervical os narrows and the mucus returns to its preovulatory thick, unreceptive state.

How can the doctor tell if that mucus is receptive?

By checking the cervical mucus within two to fifteen hours after intercourse just prior to the time of expected ovulation. This postcoital test (Huhner test) is simple and painless. It consists of aspirating some mucus from the cervical canal and examining it under a microscope.

If your cervix is friendly, a certain number of living moving sperm should still be squirming around in the cervical mucus. In contrast, an unreceptive mucus will show no sperm or only dead ones in spite of the presence of motile sperm in the upper vagina.

For women whose mucus obstinately defies any sperm to sneak through, very small doses of oestrogen prior to ovulation may stimulate a greater output of normal cervical mucus. When an obvious cervical infection and discharge may be interfering, treating and clearing the infection may well solve the problem.

Are those tubes keeping you from getting pregnant?

Since fertilization of the ovum normally occurs in the Fallopian tubes, any blockage or obstruction involving the tubal passageways can make you infertile. For pregnancy to occur, at least one tube must be open and functioning normally.

There can be many reasons for blocked tubes. A gonorrhoeal tubal infection is certainly a common cause, but other pelvic infections as well as congenital tubal anomalies have been known to take their toll. In some parts of the world, notably Scotland and Israel, tuberculosis of the tubes accounts for 5 to 10 per cent of infertility problems.

Blockage of a perfectly normal tube can also occur if the tube is kinked by surrounding scar tissue or old adhesions from previous pelvic problems or surgery, for example, a ruptured appendix.

How can the Fallopian tubes be checked?

Several ways. Most commonly, either by a special X-ray of the uterus and tubes (hysterosalpingogram) or by gas (carbon dioxide) insufflation.

What exactly is gas insufflation?

A simple procedure that is usually done in an outpatient clinic. It checks the tubes by the passage of gas (carbon dioxide) through them. With a small rubber-tipped adapter inserted just inside the cervical opening, a stream of pure carbon dioxide gas is slowly released into the uterine cavity. If either or both tubes are open, the carbon dioxide gas will gradually pass through the tubal passageway and escape into the abdominal cavity. If both tubes are blocked, there will obviously be no passage of gas.

How does the doctor know whether the gas has escaped through the tubes?

He can frequently tell by the way the pressure rises and falls on the special gauge. Imagine for a moment that the tubes are drinking straws through which you blow air. If the straw is not plugged, the air will flow easily and smoothly. If the straw is bent or obstructed, no matter how hard you blow, no air will pass through it. Gas insufflation works on almost the same principle.

Verification that at least one tube is open will depend upon your experiencing a mild, temporary shoulder pain after the test.

Why the shoulder pain?

Sitting up or standing up after the examination will cause the small amount of carbon dioxide in the abdominal cavity to ascend automatically and lodge against the diaphragm (the muscle that separates the chest and abdomen). Irritation of the diaphragm from the gas will result in reflex shoulder pain. If you should lie down again, the gas will automatically shift away from the diaphragm and the pain will be relieved. But don't worry. Nature quickly absorbs that harmless small amount of carbon dioxide and you will be completely comfortable very shortly.

If you don't experience any shoulder pain, your doctor may either repeat the test at another time or else take an X-ray of the tubes. Sometimes a simple muscle spasm in the wall of the tubes can prevent any gas from escaping. A negative result is not absolute proof that those tubes are blocked.

What about an X-ray of the tubes?

A hysterosalpingogram involves taking X-ray pictures during the injection of a small amount of radiopaque dye through the cervical canal. This has the advantage of outlining the inside contours of the entire uterine cavity as well as the tubal passageways.

If there should be a blockage in either tube, its location can be accurately pinpointed. If both tubes are open, the dye will simply spill out of the ends and into the abdominal cavity.

You might have some temporary, mild uterine cramping during the test, but no shoulder pain afterward. The dye, which is heavier than carbon dioxide, will simply gravitate to the pelvic area and undergo rapid absorption.

If your tubes are blocked, can anything be done?

Since anywhere from 15 to 35 per cent of infertility problems are the result of blocked tubes (depending on whose statistics you quote), the possibility of surgically unblocking the tubes assumes prime importance.

Tuboplasty, or plastic reconstructive operations on damaged tubes are painstaking, meticulous and delicate surgery. When you consider that the tubal passageway isn't much bigger than the bristle on a hairbrush, you can appreciate why results, even in the hands of competent and experienced gynaecologists, are less than perfect.

Re-establishing the continuity of the tubes is also no permanent guarantee of success. A tube successfully opened by surgery may subsequently reseal because of scar-tissue formation or in some instances may even cause a tubular or ectopic pregnancy.

But even an open tube is not necessarily a functional and healthy tube. As you might remember from Chapter 2, the Fallopian tubes are more than just passageways. Specialized cells within their lining must also nourish the fertilized egg during its three- to four-day trip to the uterine lining.

For these reasons, success in terms of conception and full-term pregnancies cannot always be guaranteed following tubal plastic surgery.

What are your chances of getting pregnant after a tubal operation?

Pregnancy rates among women following tubal surgery vary from 7 to 40 per cent. Much depends on where the tube is blocked, how much of the total tube is affected, and the severity of the involvement. Needless to say, all these factors are vitally important in evaluating the potential success of any procedure.

As might be expected, surgery on tubes severely compromised

by extensive disease can easily fail. If there is only minimal tubal damage, results predictably are better. Your chances for success are further enhanced if the surgery is performed by a gynaecologist who has specialized in tubal surgery. Tuboplasty is not a routine operation.

What about the woman who just does not ovulate?

No young and respectable ovary will ever release a single egg unless the pituitary is in perfect working order. Lack of ovulation in women of reproductive age resulting from inadequate or poorly timed ovarian stimulation by the pituitary accounts for another 10 to 25 per cent of infertility problems.

As you may remember from Chapter 5, it takes two pituitary hormones (FSH and LH) working in absolute harmony to mature and launch an egg. Too much or too little of either hormone at the wrong time equals zero egg output.

Until fairly recently, most women who did not ovulate because of this problem were just out of luck. Adoption was the only answer. There was no magic elixir that could straighten out pituitary function or coax an egg out of those ovaries. Today, with the advent of the new fertility drugs, ovulation can be induced in about 80 per cent of such women, if they are fortunate and persistent enough to be taken on by the few specialist clinics who give this treatment.

Are you a candidate for one of the fertility drugs?

Being a candidate depends upon eliminating all other possible causes of infertility. This implies that everything else should be working for you: cervix, tubes and a fertile partner. In addition to basic blood and urine studies, a complete hormonal evaluation is also necessary to determine how well the pituitary and other endocrine glands are functioning. If lack of ovulation owing to a pituitary hormonal dysfunction is established as the only apparent reason for your failure to conceive, a fertility drug just might be the answer.

How do fertility drugs induce ovulation?

There are basically two different kinds of fertility drugs: the first induces ovulation by simply prodding the pituitary to release its hormones more effectively; the second induces ovulation by actually replacing the needed hormones.

The results of your pituitary hormonal evaluation will determine which fertility drug, if any, is the possible answer to your particular problem. If your pituitary is essentially normal but just slightly off-balance in relation to complete hormonal harmony between FSH and LH, it might need just a little nudge to function properly. Less commonly a woman may fail to ovulate because of an inadequate pituitary output of FSH and LH. Prodding the pituitary in this situation would do no good. As the old saying goes, 'You can't get blood out of a turnip'. Under these circumstances, nothing short of actual replacement of both FSH and LH will work.

What fertility drugs are available?

Currently only three: clomiphene; human menopausal gonadotrophin (HMG: known by trade names Pergonal or Humegon); and human chorionic gonadotrophin (HCG).

What is clomiphene?

Clomiphene is a synthetic drug preparation that induces ovulation by stimulating the pituitary to release FSH more freely. If your pituitary and ovaries are functionally intact but your problem is one of hormonal imbalance, clomiphene may be the drug of choice.

During six years of intensive clinical evaluation, four thousand anovulatory women were given clomiphene for a variety of menstrual and hormonal disorders, and ovulation was induced in some 80 per cent of the women so treated.

How is clomiphene taken?

By mouth, usually for five days during the menstrual cycle. However, since no two women will respond in the same manner, dose and length of treatment will vary.

If ovulation is going to occur, it will frequently be triggered within five to nine days following the last tablet. For best results, make sure your partner is around. Some women will ovulate the very first month. Others will require repeat treatment for several months. For others, clomiphene just doesn't work – no egg comes.

Should pregnancy occur, there may or may not be resumption of normal ovulation following delivery. In some instances, therefore, repeat treatment with clomiphene may be necessary should a subsequent pregnancy be desired.

What about side effects while on clomiphene?

Hot flushes sometimes occur because of increased pituitary FSH activity. In a small proportion of women, overstimulation by the pituitary may cause an ovarian cyst. Clomiphene-induced ovarian cysts, however, tend to be small and readily disappear within one to four weeks following discontinuation of treatment.

When properly used, clomiphene is a safe drug, but your chances of having a multiple pregnancy are slightly increased. Twins can be expected in about one out of sixteen clomiphene-induced pregnancies as compared with one in eighty spontaneous conceptions.

What about other fertility drugs?

HMG (human menopausal gonadotrophin) is essentially a hormonal extract of FSH from the urine of menopausal women. HCG (human chorionic gonadotrophin), on the other hand, is a hormonal extract of an LH-like substance from the urine of pregnant women. These two hormone extracts are used together in a sequential fashion to trigger ovulation by literally substituting for the two pituitary hormones, FSH and LH. Their use is primarily limited to that small group of women who are anxious to conceive but who fail to ovulate because of an inadequate pituitary output of FSH and LH. Needless to say, the cost of a single month's supply to effect ovulation can be as much as £100 or more, since these two human hormonal extracts are not synthesized commercially but have to be collected, purified and extracted.

Among women treated with these preparations, up to 90 per cent ovulate and 65 per cent subsequently conceive. As impressive as these figures may seem, only about 30 per cent of the women who do conceive actually give birth to living healthy babies. The remaining women unfortunately either abort spontaneously or give birth to grossly immature infants incapable of surviving. Furthermore, the effects of these two hormone extracts are somewhat unpredictable. (HMG, in particular, is not generally available to doctors or hospital clinics: it is restricted to those hospitals where facilities are available for close hormonal monitoring and constant supervision during treatment.) Being on this medication means having frequent pelvic examinations and many elaborate urine and blood hormonal studies to evaluate progress during treatment.

Why is such close supervision necessary?

Even with close supervision and carefully regulated dosages of HMG and HCG, there is a substantial chance of overstimulating the ovaries. As a result, large ovarian cysts can develop virtually overnight. Withdrawal of medication will usually result in cyst regression, but compared to clomiphene-induced cysts, ovarian enlargements with HMG and HCG occur with greater frequency and are potentially more serious.

What about multiple pregnancies with HMG and HCG therapy?

Unfortunately, your chances are high. Overstimulation of the ovaries can also cause super-ovulation with the simultaneous release of several eggs. Many of the famous multiple births so highly publicized in the past few years are HMG and HCG babies. Among women successfully treated with these preparations, about 30 per cent of all pregnancies will result in multiple births – twins, triplets or worse.

Undoubtedly with continuing research there will be better

and more effective ways of controlling the problem of ovarian overstimulation.

Is there any other way to induce ovulation besides fertility drugs?

For some women with the polycystic ovarian syndrome (see Chapter 9), wedge resection or the surgical removal of a portion of each enlarged ovary may correct the basic hormonal disturbance. Exactly how ovarian wedge resection works is still open to debate. More recently, clomiphene therapy has largely supplanted this surgical approach in women who want to become pregnant. Nonetheless, for some women with polycystic ovaries, surgery may still be the best answer in bringing about resumption of normal periods and monthly ovulation.

What else can make you infertile?

Endometriosis indirectly accounts for many infertility problems by interfering with the egg's passage from the ovary into the tube. (See Chapter 20 for details.)

What about the couple who seem perfectly normal but just can't conceive?

Since 1964 there has been mounting evidence to suggest that many obscure and previously unexplained infertility problems among normal, healthy couples may have an immunological basis. Stated simply, you may be producing antibodies against your partner's sperm.

Are you immune to your partner's sperm?

As farfetched as this may seem, you and your partner may be incompatible on a cellular level.

In the same manner, for example, that a smallpox vaccination stimulates the production of antibodies against that disease, sperm acting as a foreign protein substance (antigen) may provoke the formation of sperm antibodies in some women. Since sperm remaining in the female genital tract following intercourse are probably engulfed and removed by special scavenger cells, it is possible that those absorbed sperm protein fragments may subsequently stimulate antibody formation. Under these circumstances, repeated coitus with deposition of sperm in the vagina gradually allows the woman to build up more and more circulating and tissue-fixed antibodies against that foreign protein sperm material. In time, therefore, it is possible that antibodies present in the blood and in various body tissues (vagina, cervix, uterus) may rapidly inactivate any new sperm invaders long before they can ever reach the egg.

To further complicate the situation, there may be different types of sperm antigens and therefore different types of sperm antibodies. Thus, a woman exposed to repeated intercourse with different partners might possibly have a greater variety, as well as a higher level, of sperm antibodies.

Does this mean that promiscuity may be an obscure cause of infertility?

Not necessarily. Some women never develop sperm antibodies regardless of how many sexual partners they have or how frequently they engage in coitus. On the other hand, a woman with relatively little sexual exposure may have difficulty conceiving because of a significantly high level of sperm antibodies. Exactly what triggers the development of these antibodies in some women and not in others remains to be discovered. Since the immunological aspect of fertility is a very new field, much of the work is still limited and experimental. Moreover, tests for sperm antibodies are neither generally available nor perfected.

How can you know whether your infertility has an immunological basis?

Here again the answer is elusive. However, if you can get tested and are found to have a high level of sperm antibodies, your situation may be more hopeful than you think. There may still be a way to get pregnant even if you are producing antibodies against your partner's sperm.

How can you possibly get pregnant if you have sperm antibodies?

By temporarily preventing further exposure to sperm. It stands to reason that if you can build and maintain a high antibody level against sperm by repeated intercourse, then it follows that by avoiding further contact with sperm your antibody level should drop. In brief, there are only two possible methods whereby this can be accomplished: stay away from all sex or have your partner wear a condom during intercourse for at least nine to twelve months.

Among couples apparently unable to conceive because of a sperm-antibody problem and who subsequently elected to try the condom method, 100 per cent of the women showed marked reduction in their sperm antibody level after one year of protected coitus. Even more exciting, approximately 60 per cent of these women subsequently became pregnant after their partners discarded the condom.

Therefore, if there doesn't seem to be any apparent reason for your infertility, this method of protective coitus may be worth a try.

Suppose it doesn't work – then what?

In regard to couples who may have other obscure reasons for their infertility, medical science may soon provide an answer even for them. But sometimes the reason for failure to conceive is emotional distress caused by trying too hard to get pregnant. It has happened that 'infertile' women who have abandoned hope and stopped trying – including some who have even adopted children – have then become pregnant.

16. How to Avoid Pregnancy

Ever since man and woman discovered that one plus one makes three, they have been searching for the ideal contraceptive. According to recent statistics, it has taken five thousand years to achieve the estimated present world population of 4000 million. At the current rate of human fertility this figure will be almost double in another thirty years.

If you already have that hemmed-in feeling, be thankful that you won't live to celebrate the year of the big squeeze, 2772. With a predicted one square foot of terra firma per person, human beings will be forced either to copulate in the vertical position or to find more breeding room. And so, while the search goes on for the ideal contraceptive . . .

Can a fertile couple lead a full sex life and be sure of avoiding pregnancy?

All contraceptive methods can and have failed on the basis of human error, product failure or a combination of both, so there is really no absolutely guaranteed way to avoid pregnancy. But don't give up hope yet. There are many ways to thwart the meeting between egg and sperm. All it takes is a little motivation, some basic information and the selection of the contraceptive method best suited to your individual needs.

What methods are used to try to prevent conception?

Here is a list of methods. (Only the first two are markedly efficient, numbers 3 and 4 are most effective when used together and the final three come far behind in terms of preventing pregnancy.) (1) suppressing ovulation through various hormonal medications; (2) making the lining of the uterine cavity unreceptive to egg or sperm; (3) imposing a physical barrier to prevent migration of sperm; (4) destroying or inactivating sperm by the use of various chemical substances; (5) withdrawing the penis from the vaginal canal prior to ejaculation; (6) flushing the vaginal canal with various solutions immediately after intercourse; and (7) abstaining from sexual intercourse during the woman's fertile period.

How can you select the best method of contraception for yourself?

Begin by evaluating your persona requirements. Do you need constant protection or is intercourse an infrequent event? Is pregnancy to be avoided at all costs or will you accept some risk by using a less effective contraceptive method? Can you depend on partner cooperation or is it all up to you? And equally important, are you sufficiently motivated to be bothered with creams, foams or perhaps a diaphragm?

Selecting the best method for your needs also depends on knowing what contraceptive methods are available and the advantages and disadvantages of each.

Are you as safe as you would like to be?

All birth-control methods are evaluated on their ability to prevent pregnancy based on 100 women years. For example, the table below states that an intrauterine device has a 3 per cent average pregnancy rate per 100 women years; this means that if 100 fertile and sexually active women use an IUD for one year, three of them will probably become pregnant. Stated another way, if you use an IUD for one year, you have about 3 chances out of 100 of becoming pregnant.

The range of possible risk (right-hand column) is much more variable. This is where human error really gets into the picture. Take the diaphragm, for example. How you use it may well make a difference between a 5 per cent risk or a 28 per cent risk of pregnancy.

As you will soon see, regardless of the contraceptive method you choose, there are ways of decreasing your potential risk of pregnancy. In short, being safe depends not only on what method you use but how effectively you use it.

CONTRACEPTIVE METHODS AND PREGNANCY RISK

Method	Average pregnancy rate per 100 women years	Range of possible risk per 100 women years
Oral contraceptives ('the pill')	less than 1%	(combined) 0·% (sequential) 1·4
'Minipills' (progestogen only)	3	?
Intrauterine device (IUD) (loop, coil, shield, etc.)	3	2–7
Cap (diaphragm) and spermicide	12	5–28
Sheath (condom, rubber, French letter, Durex)	15	8–15
Coitus interruptus (withdrawal)	16	?
Rhythm	16	15–34
Foams, jellies, suppositories	variable	4–40
Douching (after intercourse)	over 40	
No method	80	

What exactly are oral contraceptives ('the pill')?

Various combinations of the two female hormones, oestrogen and progesterone, in synthetic form. Of the many different contraceptive pills currently available, most are a combined preparation and some a sequential preparation. A combined preparation simply means that *all* the pills contain both an oestrogen and a progestogen. In contrast, a sequential preparations has two different kinds of pill: the first fifteen tablets contain only oestrogen, whereas the remaining five or seven tablets have both an oestrogen and a progestogen.

Both types are highly effective, but because of the higher risk of pregnancy with sequential preparations, their use has become limited.

Why are the pills so effective in preventing pregnancy?

They keep you from ovulating. No egg, no pregnancy. The hormone content of the pill (oestrogen and progestogen) prevents the pituitary from stimulating the ovary by suppressing the output of pituitary hormones (FSH and LH) necessary to mature and launch an egg. (See Chapter 5.)

How should the pills be taken?

Regularly and as prescribed. Most of the newer preparations now contain either twenty-one or twenty-eight pills per package.

For those of you on a twenty-one-day package, begin the very first month's supply on the fifth day of your menstrual cycle, counting day one as the first day your period begins. Take one pill every day until the package is finished (twenty-one days). Wait a full seven days, then start your next month's supply. Once you start taking the pills, your schedule will be three weeks on the pill and one week off the pill regardless of when your period comes. Therefore, each new twenty-one-day package will always start on the same day of the week. In other words, if you started your first month's supply on a Saturday, the following month's supply will also start on a Saturday.

During the seven days off the pill, you should have your period. In time, your flow may become more scanty but this is perfectly normal when you are taking most oral contraceptives. If you should miss a period, be sure to resume the pills anyway. If, perchance, you should miss two periods in a row, better check with your doctor. You probably aren't pregnant, but perhaps a different preparation would suit you better.

If you are on a twenty-eight-day package, your schedule is even simpler. Once you start the pills, continue to take one pill every day without interruption. Just make certain that you take the pills in their proper sequence. The last seven pills (for days twenty-two to twenty-eight inclusive) have no hormonal content, only iron in some instances. Twenty-eight-day pill packages were devised for the woman who finds it easier to remember to take a pill every day. Regardless of whether you are on the twenty-one- or twenty-eight-day package, your periods will usually come every twenty-eight days because they are now being artificially regulated.

How soon do the pills protect you?

The very first month, providing you begin on the fifth day of your period and don't forget or skip any pills. However, most doctors prefer to be cautious, and advise using an additional method of contraception as well as the pill in the first month only. Indeed, if you normally (without medication) have short cycles averaging less than twenty-five days, you should definitely use some additional method of protection during the first month on oral contraceptives. Since ovulation normally occurs two weeks before the anticipated next period, women having relatively short cycles may ovulate on day eight to nine; therefore, if the pill is started on day five as prescribed, the amount of hormonal medication (only four days) may be insufficient to suppress ovulation for the first month. In the second month, however, you should be completely protected by the pill.

Are you still safe from pregnancy if you forget a pill?

Since the pill prevents you from ovulating at mid cycle, the most crucial pills *not* to forget are the first ten or twelve. Missing a pill during this time is definitely more risky than forgetting a pill towards the end of your month's supply.

Should you inadvertently skip a pill, be sure to take two pills the following day. If you miss more, check with your doctor and plan to use some additional protection. Missing a pill or two may also cause some spotting or bleeding.

Therefore, to help you remember, make it a habit to take the pill at a certain time every day, either in the morning at breakfast or at bedtime. Some women find it helpful to post a big reminder in some conspicuous place.

How long can you stay on the pill?

At the present time, there is no set limit. Although some doctors advise coming off the pill every eighteen months or so for two or three cycles, there are no known harmful effects from continuous and prolonged use of oral contraceptives. Many women have been on the pill for years without apparent problems.

However, if you have completed your family and perhaps still need contraceptive protection for another five to ten years or so, it might make sense to consider a more permanent solution, such as tubal ligation for yourself or even a vasectomy for your partner, as oral-contraceptive pills are potent hormones that affect the whole of your body.

For maximum interval protection between pregnancies, the pill is the ideal contraceptive. Once the pill is stopped there is usually a prompt return of normal ovarian and pituitary function.

How soon can you get pregnant after stopping the pill?

Almost immediately. About 60 to 70 per cent of fertile women will become pregnant within three months after stopping the pill. Contrary to what many believe, your general fertility will not be increased as a result of having been on the pill. If you had prior difficulty conceiving, you may again experience the same problem.

Do your periods return to normal once you stop the pill?

If your periods were previously regular, they will probably return to normal. If your periods were previously irregular and unpredictable, they may resume their old pattern. Nonetheless, the first period off the pill may be delayed one or two weeks. On occasion, resumption of menstruation may be further postponed because the suppression of pituitary function by the pill may continue for a time despite cessation of medication. Although this is fairly uncommon, it tends to occur more frequently among women whose periods were never really regular.

What about common side effects from the pill?

While oral contraceptives have become the chemical scapegoat for a variety of physical and even emotional problems, there is no doubt that many women do experience a variety of adverse effects. Since these range through aches, pains, headaches, feelings

of fatigue, nervousness, depression, dizziness, excess weight
gain, constipation, stomach upsets, rashes, falling hair, insomnia
and changes in sex drive it is very difficult to pin down exactly
which can be directly attributed to the pill. For instance, in one
clinical study involving 100 women taking the identical oral
contraceptive for the same duration, approximately eighty-five
did not notice any change in libido. Of the remaining fifteen,
eight complained of a decreased interest in sex and seven hailed
the pill as a new aphrodisiac.

Established side effects from oral contraceptives are definitely
related to the total hormone content per pill and to the relative
proportion between the oestrogen and progestogen. When the
pill first became available in 1960, many women were disenchanted because of undesirable symptoms suggestive of early
pregnancy – extra weight gain, nausea, bloating, fluid retention
and at times even an increased pigmentation of the skin, especially around the face (chloasma). Fortunately, research scientists
soon discovered that a lower total hormone content could minimize unpleasant side effects without jeopardizing contraceptive
effectiveness.

Today, with the new low-dose preparations, most women who
need efficient protection against pregnancy are ready to continue
the pill despite these kinds of side effects. Some may have to live
with breakthrough bleeding or irregular spotting and quite a few
may find it difficult to control their weight gain while on the pill.
However, a change in brand can often help.

Is there a pill just right for you?

With so many different brands among which your doctor can
choose, prescribing the right pill may well make all the difference in your comfort. As with any medication, no two women
will respond exactly the same way.

In general most women do well on a preparation in which the
oestrogen and progestogen content are fairly well balanced. A
few women may need a pill containing either more oestrogen or
more progestogen. Take, for example, the woman with a slightly
higher than normal premenstrual oestrogen level. For her, fluid

retention, tender breasts and heavy periods may always have been a problem. With such a history she would probably do better with a pill containing more progestogen and less oestrogen. In contrast, the woman with premenstrual pimples, normally scanty periods and small breasts might benefit from a pill having more oestrogen and less progestogen. Under any of these special circumstances, your doctor should be able to prescribe a pill almost tailor-made to your needs.

Can oral contraceptives cause any serious problems?

There is no denying that serious problems and even fatal catastrophes have befallen women while on the pill. Thrombosis (blood-clot formation) with pulmonary embolism (clot to lung) and strokes have been the cause of death in a few instances.

If you are one of the 2 million British women currently taking oral contraceptives, or among those contemplating starting the pill, it is time you considered some facts and rationally evaluated the potential risk you may or may not be running.

Is the pill associated with an increased risk of blood clots?

Since 1969, when the Committee on the Safety of Drugs stated that the risk of thromboembolic episodes while on the pill was directly related to the size of the oestrogen dose, the vast majority of pills now prescribed in Britain are of the low-oestrogen brands, which have the same contraceptive effect with a lower risk of thrombosis. Nevertheless, a woman taking the pill is still about five times more likely to be admitted to hospital for deep-vein thrombosis – of the leg, for example – than a woman not taking the pill. Yet this increased risk should be seen in perspective: it means five times an extremely small risk. Statistically there are fifty more chances in 100 000 that you will have a blood clot when you are taking the pill.

Is there any risk of death being caused by the pill?

Let us assume for the moment that the most frightening reports are true and that there is a direct cause-and-effect relationship between the pill and blood clots. This would imply that every woman taking the pill would be seven times more likely to die from a blood clot to the lung or brain than a woman not taking the pill.

If this were true, how big a risk statistically is seven times more? It would mean that if you are between the ages of twenty and thirty-four and are on the pill, you have 1·3 chances out of 100 000 of dying from a thromboembolic catastrophe this year. If you are over thirty-five, your risk increases to 3·4 chances out of 100 000.

What is seldom mentioned is the fact that in England and Wales alone, out of 100 000 pregnant women, approximately 13 die each year as a *direct* result of pregnancy or childbirth. And the mortality rate among women legally aborted is currently about 7 deaths per 100 000 a year. Conclusion: staying on the pill and avoiding pregnancy seems safer than being pregnant or having a legal abortion.

Needless to say, until the controversy is definitely settled, the pill should not be taken by women with a past history of thrombophlebitis or thromboembolic problems. For women currently on the pill, possible warning signs of an early thrombophlebitis, such as vague pains in the legs or lower abdomen, should not be ignored. Similarly, any unusual chest pain, shortness of breath, or disturbances of vision should be reported immediately to your doctor. Just because you have been on the pill for *x* number of years without adverse effects does not necessarily mean that you are immune from developing a blood-clot problem.

Is there any association between the pill and cancer?

There is absolutely no evidence that birth-control pills will cause or initiate cancer of any organ in the human body. However, in women who already have a known malignancy involving either the breast or the endometrium (uterine lining), oestrogenic substances may in certain cases stimulate the growth of dormant cancer cells. Under these circumstances, birth-control pills should be avoided.

Are periodic physical examinations necessary while taking the pill?

Yes, indeed. No conscientious doctor will prescribe the pill or renew a prescription for any extended period without a thorough gynaecological check-up including a breast examination and a cervical smear.

At times, migraine headaches, diabetes and a tendency towards high blood pressure can be aggravated by oral contraceptives. Similarly, fibroid tumours of the womb, if present, may enlarge more rapidly as a result of oestrogen stimulation.

For these and other reasons, your doctor or Family Planning clinic will suggest that you go back at least every six to twelve months and your prescription will be arranged accordingly. Should you have any problems or complaints between visits, inform your doctor or the clinic promptly. If you plan to stay on the pill, be sure to arrange your next appointment for before your prescription runs out.

In the final analysis, birth-control pills continue to be for millions of women not only safe but also the most effective contraceptive method available.

What are 'minipills' and how are they different?

In contrast to other oral contraceptives, the minipills (of which there are three currently available) contain progestogen only and are taken on a continuous daily basis. Moreover, their contraceptive effectiveness (97 per cent) does not depend primarily on suppression of ovulation. In fact, most women taking the minipills continue to ovulate.

How, then, do the minipills prevent pregnancy?

Primarily in one of two ways: sperm penetration through the cervical canal is inhibited by alterations in the property of the cervical mucus (see Chapter 15), and tissue changes involving the lining of the womb make implantation of the egg unlikely if ever it does get fertilized.

Are there any advantages or disadvantages to taking the minipill?

Since the minipill does not contain any oestrogen, some of the side effects associated with combined and sequential oral contraceptives may be minimized. Whether this also means a decreased risk of thromboembolic problems currently attributed to the synthetic oestrogen content of these other preparations is not yet known. Only time and more extensive studies will furnish that answer.

On the minus side of the ledger, the minipill has two disadvantages: annoying breakthrough bleeding and, at times, irregular menstrual cycles. Researchers are trying to overcome these problems, but here too, much work remains before the perfect minipill becomes a reality.

What is an intrauterine device (IUD)?

Intrauterine means within the womb. The devices are made of soft, flexible plastic material that comes in a variety of fanciful shapes. (See Figure 21.) When properly fitted and retained within the womb, an IUD is second only to the pill in contraceptive effectiveness, or just about 97 per cent foolproof.

How does an IUD prevent pregnancy?

In a most devious and indirect manner. Studies have shown that shortly after the IUD comes into physical contact with the lining

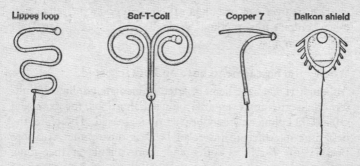

Lippes loop   Saf-T-Coil   Copper 7   Dalkon shield

21.   *Intrauterine devices*

of the womb, a local tissue reaction creates an environment hostile to both egg implantation and sperm. In effect, the IUD, which acts as a giant foreign body, stimulates an outpouring of intrauterine scavenger cells (macrophages). Alien intruders such as sperm or even an egg, should it be fertilized, are quickly engulfed and dispatched by these scavenger cells.

Can any woman be fitted with an IUD?

Until fairly recently, fitting nulliparous (never pregnant) women with an IUD posed some problems. Insertion was frequently difficult and subsequent distortion of the uterine cavity by the IUD almost invariably caused painful cramping and heavy bleeding. Today, with new and improved IUDs in various shapes and sizes, almost any women can be properly fitted, though few doctors will recommend this method of contraception for women with pelvic or menstrual trouble.

How long can you wear an IUD?

IUDs containing copper should be replaced every two years. On the other hand, if you have been fitted with one of the simple plastic devices such as a Lippes loop or Saf-T-Coil and are having no problems, there is no specific time limit.

What are the advantages of using an IUD?

Convenience. Once an IUD is inserted, your contraceptive worries are over – or just about. If you can't take the pill or find other contraceptive methods generally unsatisfactory, an IUD may be your answer.

When's the best time to have an IUD inserted?

Although IUDs have been inserted immediately following full-term deliveries and even after induced abortions, the expulsion rate (IUD falling out) may be slightly increased. Therefore, the best time in which to insert an IUD is during menstruation. Because the cervix is softer and more pliable at that time, insertion is somewhat easier. In addition, the presence of menstrual bleeding will further assure your doctor that you probably aren't *early pregnant*.

If you are early pregnant, can inserting an IUD cause an abortion?

No reliable figures are available. Inadvertent abortion might be possible. Then again, a healthy and well-implanted egg may continue to grow even when nudged by an IUD.

How is an IUD inserted?

Carefully and with sterile precautions. Although the technique will vary among doctors, the procedure is quite simple.

Once the cervix is exposed and cleansed with an antiseptic solution, the depth of the uterine cavity is checked by passing a small probe through the cervical canal. This manoeuvre tells your doctor how deep to insert the device and also which size IUD will fit best.

Most IUDs now come in sealed, sterilized packs with a disposable introducer not much thicker than the head of a kitchen match. The introducer with the preloaded IUD is simply inserted through the cervical canal and gently advanced into the uterine cavity. When the proper depth is reached, the introducer is detached and presto, the IUD is in place. The whole procedure rarely takes longer than three minutes.

Will it hurt much?

This varies widely. It depends on the particular device chosen, the way it is inserted and the woman's own pain threshold. Most of the discomfort actually results from a slight stretching of the cervical canal as the device is advanced inward. For this reason, insertion is easiest and usually relatively painless for women who have had a full-term vaginal delivery. For women who have never been pregnant or mothers with a tight cervical canal, the procedure can be temporarily uncomfortable or markedly painful. Some women may notice definite cramping pains for a while after insertion.

Since there is no way that you or the doctor can know in

advance how you will react, it is a good idea to take an afternoon off and arrange to have a friend with you to see you get home all right. Walking, driving or using public transport might be difficult.

What kind of problems can you expect with an IUD?

You might never have any problems. Otherwise, intermittent spotting between periods and occasionally heavier and longer periods during the first two or three months are not unusual. Thereafter, the bleeding should taper off and your monthly flow resume a more normal pattern. But in some women fitted with an IUD, persistent and annoying bleeding with or without uterine cramping may necessitate removal of the device.

You should also be alert to the possibility of losing your IUD. IUDs have a greater tendency to fall out or be expelled during the first few months following insertion and particularly during menstruation. Needless to say, the expulsion of some devices may go completely unnoticed.

To be on the safe side, you should periodically check to see if your intrauterine device is where it belongs.

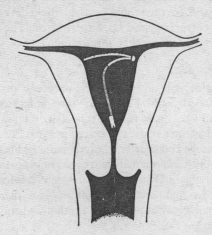

22. *Intrauterine device in place*

How can you tell whether your IUD is still in place?

Find the nylon thread. All IUDs are attached to a small, stiff thread that protrudes into the upper vagina for about one to two inches. To locate the thread, sweep your finger deep inside the vagina as far as you can reach or else simply feel around the cervical opening. (See Figure 22.) Some women appoint their partners as guardian and keeper of the thread. Regardless of who assumes the responsibility, check at least after every period and preferably more frequently during the first few months.

If nobody can find the thread, better see your doctor. In the meantime, be sure to use some other form of contraception just in case.

Can that IUD thread ever bother your partner?

A few men do complain of being pricked by the thread during coitus. In this situation, arrange to see your doctor, he or she can usually remedy the problem by shortening the thread. In the meantime using a position which makes penile penetration less deep will help your partner.

Can you still use tampons if you have an IUD?

Absolutely. You will not inadvertently pull out the IUD. There is no way that the nylon thread can wrap itself around the tampon. It's been tested scientifically and found to be impossible.

What happens if you become pregnant with the IUD in place?

Although more than one IUD has been delivered with a normal full-term baby, the incidence of spontaneous abortion (miscarriage) is significantly higher if the device is left in place. Moreover, certain IUDs have been implicated as the cause of serious uterine infections during pregnancy. Therefore, if you think you might be pregnant and do have an IUD, be sure to check promptly with your doctor. Under these circumstances, removal of the device might be advisable.

262 From Woman to Woman

Can there be any serious complications from an IUD?

Complications such as perforation of the uterus at the time of insertion or subsequent migration of the IUD through the uterine wall and into the pelvic cavity have been reported. Pelvic infections, however, are rarely caused or precipitated by an IUD. Moreover, with the newer and more resilient intrauterine devices, most serious complications are becoming exceedingly uncommon.

Is there any association between an IUD and the subsequent development of pelvic cancer?

Here again, there is no evidence that an IUD can cause uterine and/or cervical cancer.

Are there any better and more effective IUDs now available?

Yes. The Grangard, or Copper 7, seems to be one of the most effective of the newer intrauterine devices. Shaped like the number 7, this tiny plastic device is wound with a fine copper wire. The copper apparently reduces uterine muscle irritability (cramping) in addition to exerting a marked antifertility effect. The device has a low expulsion (fall-out) rate – 4–6 per cent – high contraceptive effectiveness – close to 99 per cent – and minimal side effects.

What about slow-release progesterone IUDs?

These devices are only under research at the moment and are not yet available for general use.

Although inserted into the uterine cavity and technically classified as IUDs, they work on an entirely different principle. Unlike the conventional IUD, this T-shaped plastic device is filled with tiny progesterone crystals. The progesterone is slowly released in small daily doses and exerts local changes on the cervical mucus and lining of the uterus. As a result, the cervical mucus becomes unreceptive and thereby prevents the successful penetration of the sperm. (See Chapter 15.) Furthermore the lining of the uterus is sufficiently altered so as to prevent implantation of an egg, should fertilization occur.

One of the obvious advantages of this system is that the progesterone released into the uterus does not interfere with ovulation or affect the whole body. The overall pregnancy rate per 100 woman-years is a remarkably low 0·5 per cent. This means that progesterone IUDs are almost as effective as oral contraceptives but have none of their undesirable side effects. In addition, the expulsion rate and the pain or bleeding sometimes associated with the conventional IUD are considerably reduced.

The main disadvantage of the slow-release progesterone IUDs is their loss of efficacy after 400 days, or about thirteen months; thus, yearly replacement of the device is necessary.

What did women in grandmother's day do to avoid pregnancy?

Long before the pill and the IUD came on the scene, women imposed some mechanical barrier between the cervix and semen. Back in the 1700s, a resourceful woman could always rely on her lemon recipe. Half a squeezed lemon inserted over the cervix at bedtime was marvellously effective. It blocked the cervical canal, and the citric acid probably acted as a spermicidal agent.

With the vulcanization of rubber, however, not only did the world start spinning on tyres, but sexuality too was given a new bounce. Today, sheaths and diaphragms and caps made of pliable and durable latex rubber have become an acceptable contraceptive method for many couples.

What is a diaphragm?

A dome-shaped latex rubber device mounted on a circular base containing a metal spring. (See Figure 23.) It is often known as a 'Dutch cap' but this is confusing, as other smaller devices, made of thicker rubber and without springs, are technically called caps: their aim is the same – to cover the cervix and prevent sperm getting into the womb. A diaphragm or cap must be professionally fitted and requires a prescription for purchase.

A properly fitting diaphragm when correctly inserted should

cover the entire cervix and upper vagina. It should also remain in place despite straining on your part or vigorous penile thrusts. Equally important, it should be so comfortable that you and your partner are completely unaware of its presence. If it interferes with intercourse you haven't been properly fitted and may need a different size or a different shape.

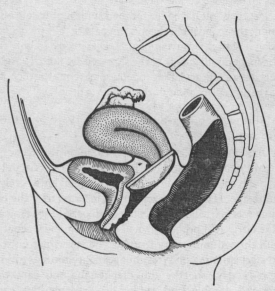

23. *Diaphragm in place*

How do diaphragms differ?

On two counts: size, which in most women averages between 70 and 85 millimetres in diameter, and the type of metal spring used in the base. The metal spring (either a flat or a coiled type) serves to decrease or increase the flexibility of the diaphragm so as to conform more precisely to the contours of the vagina. To be effective, a diaphragm must be specifically fitted to the size and shape of your vagina.

Can all women be properly fitted?

Not always. Some women just make poor diaphragm candidates because of a too relaxed vagina with poor muscular tone. If this is the case, a diaphragm is apt to slip out of place at the wrong time, or even be difficult to insert properly. A tipped (retroverted or retroflexed) uterus may also at times make proper insertion difficult.

At the other extreme is the young woman with a fairly snug vaginal opening. Initial attempts at both squeezing in and removing the diaphragm can be an exercise in patience and perseverance. Then, of course, there is a third group of women who can be properly fitted but who instinctively dislike inserting any object into the vagina. They too would do better with some other contraceptive method.

How reliable is a diaphragm against pregnancy?

Very reliable if you use it properly at all times. Diaphragms can be 95 per cent effective. Most of the other 5 per cent diaphragm failures probably result from improper use of spermicidal jelly, careless insertion of the diaphragm, premature removal or just plain neglecting to use it.

How can you use a diaphragm most effectively?

If you are being fitted for your very first diaphragm, make sure you understand how to insert it properly (cervix covered) and remove it easily *before* you leave the clinic or doctor's surgery. Most women find that handling a diaphragm is awkward at first.

To make your diaphragm as effective as possible, you will also need a tube of spermicidal cream or jelly, which is provided by the clinic or can be purchased at any chemist without prescription. Although it makes no difference which side of the rubber dome will be in direct contact with the cervix (dome up or dome down), it is important to use an adequate amount of spermicidal cream or jelly. Before every insertion squeeze about one teaspoon of jelly onto the side of the diaphragm that will be against the cervix and smear some more around the entire rim.

For best results smear a little jelly on the other side of the diaphragm too. The spermicidal jelly will effectively kill sperm as well as form a protective seal around the rim of the diaphragm.

The diaphragm must be in place before every act of intercourse. If, following insertion, there is a delay of an hour or more before coitus, or if you have repeated intercourse, it is advisable as an added precaution to insert additional spermicidal cream with an applicator – but without removing the diaphragm.

If yours is an active sex life, you may find it easier to slip in your diaphragm before going to bed every night. With a little practice, it will take you less than fifteen seconds. On the other hand, you may find that it is easiest to keep the diaphragm in for twenty-four hours at a time, removing it each day for washing, of course. This means that with a tube of spermicide in your bag you will be protected from pregnancy and free to have intercourse when and wherever.

When should you remove the diaphragm?

Not for at least eight hours after the *last* intercourse. (Douching is not necessary. However, if you prefer to douche, wait at least eight hours following intercourse. Otherwise you might flush away the contraceptive protection afforded by the vaginal jelly or cream.) After removing your diaphragm, you should wash it in warm water, dry it thoroughly, and put it back in its compact.

Prolonged wearing of the diaphragm is not harmful, but it is a good idea to remove and wash it every twenty-four hours as part of your normal hygienic routine.

How often should you have your diaphragm checked or changed?

Even with good care, your diaphragm should probably be replaced at least every eighteen months. Ideally, every year. It is also advisable to examine it every now and then for any tiny defects or holes that may appear along the rim.

Any change in your vaginal dimensions will also mean that you'll need a refitting. If you have recently had a baby, have gained or lost ten or more pounds (over 4·5 kilograms), are newly married or otherwise have begun an active sex life, you may need a diaphragm of a different size.

What are the disadvantages of using a diaphragm?

Success with a diaphragm requires motivation. You must be willing to take the time and accept the minor inconvenience of using your diaphragm properly.

Are there any advantages of using a diaphragm?

Certainly. Although usually less effective than either the pill or an IUD, used properly the diaphragm can compete favourably as a reliable method of contraception. What is more, unlike either of the other methods, there are no contraindications to its use or any side effects to worry about.

A properly fitted diaphragm cannot get 'lost inside', create infection or interfere with intercourse.

What is a condom?

Whatever name you use – French letter, Durex, sheath, rubber, protective, prophylactic – a condom is a fine delicate sheath made from latex rubber that completely covers the penis during intercourse. Thus, the condom, by serving as a reservoir to receive the entire ejaculate acts as a mechanical barrier to pregnancy.

The use of the condom places the responsibility for avoiding pregnancy squarely on the man. For every 100 fertile couples who use this method exclusively for one year, approximately 16 per cent of the women will become pregnant. Here again, a few extra precautions can reduce the risk of pregnancy.

What precautions?

Following ejaculation your partner must take care in withdrawing the penis from the vagina. Pulling out too abruptly may cause the condom to slip off or allow the semen to escape. To be on the safe side, he should grasp the condom firmly as he withdraws.

For additional security, and especially at mid cycle, many women combine the use of a condom with a vaginal spermicidal cream. With this kind of double protection, your chances of becoming pregnant should be minimal.

What are the disadvantages of using a condom?

It might tear at the wrong moment. In addition, since a condom must be rolled onto an erect penis, the biggest disadvantage by far is an interruption of sexual play. For the highly aroused woman in particular, this can be an annoying intermission. In men who may have difficulty in obtaining and maintaining an erection, the need to fiddle with a condom may be their undoing. Then, too, good-quality lubricated condoms are not inexpensive. Considering the fact that they are throw-away items used only once, having an active sex life and relying exclusively on condoms can be a drain on a young couple's budget.

The condom also tends to lessen sexual sensation. Men especially complain of decreased penile sensitivity. For some couples, however, the use of a condom for this very reason is a distinct advantage.

Why would decreased penile sensitivity be an advantage?

According to some sexologists, 98 per cent of women would achieve orgasm if their partners could sustain an erection intra-vaginally for at least fifteen minutes. This may be like putting sexual enjoyment on a computer basis, but nonetheless, a rubber protective by decreasing penile sensitivity, may allow some men to sustain an erection longer. Aside from perhaps improving sexual performance, using a condom as a method of contraception has other advantages.

What other advantages?

No prescription is needed and condoms can be purchased at barbers, most chemists and even from vending machines. Furthermore, condoms are also the best protection against contracting venereal disease.

What about coitus interruptus?

This requires masterful self-control by your partner. Withdrawing from the vagina before ejaculation also demands experience and know-how. As mentioned earlier, penile urethral secretions prior to ejaculation may contain sperm (as many as 50 000), but chance impregnation under these circumstances is less likely to occur than from other unintentional slip-ups. Most failures – and this method does have a 16 per cent risk of pregnancy – are primarily the result of withdrawing too late. Lack of precision timing can also cause inadvertent ejaculation of semen against the outside vaginal opening rather than directing it well away from the vulva. One factor which may persuade you against coitus interruptus is that it is just that – interrupted intercourse. It can leave the woman roused but just short of orgasm. (See Chapter 14.)

Yet it is surprising that, with the range of contraceptives now available, many couples still rely on this highly unsatisfactory method of family planning.

Anyone for the rhythm method?

The prevention of pregnancy by the avoidance of sexual intercourse during your fertile days is a wonderful theory. In practice, the pregnancy risk is 15–34 per cent, which means a lot of conceptions for a so-called contraceptive method.

The big question remains, how can you know for sure the moment of ovulation? Keeping basal-body-temperature (BBT) charts is tedious and rarely satisfactory. Even BBT charts can fail on occasion. Checking for changes in cervical mucus consistency, although fairly reliable according to reports, does depend upon knowledgeable subjective interpretation. The astrological concept of calculating your fertile period by the sun–moon angle at the time of your birth will have to be investigated further.

Is there another way to calculate your fertile period?

Since you already know that ovulation tends to occur fourteen days (plus or minus two days) before your next period and that a sperm can survive at least forty-eight hours and the egg twenty-four hours, impregnation is theoretically possible in an ideal twenty-eight-day cycle from days ten to seventeen inclusive. But – and this is an important consideration – how many of you are so regular that you can unerringly predict the date of your next period? Precious few. This is where the magic formula comes in!

Are you ready for the magic formula?

To make the rhythm method work most efficiently, you should keep a record of the *length* of your menstrual cycles for at least eight months and preferably longer. By making a note of the first day of every period for eight consecutive months, you can calculate the length of each menstrual cycle. For example, if your period starts on April 2 and your next period comes on April 27, that cycle length is twenty-five days.

Once you have gathered this valuable information, you are now ready to apply the formula. Pick out your longest cycle and subtract the number 11. Pick out your shortest cycle and subtract the number 18. The days in between are your unsafe days or your fertile days – no intercourse.

If, for example, your longest cycle ran thirty-four days and your shortest cycle ran twenty-seven days – 34 minus 11 equals 23, and 27 minus 18 equals 9. You should therefore avoid intercourse from day nine up to and including day twenty-three of every cycle.

If your cycles varied from twenty-three to twenty-eight days, you'd have to abstain from day five up to and including day seventeen – 23 minus 18 equals 5, and 28 minus 11 equals 17. Under these circumstances conception could occur in some women during their period even though the risk of impregnation during the first five days of menstruation is exceedingly remote – less than one chance out of 1000. However, if you consistently have short cycles or if your periods are completely irregular, having intercourse after the fifth day from the start of menstruation (whether or not you are still bleeding) definitely increases the risk of pregnancy.

By now, you can understand how any fluctuation in cycle length can greatly prolong the duration of your safe time – up to a full two weeks or longer. Under these circumstances, the rhythm method becomes an exercise in sexual abstinence.

Nevertheless, if your cycle lengths are completely irregular and you depend on the rhythm method because of personal preference or religious convictions, there is a way to avoid pregnancy without prolonged sexual abstinence.

How is that possible?

By controlling the moment of ovulation. Knowing when you ovulate can certainly help limit the days of sexual abstinence.

Recent studies have shown that in women given a very small dose of oestrogen from days nine to sixteen inclusive of the menstrual cycle, ovulation consistently occurred within a five-day period (days thirteen to seventeen). Previously, ovulation in these women had been completely unpredictable. In addition, the small repeated dose of oestrogen proved safe and without side effects. This method, however, is not a routine procedure. As yet, it has been used only in selected cases by a few doctors.

Are there any hazards in using the rhythm method?

The main hazards of the rhythm method are emotional. If you have regular periods it may be easy enough to avoid intercourse for those eight days each month. If your cycles vary from thirty-four to twenty-seven days you will need to avoid coitus for over two weeks in every four. Couples with strong motivation can make it work, but many find the discipline too much of a strain.

There is also a small risk of having an abnormal pregnancy if you do get pregnant. Since ovulation is normally geared to occur around mid cycle, any egg that is released either before or after its expected time has a somewhat greater chance of being abnormal. This is particularly true in the egg that is 'over-ripe' and released after its expected time. Inadvertent fertilization of such an egg does increase a woman's chances of having either a spontaneous abortion or a congenitally abnormal child.

What about spermicides?

These include various chemical preparations obtainable without a prescription and marketed as jellies, creams, aerosol foams, suppositories or foaming tablets. All of them are inserted into the vagina before intercourse and act by killing sperm on contact as well as by inhibiting their migration through the cervical canal.

How really effective are these preparations?

When used as the sole method of birth control over a twelve-month period, the chances of becoming pregnant range anywhere from 4 to 40 per cent.

Of all the vaginal spermicides, aerosol foams are probably the most effective against pregnancy – up to 96 per cent according to some clinical studies. Moreover, they are less messy, easy to use, go to work instantly, and can be inserted as long as one hour prior to intercourse.

Spermicidal jellies and creams are best used in conjunction with either a condom or a diaphragm. When used alone there is a 20–30 per cent chance of conceiving within one year.

Foaming vaginal tablets and vaginal suppositories (also called pessaries) are the least reliable. Following insertion, the tablet needs at least five minutes to start foaming, and the suppository a good fifteen minutes to melt. Failure to wait the prescribed time undoubtedly contributes to the 30–40 per cent pregnancy risk. Should intercourse be delayed thirty minutes or more, another tablet or suppository must be inserted.

Regardless of the spermicide you use, all of them must be reapplied if you are going to have intercourse a second time. There is only enough spermicide in any one application to take care of the sperm in one ejaculation. As an additional precaution, if you must douche after intercourse, wait at least eight hours. Otherwise you'll wash away any protection you might have.

Is douching all right as a contraceptive method?

No. With a pregnancy risk well over 40 per cent, douching as a method of birth control might as well be forgotten. Besides, jumping out of bed right after intercourse to douche has the distinct disadvantage of interrupting what can be for many couples a moment of deep and tender intimacy.

What about the 'morning-after' pill?

The 'morning-after' pill is in reality ten tablets of diethyl-stilboestrol (DES), a synthetic oestrogen. High doses of oestrogen, when taken twice a day for five days, prevent implantation of the fertilized egg by altering the uterine lining. To be effective, the medication must be started within seventy-two hours after an unprotected act of intercourse presumed to have occurred around the time of ovulation.

The use of this drug is *not* an alternative form of birth control, nor is it without undesirable side effects. DES in high doses can cause nausea, vomiting and changes in the next expected period. It may also harm the embryo if a fertilized egg is implanted despite the treatment. Currently, the use of the so-called morning after pill is strictly an emergency measure and largely limited to the prevention of pregnancy in rape victims.

What about family planning for the woman who has just given birth?

Many women find that they are not much interested in intercourse just after they have given birth, and most couples don't resume intercourse at least until after the check-up six weeks after delivery. However, since ovulation can occur by the thirtieth day following a full-term delivery, another pregnancy is possible if unprotected intercourse occurs as soon as the fourth week. The selection of a contraceptive method for a recently delivered woman will partly depend on when she resumes intercourse as well as on the type of method she prefers.

For women intending to go on the pill, the vast majority of them will start taking it on day five of the first menstrual cycle following delivery. Where reliable protection against pregnancy is needed in advance of the first period (which may be delayed as long as twelve weeks), doctors may advise starting the pill about four weeks after the delivery.

If the woman wants to use an intrauterine device, the best time for insertion is during the first or second period after delivery.

For women who prefer using a diaphragm, it is advisable to wait at least three months after childbirth before being re-fitted. This interval allows the vagina and its supporting tissues to return to normal and thus assures a better diaphragm fit.

Other contraceptive methods such as the condom, vaginal foam and even coitus interruptus (withdrawal) can be used as needed.

What about family planning in the woman who is breast feeding?

With the exception of the pill the last section also applies to the breast-feeding mother.

If you want to breast feed and are determined to use the pill you should consult carefully with your doctor. You will also have to accept that this form of contraception will reduce your milk supply.

It is preferable to select a contraceptive method other than the pill if you intend to breast feed for more than a month.

Doesn't breast feeding suppress ovulation?

To a certain extent, yes, but breast feeding should not be relied upon as a method of contraception. Some lactating mothers may ovulate within the first three months after giving birth, while in others ovulation may be postponed for several months. The fact that a woman ovulates two weeks before an anticipated period makes it possible for her to become pregnant again without ever having had a period after delivery. Therefore, if you are breast feeding and want to avoid another pregnancy, use some form of contraception as soon as you resume intercourse.

Are there any newer contraceptive methods on the horizon?

Researchers are experimenting on a wide variety of contraceptives – long-term hormone injections, antisperm antigen injections and a pill for men. For the moment, however, no method under investigation is free of significant shortcomings.

Thus, while we await the ideal contraceptive – something completely acceptable to all women, absolutely safe with no side effects, 100 per cent effective against pregnancy, inexpensive, readily available, requiring little or no motivation and forethought and easily reversible – we must be content with what we have. For the thoughtful woman, the selection of any one method of birth control over another is still a matter of her knowing and assessing the advantages, disadvantages and potential risks involved.

17. Sterilization

What if your family seems complete, you have five, ten or fifteen reproductive years ahead, and you want to ask your doctor for sterilization? In practice, many doctors will be understandably chary of advising *voluntary* sterilization. That family which seems to you complete could be wiped away by a fire or car crash – you would be left with none. The loss of even one child could not be replaced. Moreover, that marriage which seems to you so stable may yet end in a divorce. You could not conceive another baby for a later partner. While obviously the decision is a personal one, these are the kind of questions a doctor will expect you and your partner to have taken into account. The signatures of both partners in a marriage are usually requested for a voluntary sterilization in order to record that they are both giving their consent to the operation. Single women (unless they are mothers of six!) and married or divorced women with no children will find doctors unwilling to recommend anything but contraception.

What is the definition of sterilization?

To render incapable of reproducing. In women, voluntary sterilization implies surgical interruption of both Fallopian tubes. Without a functional tubal passageway, there is no way for the sperm to meet the egg.

Sterilization in the male involves an interruption of his tubes, the vas deferens. The procedure is called a vasectomy and consists of blocking the vas deferens, or the two passageways along which sperm travel from the testicles to the penis.

Isn't sterilization the same thing as castration?

Absolutely not. Castration involves either the surgical removal of the gonads (both ovaries or both testicles) or in special circumstances the destruction of these organs by specific X-ray technique (irradiation). Castration, therefore, not only renders the individual permanently sterile but eliminates the production of sex hormones by these glands.

How is sterilization in the woman accomplished?

At present three different operations are being used to block the Fallopian tubes: abdominal tubal ligation, vaginal tubal ligation and electrocoagulation of the tubes via laparoscopy.

The procedure used will depend primarily on the gynaecologist's preference and whether the sterilization is done immediately following childbirth or at some other time.

What is an abdominal tubal ligation?

Tubal ligation or, specifically, abdominal tubal ligation is far the most common operation used for voluntary sterilization. It entails making an abdominal skin incision just big enough to provide operating space. If the operation is done immediately after childbirth, the incision will usually be located about one or two inches below the navel, or at the same level where the Fallopian tubes branch off on either side from the top of the uterus. After childbirth the uterus is still quite large, almost as big as a grapefruit. The Fallopian tubes therefore ride fairly high in the abdomen.

In nonpregnant women who have a normal-size uterus, the incision will of course be much lower and can even be hidden in the pubic hair line just above the mons.

Does a tubal ligation simply mean tying the tubes shut?

No. The term tubal ligation is a misnomer. Almost without exception, a tubal ligation involves the surgical removal of a portion of each tube. The two cut ends of each tube are then pinched shut and individually tied. The exact technique will vary among gynaecologists, but the result is the same: an anatomical disruption in the continuity of the tubes. Thus, the passageway is not only blocked but part of it is missing.

When is the best time to have an abdominal tubal ligation?

Almost any time you decide that sterilization is for you. For most women the ideal time is just after childbirth. The operation can take less than thirty minutes and your total stay in the hospital for both delivery and tubal ligation will still average only a week. Tubal ligation at the time of delivery avoids the inconvenience of another stay in hospital.

If you have natural childbirth and request tubal ligation, the procedure will be done as soon as possible following delivery. This, however, will require putting you to sleep with a general anaesthetic.

If you are delivered by Caesarean section and want your tubes tied, the procedure can of course be done at that time and through the same incision.

Should you decide you want a tubal ligation after delivery, make sure to tell your doctor well in advance of your delivery date. This will give him ample time to discuss the operation with you and to arrange it with the hospital.

What about a vaginal tubal ligation?

A vaginal tubal ligation can be done concurrently with an early abortion, but this method of sterilization is never performed immediately after a full-term delivery. Following childbirth, the vaginal tissues are too congested, and even more important, the Fallopian tubes are way out of reach.

Vaginal tubal ligations are therefore usually limited to

nonpregnant women. Since this procedure is done entirely through the vagina, operating space is more limited. Being a candidate for a vaginal tubal ligation requires normal pelvic organs and a fairly roomy vagina. Only the gynaecologist can decide if you are suitable for this operation.

How can the tubes be tied through the vagina?

By means of a small incision in the upper vagina just behind the cervix, the abdominal cavity is entered through a space between the uterus and the rectum. Once the tubes are located, they can then be grasped and a portion of each tube removed and the cut ends tied shut. Sometimes the gynaecologist will elect simply to remove the fimbria (see Chapter 2) from each tube and tie the free end.

A vaginal tubal ligation has certain obvious advantages. There is less discomfort after surgery and, of course, no visible scar or stitches to take out. Most women can be discharged from the hospital within forty-eight to seventy-two hours.

Are there any disadvantages to vaginal tubal ligation?

Yes. The operation at times can be technically very difficult. Then too, there is always the risk that the abdominal cavity will become infected with vaginal bacteria despite sterile precautions.

What about the laparoscopy method for sterilization?

With few exceptions, this operation is mainly used for women not recently pregnant. Hailed by the press as 'belly-button' surgery, electrocoagulation of the Fallopian tubes via laparoscopy is now being done in some hospitals. To date the technique has been perfected by relatively few doctors. Nonetheless, its popularity seems to be growing.

Exactly how is laparoscopy used?

Under general anaesthesia, pure carbon dioxide gas is slowly released into the abdominal cavity through a small puncture wound just below the umbilicus. Since the patient's body is also tilted head down, the carbon dioxide gas not only inflates the abdominal cavity but displaces the bowel away from the pelvic organs, thus exposing the uterus and tubes. The puncture wound is then sufficiently enlarged to permit the passage of the laparoscope, a slender tube shaped like a telescope and equipped with a bright heatless light.

Once the tubes are clearly visible through the laparoscope, a second instrument, the operating scope (coagulating instrument) is inserted either through the same puncture wound alongside the laparoscope or, more commonly, through a second puncture wound in the lower abdomen. By carefully manipulating the Fallopian tubes with the operating scope, each tube is gently lifted and seared (coagulated) in two or three places. Some gynaecologists also cut out the segment of coagulated tube. At the end of the operation, the carbon dioxide gas is simply allowed to escape and any remaining gas is harmlessly absorbed.

What are the advantages and disadvantages of this technique?

Since tubal coagulation is done primarily on women not recently pregnant, most women can be discharged within two days if all goes well.

But electrocoagulation of the tubes via laparoscopy should never be considered a minor operation. On occasion there have been serious complications, such as intractable abdominal bleeding and bowel injuries necessitating further surgery. In a few isolated instances there have even been deaths directly attributed to this operation.

Is electrocoagulation of the tubes a reliable method of sterilization?

According to statistics gathered over the past five years, the failure rate following such a procedure is running approximately 0·2 per cent, a figure that compares favourably with other methods of tubal sterilization.

Is there any other method of tubal sterilization?

Yes, hysteroscopic sterilization. This new method involves the passage of a narrow, telescope-like instrument through the cervical canal and into the uterine cavity. Thus, once the minute openings of the two Fallopian tubes are located, a tiny cauterizing instrument is passed through the telescope and the tubal openings are coagulated under direct vision.

The advantages of this method are many: the operation can take only five minutes; it requires no incision or elaborate surgical equipment. Although relatively few women have undergone this operation, success in terms of complete tubal blockage is running close to 95 per cent.

How soon can you resume intercourse after sterilization?

That depends on the procedure used, how comfortable you are and what your doctor tells you. In general, restrictions against intercourse following a tubal ligation after childbirth will, of course, be those imposed because of the delivery rather than the ligation. For the nonpregnant woman who undergoes sterilization via laparoscopy or by abdominal tubal ligation, intercourse can be resumed within one to two weeks (if she is sufficiently comfortable). On the other hand, a vaginal tubal ligation usually requires at least four to six weeks of sexual abstinence to assure proper healing of the upper vaginal incision.

Unlike a vasectomy in the male, there will be no temporary need for contraception following the tubal procedure. As soon as the Fallopian tubes are closed, you are protected against a possible pregnancy.

Will having a tubal sterilization affect your sex life?

Absolutely not. In fact, it may even improve relations. With the worry of pregnancy off your mind, you may find intercourse much more pleasurable.

What about your periods and female sex hormones?

Regardless of whether your tubes are cut, pinched, tied or coagulated, the uterus and ovaries are not affected. You will continue to ovulate, menstruate and have a perfectly normal output of female hormones. Physiologically, you will be exactly the same as before with only one exception. You won't be able to become pregnant.

What happens to the eggs that are released by the ovaries?

With no place to go and no sperm to meet, they just disintegrate and are harmlessly absorbed.

If you change your mind and want another baby, can the tubes be reopened?

No. The results of attempts at tubal reconstructive surgery following any form of sterilization have been very disappointing. Indeed, the fact that you have felt the need to ask this question would suggest to most doctors that you don't want to take this final action. It can never be overemphasized that a request for tubal ligation or tubal coagulation is a serious step.

Rushing into voluntary sterilization, especially if you are still quite young, without serious thought and consideration, is foolhardy. Unless you are absolutely convinced that you will never want any more children, better reconsider any decision for sterilization. All of these tubal operations are intended to be permanent and irreversible.

However, for those of you seeking an alternative solution to your contraceptive problem . . .

Should you talk your partner into a vasectomy?

You can do no more than subtly suggest that he could solve your birth-control problem: the decision to have a vasectomy should be entirely his. If he can't volunteer cheerfully and willingly, forget it.

More and more men are now having this operation, so there may come a time when your partner too might consider it a good idea.

Who should your partner see about a vasectomy?

His doctor may be able to refer him to a special clinic – or he can contact the local Family Planning clinic, who will know what services are available in your area.

What is a vasectomy?

The male equivalent of a tubal ligation. All sperm are transported from the testicles to the penile urethra (urinary channel) through the two vas deferens. A vasectomy is simply an interruption of these passageways at their most anatomically accessible place – just under the skin on either side of the scrotum. In fact by gently rolling the scrotal skin just above the testicles on either side (if your partner will let you), you can easily feel those two hard cordlike structures.

Under a local anaesthetic, a small skin incision is made on either side of the scrotum; a segment of each vas deferens is removed and the free ends are tied shut.

How is a vasectomy performed?

A vasectomy is a twenty- to thirty-minute operation usually done in a clinic or hospital outpatient department.

Most men experience little physical discomfort and can usually resume normal activities within one or two days. But after the operation, it will still be necessary to continue using some form of contraception, at least for a while.

Why is birth control still necessary immediately after a vasectomy?

Unlike women who release one egg a month, men will still have millions of sperm swarming above the point where the vas were tied. This means that either you or your partner must continue to use some form of birth control until he gets the all-clear from his doctor. In most men, it takes at least six weeks to two months of regular intercourse to discharge the remaining sperm. Usually the doctor or clinic will ask for two semen specimens, one two to four weeks after the first, and will only give the all-clear if the second specimen is sperm-free.

Will your partner be the same sexually?

Vasectomy will not interfere with the output of male hormones or the ability to perform sexually. Your partner will still be able to have an erection, reach a climax and ejaculate. If he did it before, he'll do it again.

Is there a change in the amount of semen ejaculated after vasectomy?

No, the same as before. Semen or seminal fluid is actually a mixture of secretions from the prostate and seminal vesicles. At the moment of orgasm these secretions will still be discharged through the penis.

Are vasectomies reversible?

No. And here again, if you feel the need to ask this question, do you really think the operation is a good idea in your case? Although it is *possible* to reconnect the vas deferens in approximately 70 per cent of the men so that sperm can again be ejaculated with the semen, fewer than 25 per cent will actually be fertile.

The reason for this low fertility rate is related to the presence of sperm antibodies. Following vasectomy, various sperm protein fragments can apparently be absorbed by the bloodstream, causing the subsequent production of antibodies. Therefore, even though the vas deferens may be made anatomically intact again and sperm can be discharged from the testes through the penis, the presence of sperm antibodies causes markedly impaired fertility.

Thus, it is obvious that the decision for vasectomy should be as carefully considered as that of any tubal sterilization.

In conclusion, voluntary sterilization of either partner should be limited to those individuals emotionally mature enough to know their own minds and who, after careful consideration and forethought, sincerely desire an effective and permanent solution to their contraceptive needs. If you and your partner are absolutely convinced that you don't want any more children under any circumstances, then sterilization may be the answer for you.

18. Abortions: Spontaneous and Induced

Currently more than 180 000 legal abortions are being done each year on residents in Britain. For every four babies born, there is one legal abortion.

There is no doubt that abortion is one of the most emotionally charged issues of this decade. In Britain the workings of the 1967 Abortion Act, which made legal abortions more freely available, was broadly supported by the report of the Lane Committee in April 1974. Since then there has been persistent lobbying in Parliament for an amendment of the 1967 Act to clamp down on abortion for 'social' rather than medical reasons, and a Select Committee has been set up again to examine the amendment. But no matter what your personal attitudes may be, a woman seeking termination of an unwanted pregnancy needs emotional support and wise counsel.

What is an abortion?

The interruption or loss of any pregnancy (regardless of the cause) that occurs before the foetus is viable, that means, before the infant can survive outside the mother's womb. For medical–legal purposes foetal viability has been arbitrarily established at twenty-eight weeks. (The Lane Committee recommended that this limit be reduced to twenty-four weeks.) Any foetus delivered after the twenty-eighth week of pregnancy is therefore considered capable of surviving and is no longer classified as an abortion.

What about miscarriages?

A miscarriage is a spontaneous (natural) abortion. Induced abortions (termination of pregnancy) are brought on by artificial means. More about the methods of induction shortly.

How common are spontaneous abortions (miscarriages)?

Very common. About 10 to 15 per cent of all pregnancies are spontaneously aborted. For the woman involved, the majority of spontaneous abortions are really a blessing in disguise. If nature hadn't equipped women with a built-in mechanism to flush away a defective embryo, there would be many more congenitally abnormal babies.

What causes most miscarriages?

Any number of things. Gross chromosomal defects in either the egg or sperm account for about 25 per cent of the losses. Aside from these genetic errors, which would be completely incompatible with life, the remaining 75 per cent are probably a combination of various factors: faulty implantation of an otherwise normal egg, inadequate hormonal or nutritional support of the growing embryo or, less commonly, a maternal infection during the vitally important early weeks.

When are you most apt to miscarry?

During the first twelve weeks following conception. Once you pass the magic three-month limit, chances are excellent that your pregnancy will remain intact.

This does not mean that you should curtail your normal activities during those first three months. Any good fertilized egg once firmly entrenched within the uterine lining is hard to shake loose. If running, bicycling, swimming or even judo is part of your usual routine, there's no need to stay home and take up basket weaving.

The old myth of avoiding intercourse during those days when you would normally menstruate (if you weren't pregnant) can also be discarded. It stands to reason that if an early pregnancy could be so readily disturbed, there wouldn't be the current line-up of women seeking induced abortions.

How soon can you tell whether you are pregnant?

Unless you happen to be keeping an accurate basal body temperature chart as described in Chapter 6, you will probably be at least two to three weeks pregnant before getting your first real clue – missing a period. Not remembering when your last period was or having somewhat irregular cycles can further delay early recognition of pregnancy.

So-called morning sickness or nausea doesn't usually start until the fifth week of pregnancy, but don't depend on that. Half the women who are pregnant are never bothered with gastro-intestinal upsets. Breast tenderness and engorgement as well as having to urinate more frequently are also unreliable signs of early pregnancy.

How else can you tell if you are pregnant?

By a urine pregnancy test. Currently, pregnancy tests are available from your own doctor, some chemists, non-profit-making clinics (some also do a mail-order service) Family Planning clinics, student health centres and from commercial pregnancy-testing laboratories. Do-it-yourself pregnancy test kits are not recommended because it is too easy to get a wrong result.

Most pregnancy tests depend upon detecting the presence of placental hormones (human chorionic gonadotropins, HCG) excreted in the urine. However, since it normally takes twenty-one days following implantation of the fertilized egg for these hormones to be detectable in the urine (with current laboratory methods), a fairly reliable yes (you are pregnant) or no (not this time) answer from this test depends on your being at least three weeks pregnant or approximately ten days late for a period. In addition to the time factor, the accuracy of any pregnancy test can be adversely affected by the presence of protein in the urine, concentration of the urine and so on. *Needless to say, you can be pregnant and still have a negative pregnancy test.* For this reason and particularly if you would want an abortion if you were pregnant, check with your doctor for confirmation as soon as possible.

Isn't there a more accurate pregnancy test available?

Yes, but it is not available everywhere. This new pregnancy blood test is proving to be 100 per cent reliable as early as the first day after a missed period. In fact, it can accurately detect pregnancy within four to six days following conception or, in other words, before the fertilized egg even implants. Unlike conventional pregnancy tests that check for the presence of placental hormones (human chorionic gonadotropins, or HCG) in the urine, this new blood test detects an HCG-like substance presumably produced by the fertilized egg. The test itself takes less than one hour to run and requires only a minute amount of blood drawn from a single finger prick.

How early can your doctor confirm that you are pregnant?

Rarely earlier than six weeks by just examining you. Around this time the only physical finding indicative of a possible early pregnancy will be a somewhat softer uterus and cervix. After four weeks there is a perceptible increase in uterine size. At six weeks the uterus is usually sufficiently enlarged in most women to establish a presumptive confirmation of pregnancy. Reliance on the bluish discolouration of the vaginal mucosa and cervix as an objective sign of early pregnancy can be misleading. This colour change may also precede menstruation or be present whenever there is increased venous congestion of the genital tissues.

However, should your pelvic examination and pregnancy test both be inconclusive and you are still concerned about the possibility of an unwanted pregnancy, you should have another urine pregnancy test.

Yet perhaps you are just late with your period.

Isn't there a pill that can bring on a late period?

Yes, but it will work only if you are *not* pregnant. In these cases, uterine bleeding can usually be induced by the hormone progesterone. Within three to ten days after receiving the hormone pills, the uterine lining will slough and a period will start. No menses (absence of bleeding) will be presumptive evidence of pregnancy.

If you are pregnant, will the pills hurt the baby?

There is recent evidence to suggest that the use of any synthetic progesterone or oestrogen–progestogen compound during the early weeks of pregnancy may (in a few isolated instances) result in a congenitally malformed infant. Therefore, until further investigations either prove or disprove that these compounds may adversely affect the foetus, the administration of any such hormonal agents in pregnancy testing is being discouraged.

Suppose you are pregnant and want an abortion?

Since ancient times women have sought various means to terminate unwanted pregnancies. All manner of potions, draughts and intestinal irritants have been ingested. None of these have worked. Drugs such as ergot, pituitary extract and quinine to stimulate uterine contractions also fail to abort an early pregnancy. The hazardous practice of forcing objects through the cervical canal can be lethal for both mother and foetus. Perforation of the uterus, bladder or bowel, as well as massive uncontrollable haemorrhage or overwhelming infection with septic shock are just a few common causes of death from these do-it-yourself methods. The injection under pressure of chemical or soap solutions into the uterine cavity by means of a douche has also been responsible for instantaneous death as the result of a massive embolus to the brain. The cavity of the pregnant uterus is lined with multiple thin-walled blood vessels which allow any material injected under pressure to diffuse rapidly into these vascular channels and thus be carried by the bloodstream to the brain. Sadly enough, the occasional sexual practice during love play of blowing air into the vagina of a pregnant woman has similarly caused her sudden death via a massive air embolism of the brain.

Regardless of your reasons for wanting to have an abortion, don't ever try to do it yourself or have it done illegally. Hospital and morgue records are replete with cases of women who, in desperation, unwittingly and tragically signed their own death certificate. The very nature of the pregnant uterus, with its soft walls, its tremendously increased blood supply, and the presence of large blood vessels within the uterine lining, makes any of these ill-advised abortion attempts little better than outright suicide.

Today, no woman need resort to these dangerous practices, jeopardizing her health or her ability to bear children. You can get a legal – and safe – abortion through the National Health Service (go to your doctor to be referred to a hospital gynae-cologist), through a charitable pregnancy advisory service or through the private sector.

When should an induced abortion be done?

As early as possible. For the woman who views abortion as her only 'way out', it is medically and psychologically important that she should reach her decision quickly. In Britain it is regarded as highly desirable that an induced abortion be done before the twelfth week of pregnancy. If you leave it until later you may find it more difficult to get one, for beyond three month's gestation the increased size of the uterus makes the termination of a pregnancy much more complicated.

How late is too late to be legally aborted?

In law, after twenty-eight weeks. (And the Lane Committee recommended that the limit should be reduced to twenty-four weeks.) In practice, very few surgeons would be prepared to carry out an abortion after the third or fourth month save in exceptional circumstances or unless there was a valid medical indication. In this kind of case, they would have to be satisfied that the continuation of the pregnancy would be seriously detrimental to the woman's physical health.

How are abortions done?

At the present time there are several medically sanctioned methods for terminating pregnancy, from simple vacuum aspira-tion of the contents of the uterus to major surgery in a few selected women.

For pregnancies of less than twelve weeks, vacuum aspiration is becoming the method of choice.

What is the vacuum aspiration method of abortion?

Removal of the contents of the uterus by suction. In contrast to the conventional and older D and C (dilatation and curettage) method, termination of an early pregnancy (less than twelve weeks) by vacuum aspiration is faster, easier, safer and involves less blood loss. Cervical dilatation, or stretching of the cervical canal, is minimal and frequently not even necessary.

In brief, once the woman is either sufficiently relaxed under a local cervical anaesthetic or asleep under a light general anaesthetic, the operation rarely takes longer than five minutes in most cases. For certain selected women with a very early pregnancy (less than eight weeks), anaesthesia may not even be necessary.

A slender, flexible plastic tube (cannula) is passed through the cervical canal and into the uterine cavity. A controlled negative pressure is then transmitted through the cannula by means of a special vacuum pump, and within seconds the entire contents of the uterine cavity can literally be sucked out.

Is a stay in hospital necessary?

Usually. A few districts now have outpatient clinics especially equipped to handle abortions on a 'come in the morning and go home in the afternoon' basis. It is likely that outpatient treatment for early abortions will become more widely available in future.

How will you feel physically after this procedure?

Remarkably well. Ninety-five per cent of the women have no associated pain following vacuum aspiration, and bleeding, if any, is usually confined to vaginal spotting for a few days. In most cases you can expect your next menstrual period within four to six weeks.

Check with your doctor about when you can resume intercourse.

Since ovulation can occur as early as day ten following termination of a pregnancy by either abortion or miscarriage, your doctor will probably want to discuss birth control with you. If you should have any questions or problems after your abortion, be sure to contact your doctor. And don't forget to keep your follow-up appointment.

What kinds of problems could you have?

In some 5 per cent of the women so aborted, there may be temporary heavy vaginal bleeding or lower abdominal tenderness with fever. Although these problems are more apt to occur in late first trimester abortions (ten to twelve weeks), neither condition is usually serious, providing you seek prompt medical attention. Appropriate medication on an outpatient basis can successfully remedy the situation in almost every case.

Can there be any serious complications associated with early abortions?

Despite the excellent safety record of first trimester abortions (up to the twelfth week), there is a slight risk of uterine perforation or the inadvertent passage of the cannula through the soft uterine wall. Many uterine perforations, however, can and do heal spontaneously without causing further problems. Nonetheless, a uterine perforation can be complicated by haemorrhage, needing immediate abdominal surgery. For this reason, even outpatient abortion facilities are required to have trained medical personnel as well as major operating facilities readily available in case of an emergency.

What about dilatation and curettage (D and C)?

This operation is done under a general anaesthetic. It involves dilating (stretching) the cervix and scraping out the contents of the womb with an instrument called a curette. The woman will stay at least twenty-four hours, and perhaps up to three days in the hospital or nursing home, longer if there are complications such as heavy bleeding. Some women are likely to have bleeding similar to a period for two or three days afterwards.

What happens if you are more than three months pregnant and want an abortion?

Past the third month of pregnancy, both the uterus and the foetus undergo rapid development. The growing foetus begins to assume a more obvious human form. In addition, the uterine walls become thinner (more stretched) and the uterine cavity inside becomes correspondingly larger.

At this stage of pregnancy, it therefore becomes increasingly difficult to aspirate the entire uterine contents through a small cannula. Similarly, a dilatation and curettage under these circumstances, although possible, is much more hazardous. Blood loss is apt to be excessive and inadvertent perforation of the thin uterine wall much more likely. For these reasons, a different method of abortion now becomes necessary.

How are more advanced pregnancies aborted?

Most commonly by the injection of a prostaglandin solution into the uterine cavity, and specifically into the amniotic sac (bag of waters). Chemically classified as fatty-acid derivatives, prostaglandins are hormone-like substances normally found in various body tissues. To date, of the fourteen different prostaglandins known to occur in the human body, two have proved effective in aborting early unwanted pregnancies as well as in inducing normal labour at term. In women sixteen- to twenty-weeks pregnant, studies indicate that the injection of one of these prostaglandins into the amniotic sac may provide a safer and faster means of inducing labour than the use of conventional saline injections, which are still widely used. The methods of operation for both saline and prostaglandin abortions are broadly the same.

However, success with this method of abortion (amniocentesis) requires a fairly well developed amniotic sac, which usually means waiting at least until the sixteenth week of pregnancy. For the woman who delays seeking help beyond her third month, the necessity of having to 'wait it out' until her sixteenth and sometimes eighteenth week of pregnancy, plus the anticipation of going through a miniature labour, makes late abortions much more traumatic for everyone concerned.

How are saline abortions done?

Following completion of necessary laboratory work (blood and urine tests), most women will be admitted directly to an induction unit in the hospital or nursing home. Under a local anaesthetic a needle with an attached catheter is passed through the abdominal skin and directed downward through the uterine wall and into the amniotic sac. When the catheter is properly positioned, the doctor then withdraws a certain amount of amniotic fluid and replaces it with a sterile saline solution. The procedure rarely takes longer than fifteen minutes, and the patient is then returned to her assigned hospital bed – to wait.

What does the saline solution do?

It kills the foetus and provokes labour. Since there is normally a delay of several hours between the saline injection and the first uterine contraction, most women will not deliver for at least twenty-four to thirty-six hours. Labour is usually short and pain killers and sedation are given as needed.

If everything goes as anticipated, the average stay in hospital or nursing home is two and sometimes three days depending on how long it takes to effect delivery. Most women will have some vaginal bleeding similar to that seen after a full-term delivery. Menstruation will probably resume within six to ten weeks.

Can there be any problems associated with amniocentesis?

Unlike early pregnancies, which can be easily and safely terminated in virtually every case, abortion by amniocentesis is not a benign procedure. Complications both minor and major can run as high as 30 per cent.

Besides fever and abdominal pain, one of the more common problems is related to delivery of the placenta (afterbirth). In 15 to 25 per cent of the women so aborted, the placenta becomes entrapped within the uterine cavity or only partially separates.

Although not usually a serious problem, it may necessitate a dilatation and curettage (D and C) under general anaesthesia to remove the retained tissue.

What about serious complications from saline amniocentesis?

Haemorrhage, severe infection or toxic reaction to the saline solution are not that uncommon. Inadvertent injection of the saline solution into a blood vessel has also taken its toll.

Since the majority of serious complications as well as most fatalities (7 deaths per 100 000 legal abortions) occur in women being aborted by saline amniocentesis, a few doctors prefer an alternative method of terminating second trimester pregnancies in selected women.

How else can a pregnancy over twelve weeks be aborted?

Via *hysterotomy* – a miniature Caesarean section. With this operation the foetus and attached placenta are removed through a small incision in the uterus. Thus, the foetus, although usually born alive, rapidly succumbs within a few moments because of its gross immaturity.

In younger women requesting sterilization at the time of their abortion, a hysterotomy in combination with a tubal ligation may be the operation chosen for pregnancies beyond fourteen weeks gestation.

On the other hand, if the woman may someday want children, hysterotomy as a method of abortion has definite drawbacks.

What are the disadvantages in being aborted by a hysterotomy?

There is, of course, the longer hospital stay because of major abdominal surgery. Second, the presence of a scar in the uterine wall usually necessitates Caesarean sections for future delivery of full-term infants. Despite good healing following hysterotomy, any incision through the entire thickness of the uterine wall is always a future site of potential weakness during a subsequent pregnancy. For this reason a Caesarean section at term would eliminate possible separation of the old scar (uterine rupture) under the stress of forceful labour contractions.

Needless to say, aborting pregnancies after the twelfth week by either hysterotomy or amniocentesis leaves much to be desired. Currently, intensive clinical research is being directed toward making late abortions relatively safer and easier.

Is a better contraceptive the current answer to preventing unwanted pregnancies and abortions?

Apparently not, for despite the effectiveness of available birth-control methods, the vast majority of women seeking an abortion will readily admit to not having taken any contraceptive precautions. There is no question that among unmarried women a single, unexpected act of coitus does account for many unwanted pregnancies. But other than this group, there are still thousands of sexually active and knowledgeable women who, although they have easy access to a reliable contraceptive method, consistently fail to protect themselves for a variety of psychosexual reasons.

Pregnancy, although unwanted, may for some be proof that they have been loved and desired. For others, the use of any form of birth control detracts from the spontaneity of the moment and the feeling of total commitment to their sexual partner. Not uncommonly because of religious reasons, a woman may consider birth control unnatural and therefore sinful. A denial of reality is sometimes seen in young, healthy women who are absolutely convinced that they are immune to pregnancy. And yet, following abortion, they again become pregnant within a few weeks out of fear that the first abortion did indeed leave them infertile. Others delight in sexual roulette, finding coitus more exciting when it carries a real risk of pregnancy.

Among teenagers, however, lack of proper sex information and inability to obtain a reliable contraceptive are important contributing causes to the growing number of unwanted pregnancies. But here again, it seems that psychosexual reasons, both conscious and unconscious, prevent many from using birth control even when freely and confidentially available. Adolescence, with its tremendous awakening of sexual needs in combination with intellectual and emotional immaturity, is a difficult period in which to appeal to rational judgement.

In the final analysis, there will always be women seeking abortions. The wider dissemination of birth-control information, easy availability of effective contraceptives and wise counsel will never eliminate the problem of unwanted pregnancies, but at least they will bring us somewhat closer to the best possible solution.

Part 6

Changes in the Natural Woman

19. Four Ordinary Disorders

There are four common, yet frequently misunderstood, problems that can happen to any woman: genital warts, cervical cysts, fibroid tumours of the uterus and benign ovarian growths. Since these problems can and do occur independently of one another, let's start at the vulva and then proceed to the cervix, uterus and ovaries.

What are warts doing on the vulva?

You may know that a virus is responsible for the common skin wart. But did you know that another closely related virus can also cause warts to grow and thrive around the moist vulvar folds and, frequently, inside the vagina?

Genital warts are nothing new. They have been plaguing both men and women for centuries. Until recently they were called venereal warts because of the belief that the responsible virus was transmitted exclusively by sexual intercourse. However, the virus on occasion can be acquired without such intimate contact. Be that as it may, genital warts are becoming increasingly common, especially among sexually active women between fifteen and thirty.

What do genital warts look like?

Genital warts frequently make their debut as tiny, discrete pinkish-tan growths not much bigger than a grain of rice. At first only two or three may be noticed around the vaginal opening or clustered along the labia. However, where conditions are favourable for their growth, genital warts can flourish and spread.

What makes them flourish?

Scratching because of itching or minor irritation can spread the virus to other vulvar areas and thus cause new warts to appear. Moreover, once the warts have gained a foothold, excessive vulvar moisture seems to be the most important factor in their continuing growth. Among women with vaginal infections and abnormal discharges, genital warts can be particularly annoying. Similarly, increased genital secretions such as occur during pregnancy or from taking contraceptive pills can also cause genital warts to thrive and flourish. During pregnancy especially, what might have started out as only two or three small warts can mushroom into several cauliflowerlike masses.

Can these warts ever be serious?

Other than being unsightly and a source of local irritation and itching, they seldom cause problems. If neglected, however, large warts may become infected as a result of scratching or poor vulvar hygiene. On rare occasions neglected warts have been known to cover the entire vulva and even block the vaginal opening.

What can be done about genital warts?

As long as excessive vaginal secretions or discharge continue to bathe the vulvar area, it is difficult to eradicate genital warts permanently. Some warts can even disappear spontaneously by simply clearing the vaginal infection or minimizing vaginal secretions. For women on oral contraceptives, this may mean stopping medication temporarily. Such clothing as nylon underwear and tights, which tend to trap moisture, are also best avoided. If genital warts appear during pregnancy, successful eradication may have to wait till after delivery.

More specific treatment will vary depending on the size and number of warts. For very small warts, two or three topical applications of a special solution (podophyllum) at weekly intervals may be all that is necessary. The applications are painless and within a few days the warts usually slough off. Where there may be several large clusters of warts, treatment by freezing, cauterization or surgical removal may be the best solution. Regardless of the treatment selected by your doctor, the vulva, because of its rich blood supply, heals remarkably well and fast and without any apparent scarring.

What's all this talk about cervical cysts?

Of all the possible happenings along the female tract, cervical cysts, also known as Nabothian cysts (or follicles), are by far the most common. In fact, cervical cysts are so prevalent that they can almost be considered normal. Nonetheless, the word 'cyst' for many women seems to have an ominous pathological ring. And if something sounds pathological, can major surgery be far behind? For this reason, let's clarify all the confusion and needless worry.

What exactly are cervical cysts?

Nothing more than plugged-up cervical glands filled with mucus secretions. Cervical cysts can occur singly or in groups, depending on how many cervical glands are involved. They rarely get any bigger than a small pea and usually appear as white pimple-like elevations on the surface of the cervix. Cervical cysts are to the cervix what pimples are to the face. They are not the least bit serious, but their presence indicates some past or recent cervical infection or irritation.

Is treatment always necessary?

No. But treatment will make your cervix pink and beautiful again. Since cervical cysts are associated with cervical irritation or infection (cervicitis), most doctors will elect to treat such a condition. In addition, any bothersome discharge because of chronic cervicitis should also be eliminated.

Because the surface of the cervix is relatively insensitive to pain, most cysts can be comfortably and readily treated by cauterization. Cauterization, by destroying the infected tissue and allowing trapped mucus secretions to drain, permits areas of chronic inflammation to be replaced by new and healthy cervical tissue within four to six weeks. If you should notice a watery discharge or a pink staining for several days following cauterization, don't be alarmed. This is perfectly normal and will rapidly disappear as your cervix heals.

But let's move on and consider more serious gynaecological problems – specifically, fibroid tumours of the uterus, which may at times require major surgery.

What exactly are uterine fibroids?

Benign (nonmalignant) growths made up of muscle and fibrous tissue. Although it is possible to have just one fibroid tumour, multiple tumours are much more common. In most women, fibroid tumours (also known as fibroids, myomata or leiomyomata) generally begin as several small seedings embedded throughout the thick muscular wall of the uterus. As these seedings progressively enlarge and become more nodular, they can encroach upon the uterine cavity and/or grow outward and distort the normally smooth outer contour of the uterus. (See Figure 24.)

With regard to size, fibroids can vary tremendously. Some have even weighed as much as 20 pounds (9 kilograms).

What causes fibroid tumours?

Nobody knows for sure, but their growth seems to depend on oestrogen stimulation. Thus, as long as a woman is still having regular periods, fibroid tumours will usually continue to enlarge. Contraceptive pills, especially those with a high oestrogen content, can also accelerate their growth. As a general rule, however, most fibroids grow slowly even among women using oral contraceptives.

Once the menopausal years begin and oestrogen output decreases, fibroid tumours will cease to grow and in many instances shrink in size.

How common are fibroids?

With the exception of pregnancy, fibroid tumours are the most common cause of an enlarged uterus. Although infrequent in women under twenty-five, the incidence of fibroid tumours increases sharply thereafter. Approximately 20 to 25 per cent of all women over thirty have fibroids, some of them seriously enough to warrant a hysterectomy (removal of the uterus). But having fibroids does not necessarily mean surgery, nor do these tumours always cause problems. Symptoms, if any, will depend on the size of the tumours and their location within the uterus.

Do fibroid tumours ever become malignant?

Very rarely. In fact, to perform a hysterectomy on the basis that a fibroid tumour may become malignant is not justified. According to recent statistics, less than 0·4 per cent of all fibroids ever become cancerous, and then predominantly in women well past the menopause.

Can a woman with fibroid tumours ever become pregnant?

Yes, indeed. Fibroid tumours as a rule do not interfere with fertility. The one possible exception would be where the tumours actually block the Fallopian tubes, thereby preventing sperm from meeting the egg.

However, once pregnancy is established, previously small and asymptomatic fibroids frequently enlarge because of higher oestrogen levels and the increasing uterine size. Under these circumstances, other problems may occasionally arise.

How can fibroids interfere with pregnancy?

Although many women have successfully delivered a full-term baby in spite of their fibroids, these tumours can create difficulties during pregnancy. If, for example, the fibroids bulge or jut into the uterine cavity, the baby may have insufficient room to grow properly. In these instances, premature labour and delivery, sometimes as early as three to five months before term, are not uncommon.

In women who do carry to term, normal vaginal delivery may not always be possible. Thus, where tumours block the birth canal or even cause the baby to lie in an abnormal position, a Caesarean section may be necessary. Following delivery fibroid tumours usually shrink to the size they were before the pregnancy.

Are fibroid tumours a common cause of abnormal bleeding?

No. Surprising as it may seem, fibroid tumours do not usually cause bleeding or spotting between periods. However, if the tumour or tumours bulge into the uterine cavity, heavy and long periods with the passage of large clots can occur. Tumours that in any way distort the normal contours of the uterine cavity can cause heavier menstrual blood loss by increasing the bleeding surface of the uterine lining. (See Figure 24.)

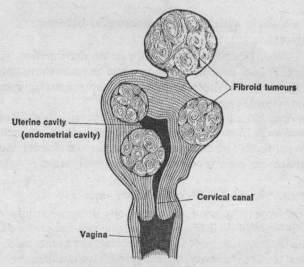

24. *Womb with multiple fibroid tumours*

What about other problems?

Large fibroids can cause a sensation of pelvic fullness or discomfort. At times a fibroid may press against the nearby bladder and thereby limit the amount of urine it can hold comfortably. Although this in itself is rarely serious, it can create an annoying problem – having to urinate more frequently. Less commonly, a large fibroid may interfere with normal bowel evacuation by pressing against the rectal wall. Even small tumours can create problems if they press against a particularly sensitive area. Nagging backaches, for example, can occasionally be caused by a small fibroid pressing on pelvic nerve fibres.

Yet despite these potential problems, the majority of women with fibroid tumours are remarkably free of symptoms.

Can a woman have fibroid tumours and not know it?

Absolutely. In fact, for many woman, fibroid tumours are inadvertently discovered during routine pelvic examination.

Can the presence of fibroid tumours usually be detected?

Most fibroids distort and enlarge the uterus. Nonetheless, it is possible for a uterus to seem perfectly normal on pelvic examination and yet have its cavity distorted by a single small fibroid. Suspicion that such a fibroid exists may be aroused by an unaccountably profuse menstrual flow. Under these circumstances, an X-ray of the uterine cavity (hysterosalpingogram – see Chapter 15) or a D and C (dilatation and curettage) would be necessary to confirm the diagnosis. However, fibroid tumours that jut into the uterine cavity (submucous fibroids) cannot be 'scraped away' by curettage, as they are embedded in the muscle wall.

What can be done about fibroids?

Treatment will depend on several factors: the size and site of the tumours, the problems they are causing, your age and whether or not you want children.

If your fibroids are relatively small and asymptomatic, your doctor will advise 'watchful waiting', for they may well grow slowly and never give you much trouble, in which case it is best to leave well alone. Regular pelvic examinations will usually be sufficient to keep track of any changes. The fact that fibroids regress during the menopausal years makes this conservative approach worthwhile for a great many women.

If the tumours are large and troublesome, however, surgery may be necessary.

If you have troublesome fibroids, is removal of the uterus necessary?

Not always, but fibroid tumours that create general pelvic discomfort or consistently cause heavy menstrual bleeding are usually handled by removal of the uterus (hysterectomy). For older women hysterectomy is frequently the treatment of choice. But even in such situations, hysterectomy may not always be the best answer.

Why not?

Even among women who have completed their family, removal of the uterus may be regarded as a threat to their feminity, sexuality or self-image. The fact that fibroid tumours are benign lesions makes it especially important that a woman's reaction to possibly losing her uterus be carefully evaluated before a hysterectomy is advised.

Unfortunately, few women are aware that there is an alternate surgical treatment for symptomatic fibroid tumours.

What is the alternative treatment?

Myomectomy or multiple myomectomy – removal of the fibroid tumours without sacrificing the uterus. Although this procedure is usually reserved for the younger woman with symptomatic tumours or for the woman whose fibroids may possibly interfere with pregnancy, myomectomy can nonetheless be done on any woman, providing that the uterus is not involved too extensively.

Why, then, are hysterectomies done for fibroid tumours?

As effective as myomectomy can be, there is a good chance that a new crop of fibroid tumours may develop, particularly in the woman under forty-five. Then too, if fibroids are really causing problems, most women, especially if they are over forty, would just as soon have the problem permanently resolved. Furthermore, the surgery involved in a myomectomy is technically more difficult and can involve greater blood loss than hysterectomy.

Apart from these considerations, fibroid tumours are sometimes associated with endometriosis (see Chapter 20) or other pelvic conditions. Under these circumstances, removal of the uterus, particularly in the older woman, may also be indicated on the basis of these coexisting conditions.

What happens if you have a hysterectomy?

Much confusion still exists as to what a hysterectomy really entails. Whether your doctor chooses to call the operation a simple hysterectomy, a complete hysterectomy, a pan-hysterectomy, or a total hysterectomy, all of these terms mean or should mean exactly the same thing, namely, removal of the body of the uterus plus its cervix. Unfortunately even doctors sometimes become casual in their terminology and may at times use one of these terms to include removal of the tubes and ovaries. So check with your own doctor just what he or she means by a particular term. Regardless of the qualifying adjective preceding the term hysterectomy, the procedure should refer only to removal of the entire uterus.

The two exceptions to the above are the so-called partial hysterectomy and radical hysterectomy. In partial hysterectomy the cervix is left in place and only the body or upper portion of the uterus is removed. Partial hysterectomies, although popular thirty years ago, are rarely if ever done nowadays, and only under very extraordinary conditions. A radical hysterectomy, on the other hand, entails removal of the uterus plus adjacent pelvic lymph nodes. This extensive surgical procedure is reserved strictly for certain pelvic malignancies.

Having a hysterectomy therefore means no more periods and no more pregnancies. Other than that, a hysterectomy will not interfere with ovarian function or female hormone production.

In other words, you will not go through the menopause any sooner than nature intended by simply losing the uterus.

Is there a special term to indicate removal of the tubes and ovaries?

Yes, indeed, a very long, fancy term: bilateral salpingo-oophorectomy. *Salpingo* refers to the Fallopian tubes; *oophor* to the ovaries; *ectomy* to removal of; *bilateral* simply means both sides. Therefore a bilateral salpingo-oophorectomy means removal of both tubes and ovaries.

But having a hysterectomy, especially for fibroid tumours, does not mean that your ovaries have to be removed as well. There are few pelvic conditions that require sacrificing normal ovaries. Nonetheless, if you are advised to have a hysterectomy, make a point of finding out exactly what operation is planned. And don't sign any operating consent form until the operation has been thoroughly discussed and explained to you.

Removal of the ovaries with a sudden and abrupt loss of oestrogen can be a shock to any woman's system even if she is close to fifty. After all, the ovaries do continue to produce some oestrogen even up to the age of sixty and beyond. Unlike normal menopausal symptoms that gradually appear as oestrogen levels decrease slowly over a period of years, symptoms from a surgically induced menopause can be dramatic and are not so easily controlled with oestrogen replacement therapy. There is nothing like your own two ovaries producing their own oestrogen.

Why, then, do gynaecologists sometimes remove ovaries that are themselves normal?

Primarily to prevent the possible later development of ovarian cancer. There is no denying that cancer of the ovaries is a dangerous malignancy, but fortunately it is not very prevalent.

In the final analysis, where there exists no current and valid reason for castration at the time of hysterectomy, the decision of whether or not to remove normal ovaries should belong to the individual woman.

What about ovaries that aren't normal?

When nature blessed women with ovaries, she packed inside those prune-sized organs not only a fantastically complex hormone factory complete with an egg-processing plant, but she also endowed each ovary with the potential to develop all manner of cysts and tumours. When you consider that the ovary, even from infancy, can harbour about twenty different types of growths, both benign and malignant, it is little wonder that the finding of an enlarged ovary on pelvic examination can be a problem in diagnosis. To make the problem of ovarian growths even more complex, some can disappear as readily as they appeared while others can grow to fantastic sizes if left unattended.

How big can an ovarian growth become?

Large enough to fill the entire abdomen. One such ovarian tumour made medical history back in 1809 when a dashing and fearless frontier surgeon, Dr Ephraim McDowell, performed the world's first removal of an ovarian tumour in Danville, Kentucky. Working under primitive conditions and without a whiff of anaesthesia, he skilfully extracted a 22·5-pound (10·2-kilogram) ovarian tumour while the intrepid patient, Jane Todd Crawford (tired from a three-day trip on horseback to reach the good doctor), distracted herself by reciting psalms during the surgical ordeal. Happily for all concerned, Mrs Crawford made a rapid and uneventful recovery and Dr McDowell joined the select group of medical notables.

In contrast to such a phenomenon, most benign ovarian growths are rarely that spectacular.

What about ovarian cysts?

Each year thousands of women are told, 'You have an enlarged ovary'. But in spite of all the diagnostic possibilities to account for an enlarged ovary, such a finding in an otherwise healthy woman during the childbearing years is most likely to be a physiological cyst, that is, either a follicle or a corpus-luteum cyst.

What exactly are physiological cysts and why are they so common?

As you may recall from Chapter 5, all functioning ovaries normally contain small cystic structures (follicles) in various stages of growth or degeneration. Thus, in order for one ovarian follicle to mature and release its egg (ovulation) during any single menstrual cycle, countless other follicles fail in the attempt and rapidly disintegrate into microscopic specks of scar tissue. As long as these follicles behave properly, none of them will grow any larger than a fraction of an inch in size. Occasionally, however, and for some usually obscure reason, the chosen follicle may fail to release its egg or one of the competing follicles may refuse to disintegrate. In either case, the disturbed follicle may continue to enlarge and fill with clear fluid (follicle cyst).

Similarly, a cyst can develop from the remnants of the follicle that has extruded its egg, thus forming a corpus-luteum cyst.

Do these particular cysts ever cause problems?

Since most physiological cysts rarely get bigger than the size of a lemon, dull, aching pelvic pain sometimes associated with larger ovarian growths may be absent.

Follicle cysts seldom cause problems. In fact, they frequently disappear spontaneously after one or two menstrual cycles. For this reason many gynaecologists will simply advise a repeat pelvic examination within two or three months. If, however, the cyst should remain and increase in size, or start to cause pain, etc., surgery may be indicated.

Corpus-luteum cysts, on the other hand, are more likely to cause menstrual irregularities as a result of hormonal disturbances. At times, therefore, intermittent spotting or bleeding and even a delay in menstruation is possible. Corpus-luteum cysts can also regress, but on occasion they may rupture and cause internal bleeding sufficiently heavy to necessitate immediate surgical removal of the cyst.

With regard to other ovarian growths, surgery is usually advisable even in the absence of symptoms.

Why is surgery usually necessary when dealing with other ovarian growths?

Regardless of how competent a gynaecologist may be, there is no way of accurately determining by pelvic examination alone whether an ovarian mass is benign or malignant. Shape, size and consistency of the growth may be helpful in this regard, but these physical findings can be deceptive.

Symptoms, at least initially, are also of little diagnostic value. Menstruation, for example, usually remains normal with either a benign or malignant ovarian growth. Then too, any ovarian tumour or cyst, if sufficiently large, can cause pelvic or lower abdominal discomfort. In certain cases X-rays of the pelvic area may provide additional clues to the nature of the ovarian mass, but here again the findings are frequently unreliable. Thus, only by surgically removing the ovarian growth and examining the tissue under a microscope can an accurate diagnosis be made.

Fortunately, very few ovarian growths prove to be malignant. Even assuming one could be certain that a particular ovarian mass was benign, surgery would still be advisable. Apart from the fact that ovarian tumours and cysts can occasionally rupture, bleed, become infected, twist, or cause pelvic havoc, there is another important reason to favour early surgical intervention.

What reason is that?

In contrast to most physiological cysts, other ovarian growths, whether they be cysts or solid tumours, will usually continue to enlarge and ultimately cause serious problems. Continuing growth of such an ovarian mass, for example, can gradually constrict and press against the surrounding normal ovarian tissue and reduce its blood supply. Thus, in time, with less blood flow and nourishment reaching the otherwise normal and uninvolved portion of the ovary, it may eventually atrophy, shrink and cease to function. Therefore, delaying or postponing surgery in these cases may unnecessarily jeopardize the entire ovary. On the other hand, fairly prompt removal of such a tumour or cyst can avoid this potential problem and allow the doctor to spare the remaining portion of ovary.

It is only natural for anyone to want to avoid surgery, particularly if pain and other symptoms are absent. But ovaries are far too precious to be inadvertently compromised by prolonged 'watchful waiting' under these circumstances. For when it comes to a 'true' ovarian mass in contrast to a physiological cyst, surgical removal of the offending tumour or cyst (ovarian cystectomy), with preservation of normal ovarian tissue whenever possible, is still the best treatment.

20. Endometriosis

Ever since endometriosis (pronounced endo-me-tree-o-sis) first came to the attention of gynaecologists more than a century ago, it has continued to be one of the most puzzling of all pelvic diseases. Not only can it cause a variety of symptoms and mimic other pelvic conditions, but it can take the joy out of any woman's sex life. The fact that endometriosis afflicts about 5–10 per cent of women, and mainly during their prime years (twenty-five to forty-five), that it can be responsible for menstrual misery, infertility and severe pain during sexual intercourse gives it a well-deserved place in any book on female problems.

What exactly is endometriosis?

A condition where fragments of tissue from the uterine lining (endometrial tissue) are deposited, become embedded, and grow outside the confines of the uterine cavity. Although the exact cause is unknown, endometriosis is most likely the result of tiny shreds of endometrial tissue finding their way through the Fallopian tubes and into the pelvic cavity during menstruation. Thus, as these tissue fragments from the uterine lining spill onto the ovaries and implant themselves along the outer surface of the uterine wall and elsewhere in the pelvic area, various problems can be precipitated.

How do these tissue fragments create problems?

Endometrial tissue in these unusual locations behaves much like the tissue lining the uterine cavity. In other words, these newly deposited tissue fragments also swell, thicken and bleed cyclically under the influence of ovarian hormones.

Even more peculiar is the tendency for this misplaced tissue, although noncancerous, to grow and spread to neighbouring pelvic organs. Tissue fragments, for example, deposited along the outer back wall of the uterus, may gradually invade the nearby bowel wall. Nature, in an attempt to protect the surrounding pelvic organs from further involvement, covers these areas of endometriosis with scar tissue. In women with severe endometriosis of long standing, the scar tissue can literally cement the bowel to the female pelvic organs.

What kind of symptoms does endometriosis provoke?

For most women the onset of increasingly painful periods after perhaps years of relative comfort is probably the earliest and most common complaint. Cyclic bleeding from these abnormally located endometrial tissue fragments within the pelvic cavity, in contrast to menstrual cramps, causes a steady dull-to-severe lower abdominal pain. At first the pain occurs just before or during menstruation. Later on, as more and more of the implants accumulate, swell and press against the confining scar tissue, a nagging soreness in the lower abdomen can precede menstruation by two and even three weeks. For women severely afflicted, the week following menstruation may be the only time of relative comfort. Another puzzling aspect of the disease is that women with minimal endometriosis sometimes have the most pelvic distress.

Approximately 40 per cent of the women with endometriosis will also be infertile despite regular periods, normal monthly ovulation and open Fallopian tubes.

Why are these women infertile?

For pregnancy to occur, the released egg must find its way into one of the Fallopian tubes. In women with endometriosis, scar tissue may impair the normal mobility of the Fallopian tubes. Needless to say, if the tubes are bound down by fibrous adhesions, they can't possibly swing over to the ovary and scoop up the egg at the time of ovulation.

In three out of four women with endometriosis, infrequent coitus because of severe pain during sexual intercourse also contributes to a low conception rate.

What kind of pain on intercourse and why?

Not just any pain, but on deep penile penetration a sharp, shooting pain somewhat like being impaled on a knife. Since endometriosis frequently involves the uterine ligaments, which are richly invested with multiple nerve fibres, even the slightest touch or pressure against these affected ligaments can cause marked discomfort. During sexual intercourse, therefore, each penile thrust against the upper vagina or cervix brings about acute and unbearable pain by stretching the involved uterine ligaments. Under such circumstances intercourse, though previously enjoyable, may now by necessity be avoided or, in some instances, only tolerable for two or three days immediately following menstruation. Partners may attempt different coital positions to limit the depth of penile penetration, but at best endometriosis can be a real sexual turn-off.

How can your doctor tell whether you have endometriosis?

The first real clue is the symptoms themselves. If your history includes increasingly painful periods, dyspareunia (painful intercourse) and the inability to conceive, endometriosis is a likely suspect. Where pain on deep penile penetration is a major concern, the uterine ligaments can frequently on pelvic examination be felt as thick, beaded cords. Furthermore, the pain experienced during intercourse can readily be reproduced by manually stretching the affected ligaments.

Where the diagnosis is more obscure, visual inspection of the pelvic organs (under local or general anaesthesia) may be necessary. For this purpose a small, slender telescope-like instrument can be passed through either the upper vagina or, more commonly, a small puncture wound in the abdomen. Using this procedure (laparoscopy), the diagnosis can be confirmed and the extent of the disease better evaluated.

Are some women more susceptible to endometriosis?

Yes. Endometriosis occurs only in women who menstruate and ovulate regularly. Therefore, the longer a woman goes without any interruption in normal ovarian function, the greater her chances of eventually developing endometriosis. A woman who ovulates regularly and who postpones pregnancy over a period of several years is more likely to be a candidate.

As an aside comment, the use of tampons during menstruation does not play a role in the development of endometriosis. Whatever the mechanism is that causes menstrual debris (including endometrial tissue) to back out through the Fallopian tubes, tampons are off the suspect list.

Fortunately, however, endometriosis need not wrap up one's sex life in moth balls, nor is it necessary for any woman to be increasingly incapacitated with pelvic pain and menstrual misery. For the women who do ultimately develop endometriosis much can be done. And sometimes endometriosis can even be nipped in the bud before real problems develop.

Can the problems of endometriosis really be avoided?

For the young woman who already has symptoms of early endometriosis, the best advice is to get pregnant as soon as possible – if at all feasible. It is truly amazing how the absence of ovulation and menstruation during the months of pregnancy will effect an almost miraculous cure. Areas of endometriosis rapidly shrink and frequently disappear. In fact, after delivery, it may never again be a problem. In women who do have recurrences, however, spacing their children closer together rather than waiting three or four years between pregnancies is also helpful in preventing flare-ups.

Avoiding the progression of endometriosis therefore narrows down to interrupting periodically normal ovarian function. For this reason, the symptoms of endometriosis may spontaneously improve with the advent of the menopause.

Is there any way to avoid endometriosis completely?

Possibly. Although unproved, long-term use of contraceptive pills with suppression of ovulation for extended periods of time may be a factor in preventing endometriosis from developing in susceptible women. In addition, since most contraceptive pills also tend to decrease menstrual flow, the chances of significant amounts of menstrual debris backing out through the Fallopian tubes are greatly lessened. Nonetheless, where endometriosis already exists, the use of the pill in the doses conventionally prescribed for contraceptive purposes is usually inadequate to control the progression of symptoms.

What, then, is the treatment for endometriosis?

Symptoms from minimal endometriosis may at times spontaneously improve without the benefit of either pregnancy or special medication. In other instances, progressively increasing pelvic pain makes treatment necessary. Under these circumstances, the next best thing short of pregnancy is the creation of a state of false or pseudopregnancy. This usually means preventing both ovulation and menstruation by hormone therapy administered by mouth (or by injections at regular intervals) over a period of several months. Here again, endometrial implants melt away and pelvic pain disappears. Sex too can once again be enjoyed. Following hormone treatment approximately 60 per cent of the women remain completely comfortable for as long as four to six years after stopping all medication.

As effective as hormone therapy can be, it is not always the solution.

Why not?

Once the medication is stopped there is always the possibility of recurrence. In other words, once ovulation and menstruation resume, areas of pelvic endometriosis may be restimulated or new areas may even form with the subsequent return of all the old problems. Less commonly, long-term hormone therapy may cause unpleasant side effects (weight gain, fluid retention, etc.) or actually be contraindicated because of other existing pelvic or medical conditions.

In women who wish to become pregnant, hormone therapy will also be of little value if scar tissue around the Fallopian tubes is preventing proper pick-up of the released egg.

Where any or all of these problems exist, conservative surgery may be the answer.

Conservative surgery - what's that?

A sometimes long and meticulous surgical operation performed through a lower abdominal incision. Since endometriosis is usually first diagnosed in women between the ages of twenty-five and thirty-five, conservative surgery further implies the preservation of the reproductive organs while ideally preventing recurrences of the disease by eliminating all areas of endometriosis. For example, endometrial implants on the ovaries (endometrial cysts) can be removed, leaving normal ovarian tissue intact. Similarly, endometrial implants along the uterus and pelvic ligaments can be excised or cauterized and thereby permanently destroyed. If the uterus is tied down by scar tissue, it can be freed and resuspended in a more normal position. As a further precaution against the recurrence of pelvic pain, some gynaecologists may also strip away the tiny nerve fibres that carry pain impulses from the uterus (presacral neurectomy).

Last but not least, scar tissue around the Fallopian tubes can be removed and the normal mobility of the tubes restored.

How successful is conservative surgery in endometriosis?

Where endometriosis is the only cause of infertility, approximately one third to one half of all women who undergo conservative surgery may happily conceive within three to six months following the operation. When the surgery is performed primarily to relieve pain, results will vary from woman to woman.

Successful eradication of all areas of endometriosis can at times be difficult. For this reason temporary hormone therapy following surgery is frequently necessary to prevent recurrent minor flare-ups. Nonetheless, in some of the women so treated, the subsequent recurrence of intractable pelvic pain will ultimately necessitate more radical surgery to effect permanent relief.

Regardless of the outcome, conservative surgery is recommended whenever possible in the woman under forty.

What kind of radical surgery is sometimes necessary?

In a minority of women with long-standing and extensive pelvic endometriosis, removal of the uterus and at times even the ovaries may be the only effective way to eliminate all pain. As drastic as this procedure may seem, would it be less drastic to allow such a woman to remain a pelvic cripple, as well as unable to tolerate sexual intercourse?

Should removal of the ovaries be necessary, however, oestrogen replacement therapy can be given without running the risk of re-activating the condition. Today, fortunately, with better techniques for early diagnosis and more effective hormone therapy, extensive surgery for this disease is becoming increasingly less necessary.

In summary, endometriosis remains a baffling problem, potentially capable of creating pelvic havoc and sexual disharmony. As in all problems to which women are heir, early treatment still offers the best chance for complete recovery.

21. The Menopausal Years

At no other time in a woman's life is there such a complex interplay between physical and psychological factors as during the menopausal years. Along with the physical stress brought about by hormonal imbalances, the psychological and emotional reactions of each woman to this normal transition will vary depending upon her previous life style, attitudes and self-image.

For centuries women have been programmed to accept their ability to reproduce and raise children as their prime function in life. Even today, any woman who persists in asserting her identity to the detriment of her conventional role runs the risk of being ridiculed or labelled either neurotic or blatantly unfeminine. Because of these deeply ingrained sexist attitudes together with our society's preoccupation with youth, is it any wonder that many women regard the menopause as the beginning of the end?

It is all too easy to equate ageing with the chronological passage of time and to compartmentalize our lives and attitudes on the basis of years lived. Thus, at thirteen we become teenagers, at eighteen are magically transformed into adults, at forty are resigned to being middle-aged, and at sixty are arbitrarily tossed onto the dump by mandatory retirement.

But is ageing solely a function of time, as our culture would have us believe? Surely all of us have known women whose vitality and appearance surprisingly belied the date on their birth certificate. In addition to the passage of time, the rate of physiological ageing among all individuals also depends on the dynamic interplay of genetic, environmental and psychological factors. If you believe that being forty, fifty or sixty constitutes being old, then regardless of anything else, you will assuredly feel and act accordingly. For how we think and what we truly believe profoundly affect our bodily functions and influence our ability to handle change.

In 1900 the life expectancy of the average British woman was about fifty years. Today, women in this country have a reasonably good chance of reaching the age of seventy-five. This means that a forty-five-year-old woman has probably another thirty years, or more than half of her adult life, yet to live. From these figures it is evident that the menopause, rather than being the beginning of the end, should be viewed in its true perspective, as a normal transition and a new beginning in the middle of adult life – a time to pause and evaluate what we have done with our lives, but more important, what we hope, plan and expect to accomplish during the many potentially rewarding years that lie ahead.

Is the menopause the same thing as the 'change of life'?

Not exactly. Although these terms are frequently interchanged, the word menopause simply means the permanent cessation of all menstruation as ovarian function declines. The so-called change of life represents the sum total of all normal hormonal readjustments, from the gradual decline in oestrogen production through the body's adaptation when it reaches a new and different state of hormonal balance. In most women the change of life (menopausal years or climacteric) usually spans a four- to six-year period, whereas the actual menopause is only an isolated event in this normal physiological transition.

How can you know when you are beginning the menopausal years?

Trying to pinpoint the beginning of the menopausal years is as difficult as deciding at what moment a girl becomes a woman. Since it takes years for the ovaries to withdraw all hormonal support, early symptoms related to decreasing oestrogen levels may initially be very subtle. Women who fully expect to 'fall apart' as soon as they hit forty naturally blame every change in mood, feeling of depression or vague ache and pain previously taken in stride on the 'change'.

Actually, the first real indication that the ovaries are beginning to slow down is usually a change in menstrual pattern. For most women these menstrual irregularities commonly start between forty-five and fifty, but in a few instances they can begin as early as thirty-five or as late as fifty-five.

In what way are your periods likely to change?

They frequently become increasingly unpredictable. A few women will experience an abrupt cessation of all menstruation. Others will tend to have lighter periods that gradually become further apart until they cease altogether.

Some women, however, do experience more distressing irregularity. In these instances, length of flow, amount of bleeding, as well as intervals between periods can be extremely variable. Thus it is not too unusual to have one heavy period, whereas the following period may be relatively light. Length of menstrual cycle can also fluctuate, with periods coming as frequently as twenty-one to twenty-four days alternating with a delay of six to eight weeks or longer.

How can you be sure whether that irregular bleeding is really normal?

Other than checking with your doctor, there is no way to be absolutely certain. Nonetheless, there are certain types of bleeding that should be considered abnormal until proved otherwise: bleeding or spotting recurring at intervals of less than twenty-one days, persistently heavy, flooding periods or bleeding lasting longer than eight days. In addition, any spotting after intercourse or the sudden reappearance of bleeding after having seen nothing for six months or longer should also be evaluated by your doctor.

How long do these menstrual irregularities usually last?

Anywhere from a few months up to one, two and even three years. If it has been twelve months or more since your last menstrual flow, you can now consider your periods to be permanently over. Any recurrence of bleeding or spotting after twelve months should not be considered normal.

When is it safe to stop using birth control?

If you are not on birth-control pills and are still menstruating (no matter how irregular your periods may be), ovulation and pregnancy are still possible. Your ovaries may be slowing down, but they haven't given up yet. Using contraceptive protection will also relieve you of unnecessary anxiety when periods are skipped or delayed.

As a general rule, if you are forty-eight or over and have had no periods for at least six months, you are probably safe from pregnancy. If you are younger than forty-eight, it is best to continue using some form of birth control unless it has been twelve months or more since your last period.

For the older woman taking the pill, periods will probably continue to be regular as long as the uterine lining can still respond to hormonal stimulation. It is thus possible for a woman to have artificially induced periods beyond the menopause.

When your periods finally do stop, does that mean your ovaries no longer function?

Not necessarily. The ovaries continue to produce some oestrogen for ten, fifteen and even twenty years after all periods have ceased. Every woman has her own biological timetable. For example, a woman may stop menstruating at age fifty and yet at age sixty her vaginal and vulvar tissues may be comparable to those of a much younger woman because of small but continuous oestrogen stimulation. In contrast, a woman whose ovaries retire at an earlier age may already show thinning of the vulvar and vaginal tissues within five years after her last period.

In general, most women continue to produce some ovarian oestrogen for at least ten to fifteen years after they have stopped menstruating. For this reason gynaecologists when performing a hysterectomy on a menopausal woman will spare normal ovaries whenever possible. Preserving the ovaries prevents a too abrupt loss of oestrogen and thereby allows the body to effect a smoother hormonal readjustment in its own time. There is still, of course, oestrogen from adrenal gland sources, but the output is usually too minimal to exert any appreciable effect on the breasts and genitalia.

What about other menopausal symptoms?

For 20 per cent of women the cessation of menstruation may be the only apparent sign of having been through the menopause. Another 65 per cent of women, although occasionally bothered with menopausal systems, will be able to cope with them effectively with minimal help. For the remaining 15 per cent, however, true menopausal symptoms such as hot flushes, sweats, insomnia, tingling of the hands and feet, headaches, occasional heart palpitations and fatigue may be sufficiently distressing to warrant appropriate treatment and counsel.

Are hot flushes really common?

Next to menstrual irregularities, hot flushes head the list of menopausal complaints in four out of five women. Although not the least bit serious, hot flushes can be disconcerting. One moment you can be cool and comfortable and in the next over-whelmed with a spreading sensation of fiery heat from the waist up, accompanied by drenching perspiration and a marked flush-ing of the face and neck. Hot flushes can be infrequent and dis-appear altogether within a few weeks. In other women, they can occur ten to fifteen times a day, lasting up to a full minute and persist for months.

For some perverse reason, hot flushes also take great delight in striking after hours. A woman who has hot flushes during the day may still spend most of the night throwing off the covers and rushing to the nearest window. Fortunately for all concerned (including bed mates who also lose sleep), frequent and bother-some hot flushes are among the most easily controlled of all menopausal symptoms (more about this later).

How does a decrease in oestrogen cause hot flushes?

By upsetting the hormonal balance between the ovary and the hormone headquarters (pituitary and hypothalamus) in the base of the brain. (See Chapter 5.) Try imagining for a moment a giant seesaw. On one side are the pituitary hormones (FSH and LH); on the other are the ovarian hormones (oestrogen and progesterone). For thirty-five years or so, regular menstrual cycles have depended upon the pituitary and ovarian hormones seesawing back and forth in perfect harmony. Thus, each time the ovaries produced more oestrogen, down went the level of pituitary hormones; when the ovaries put out less oestrogen, up went the level of pituitary hormones.

But now as the ovaries begin slowing down during the menopausal years, this beautifully balanced seesaw is thrown off kilter. With less and less oestrogen being produced by the ovaries, the pituitary responds by pouring out five, ten or even a hundred times more FSH than ever before in a desperate attempt to stir up the sluggish ovaries. In no time at all the hypothalamus also becomes affected.

What does the hypothalamus have to do with hot flushes and other menopausal symptoms?

Since the hypothalamus, or master gland, is ultimately responsible for the smooth functioning of the pituitary, it too becomes irritated by lack of sufficient oestrogen to balance the hormonal seesaw. As the hypothalamus also controls such bodily functions as sleep, heat regulation, energy levels and the vast network of special nerves that feed into every organ and blood vessel (autonomic nervous system), it is little wonder that temporary disturbances in this important control centre can precipitate such a variety of symptoms.

Thus hot flushes, tingling sensations, insomnia, heart palpitations and occasional migrainelike headaches can frequently be traced to temperamental outbursts of an oestrogen-hungry hypothalamus. In addition, intermittent fatigue after relatively minor physical exertion may also be the result of sporadic malfunction of this master gland.

Do the 15 per cent who are severely bothered with menopausal symptoms experience all of these problems?

Heavens, no. No woman will ever have all of these problems or even most of them. Moreover, menopausal symptoms are not constant sources of irritation. Even in the absence of any specific hormonal treatment or oestrogen replacement, there will be intervals of complete comfort followed eventually by permanent relief, usually within three to five years, as the body readjusts to a different hormonal tempo.

Why, then, do some women become tense and irritable?

Physical stress as such as certainly one factor. If, for example, you are intermittently seized with devastating hot flushes, have trouble sleeping at night and suffer from recurrent migrainelike headaches, is it any wonder that at times you may be tense and irritable?

Headaches, especially the ones described as 'sick headaches', which seem to radiate all the way down to the toes and last forever, are occasionally sources of real apprehension. A woman so afflicted may well believe that she is losing her mind.

The fact remains that symptoms truly related to an oestrogen deficiency will respond to oestrogen therapy. Not so for other problems.

What other problems?

The menopause unfortunately coincides with 'middle age', which in itself can be a trying period especially for the biologically oriented woman.

For example, the woman who has attached too much importance to being youthful and sexually attractive may regard the menopausal years as a prologue to old age, with its attendant loss of everything she considers worthwhile. If, in addition, her life interest has revolved around being a wife and homemaker, her apprehension can be further aggravated by a husband frequently too busy with work to give her the reassurance and attention she needs. Children, if any, are likely to be approaching maturity and anxious to set out on their own. Seemingly no longer needed by either children or husband and lacking any real appreciation of her individual worth, she may view her situation with dread and anxiety. Thus, emotional, psychological and sexual maladjustments hitherto submerged in a sea of activity may now bubble to the surface and erroneously be blamed on the 'change'.

The woman who has not borne children, who is unmarried and who has had little or no sexual experience may not be spared her own reactions to the change of life. She may be all the more upset if she was unaware that her self-image included her capacity to procreate. Hence the shock of finding herself upset by the change of life can be more disconcerting than the symptoms of the change themselves. Difficulties at work or with relations and friends can often be precipitated at this stage, and they may be quite bewildering if their cause is not immediately obvious.

What about sexuality in the woman over fifty?

Assuming that you have a compatible partner, your enjoyment of the sex act during or after the menopausal years will depend upon your previous coital experiences, your mental and emotional attitude toward love making and your self-image. If, for example, you believe that advancing age or perhaps the surgical removal of some female organ makes you less sexually desirable, then your capacity to enjoy coitus will be adversely affected. Yet sexual drive or libido in women is only partially dependent on functioning ovaries or the presence of oestrogen. Psychological factors play a far greater role.

In brief, feeling sexy and being able to perform sexually are not limited by age or lack of female hormones. Women can enjoy sexual intercourse and remain orgasmic all the days of their life. In fact, for some women, sex is even better after the menopause.

In what way can sex be better after the menopause?

When pregnancy is no longer possible, many women experience a renewed interest in sex. Furthermore, by the time most women reach their middle fifties, major family responsibilities are frequently over. Thus, with less worry, more spare time, and perhaps financial security at last realized, many women can enjoy sex on a more mature and emotionally gratifying plane.

Why, then, do some women withdraw from sex as they grow older?

There are any number of reasons. Even in this supposedly enlightened age, sex is still popularly regarded as the sole prerogative of the 'young'. For the older couple who perhaps grew up with this misconception, feelings of guilt or shame because of wanting or needing sex may gradually suppress all overt sexuality.

For other women, the marital bed may never have been a source of joy and delight. After years of personal sexual maladjustment or consistent lack of gratification because of a clumsy and inept husband, advancing age may now serve as an attractive and legitimate excuse to shy away from further contact.

One must also remember that as a woman becomes older, her partner is also ageing. In men over fifty-five especially, psychological impotence or repeated difficulty in obtaining or sustaining an erection invariably leads to complete abandonment of coitus. This is indeed unfortunate for the woman desiring physical intimacy. Then too, in this age category many women are widowed or divorced. Frequently considered too old by society's double standards to find a suitable mate, the older divorcee or widow desiring sexual activity must either suppress her feelings or find an alternate outlet. The fact that many women resort to masturbation under these circumstances is certainly understandable.

However, in women who have the opportunity for a satisfying sexual relationship, local genital changes as a result of oestrogen deficiency can create problems during intercourse.

How does a lack of oestrogen affect the vulva, vagina and uterus?

It is important to realize that changes such as thinning and loss of elasticity in the vulvar, vaginal and uterine tissues occur only after a long and significant lack of oestrogen. Therefore, unlike other menopausal symptoms (hot flushes, etc.) genital organ changes occur much later. It may be as long as five to fifteen years after the menopause before any of the genital changes become apparent. Much depends upon how well the ovaries continue to function and whether or not supplemental oestrogen is taken.

With regard to the external genitalia (vulva), pubic hair becomes sparse and there is a gradual loss of fatty tissue. The lips (labia) become thin and flat and lose some of their elasticity. The clitoris, which previously was partially covered and protected by the labia, subsequently becomes more exposed. Although this now makes the clitoris appear relatively larger and more prominent, it too actually decreases in size.

Lack of oestrogen also causes the uterus to shrink in size and the vagina to undergo atrophic changes in the postmenopausal woman. In time, therefore, with thinning of the vaginal walls, loss of elasticity, and a decrease in blood supply to the area, the vagina becomes shorter, narrower and less capable of producing adequate lubrication during sexual excitement.

In what way can these local genital changes interfere with sexual enjoyment?

If the vaginal opening becomes relatively smaller and in some cases insufficiently lubricated, penile entry may be uncomfortable. Decreased elasticity of the vaginal walls also prevents the proper dilatation and expansion of the vagina. This in itself can make attempts at deeper penile penetration a potential source of discomfort.

When there is also marked thinning of the vaginal tissues, repeated penile thrusts can irritate the nearby urethra and bladder. Under these circumstances and particularly in elderly women, burning on urination and bladder spasms may be noticed immediately after intercourse. (See Chapter 13.)

During extended intercourse, a few women may even complain of clitoral irritation. In the postmenopausal woman whose clitoris is relatively more exposed because of labial atrophy, this exquisitely sensitive organ now becomes vulnerable to more direct stimulation during coitus. Needless to say, too intense, too prolonged, and too direct stimulation, rather than being exciting, can actually be distressing and unpleasant.

Less commonly, acutely painful uterine cramping during orgasm, and particularly in women past sixty, can be another reason for avoiding coital contact. Although the exact cause of this phenomenon is not completely understood, it can be corrected by appropriate hormonal therapy.

The maintenance of a fairly active sex life in the postmenopausal woman will definitely help avoid some of these problems during intercourse.

How can having sex avoid sex problems?

Even when there are vaginal atrophic changes, there is nothing like regular intercourse to help keep the vagina dilated and flexible. Vaginal lubrication, although decreased in amount, may still be sufficient to permit easy penile penetration. If, however, lubrication is insufficient, K-Y lubricating jelly (nonprescription) applied around the vaginal opening prior to coitus can be helpful.

But despite these measures, irritation and discomfort during or following coitus has made more than one woman with a healthy sex drive and a capable partner finally desist from further attempts at intercourse.

Fortunately, however, no woman need resign herself to a life of celibacy or tolerate unpleasant physical symptoms because of waning ovarian function. Menopausal and postmenopausal problems can usually be effectively treated.

What can be done about menopausal and postmenopausal problems?

Regardless of whether a woman is just beginning the menopausal years or is several years past menopause, symptoms and distress referable to an oestrogen deficiency can be immeasurably helped by hormone replacement therapy (HRT) with oestrogen alone or oestrogen and progestogen combined.

As research into hormone replacement therapy is still continuing, your doctor may well choose to refer you to one of the few specialist HRT clinics.

What can a woman expect from hormone replacement therapy?

Contrary to what many women believe, taking oestrogen will neither delay the onset of the menopause nor prolong this normal period of transition. The primary purpose of oestrogen replacement during the menopausal years is to help women go through this temporary phase more smoothly and to retard and perhaps even prevent the later development of other oestrogen-related deficiency problems. With or without supplemental oestrogen, the body will still follow its own biological timetable and adapt normally and naturally to waning ovarian function.

Women who expect oestrogen to stop the clock, or prevent hair from turning grey, or skin from wrinkling, will be sorely disappointed. As wonderful as oestrogen is, the secret of perpetual youth has yet to be discovered. Nevertheless, if a true oestrogen deficiency does exist, oestrogen can help keep the skin, hair and blood vessels in better health. Breast tissue will also keep its firmness and elasticity longer than it would otherwise. Taking oestrogen will also help avoid the redistribution of fat, or that 'middle-age spread', provided, of course, that you watch your diet and exercise regularly.

Other complaints during the menopausal years, such as excessive weight gain, lapses of memory, emotional instability and loss of sexual interest, are rarely the result of hormonal deficiency of itself.

How can oestrogen help in the early menopausal years?

Hot flushes and sweats in particular can frequently be eliminated or markedly reduced in frequency and intensity. Less common complaints, such as tingling sensations, headaches, insomnia and heart palpitations, can also be controlled if they are truly related to an oestrogen deficiency. Thus, in many instances, nervousness, irritation and even depression stemming from these physical stresses can be relieved by oestrogen.

In cases where various psychosomatic complaints masquerade as hormonal deficiencies, oestrogen therapy may prove disappointing. In women who manifest extreme anxiety or nervousness (not related to oestrogen deficiency), the temporary use of tranquillizers or mild sedatives can afford needed relief.

Can hormone replacement therapy ever increase a woman's sex drive?

Only indirectly. If there are times when your sexual desire is low because of hot flushes and such, oestrogen can help by making you more comfortable physically. Even the most sensuous woman can be an unenthusiastic lover when she feels out of sorts. Other than that, oestrogen is no panacea for a sagging libido, nor will it transform a previously unresponsive woman into an orgasmic nymphomaniac.

For the older woman, however, who is involuntarily celibate because of genital atrophic changes, oestrogen therapy can really improve her sex life.

How can oestrogen help postmenopausal sexual problems?

It is truly amazing how oestrogen replacement therapy can re-vitalize atrophic vaginal and vulvar tissues in the older woman. Within a remarkably short time the vaginal walls become thicker, more pliant and easier to stretch. Fatty tissue previously lost from the labial folds can be partially regained. Thus, with better vulvar padding the clitoris can once again be protected from too direct and oftentimes irritating stimulation. In addition, with more blood now coursing through these tissues, effective vaginal lubrication during sexual excitement occurs more rapidly and lasts longer. A better blood supply to the entire genital area also intensifies and prolongs a woman's sexual response.

Are birth-control pills useful for controlling menopausal symptoms?

Where there is still a possibility of pregnancy, the use of oral-contraceptive pills in the premenopausal woman can be helpful not only in regulating periods, but also in controlling symptoms such as hot flushes. However, by the time most women reach fifty, the chance of impregnation is fairly remote so that most doctors favour using less potent oestrogen therapy to control menopausal symptoms.

How do birth-control pills differ from other types of hormone replacement therapy?

Birth-control pills (either combined or sequential, see Chapter 16) are synthetic preparations and contain relatively high doses of oestrogen in order to prevent ovulation. The fact that high doses of synthetic oestrogen can be associated with unpleasant side effects, including the possible risk of blood-clotting problems, makes their use totally unnecessary in women who are no longer concerned about the possibility of pregnancy.

For the older woman who needs only to supplement her waning oestrogen in order to control distressing menopausal symptoms, small doses of oestrogen from natural sources are far superior, safer and better tolerated than any birth-control pill.

How is oestrogen therapy usually given?

When it comes to menopausal symptoms, oestrogens extracted from natural (animal and plant) sources rather than synthetic preparations seem to provide the most relief. Oestrogen is usually given by mouth on a cycle basis (three weeks on medication and one week off). How much you need will depend upon the severity of your symptoms. During the week off medication you should not have any appreciable return of menopausal symptoms. If you are no longer having periods, taking oestrogen cyclically rather than continuously will also help prevent excessive stimulation of the uterine lining, which can cause irregular bleeding.

To avoid the results of over-stimulation of the uterine lining, some doctors prefer to give a three-week course which includes a progestogen for five days. This ensures proper withdrawal bleeding during the week off medication. So the HRT regimen chosen for you may give you regular light periods.

Oestrogen by injection, on the other hand, is much less commonly used for several reasons: it requires frequent visits to your doctor, the medication is more expensive and, most important, the effects are less predictable than with oestrogen taken orally. For the most part, oestrogen by injection is usually reserved for the rare woman who cannot tolerate or properly absorb oral medication.

What about oestrogen in the form of creams or suppositories?

Although oestrogen in cream or suppository (pessary) form can be locally absorbed, oral oestrogen is far more effective in rejuvenating vaginal and vulvar tissues. Nonetheless, these topical applications are helpful in treating relatively minor vaginal or vulvar problems in oestrogen-deficient women. Not infrequently their only complaint may be occasional vaginal dryness and itching (not necessarily associated with intercourse). In these cases, intermittent applications when necessary of an oestrogenic vaginal cream may be sufficient to provide prompt and complete relief.

Medicinal oestrogen products, however, are available only by prescription and should not be confused with cosmetic creams containing oestrogen. By comparison, these so-called hormone creams sold for beautifying purposes contain only minimal amounts of oestrogen.

Are there any problems associated with hormone replacement therapy?

When taken as prescribed, menopausal hormone therapy is both safe and effective. At times, however, over-stimulation of the uterine lining by oestrogen can cause irregular bleeding. Although this is no cause for alarm, it may raise the question of whether the unexpected bleeding is the direct result of hormone therapy or caused by an unsuspected uterine polyp or other growth. As mentioned earlier, oestrogen of and by itself does not cause cancer. Nevertheless, the fact that cancer of the uterine lining (see Chapter 23) is more prevalent among older women makes any unexpected bleeding or spotting a matter that deserves prompt evaluation. At times, simply lowering the oestrogen dose or temporarily stopping all medication will resolve the bleeding problem. More commonly, your doctor will probably suggest other tests or even a D and C just to make certain that all is well.

In any event, never increase your oestrogen dose on the mistaken belief that if a little oestrogen makes you feel good, more oestrogen will make you feel great. Too much oestrogen can, in addition, cause occasional breast tenderness and engorgement.

How long can a woman stay on HRT?

If oestrogen makes a woman feel and look better and there are no contraindications to its use, oestrogen can be taken indefinitely. Apart from controlling menopausal symptoms and keeping the genital tissues in good condition, oestrogen may also be a factor in protecting women against various degenerative diseases, such as hardening of the arteries, heart attacks, strokes, arthritic changes and softening of the bones (osteoporosis).

Needless to say, not all doctors are in agreement about how long oestrogen replacement therapy should be given. Regardless of their individual philosophy, each woman should be evaluated and treated on the basis of her own specific needs.

In the final analysis, the menopause need not be a time of dread or apprehension for any woman. Much can be and is being done. Hormone replacement therapy as well as other medication can handle the temporary physical stresses. Equally important, rapidly changing and more realistic attitudes regarding the role of women and expanding options for creative living are also going to temper the psychological and emotional stresses of this period. It is already an undeniable fact that career women or those having interests in addition to their roles as homemakers are the ones most likely to breeze through the menopausal years.

Perhaps when all women realize that their ability to live fully rewarding and sexually gratifying lives does not depend upon the reproductive function, the myths surrounding the menopausal years will at long last be laid to rest.

22. Breast Problems: Benign and Malignant

Thousands and thousands of British women go to their doctors each year to report breast lumps and most of the different kinds of lumps are entirely harmless. Only a small proportion of women – that means approximately nineteen thousand out of the seventeen million odd at risk each year – are discovered to have cancer of the breast. Yet if cancer is found in the early stages, it can very likely be cured. Doctors are concerned that women should seek early treatment, as with modern drugs, surgery and radiotherapy, they know that the mortality rate can be reduced.

It is not enough to rely on being examined during your occasional visits to your doctor. You as a woman should become an expert in checking your breasts. Meticulous routine self-examination is the best way to know what is normal for you.

How often should you examine your breasts?

Regardless of your age, make it a point to examine your breasts at least once a month. If you are still menstruating regularly, the best time to check your breasts is during the week following your period. Examinations done premenstrually or during your period can be less reliable because of breast engorgement or tenderness. You should also pick a time and place when you can be undisturbed and unhurried. Although many women period-ically check their breasts while bathing or taking a shower, this in itself is insufficient to ensure a thorough examination.

What is the technique for thorough breast self-examination?

Under good lighting, strip to the waist and either sit or stand in front of a mirror. With your arms resting naturally at your sides, observe both breasts for any differences in size, shape and con-tour. As some of you may have noticed, one breast might be somewhat fuller. This may be perfectly normal. Needless to say, what we are concerned with is the detection of differences that were not previously observable. Pay particular attention to the nipples. Do they look the same? Are they symmetrical and at the same level, or does one nipple seem to be pulled to the side? Unless you have always had an inverted nipple or nipples, the retraction or turning in of one nipple is not normal. Similarly, any dimpling of the breast skin should also be noted. Now raise both arms overhead and repeat the same observations. Elevating the arms exposes the undersurface of the breasts and further helps detect any changes in contour or symmetry.

Following this simple mirror inspection, the next and most important step is feeling or palpating the breasts.

How should you palpate your breasts?

Since any breast irregularity can be detected more easily by allowing the breast tissue to flatten against the chest wall, this part of the examination is best done lying down. If your breasts are heavy or pendulous, placing a small pillow beneath the shoulder on the side to be examined will also help distribute the weight of the breast more evenly along the chest wall.

To examine the left breast, lie on your back with your left hand beneath your head and your elbow resting comfortably out to the side. With the right hand, using only the flat surface of the four fingers, palpate the breast tissue between your fingers and the chest wall with a gentle rotary motion. Although there are various ways to ensure a thorough examination, if you think of your breast as representing the face of a clock with each hour equal to one segment of breast, you are less likely to overlook any irregularity. For example, begin at twelve o'clock and work your way from the outside of the breast to and including the nipple. Then move on to one o'clock and through the remaining ten segments, always starting from the outer edge of the breast and moving towards the nipple. To examine the right breast, repeat the process using the left hand.

In addition, check each nipple for any discharge by gently squeezing it between the thumb and index finger.

What do normal breasts feel like?

Since breasts vary in texture and consistency depending on your age, hormone levels and amount of fatty tissue, don't be discouraged if initially you can't tell for sure what you are feeling. Small breasts, for example, may feel more glandular, whereas large breasts may feel soft and doughy. Other women may even notice tiny gritty areas scattered throughout both breasts. In any event, regular self-examination will allow you to become familiar with what your breasts feel like normally. Thus, with practice you will be able to detect any lump, thickening or irregularity that may subsequently appear.

Do breast lumps occur more frequently in certain breast areas?

Although a breast tumour or cyst, whether benign or malignant, can occur in any area of either breast, many breast cancers first appear in the upper outer quadrant. This corresponds to the area between twelve and three o'clock on the left breast and between nine and twelve o'clock on the right breast. For this reason, it is especially important that these areas be meticulously examined.

The fact that breast problems are so prevalent also makes it important to know something about the three most common breast lesions: cystic mastitis (fibrocystic disease), fibroadenomas and cancer.

What is cystic mastitis?

A common benign (noncancerous) condition characterized by the presence of multiple small cysts interspersed with mild fibrous thickening of the breast tissue. The cause of these cysts is not completely understood, but their development does seem to depend upon cyclic oestrogen stimulation of the breast tissue. Fibrocystic disease affects well over 30 per cent of all women during the reproductive years. However, with decreasing oestrogen levels after the menopause, the incidence of this condition drops rapidly.

What kind of problems does cystic mastitis cause?

Sometimes none at all. It all depends on the size and number of cysts and how much breast tissue is involved. In many women the cysts may be so small as to go completely unnoticed. However, where several small cysts are clustered together they may become more prominent and quite tender premenstrually because of fluid retention. A larger single cyst in particular may cause more local discomfort because of a rapid distention of its capsule with fluid. In these instances, such a cyst may enlarge noticeably prior to menstruation and shrink with the onset of the period. The fact that these cysts can cause breast tenderness, as well as fluctuate in size depending upon the phase of the menstrual cycle, is an important distinguishing feature of the condition.

Can these cysts ever disappear spontaneously?
Tiny cysts may disappear, but larger ones will frequently persist.

Can anything be done for breast discomfort caused by cystic mastitis?
When fibrocystic areas become sore, tender and sensitive to the touch because of premenstrual fluid accumulation, restriction of one's salt intake and sleeping in a good uplift bra during the week before menstruation will definitely help. If symptoms are more severe, ice packs applied to the breasts two or three times a day for five to ten minutes or even diuretics when necessary can give additional relief. More recently, the use of an oestrogen–progestogen combination has proved remarkably effective in relieving the distress associated with fibrocystic mastitis in a few selected cases.

If, however, there is one dominant lump or cyst, more definitive treatment is usually necessary.

Why is that?
Needless to say, the presence of any persistent lump or mass, especially if it is solitary, should never be ignored. The lump may feel and act like a benign cyst, but a definite diagnosis cannot be made by palpation alone.

Then too, breast cancer can coexist in the same breast with fibrocystic mastitis. On occasion a large, single, benign cyst may even overlie a beginning breast cancer, thus obscuring its presence and preventing early detection by palpation. For these reasons it is important to establish a definite diagnosis when dealing with any breast lesion.

How are these benign cysts sometimes treated?
Until recently, surgeons routinely excised any breast lump, cyst or irregularity to establish a diagnosis. Today needle aspiration, that is, draining the cyst through a small puncture, is more often

used to establish the diagnosis without the need of resorting to surgery. Many surgeons carry out this procedure at a woman's first visit to their office or outpatient clinic for diagnosis. While needle aspiration is not very pleasant it does save a woman the distress of waiting for several days between seeing the surgeon and being called to hospital for biopsy.

If the cyst disappears completely following withdrawal of its contained fluid, it was obviously not cancerous and a biopsy is unnecessary. The fact that some women may develop several such cysts during their lifetime makes needle aspiration under these circumstances preferable to repeated excisional biopsies. If, however, following aspiration, the cyst remains palpable or is in any other way suspicious, further studies are necessary.

Can needle aspiration of breast cysts ever be harmful?

Even if the supposed cyst should prove to be a solid tumour and is diagnosed on subsequent biopsy as breast cancer, an unsuccessful attempt at needle aspiration will not cause malignant cells to spread. Needle aspiration of breast cysts (whether or not totally successful) is a safe procedure that is being used by more and more surgeons.

Suppose the breast lump is solid and not cystic, what then?

Here again, much useful information can be gleaned by physical examination of the breast mass in question. If the lump is firm, well circumscribed and *freely movable* within the breast tissue somewhat like a marble, chances are excellent that it is probably a fibroadenoma or at least a benign lesion.

What is a fibroadenoma?

A common benign breast tumour usually found in women under thirty-five and not infrequently in teenagers. Most fibroadenomas occur singly and vary in size from 1 to 2 inches (2·5–5 centimetres) in diameter. On occasion, however, they can grow larger and even be multiple, but this is rare. Since they are not tender and do not cause symptoms, they are often discovered inadvertently by the woman or else detected on a routine physical examination.

What can be done about a fibroadenoma?

If the nodule is discovered in an adolescent girl, local excision may be postponed until later. Premature removal of such a lump in a teenager could conceivably interfere with the proper development of the breast. If, however, the lump progressively enlarges or is discovered in a teenager with fully developed breasts or in an older woman, most doctors will recommend an excisional biopsy (removal of the entire nodule through a small incision).

Why is removal of a fibroadenoma usually advised?

Despite the fact that fibroadenomas never become cancerous, there is no way of being completely sure that the lump in question is indeed a fibroadenoma short of actually examining the tissue under a microscope. Deferring surgery or 'watchful waiting' could in these instances (and especially if the women is over twenty-five)' be detrimental. More than one cancer has physically masqueraded as a clinically benign lesion.

Nevertheless, there are certain diagnostic techniques that can be extremely helpful in distinguishing between benign and cancerous tumours.

What diagnostic techniques?

Recent refinements in breast X-ray techniques (mammography) and thermography are beginning to make possible the detection of early breast cancers.

Thermography – what's that?

A simple and rapid method that detects temperature differences within the breast tissue. Malignant tumours, because of accelerated cellular activity, will emit more heat than normal breast tissue. Thus, by means of an infra-red scanning apparatus, any subtle changes in heat production within the breast can be localized and visualized on a special screen.

Thermography requires no exposure to radiation, is (of course) entirely painless and is effective irrespective of breast size. Unfortunately its accuracy is limited. Most studies report that 85 per cent of existing breast malignancies are spotted by thermography – but that means that 15 in every 100 are missed. Less serious but nonetheless terrifying for the patients are the number of 'false positive' readings. 'Hot spots' suggesting a malignancy have been found in up to 35 per cent of women who turned out to have benign breast lesions, and up to 15 per cent of women who had entirely normal breasts. Exactly why this should be is not yet known.

What about the new breast X-ray techniques?

Xeroradiography of the breasts is currently the best new ancillary method for detecting very early breast cancer. In contrast to conventional breast X-rays (mammograms) xeroradiography can pinpoint minute malignant changes with far greater accuracy, speed and reliability than ever previously imagined. In addition to minimal exposure to X-ray, breast prints by this technique can be processed within ninety seconds and are far easier to interpret. The entire examination rarely takes longer than twenty minutes.

In many instances xeroradiography and conventional breast X-rays have detected cancers prior to their being physically evident. In one particular clinical study in which 132 breast cancers were discovered, forty-four would have been completely missed if breast X-rays had been omitted. Even more startling is the growing evidence that some breast cancers may actually exist for as long as two to eight years before being palpable as a tiny (less than one-half inch), discrete lump or thickening.

But as accurate as xeroradiography can be (close to 90 per cent), breast tumours that are palpable on physical examination may on rare occasion go undetected radiographically. Needless to say, if the battle against breast cancer is to be won, reliance must still be placed on regular, meticulous breast examinations, ancillary diagnostic methods (xeroradiography, etc.), plus immediate biopsy of any suspicious area.

Is breast cancer really that common?

Within the next twelve months approximately 12 000 women in Britain will die of breast cancer and an estimated 19 000 new cases will be diagnosed. It is the most common form of cancer affecting women. Cancer of the breast is generally found in women over the age of twenty-five, but far more commonly in women over forty-five.

Yet despite extensive surgical operations, super-refined radio-therapy and new wonder drugs, the mortality rate from breast cancer is not declining. If anything, it may be slowly increasing.

Why have new kinds of treatment failed to improve survival rates?

For the simple reason that many cancers when first diagnosed have already spread (metastasized) beyond the confines of the local lymph nodes. Although the new and sophisticated diagnostic methods can detect distant tumour spread, small metastatic lesions may occasionally be missed. Thus, at the time of initial treatment for the primary breast tumour, clinically unsuspected cancer may already exist elsewhere in the body. Under these circumstances no amount of breast surgery or radiotherapy, regardless of how effective in eradicating the original (primary) tumour, can effect a cure.

How long can a breast cancer remain localized?

Unfortunately there is no way of determining this with any degree of accuracy. Generally speaking – but there are always exceptions – the smaller the tumour the greater the likelihood that the cancer is still confined to the breast proper.

If untreated, however, malignant cells will invariably spread to other parts of the body in time.

Where and how does cancer of the breast spread?

Most breast cancers will initially spread to adjacent lymph nodes, which act as temporary filters or traps for the malignant cells. Exactly where the tumour seeds (spreads) depends in part on its

location. Thus, for example, a cancer in the upper outer quadrant of the breast will usually spread to the nearby axillary
(underarm) nodes. Tumours situated closer to the nipple or
along the inner aspect of the breast tend to involve the nodes
lying behind the breast bone (internal mammary lymph nodes).
However, owing to the fact that the lymphatic drainage of the
breast is such an intricate, interconnecting system of tiny capillarylike channels, tumour cells can seed almost anywhere and at
times even spread to the opposite breast and axillary area.

In more advanced cases, malignant tumour cells can spread to
the lungs, bone, liver and other organs.

What, then, is considered an early breast cancer?

A cancer that is potentially curable – that is strictly localized in
the breast or else involves only the local lymph nodes of that
breast. In other words, all other studies such as chest X-rays,
bone surveys (simple X-rays of the bony skeleton), and other
available diagnostic methods to detect instant spread should be
unequivocally negative.

Theoretically, therefore, with no objective evidence of distant
tumour spread (metastasis), surgical removal of the cancerous
tissue and/or radiation therapy to destroy the local cancer should
be 'curative'. Needless to say, before any potentially curative
treatment is undertaken, tests should be made to determine that
the cancer is indeed early and has not spread beyond the confines
of the area to be treated.

Why should diagnostic studies to determine distant tumour spread be done prior to treatment?

Mastectomy (breast removal) and particularly radical mastectomy is an emotionally and physically devastating experience
for any woman. Therefore, if radical surgery in particular is to
be done, a woman should be reasonably assured that she has a
good chance for potential cure. Many woman (though perhaps
not all women) would prefer to know if their chances of eventual
cure or even many years of life, were small. Given this shattering
news, they would elect to live out their remaining years with

palliative treatment or minimal surgery. What, they might ask, is the point of undergoing radical surgery if the disease has, or even may have, already gone beyond the point where surgery can help?

In the past five years, bone-scanning techniques (radio-nuclide imaging) have proved enormously helpful in pinpointing minute tumour invasion of bony structures. Far more accurate than conventional X-ray pictures (bone surveys), these new scanning techniques can detect cancerous changes months before they ever become obvious by ordinary X-ray methods. In fact, as a result of these screening techniques, it is becoming increasingly apparent that metastatic spread to bone in women with a supposed 'early cancer' is more common than previously believed.

Perhaps as these newer diagnostic techniques become more generally available in hospitals and are used before surgery on patients for whom a strong clinical suspicion of cancer exists, the old operating-theatre routine, 'If it's cancer, we'll just go ahead and do a radical', will come to an end.

What does a radical mastectomy involve?

Until recently the vast majority of early or minimal breast cancers were treated by radical mastectomy. How the individual woman felt about losing her breast, or the possibility of her being physically incapacitated because of a swollen arm or weak shoulder, was immaterial. Radical mastectomy, as originally devised by Dr William Halsted in 1882 was for many years universally considered the only medically acceptable and legitimate treatment for early breast cancer.

It was logical to assume that if breast cancers first spread to the adjacent axillary area, then radical mastectomy – that is, the removal of the entire breast, chest wall muscles (pectoralis major and minor muscles), and all underarm (axillary) lymph nodes – would give a woman the best chance for cure.

In the 1930s, however, with the discovery that a portion of the breast's lymphatic system drains into lymph nodes situated beneath the breast bone (internal mammary nodes), it became apparent that radical mastectomy would fail to cure women surgically if their breast cancer had already spread to these particular nodes. Consequently a few surgeons reasoned that by extending the operation to include removal of the internal mammary lymph nodes, more women would be 'cured'. But follow-up results from the extended radical mastectomy failed to show any significant improvement in survival rates. With few exceptions this extended and traumatic procedure is rarely done nowadays.

Today, a real controversy exists among surgeons regarding what constitutes the best treatment for early breast cancer. From statistics on survival and recurrence rates among women with supposedly early breast cancer, it is apparent that the conventional radical mastectomy as routinely performed on thousands of women each year leaves much to be desired. Even when one quotes the most favourable statistics for radical mastectomy as performed in the United States, 85 per cent of the women with *no* axillary involvement will survive for five years, and in ten years, only 70 per cent will still be living. Among women with cancerous underarm (axillary) nodes at the time of radical mastectomy, the figures drop precipitously to a 60 per cent overall five-year survival rate and a 41 per cent ten-year survival rate.

It is also important to note that among many women who have had no recurrence of the disease ten years or more following radical mastectomy, the microscopic examination of all tissues removed at the time of surgery failed to show any extension of the malignancy beyond the confines of the primary breast tumour. In other words, all adjacent tissues that were sacrificed during the radical mastectomy in these instances were found to be healthy and free of any cancer cells. For this reason many cancer specialists believe that equally good results in terms of survival rates can be effected by less radical surgery in selected women with a clinically early breast cancer.

What other operations can be used for early breast cancer?

Modified radical mastectomy, for one thing. The breast and axillary nodes are removed but the chest wall muscles are preserved. By sparing the pectoral muscles, shoulder and arm strength remain normal and cosmetic deformity is substantially minimized. In other cases the operation is limited to simple mastectomy (removal of the breast only) or partial mastectomy. With regard to women undergoing partial mastectomy or removal of a portion of one breast including the overlying skin, reconstructive surgery at the time of the operation can minimize the deformity to a certain extent. In a few selected women who are emotionally unprepared to accept any of these procedures, a lumpectomy – that is, an excisional biopsy (removal of the entire breast tumour along with a margin of normal tissue) with or without follow-up radiation therapy – is being done.

What about survival rates with these lesser operations?

Among women undergoing a modified radical mastectomy, five- and ten-year survival rates are as good and in some series superior to those achieved by radical mastectomy.

In women with no clinical evidence of axillary node involvement, simple mastectomy (removal of the breast only) and partial mastectomy have effected an 85 per cent five-year survival rate.

Simple excision of the breast lump (lumpectomy) followed by radiation therapy has also brought forth startling statistics. In one series conducted in Finland in 1954, the five-year survival rate in 127 patients so treated was 85 per cent. More recent studies in the United States showed that in women undergoing local excision and radiation, five-year survival rates ranged from 70 to 50 per cent depending upon the absence or presence of clinically evident axillary node involvement. As yet, however, studies on women submitting only to local excision (lumpectomy) followed by radiation therapy are still too limited to be of statistical value.

The controversy among surgeons will continue as to whether any of the lesser methods can consistently equal or better the ten-year survival rates now obtained by radical mastectomy. However, almost all cancer specialists agree that success in terms of curing an early breast cancer depends primarily on the extent of the disease at the time of initial treatment. Some experts even go so far as to say that once the tumour has extended beyond the breast and local lymph nodes, *survival rates* are not affected regardless of the local surgical and/or radiation treatment undertaken. In other words, once the cancer has seeded to distant areas in the body, a woman's chance of *survival* will be essentially the same whether she undergoes a radical mastectomy or a lumpectomy.

Can other factors affect survival rates in breast cancer?

It can never be stressed too strongly that the earlier a breast cancer is detected and treated, the better the chance for cure. And yet, there are so many variables in breast cancer that regardless of the local extent of the disase at the time of diagnosis, no one can predict with any accuracy the eventual outcome for the individual woman. Factors such as size and location of the tumour as well as axillary-node involvement have, of course, important prognostic implications. Then too, breast cancers also differ in type and degree of malignancy. A large bulky tumour, for example, may have a very low potential for early spread, whereas a lump that is barely palpable may on rare occasions have already seeded beyond the confines of the local lymph nodes. Moreover, in some women the breast cancer may be multicentric. This means that in addition to the obvious tumour, there may be small nests of malignant cells elsewhere in the breast which can neither be felt nor seen by X-ray. In such a case, simple excision of the dominant lump would obviously fail to effect a surgical cure.

Perhaps of even greater significance in terms of patient survival is the body's immune system, that is, its inherent ability to fight malignant disease and foreign invaders. Although this is one of the most difficult variables to assess clinically, a functioning immune system may well make the difference between cure or failure in women undergoing identical treatment for identical tumours. Furthermore, certain breast cancers may grow more rapidly because of hormonal stimulation (oestrogen in particular). Other breast malignancies exposed to the same hormonal influence may be totally unaffected or even tend to remain in check. Age as well as general health of the woman also affects the ultimate survival rate.

Aside from these physical and biological variables (of which only a few have been mentioned), there is growing awareness that a woman's psychological and mental attitude towards her illness plays a significant role in the eventual outcome. In ways as yet unknown, attitudes of despair and hopelessness do lessen the body's resistance to malignant disease. On the other hand, there are many documented instances where a positive and optimistic mental outlook and a strong will to live have worked seeming miracles in women who by all objective medical findings had little or no hope left.

Does anyone know what actually causes breast cancer?

Unfortunately no – at least not yet. Nonetheless, there is increasing evidence to indicate that breast cancer may be caused by a particular virus particle. How this virus is acquired or transmitted or if, indeed, a virus is responsible for the various types of breast cancers – these are all matters currently under intensive clinical and research investigation. Much of this evidence is, of course, based on animal studies. For instance, the same virus particles capable of inducing mammary cancer in mice have been recovered in the breast tissue of some women with proved breast cancer. Moreover, these very same virus particles in a few instances have also been recovered in the milk of lactating women with no evidence of breast cancer. The question is therefore being raised – could transmission of these virus particles during breast feeding account for the subsequent development of breast cancer among female offspring as in the case of laboratory mice? This fact has led some investigators to caution women who have these particular virus particles in their milk against breast feeding female offspring. At the moment, however, so few facilities are available for testing human breast milk in this regard that some doctors are simply advising against the breast feeding of any female offspring where there is a family history on either side of breast cancer.

With regard to genetic and hormonal factors that may conceivably play a role in the development of breast cancer, much has yet to be learned. Currently there is no way of accurately pinpointing the woman destined to develop breast cancer. Nonetheless, breast cancer does seem somewhat more prevalent among certain women as compared to others.

Which woman is statistically most likely to develop breast cancer?

The woman most likely to develop breast cancer is Caucasian, between thirty-five and sixty-five, with few or no children, or has postponed pregnancy until after the age of twenty-eight. In addition she probably began menstruating at a relatively early age and possibly had previous breast problems such as cystic mastitis. With regard to family history, having a mother or sister with breast cancer increases a woman's risk of this disease two or three times over that observed in the general female population.

It should be emphasized, however, that the above profile is at best only a general guide. No woman is immune to breast cancer. But by the same token, fulfilling all of the aforementioned criteria does not imply that a woman is destined to develop this malignancy. Suffice it to say, if survival rates for breast cancer are going to improve, all women should be aware of how best to protect themselves.

How can you as a woman protect yourself against breast cancer?

You must take an active role in your own well-being and not rely entirely on periodic examinations by your doctor. Specifically this means monthly examinations. With rare exceptions, almost all early breast cancers are completely painless. Therefore, unless you conscientiously examine yourself regularly, the presence of a breast malignancy may go undetected. Equally important, you should promptly report any lump, thickening, or irregularity regardless of how vague or indefinite it may seem to you. Do not wait to see if it enlarges.

Furthermore, any discharge from the nipple (other than milk in a woman who has recently delivered) is not normal, particularly if only one nipple is involved. Any persistent burning and itching of the nipple or local skin changes involving the nipple area, such as redness, flaking, weeping eruptions and crust or scab formation, can also be warning signs of an early breast cancer. With regard to other skin changes, any dimpling, puckering or reddening over any portion of either breast also demands prompt professional attention.

At present, breast cancer is not only the leading cause of death from cancer among women, but also the most common cause of death among women between the ages of thirty-five and forty-four in England and Wales. So it would be ideal if every woman over the age of twenty-five could also have a xeroradiographic examination of the breasts. For women over thirty-five, such an examination annually would undoubtedly save many lives by detecting minimal breast cancers before they were even physically palpable.

Mass screening of all women on this scale would require the expansion of existing screening facilities into a nation-wide breast-screening programme. This is not feasible with the money and people available. In the meantime, experimental screening centres are aiming to use their limited resources by screening women statistically most likely to be at risk of breast cancer.

If you have early breast cancer, can you have a choice of treatment?

As has just been described, no surgical procedure and/or radiation therapy can guarantee any woman complete cure however minimal her disease. At best, all treatment currently available for early breast cancer carries with it some risk of ultimately being ineffective. Thus, for all practical purposes, nobody really knows, nor can anyone predict which treatment (whether it be radical mastectomy or a procedure as minimal as excisional biopsy) will or will not prove 'curative' for the individual woman with early breast cancer.

Many surgeons still insist that radical mastectomy is the preferred treatment. Other surgeons, and they are becoming increasingly more numerous, favour modified radical mastectomy and in some women simple or even partial mastectomy. Regardless of what you are advised would be the best treatment for your particular situation, only you have the final say. No surgeon can perform any operation without your express, written consent. If you are mentally and emotionally unprepared to undergo extensive breast surgery and are willing to accept the greater risk that some experts believe these lesser procedures may carry, then that is your right as an individual to decide. Too many women have allowed an early and potentially curable breast cancer to spread because they delayed seeking medical attention out of fear and dread that their only option was radical mastectomy. In the final analysis, the best treatment of early breast cancer for the individual woman is not only the eradication of the physical disease but the preservation of a life that she deems worth living.

23. Cancer of the Female Pelvic Organs

No organ in the human body is immune to malignant changes. Each year approximately fourteen thousand women in Britain are found to have a cancer of the female pelvic organs. But whether that malignancy involves the cervix, uterus, ovary, tube, vagina or vulva, cancer is curable if it is discovered early, and there are thousands of women who can personally testify to that fact.

With the fantastic strides being made in cancer research, more has been learned about the cause, treatment and prevention of cancer since 1970 than in the previous five decades. Experts now predict that within our lifetime the mystery of how and why perfectly normal cells become cancerous will be uncovered. Already there is mounting evidence that viruses are implicated in many of the one hundred different types of cancers known to afflict humans, and the same may be true for cancer of the cervix, the most common pelvic malignancy.

Within the next twelve months approximately two-and-a-half thousand British women will die of cervical cancer and an estimated four-and-a-half thousand new cases will be diagnosed. Since the cervix is so accessible to examination and the cervical smear (cytotest) such a simple and effective method of detecting cervical cancer, it is indeed tragic that any women need die of this disease. All too often, reluctance to be examined and the mistaken notion that lack of symptoms means being free from cancer are common stumbling blocks to early detection. In 1970 just about 2 million women in this country had a smear test – and that out of an estimated 17 million women at risk. Ironically, the woman most likely to develop cervical cancer is also the one most apt to avoid periodic examinations even when freely offered.

Which women are most likely to develop cervical cancer?

Cancer of the cervix may one day be considered a venereal disease. As shocking as this statement may be, it is an undeniable fact that sexual intercourse is somehow involved in the development of cervical cancer. Although proof is still lacking, cancer of the cervix may be caused by a sexually transmitted virus – herpes simplex virus type II. (The fact that women with high blood antibody levels to type II herpesvirus do have a greater incidence of cervical cancer as compared to other women lends support to this current theory – see Chapter 11.) Whether or not a virus is ultimately proved responsible, studies have repeatedly shown that the younger a woman is at the time of her first intercourse and the more active her sex life, the greater her chances of developing cancer of the cervix – and of developing it at an early age. The teenager, for example, who begins having frequent intercourse at the age of fifteen or sixteen and especially with multiple partners runs a significantly higher risk of developing cancer within twenty to twenty-five years. On the other hand, a woman who delays her first coitus until after age twenty and limits herself to one partner considerably lessens her risks of ever acquiring the disease. Although no woman is immune, cervical cancer is virtually never seen in nuns or other celibate or homosexual women.

How common is cancer of the cervix?

Currently from two to seven of every one thousand women tested are found to have cancer of the cervix, and most cases are diagnosed between the ages of thirty-five and sixty. Improved techniques for detection and treatment are saving more lives, and the over-all incidence of cervical cancer is gradually decreasing. Yet it is predicted that within the next few years, early cervical cancer will be seen more frequently among younger woman.

Why the predicted increase among younger women?

For several reasons. Since an early and active sex life significantly adds to a woman's chances of ultimately developing cervical cancer, increasing numbers of young women are unwittingly placing themselves in this high-risk category. There's no denying that sexual activity among teenagers and young unmarried women is definitely on the upswing. In addition, the widespread use of the pill, while allowing even greater sexual freedom, is also eliminating the use of the condom and diaphragm as contraceptive methods. Although difficult to prove conclusively, if the cervix is protected from direct contact during sexual intercourse by either a condom or a diaphragm, the risk of cervical cancer may be lessened. Then too, as more doctors and clinics are routinely taking smears (cytotests) from younger women, more early cancers are being detected.

What exactly is an early cervical cancer?

A malignancy involving only the most superficial cells of the cervix without any invasion of the deeper tissues. The malignant changes in early cervical cancer (also known as Stage O, or carcinoma in situ) are so discrete and localized as to be invisible to the naked eye. Consequently the cervix can appear perfectly normal. Equally important, early cervical cancer does not give any warning signs or symptoms. Detection therefore depends upon the microscopic examination of cervical cells by means of a smear or cytotest. (See Chapter 4.)

Fortunately, however, early cervical cancer usually progresses slowly.

How slowly?

It may take from four to ten years or even longer before an early cervical cancer invades the deeper cervical tissues. If diagnosed and treated during this extended preinvasive early stage, cervical cancer is virtually 100 per cent curable. Unfortunately, lack of symptoms makes many women neglect routine check-ups during this early stage.

What are the symptoms of a more advanced cervical cancer?

If the cancer is not diagnosed and treated during the early stage, there is gradual invasion into the deeper layers of the cervix. Although cervical cancer does not have any characteristic symptoms, irregular bleeding as well as spotting after intercourse or douching are among the most common complaints. Not infrequently, infection of the growing cervical tumour can also produce an intermittent foul-smelling blood-tinged vaginal discharge. Proper treatment at this stage can still save many women.

If the cancer remains undiagnosed, it eventually spreads beyond the confines of the cervix to other pelvic organs. Ultimately the vagina, the body of the uterus, the bladder and even the rectum can be invaded. As you can well imagine, the cure rate for these late stages drops precipitously, with the mortality rate well over 50 per cent.

Unlike the early stages of the disease, advanced cervical cancer progresses fairly rapidly. Thus the time between the onset of symptoms (irregular bleeding, etc.) and the terminal stage of the disease is frequently not longer than two or three years if left untreated.

How is cancer of the cervix diagnosed?

Where symptoms are absent and the cervix appears normal, a cytotest (cervical smear) can alert your doctor to a possible early cervical cancer. Nonetheless, whenever a cytotest is reported as abnormal or even positive for malignant cells, other studies are necessary to confirm the existence of cancer. As discussed in Chapter 4, a cytotest of and by itself does not prove or disprove the presence of a cancer. Even if the cervix looks entirely normal, staining it beforehand with a special iodine solution can help outline any areas of abnormal cells. On occasion, the use of a colposcope, an instrument that simply magnifies the surface of the cervix, can also help pinpoint suspicious areas for biopsy purposes. Final confirmation depends entirely on a biopsy.

What is a biopsy?

The surgical removal of tissue for microscopic examination. In the case of the cervix, a 'cone biopsy', involving the removal of a cone-shaped section of the cone-shaped cervix, is often carried out. This gives the pathologist a complete sample of the external cervical tissues to examine, and may act as treatment as well as examination, if later smear tests show that the tissues which were showing signs of pre-malignancy were removed by the cone biopsy.

A cone biopsy is done under a general anaesthetic. The vagina may be packed with gauze for a few hours after surgery to prevent bleeding. Hospital stay will usually be no more than forty-eight hours.

What happens if the biopsy report is positive for cervical cancer?

Recommended treatment will depend not only on the extent of the disease but also on the age of the woman and on whether or not she has completed her family.

If she wants to have children, the cone biopsy itself, or the further removal of the diseased part of the cervix may be all that is needed. The woman can go on and have her children, but she will be kept under close supervision, with smear tests taken at frequent intervals, so that any recurrence can be quickly spotted. The woman so treated must remember that it is only because early cervical cancer is confined to the surface cells and tends to remain confined to these cells for several years, that such conservative treatment is justifiable.

If the woman has completed her family, most surgeons will prefer to 'play safe' by removing the cervix and the uterus: performing a complete hysterectomy. Fortunately, cancer of the cervix does not spread to the ovaries nor is it affected by oestrogen, so the ovaries can be spared and, in later years, oestrogen therapy for menopausal symptoms can still be given with impunity.

How are more advanced cancers of the cervix treated?

If the cancer is still limited to the cervix but has invaded the deeper cervical tissues (Stage 1), there is always the possibility that some tumour cells may have already spread to adjacent pelvic lymph nodes. Treatment of the disease in this stage is usually by radiotherapy or, less commonly, by extensive surgery, including removal of pelvic lymph nodes. Although there are advantages and disadvantages to both treatments, therapy must always be designed for the individual woman. Whichever the treatment, the chances for cure run from 75 to 85 per cent.

With rare exception, more advanced cancers that extend beyond the limits of the cervix are always treated by radiotherapy.

What about cancer of the uterus (endometrial cancer)?

Despite the fact that the body of the uterus can be the site of various rare malignant tumours, cancer of the uterus commonly means a malignancy involving the *lining* of the uterus (endometrium); hence the name, endometrial cancer.

In Britain endometrical cancer accounts for approximately 3500 new cancer cases each year and 1700 deaths annually.

How does endometrial cancer differ from cervical cancer?

In many ways. Symptoms appear early. Growth and spread of the cancer is somewhat slower in advanced stages, and for this reason five-year survival rates are appreciably better than in cervical cancer. All in all, endometrial cancer is less treacherous than cervical cancer. As favourable as these facts may be, however, early detection of endometrial cancer by a cervical smear test is notoriously unreliable. Furthermore, the fact that this malignancy arises within the uterine cavity also makes it impossible either to see or feel on routine pelvic examination. For these reasons more sophisticated detection methods are necessary.

In addition, endometrial, unlike cervical, cancer does not seem related to previous sexual activity. Although the cause of endometrial cancer is still elusive, certain women seem more predisposed to its ultimate development.

Which women are more susceptible?

The women most apt to develop endometrial cancer are usually over fifty, are more likely to have had previously irregular periods, sporadic ovulation and difficulty in becoming pregnant. Equally interesting is the finding that obesity, high blood pressure and diabetes are also more common in women with endometrial cancer. Exactly why this should be is not known. Nevertheless, this particular combination of medical problems coupled with a history of menstrual irregularities and infertility has led experts to believe that endometrical cancer may be linked to some basic genetic and metabolic disturbance. In creasing evidence also indicates that the uterine lining in these women may be hypersensitive to the effects of oestrogen. For example, women who develop endometrial polyps (see Chapter 9) or other benign growths of the uterine lining also run a higher risk of ultimately developing cancer of the endometrium.

What are the symptoms of an endometrial cancer?

Since endometrial cancer is essentially a disease of older women, the most common symptom is spotting or bleeding after the menopause. Approximately 40 per cent of the women who bleed or spot after cessation of all menstruation will be found to have an early uterine cancer. The bleeding need not be heavy. Frequently it may be nothing more than an occasional pink stain on the toilet paper noticed after voiding. In any event no post-menopausal bleeding, regardless of how minimal or how infrequent, should ever be ignored. This is particularly true if the bleeding appears more than twelve months after the last period. Cancer of the uterus, when diagnosed early, is nearly 100 per cent curable.

Does cancer of the endometrium ever occur in younger women?

Cancer of the endometrium has been known to occur in women in their thirties and even in their twenties, but this is most unusual. Once women reach their forties, however, the incidence of endometrial cancer begins to rise sharply.

In the woman who is still menstruating, grossly irregular periods and/or bleeding or spotting between periods may be the first indications that all is not well. Particularly among women in their forties, excessively long, heavy or frequent bleeding episodes can also represent pre-malignant changes which, if untreated, can progress to an early cancer. Since 25 per cent of all endometrial cancers do occur in premenopausal women, it would be foolish to assume that all menstrual irregularities are the result of benign or hormonal problems.

How is endometrial cancer diagnosed?

Since virtually all early endometrical cancers will cause abnormal uterine bleeding in some form, it is imperative to report any unusual bleeding promptly. Armed with this information, your doctor can proceed accordingly. As previously mentioned, cervical smears are not reliable in detecting an early uterine cancer. More often than not, malignant cells from the lining of the womb may not be shed into the upper vagina. Detection of endometrical cancer therefore depends on sampling tissue from the uterine lining.

The gynaecologist may use one of two procedures to screen for endometrial cancer: endometrial aspiration or endometrial biopsy. Endometrial aspiration involves gently washing out the uterine cavity with a sterile solution and aspirating back into a special container the fluid and any discarded cells. The material is then examined for malignant cells. Endometrial biopsy simply means passing a tiny curette through the cervical canal and removing a strip of endometrial tissue for microscopic evaluation.

Both these procedures, however, are only screening techniques. It is still possible to miss an early endometrial cancer with either of these methods. For this reason, a D and C is always done if there is a strong suspicion that endometrial cancer may exist. Only by removing tissue from the entire uterine lining can an accurate diagnosis be established.

How is cancer of the uterus treated?

Here again, definitive treatment depends upon the extent of the disease and the woman's general physical condition. Usually the treatment is primarily surgical with various combinations of radiation therapy given either before or after surgery, depending upon the circumstances. Surgery for endometrial cancer means removal of the uterus and cervix (complete hysterectomy) as well as both tubes and ovaries (salpingo-oophorectomy). The possibility of hidden tumour cells around the ovaries and the fact that oestrogen can stimulate dormant endometrial cancer cells make removal of the ovaries necessary. Oestrogen replacement therapy in women previously treated for endometrial cancer is therefore not recommended. Nevertheless, if the cancer was very early, well confined and believed to have been completely removed, oestrogen in judicious doses has occasionally been prescribed by some doctors to control severe menopausal symptoms in younger women.

Interestingly enough, some advanced cancers of the uterus have shown remarkable regression as a result of large doses of a synthetic progesteronelike hormone.

What about cancer of the ovary?

Despite the fact that ovarian cancer is not as prevalent as cervical cancer, it is responsible for *more deaths* than any other pelvic malignancy. Each year about 4300 new cases are discovered in Britain and about 4000 women die of ovarian cancer. Yet, if it is detected while still limited to the ovary, five-year survival rates can approach 75 per cent.

Are some women more susceptible to ovarian cancer?

Other than being more common in postmenopausal women, cancer of the ovary shows no particular predilection for any group of women. It can occur in any woman at any age. Malignant ovarian tumours have even been reported in girls under five and in women over eighty.

Why is ovarian cancer so often fatal?

Malignant tumours of the ovary tend to spread rapidly. This is partly explained by the anatomy and location of the ovaries. A cancer of the uterine lining, for example, can be held partially in check by the thick muscular walls of the uterus. An ovarian cancer, on the other hand, is not bound or confined. It can therefore seed tumour cells into the pelvic cavity at a faster rate. Then too, malignant tumours of the ovary frequently involve both ovaries simultaneously.

Even more important, most ovarian cancers do not give early symptoms. Furthermore, if the woman is menstruating, her periods are usually unaffected. Also there are no adequate screening tests to detect an early ovarian cancer.

How, then, can a woman tell if something is wrong?

The first warning signs may be nothing more than persistent indigestion and a sense of pelvic fullness or lower abdominal discomfort. Often these symptoms are so vague as to be disregarded. Many ovarian cancers produce fluid within the abdominal cavity. Thus, all too frequently a rapidly enlarging abdomen and the sudden inability to fit into one's clothes are the first real indications of ovarian cancer. Less commonly, an abdominal mass or lump may be noticed but ignored until it too suddenly enlarges. More often than not, though, by this time the tumour has usually spread beyond the confines of the ovaries.

Isn't there any way to detect an early ovarian cancer?

Only by pelvic examination. Under these circumstances, however, even finding an enlarged ovary or ovaries is no proof that ovarian cancer is present. As discussed in Chapter 19, the ovary can give rise to many different growths, both benign and malignant. But the fact that ovarian cancer is such a treacherous disease makes most gynaecologists advise prompt surgical exploration for any suspicious ovarian mass. In women past the menopause in particular, the finding of an enlarged ovary is never normal.

What about the treatment of ovarian cancer?

In patients who cannot be cured by surgery alone, radiation therapy and/or antitumour drugs offer the best chance. In recent years several new drugs have shown great promise in the treatment of extensive ovarian cancer. Despite these advances successful treatment still depends on early detection by routine pelvic examination.

What about other cancers of the pelvic organs?

All other malignancies involving the female reproductive tract (cancer of the vulva, vagina and Fallopian tubes) are uncommon and occur primarily in postmenopausal women.

Nonetheless, publicity in the United States has recently focused attention on an unusual cancer – a causal link has been discovered between a particularly rare type of vaginal cancer in a few teenage girls and the fact that their mothers had taken the synthetic oestrogen diethylstilboestrol (DES) during that pregnancy. Exactly what triggered the development of vaginal cancer in certain girls, while thousands of others exposed to the same risk have apparently been spared, remains to be answered.

In summary cancer of the female pelvic organs accounts for approximately nine thousand deaths each year. And yet many of these deaths could have been forestalled with early treatment. It is estimated that if every woman had a pelvic examination every year or so, a smear test every two or three years, and if she promptly reported any abnormal bleeding during her menopausal and postmenopausal years, the death rate for pelvic cancer could be reduced considerably. So until we cross the threshold of a major breakthrough in cancer prevention and treatment, we must still rely on early detection by regular examinations. After all, don't we owe it to ourselves and to those who love us to live our lives in the best possible health?

Part 7

What's in Store for Tomorrow's Woman

24. The Future

With each succeeding decade scientific and technical knowledge accumulates at a staggering rate. What we know now may comprise only a small fraction of what will be known in the future. Many of the ideas being discussed and the research projects being carried out seem likely to bring startling benefits to women. Some will prove impractical; others will take generations to come into effect but all in all that small fraction of the scientific future which we dare to predict looks good for women.

The menopause and the quality of life

While there is no reason to expect that human life will be much prolonged beyond its natural span, there is every reason to expect that the quality of life enjoyed by the aged will improve. Women can already benefit. The distressing symptoms of the menopause can already be largely eliminated by oestrogen therapy. The immediate future will probably bring better forms of oestrogen replacement with fewer risks and side effects. Society's acceptance of the right of ageing women to full active lives, including sex lives, will undoubtedly help in making any such therapy widely available.

Determining the sex of your child

Scientists can already distinguish between sperm carrying the X chromosome which will lead to the birth of a girl and that which carries the Y chromosome which will lead to a boy. They are working on techniques whereby these types of sperm can be separated in a given specimen of semen. Once this technique is perfected, it will be possible for a couple to have a baby of their choice of sex, provided they are prepared to have it by artificial insemination with the husband's sperm.

While the use of such a technique would be comparatively expensive in medical time and expertise, and considerably more

366 From Woman to Woman

trouble for the couple than the ordinary methods of conception, it might prove a boon to those who at present have more children than they ideally want because they keep on trying for one particular sex.

Help for the infertile woman

There are numerous research projects being carried out in this area ranging from improvements in the drugs currently used to stimulate ovarian function, to possibilities of the actual transplantation of healthy ovaries. There is even talk of transplanting uteri or Fallopian tubes into women whose own equipment does not function. The acute medical and economic difficulties experienced by life-saving transplant programmes such as kidney transplants suggest that these possibilities are somewhat far-fetched. But it remains true that a woman who cannot conceive without medical help has a much better chance of getting that help now than ever before and that the help available to her will improve.

Birth control

Long-term control of conception by means of the pill, IUD, diaphragm, condom and all other present-day methods is likely to become obsolete in the quite near future. Probably our greatest hope for fully effective contraception without daily trouble or worrying side effects lies in research work on using the body's own immunological defence system. Already we know that some women fail to conceive because their bodies make antibodies against sperm. If scientists can make an antisperm vaccine for women, it could immobilize sperm and thus make conception impossible without interfering with hormonal function, ovulation or the menstrual cycle. In the meantime, the more immediate future will certainly see improvements in mini-pills (reducing side effects even further) together, possibly, with improvements in slow-release intrauterine hormone implants which will do away with the necessity to take a pill every day.

VD and cancer

Immunological techniques look promising here too. A vaccine against gonorrhoea is currently being tested: if it works the disease may become as rare as polio even in our own lifetime. It is not unrealistic to look forward to a vaccine against syphilis too.

In cancer research the picture is less clear. Many scientists no longer believe that 'cancer' is a single disease attacking different parts of the body. They believe, instead, that there are many cancers. A few of these may prove to be caused by viruses. If they do, then the control of those particular forms of cancer by vaccination might become possible.

At the same time the diagnosis of cancer will undoubtedly improve. Research work is being carried out to try to perfect methods of screening for cancers which, at present, too often go unsuspected for a long time. It is even possible that a blood test will be developed which could indicate the beginning of a cancer somewhere in the body.

The treatment of cancer will improve, too. Nuclear techniques by which malignant cells are destroyed selectively, without damage to adjacent normal tissue, are being improved as is drug therapy. In both areas scientists are working to reduce the side effects which the patient experiences.

Stress and the influence of mind on body

Emotional and psychological stress is known to play a part in many physical problems. Some diseases are actually labelled 'psychosomatic' meaning that they are bodily diseases with psychological factors playing a large part in causing and/or prolonging them. Many diseases are more likely to occur when an individual is severely stressed: a recently bereaved person, for example, is much more likely than others to become physically ill. A few research programmes are already using 'mind power', including bio-feedback techniques, to teach individual patients to control physical symptoms such as migraine or high blood pressure.

This is a difficult area but one with exciting possibilities for the future. We may yet learn so much about what causes damaging stress to individuals and what makes their stress manifest itself in physical disease rather than in bad temper, depression or acute mental illness, that we shall have a whole new range of weapons against disease in our own individual hands.

Glossary

The following glossary is intended to facilitate the comprehension of this book and this book only. Definitions are therefore intentionally limited and do not necessarily include all possible interpretations for a given term. When a more detailed definition is desired, the reader should consult either a standard general or a medical dictionary.

ABDOMEN   That portion of the body lying between the lower ribs and the groin.

ABDOMINAL CAVITY   The body cavity which contains most of the organs of digestion (intestines, liver, etc.) and the spleen. It is bounded by the diaphragm above and continuous with the pelvic cavity below.

ABORTION   Termination, loss, or interruption of a pregnancy of less than twenty-eight weeks. Types of abortion: induced (by artificial means); spontaneous or natural abortion – see MISCARRIAGE.

ABSCESS   An accumulation or collection of pus contained within a well-circumscribed area.

ACUTE   Sharp – brief and/or severe; of sudden onset.

ADENOMYOSIS   Condition in which displaced fragments of endometrial (uterine lining) tissue are abnormally embedded in the muscular walls of the uterus.

ADHESION   Fibrous band of tissue that abnormally binds or interconnects organs or other body parts.

ADNEXAE   Pertaining to the tubes and ovaries. General term used to define the tubes and ovaries.

ADRENALS   Important endocrine glands located atop each kidney; the suprarenal glands.

AMENORRHOEA   Prolonged absence of menstruation.

AMNIOCENTESIS   Removal of a sample of amniotic fluid for diagnostic purposes; sometimes used to detect certain congenital defects or to determine the sex of the unborn child. Saline amniocentesis specifically refers to the introduction of a saline (salt) solution into the bag of waters (amniotic sac) for purposes of abortion.

AMNIOTIC FLUID   Fluid contained within the bag of waters (amniotic sac) that surrounds the foetus during its intrauterine existence.

ANAL FISSURE   A deep crack or split in the mucous membrane of the anal canal (back passage).

ANALGESIC   Pain-relieving drug or substance.

ANDROGEN   General term applied to any hormone that has a masculinizing effect on either sex.

ANOMALIES   Abnormalities in structure or form.

ANOVULATION   Absence of ovulation.

ANOVULATORY CYCLE   Menstrual cycle wherein ovulation, or release of an egg (ovum), does not occur.

ANTEFLEXED   A normal forward bend of the uterus at the junction of its body and the cervix.

ANTEVERTED UTERUS   A forward tilt of the entire uterus.

ANTIBIOTICS   Large group of chemical substances (e.g., penicillin) that have the ability to destroy or inhibit the growth of bacteria or other disease-producing organisms.

ANTIBODY   Part of the body's natural defence mechanism; a substance found in the blood, other body fluids, or tissues that is manufactured by the body in response to noxious or harmful bacteria, viruses or other foreign invaders.

ANTI-CANCER DRUGS   Group of chemical sutsbances that can destroy or inhibit the growth of cancerous or malignant cells.

ANTIGEN   Any substance which, when introduced into the body, stimulates the production of antibodies.

ANUS   The body orifice through which faecal material is expelled (back passage).

APHRODISIAC   An agent or drug capable of arousing sexual desire.

APOCRINE GLAND   A skin gland that exudes a milky secretion having a characteristic but inoffensive odour; a scent gland.

ARTIFICIAL INSEMINATION   The deposit of semen into the vagina by means other than sexual intercourse for the purpose of procreation.

ASEXUAL   Not sexual; with no overt sexual interest in either sex.

ASPIRATION   The withdrawal of air, fluid, or other material from a body cavity or space by suction.

ASYMPTOMATIC   Absence of symptoms; no subjective sign of any disease.

ATROPHY   A wasting away or a diminution of size involving an organ or body part.

ATYPICAL   Somewhat unusual, not quite normal.

AXILLARY   Pertaining to the underarm or armpit area (axilla).

AZOOSPERMIA   Total absence of sperm in the semen; zero sperm production.

BACTERIUM (plural BACTERIA)   Broad term that includes microscopic organisms which, when abnormally present, may cause infection and disease.

BARTHOLIN'S CYST   A swelling or collection of fluid, mucus, or other material within one of the Bartholin's glands.

BARTHOLIN'S GLANDS   Mucus-secreting glands located on either side of the vaginal opening.

BASAL BODY TEMPERATURE (BBT)   The lowest normal body temperature recorded under conditions of absolute rest. For example, the body temperature during sleep or immediately upon awakening.

BENIGN   Mild in character; of a noncancerous condition.

BILATERAL   Involving both sides.

BIMANUAL EXAMINATION   Examination wherein both hands are used to palpate, or feel, the internal female pelvic organs.

BIOPSY   The surgical removal of tissue for purposes of diagnosis. Types of biopsy: cone – removal of a cone-shaped piece of tissue from the cervix, most commonly done for the diagnosis of a possible early cervical cancer; excisional – surgical removal of an entire lesion or growth; incisional – surgical removal of only a portion of a lesion or growth; needle – removal of only a very small segment of tissue by means of a special large-bore needle; punch – removal of a small wedge of tissue by means of a special (punch) instrument.

BISEXUAL   An individual who is sexually attracted to or who engages in sexual activity with members of both sexes.

BLADDER   The elastic, saclike organ that serves as a receptacle for urine.

BONE SCAN   Sophisticated diagnostic technique utilizing nuclear tracer elements injected by vein to pinpoint cancerous tumours or other abnormal changes in bony tissue.

BONE SURVEY   Routine X-rays of the spine, pelvis, and other skeletal parts to detect the presence of any abnormal or cancerous bony changes.

CAESAREAN SECTION   Delivery of a baby by means of an incision through the abdominal wall and uterus.

CANCER   A malignancy; broad term applied to any tumour, growth, or lesion characterized by the rapid multiplication of abnormal cells that have the ability to invade and spread to distant organs or other body parts.

CANDIDA ALBICANS   A fungus frequently responsible for vaginal infection; see MONILIA.

CARCINOMA   Cancer.

CARCINOMA IN SITU   A very early and localized cancer.

CASTRATION   Surgical removal of the ovaries or testicles, or else their destruction by irradiation therapy.

CATHETER   Any tubelike instrument used to inject or withdraw fluid from any body cavity or space.

CATHETERIZATION   Most commonly refers to the passage of a small rubber tube or other instrument through the urethra for the purpose of draining the bladder of urine.

CAUTERIZATION   The destruction of infected or abnormal tissue by heat, cold, or chemicals.

CELIBATE   One who does not engage in sexual activity.

CERVICAL CANAL   Passageway within the cervix proper connecting the vagina and the uterine cavity.

CERVICAL CYST   An abnormal retention of mucus secretions within one of the cervical glands.

CERVICAL EROSION   The term 'erosion' is actually a misnomer. Cervical erosion is the replacement of normal cervical tissue on the surface of the cervix by endocervical tissue, which is red and granular in appearance. This condition is usually the result of infection. Sometimes the term is loosely and incorrectly applied to any red or irritated cervix.

CERVICAL OS   The opening leading into the cervical canal.

CERVICAL POLYP   An abnormal but usually benign tear-drop-shaped growth of the cervix that commonly protrudes from the cervical os.

CERVICAL SMEAR   See CYTOTEST.

CERVICAL STENOSIS   A narrowing or stricture of the cervical canal.

CERVICITIS   An inflammation and/or infection involving the cervix.

CERVIX   The lower portion of the uterus (womb) that projects into the vagina, sometimes referred to as the mouth or neck of the womb. See also RIPE CERVIX.

CHANCRE   Painless ulcerating sore seen specifically in early syphilis.

CHLOASMA   The appearance of light brown patches on the skin of the face and elsewhere. Increased skin pigmentation occasionally seen in pregnant women and in women taking oral contraceptives.

CHROMOSOME Microscopic, threadlike particles of genetic material contained within the nucleus of cells.

CIRCUMCISION The surgical removal of the foreskin (prepuce) from the penis.

CLIMACTERIC The menopausal years, the period of time during which menstruation ceases and the body gradually adjusts to waning ovarian function and decreasing oestrogen production.

CLIMAX See ORGASM.

CLITORIS A small cylindrical erectile structure, extremely sensitive to stimulation and located just above the urethral opening in the female.

COITUS Sexual intercourse.

COITUS INTERRUPTUS The practice of withdrawing the penis from the vagina just prior to ejaculation (release of semen).

COLPOSCOPE Telescopelike instrument used to magnify the surface of the cervix.

CONCEIVE To become pregnant, to procreate.

CONDOM A sheath for the penis used to prevent pregnancy or infection; a rubber, a prophylactic, Durex, French letter.

CONGENITAL Existing or present from birth. Can refer to any physical or mental trait, peculiarities or diseases either inherited or caused by an adverse prenatal influence.

CONGESTION Engorgement of blood vessels resulting from an increased blood flow to the particular area or an obstruction of the return flow; poor venous drainage or circulation.

CONNECTIVE TISSUE Fibrous sheets of tissue that support and connect muscles or other body parts.

CONTRACEPTION Birth control; prevention of pregnancy.

CONTRACEPTIVE Any drug, device, or method used to prevent pregnancy.

CONTRAINDICATED Against medical advice and judgement.

CORPUS LUTEUM The yellow-coloured ovarian tissue structure formed from the remains of the ruptured ovarian follicle after release of its contained ovum (egg). Important because of its production of the hormone progesterone, which prepares the uterine lining to receive the fertilized egg.

CORPUS LUTEUM CYST A cyst of the corpus luteum; any abnormal accumulation of blood or other material within the corpus luteum.

CORRUGATED Having alternative ridges and grooves – not smooth. Frequently used to describe the surface of the vaginal walls in a woman during the reproductive years.

CRABS *Pediculosis pubis;* pubic-hair lice.

CULDOSCOPY Surgical procedure in which a slender, telescopelike instrument is passed through the upper vagina and into the pelvic cavity to view the internal female organs.

CULTURE A laboratory method to identify the causative agent or bacteria responsible for a particular infection or disease. In effect, the material to be examined (urine, blood, discharge, etc.) is incubated in special nutrients that allow any organisms or bacteria originally present in the sample material to multiply, thrive and thus be identified.

CUNNILINGUS Oral stimulation of the female genitalia.

CURETTAGE Scraping of any body cavity; for example, scraping the womb cavity for the purpose of removing tissue or new growths. A common gynaecological diagnostic procedure. See DILATATION AND CURETTAGE.

CYCLIC Occurring periodically or at regular intervals.

CYST Any saclike structure containing fluid or semisolid material.

CYSTIC MASTITIS A benign breast condition characterized by the presence of multiple small cysts and fibrous thickening of the breast tissue.

CYSTITIS Inflammation and/or infection of the urinary bladder.

CYTOLOGY The study of cells both normal and abnormal.

CYTOTEST A cell test for which cells are collected on a glass slide, stained, and then examined under a microscope for any abnormal forms. Most commonly used as a screening method for early cervical cancer.

DERMATITIS Inflammation of the skin from any cause. Contact dermatitis is an inflammation of the skin from contact with an irritant. Allergic dermatitis is an inflammation of the skin as the result of individual sensitivity to a certain substance or material.

DIAGNOSIS The determination of the cause of a specific infection, disease or other condition.

DIAGNOSTIC STUDIES Tests to determine the cause of an abnormal condition; also done to eliminate or rule out the presence of an abnormal condition.

DIAPHRAGM   A rubber, dome-shaped device worn over the cervix for the prevention of pregnancy.

DILATATION   The enlargement of any passageway; for example, the dilation of the cervical os and canal during childbirth.

DILATION AND CURETTAGE (D AND C)   Minor surgical procedure in which the cervical os and canal are temporarily enlarged to permit the passage of an instrument (curette) for any purposes of removing tissue from the uterine cavity.

DILATE   To make wider or larger, to expand.

DISCHARGE   Any abnormal or unusual drainage or secretion.

DISCRETE   Well-outlined, distinct, separate; usually used to describe certain tumours or lesions.

DISEASE   Any abnormal or pathological state that interferes with the proper functioning of the mind and/or body.

DISSEMINATED   Widespread; for example, a disseminated disease is one involving many organs or body parts.

DISTENTION   The state of being stretched; for example, abdominal distention is a swollen or expanded abdomen usually resulting from the accumulation of gas or fluid.

DOUCHING   Flushing of the vagina with a liquid solution, usually medicated.

DYSFUNCTION   Malfunction of an organ or body part.

DYSMENORRHOEA   Painful menstruation or menstrual cramps. Primary dysmenorrhoea implies painful menstruation without organic cause. Secondary dysmenorrhoea implies painful menstruation as the result of a specific pelvic problem or disease.

DYSPAREUNIA   Intercourse that is painful or difficult for a woman.

DYSURIA   Pain and/or burning on urination.

ECCRINE GLAND   A sweat gland.

ECTOPIC PREGNANCY   Any pregnancy that grows outside the uterine cavity. Most commonly used to describe a tubal pregnancy, that is, the implantation of a fertilized egg with subsequent growth of the embryo within one of the Fallopian tubes.

EJACULATION   Discharge of semen from the penis at the time of orgasm.

EMBOLISM   Obstruction of a blood vessel by a transported blood clot or embolus; for example, pulmonary embolism is the obstruction of a blood vessel in the lung.

EMBOLUS   Any undissolved material (for example, air, fat, blood clot) that travels in the bloodstream and subsequently blocks a blood vessel.

EMBRYO The offspring (product of conception) from the third to the end of the fifth week of intrauterine existence. During the first two weeks of pregnancy the product of conception is known as the ovum; from the sixth week until birth, the foetus.

ENDOCERVICAL Within the cervical canal.

ENDOCERVICAL GLANDS Mucus-producing glands of the cervix.

ENDOCRINE The ductless glands (ovaries, testicles, thyroid, adrenals, pituitary, etc.) that secrete hormones directly into the bloodstream and which profoundly affect other parts of the body.

ENDOMETRIAL Pertaining to the endometrium, the mucous-membrane tissue lining the uterine cavity.

ENDOMETRIAL ASPIRATION The withdrawal of a sterile solution introduced into the uterine-cavity for purposes of collecting endometrial cells for diagnostic purposes.

ENDOMETRIAL BIOPSY The sampling of endometrial tissue for diagnostic purposes.

ENDOMETRIAL CARCINOMA Cancer of the tissue lining the uterine cavity.

ENDOMETRIAL CAVITY The uterine cavity.

ENDOMETRIAL CYST An ovarian cyst made up of endometrial tissue implants and commonly seen in endometriosis. Sometimes also known as 'chocolate cyst' of the ovary because of the presence of old blood within the cyst.

ENDOMETRIAL HYPERPLASIA Benign overgrowth of the tissue lining the uterine cavity usually the result of long, uninterrupted oestrogen stimulation.

ENDOMETRIAL POLYP A tear-drop-shaped growth, usually benign, within the uterine cavity.

ENDOMETRIOSIS A pelvic condition in which fragments of endometrial tissue are found outside the confines of the uterine cavity; for example, on the ovaries, the back wall of the uterus or in the pelvic space between the uterus and rectum.

ENGORGEMENT Distention with blood or other fluid, congestion; for example, an engorged blood vessel.

EPISIOTOMY An incision into the perineum made to facilitate delivery of a baby.

ERECTILE TISSUE Tissue which, when engorged with blood, becomes swollen and more or less rigid, for example, the penis and clitoris during sexual excitation.

ERECTION The condition of erectile tissue when engorged with blood. Commonly used to describe the penis when distended and rigid.

ESCHERIUM COLI Bacterium normally present in the gut. It can cause trouble if it infects, e.g. the vagina or Fallopian tubes.

EXCISE To cut out, to remove surgically.

EXCISIONAL BIOPSY See BIOPSY.

EXTERNAL GENITALIA The vulva, or external sexual organs of the female. Can also apply to the external sexual organs of the male (penis and scrotum).

FAECAL IMPACTION Accumulation of hardened faeces in the lower rectum.

FALLOPIAN TUBES The two small passageways or tubes that branch from either side of the uterus and connect with the uterine cavity; the passageway where the egg and the sperm meet.

FELLATIO Oral stimulation of the penis.

FERTILE DAYS The days during which ovulation is most likely to occur.

FERTILITY DRUGS A group of natural and synthetic drugs capable of inducing ovulation in selected women.

FERTILIZATION Impregnation; specifically, the fusion of a sperm with an ovum.

FERTILIZED EGG An ovum that has been impregnated by a sperm.

FIBROADENOMA A common benign breast tumour.

FIBROIDS Benign tumours involving the wall of the uterus; also known as leiomyomata, myomasta or fibromyomata.

FIMBRIA Small fingerlike projections located at the free end of each Fallopian tube and important for ensuring that a released ovum finds its way into the tube.

FOETUS The product of conception from the sixth week to the end of pregnancy.

FOLLICLE A small ovarian saclike structure containing an ovum.

FOLLICLE CYST An abnormal accumulation of fluid within an ovarian follicle.

FOLLICLE-STIMULATING HORMONE (FSH) Pituitary hormone that stimulates the growth and development of ovarian follicles.

FORESKIN See PREPUCE.

FORNIX The upper vagina near the cervix.

FRATERNAL TWINS Nonidentical twins resulting from the fertilization of two separate eggs by two separate sperm.

FROZEN SECTION A rapid method of preparing biopsied tissue for the microscopic detection of abnormal and/or malignant cells. Frozen sections are usually done while the operation or surgical procedure is still in progress.

FUNCTIONAL DISEASE A condition in which an organ or body part is not functioning properly, but in which no lesion, tumour or change in structure can be determined.

FUNDUS The top of the uterus; that portion of the uterus lying above the level of where the Fallopian tubes branch off.

FUNGUS A disease-producing organism that feeds on organic matter; for example, *Candida albicans*, a fungus commonly responsible for causing vaginal infection.

GENERIC General or chemical name of a drug as opposed to its trade name.

GENITALIA Sexual organs; the organs of reproduction.

GENITAL WARTS Wartlike lesions along the vulva and/or inner vagina caused by a virus; can also affect the male external genitalia. Also known as venereal warts.

GESTATION Pregnancy; can refer to either a normal (intrauterine) or an ectopic (extrauterine) pregnancy.

GONAD Sex gland; ovary or testicle.

GONADOTROPIN Specifically refers to pituitary hormones directly affecting or stimulating the gonads; for example, FSH and LH are gonadotropins.

GONOCOCCUS *Neisseria gonorrhoeae*, the bacteria responsible for gonorrhoea.

GONORRHOEA A highly contagious venereal disease.

GRAM-NEGATIVE Refers to a differential stain used in the laboratory identification of bacteria. For example, a Gram-negative bacteria such as gonococcus, (*E. coli*, etc.) will stain pink when subjected to a certain dye; a Gram-positive bacteria will stain a deep purple when exposed to the same dye.

GYNAECOLOGIST A doctor who specializes in the treatment and management of problems affecting the female reproductive system.

HAEMATURIA Blood in the urine.

HAEMORRHAGE Excessively heavy bleeding, either internal or external.

HERPESVIRUSES Group of viruses responsible for various benign afflictions (cold sore, fever blisters, shingles, etc.). Currently being implicated in the development of some human cancers.

HETEROSEXUAL An individual who is sexually attracted to or who engages in sexual activity with a member of the opposite sex.

HIRSUTISM Abnormal presence of excessive facial and/or body hair, especially in women.

HOMOSEXUAL An individual who is sexually attracted to or who engages in sexual activity with a member of the same sex.

HORMONE A chemical substance produced by an endocrine gland and which stimulates or affects other organs or body parts.

HOT FLUSH A sudden flushing of the skin accompanied by perspiration and a feeling of intense heat usually involving the upper portion of the body.

HUMAN CHORIONIC GONADOTROPINS Group of hormones produced by the placenta during pregnancy and having properties similar to certain pituitary hormones such as LH and FSH (gonadotropins). The detection of these substances in the urine (chorionic gonadotropins) forms the basis of most pregnancy tests.

HYMEN A thin, semicircular strip of mucous membrane stretched across the lower edge of the vaginal entrance.

HYMENECTOMY Surgical removal of the hymen.

HYMENOTOMY Surgical incision of the hymen to enlarge the vaginal opening.

HYPOTHALAMUS A major control centre for various bodily functions, situated at the base of the brain and intimately connected with the pituitary gland.

HYSTERECTOMY Surgical removal of the uterus and its cervix either by an abdominal incision or through the vagina (vaginal hysterectomy).

HYSTEROSALPINGOGRAM Special X-ray procedure used to outline the uterine cavity and the Fallopian tube passageways.

HYSTEROTOMY An incision into the uterus, usually for the removal of an intrauterine pregnancy; a method of late abortion.

IDENTICAL TWINS Genetically identical individuals resulting from the splitting of a single ovum fertilized by a single sperm.

IMMUNE Protected against a disease or other condition.

IMMUNOLOGY The study of the body's defence mechanisms against various diseases or disease-producing agents such as bacteria, viruses, etc.

IMPERFORATE HYMEN   A hymen that completely blocks the vaginal opening.

IMPOTENT   Weak; describing a male's inability to obtain or sustain an erection for effective sexual intercourse.

INCUBATION PERIOD   The interval of time between the moment of infection and the appearance of symptoms and signs indicative of an infection.

INFANTILE UTERUS   An underdeveloped uterus; specifically, a disproportionately small uterine body as compared to the size of its cervix.

INFECTION   The contamination of any tissue with harmful bacteria or other organisms that adversely affects that tissue.

INFERTILITY   Temporary or permanent inability to conceive or reproduce.

INFLAMMATION   A condition characterized by redness, swelling, heat and pain of any tissue as the result of trauma, irritation, or infection.

INSUFFLATION   The injection of air or other gaseous material into a body cavity or passageway. Normally used as part of a test to determine whether the Fallopian tubes are open or blocked. For this, carbon dioxide is injected through the cervical canal and thus through the uterine cavity and the tubes.

INTERCOURSE   Sexual relations.

INTRAUTERINE   Within the uterine cavity.

INTRAUTERINE DEVICE (IUD)   Any device worn within the uterine cavity for the purpose of avoiding pregnancy; for example, a loop, coil, or shield.

INTROITUS   The entrance to the vagina.

INTROMISSION   The insertion of the penis into the vagina.

IRRADIATION   The use of X-rays; radium, cobalt, or other radio-active substances for either diagnosis or treatment.

KEGEL'S EXERCISES   Exercises to strengthen the pubococcygeus muscle.

LABIA   Lips, part of the female external genitalia. Labia majora, the outer lips; labia minora, the inner lips.

LACTATION   The production of breast milk.

LAPAROSCOPY   A surgical procedure wherein a slender telescope-like instrument (laparoscope) is inserted through a small abdominal puncture for the inspection of abdominal and pelvic organs.

LEIOMYOMA   Fibroid tumour of the uterus.

LESION   Any unusual or abnormal localized tissue change; for example, any sore, tumour, growth, wound, injury, etc.

LEUCORRHOEA   Nonspecific term to describe any white vaginal discharge.

LIBIDO   Sex drive.

LUTEINIZING HORMONE (LH)   One of the pituitary hormones necessary for ovulation; pituitary gonadotropin.

LYMPHATIC SYSTEM   A complex, interconnecting network of tiny capillarylike channels that drain and filter all body tissue fluid through the lymph nodes and back into the bloodstream.

LYMPH NODE   Part of the lymphatic system. Specifically, a gland which by acting as a trap or filter for bacteria, pus cells, and even malignant cells helps to localize any infection or malignancy to the area being drained.

MACROPHAGES   Large white blood cells that function as scavengers and thus protect the body against harmful bacteria and other foreign invaders.

MALIGNANT   Cancerous. See CANCER.

MAMMARY GLAND   The breast.

MAMMOGRAPHY   X-ray of the breast for the detection of abnormal tissue changes.

MASTECTOMY   Surgical removal of a breast. Types of mastectomy: radical – removal of the entire breast, chest wall muscles (pectoralis major and minor) and axillary nodes; modified radical – removal of the entire breast and axillary nodes without sacrificing the chest wall muscles; simple – removal of the breast only; partial – removal of only a portion of the breast; subcutaneous – removal of the glandular tissue of the breast without sacrificing the overlying breast skin or nipple (primarily limited to certain benign conditions).

MASTURBATION   The stimulation or manipulation of one's own or another's genitals for sexual gratification.

MENARCHE   The age at which menstruation first begins.

MENOPAUSAL YEARS   See CLIMACTERIC.

MENOPAUSE   Permanent cessation of menstruation.

MENORRHAGIA   Excessively heavy bleeding during menstruation.

MENSES   Menstrual flow.

MENSTRUAL CYCLE   The time interval from the beginning of one menstrual period to the beginning of the next. Also implies the sequence of events necessary to prepare the uterine lining for reception of a fertilized egg.

MENSTRUATION   Periodic bloody discharge from the uterine cavity as the result of specific hormonal changes.

METASTASIS   The spread of cancer cells from one part of the body to another organ or body part usually by way of the lymphatic system or bloodstream.

METASTATIC LESION   A cancerous or malignant tumour that has already spread to a distant body part or organ.

MIDCYCLE   The time in a woman's menstrual cycle during which ovulation usually occurs.

MINIPILL   Birth-control pill containing a small dose of progestogen only.

MISCARRIAGE   Loss of an early pregnancy without outside interference – that is, a spontaneous abortion as opposed to an induced abortion. Types of miscarriages or spontaneous abortions: complete – an abortion in which all the products of conception (embryo and placental tissue) are expelled; habitual – three or more successive spontaneous abortions; incomplete – an abortion in which there is still retained tissue, that is, some products of conception remain within the uterine cavity; missed – intrauterine death of an embryo or foetus, but with retention of all the products of conception for several weeks afterward; threatened – potential loss of an early pregnancy as evidenced by bleeding and uterine cramps.

MITTELSCHMERZ   Midcycle ovulatory pain. Pain and/or bleeding occurring at the time of ovulation.

MONILIA   The fungus *Candida albicans*.

MONILIASIS   Vaginal infection caused by the fungus *Candida albicans*.

MONS VENERIS   Mound of fatty tissue over the pubic bone in women and normally covered with hair.

MOTILITY   The power of spontaneous movement; one of the characteristics of normal sperm.

MUCOSA   See MUCOUS MEMBRANE.

MUCOUS MEMBRANE   Moist, glistening tissue lining the body cavities and passageways that lead to the outside. For example, the mouth, digestive tract, uterine cavity, cervical canal, vagina, etc.

MUCUS   A clear, sticky secretion from a mucous membrane.

MYOMA   Fibroid tumour of the uterus.

MYOMECTOMY   Surgical removal of a myoma.

NABOTHIAN CYST   Another name for the common cervical cyst. See CERVICAL CYST.

NEEDLE ASPIRATION   The removal of fluid or other liquid material from a cyst or body cavity by means of a needle and syringe.

NEEDLE BIOPSY   See BIOPSY.

NEOPLASM   Any new growth or tumour, either benign or malignant.

NIT   The egg of a crab louse.

NODE   See LYMPH NODE

NODULE   A small rounded lump or mass, either benign or malignant.

NYMPHOMANIAC   A woman with an insatiable and uncontrollable desire for sex.

OEDEMA   Abnormal accumulation of fluid within the body tissues that produces swelling of a part of an organ.

OESTROGEN   Hormone produced by the ovaries and responsible for female sexual characteristics.

OOPHORECTOMY   Surgical removal of an ovary.

ORAL   Pertaining to the mouth.

ORAL CONTRACEPTIVES   Birth-control pills; hormone medication taken by mouth for the prevention of pregnancy.

ORAL GENITAL SEX   Sexual stimulation of the genitals by the mouth, lips, or tongue. See FELLATIO and CUNNILINGUS.

ORGANIC LESION   See LESION.

ORGASM   Climax; the physical sensation of sexual release experienced at the culmination of coitus, masturbation, or other sexual play.

OSTEOPOROSIS   Loss of calcium and other substances from the bone, leading to its generalized softening and weakening.

OUTPATIENT   Not requiring a stay in hospital; patient whose treatment can be rendered at a clinic.

OVARIAN CYSTECTOMY   Surgical removal of an ovarian cyst without sacrificing the entire ovary.

OVARIAN RESECTION   Removal of a portion of an ovary.

OVARY   The female sex gland or gonad.

OVERT   Obvious or apparent, not hidden.

OVULATION   The release of an ovum from the ovary.

OVULATORY CYCLE   A menstrual cycle during which ovulation the occurs.

OVUM (plural OVA)   An egg. The female sexual cell produced by ovaries.

PALPATE   To discern by touching; to feel with the hands and fingers.

PATHOLOGY   The study of abnormal tissue changes and disease states.

PEDICULOSIS PUBIS   Pubic-hair lice; crabs.

PELVIC CAVITY The lowermost portion of the abdominal cavity bound by the bony pelvis and containing the internal genital organs (uterus, tubes and ovaries), bladder and rectum.

PELVIC INFLAMMATORY DISEASE (PID) Any inflammation and/or infection involving the internal female genital organs. Commonly used to describe any acute, recurrent or chronic infection of the Fallopian tubes and/or ovaries.

PENILE Pertaining to the penis.

PENIS The male organ of copulation; the phallus.

PERFORATED UTERUS A uterus in which the wall has been pierced through its entire thickness, usually inadvertently.

PERINEAL BODY The wedge of fibrous tissue, muscle, and fat between the lower vagina and rectum in the female.

PERINEUM The area between the vagina and the anus; part of the external genitalia.

PESSARY Rubber or plastic appliance worn in the vagina to support the uterus and/or vaginal walls.

PHLEBITIS Inflammation of any vein.

PITUITARY A major endocrine gland located at the base of the brain.

PLACENTA The afterbirth; the organ that nourishes the growing foetus during its intrauterine existence.

PLATELETS Specialized blood cells (also known as thrombocytes) that are necessary for normal blood clotting.

POLYCYSTIC OVARIAN SYNDROME A hormonal derangement characterized by lack of ovulation, infertility, menstrual irregularities and enlarged ovaries.

POLYCYSTIC OVARIES Condition in which both ovaries are studded with multiple small cysts.

POLYP A small, usually benign mucous membrane growth that dangles on a stalk. See CERVICAL POLYP and ENDOMETRIAL POLYP.

POSTCOITAL TEST (SIMS-HUHNER TEST) Examination of the cervical mucus shortly after intercourse to determine its receptivity to sperm.

POSTMENOPAUSAL Occurring after the menopause.

PRECOCIOUS Prematurely developed; for example, precocious puberty is sexual maturity before the age at which it normally occurs.

PRECURSOR Forerunner; any condition that precedes another condition.

PREMENOPAUSAL   Occurring prior to the menopause.

PREMENSTRUAL   Occurring prior to menstruation.

PREPUCE   The foreskin or the skin covering the glans or head of the penis; also, the foreskin of the clitoris.

PROCREATE   To reproduce, to bear children.

PROGESTERONE   The ovarian hormone produced by the corpus luteum as a result of ovulation.

PROGESTOGEN   A synthetic-like hormone preparation.

PROGNOSIS   A forecast or prediction regarding the probable outcome of a disease or injury.

PROLAPSE   A falling down of an organ because of poor or inadequate muscular and fibrous tissue support; for example, a dropped (prolapsed) uterus.

PROLIFERATIVE ENDOMETRIUM   Normal endometrial tissue lining the uterine cavity prior to ovulation as the result of oestrogen stimulation.

PROPHYLAXIS   Any measure or method that prevents or protects from a disease or other unwanted condition.

PROSTAGLANDINS   Naturally occurring compounds capable of stimulating uterine contractions.

PROTOZOA   One-celled animal organisms. See TRICHOMONAS VAGINALIS.

PSYCHOSOMATIC   Denoting a physical illness or disease that is caused, aggravated, or influenced by an individual's emotional and mental state.

PUBERTY   The age at which an individual becomes sexually mature and thus able to reproduce.

PUBOCOCCYGEUS   A broad band of muscle stretching between the pubic bone in front to the coccyx or tail bone behind that helps to support the female pelvic organs in their proper anatomical position.

PURULENT   Full of pus or containing pus.

PUS   A creamy yellow fluid; bacterial matter which has been attacked by white blood cells.

RADIATION THERAPY   Various irradiation techniques – X-ray, cobalt, radium, etc – primarily used in the treatment of abnormal and cancerous tissue.

RADIONUCLIDE IMAGING   Diagnostic technique in which malignant cells are tagged with radioactive material for purposes of identification; can also be used in the diagnosis of benign conditions. See BONE SCAN.

RADIOPAQUE Capable of being seen on X-ray; for example, dyes used in diagnostic studies.

RECTOCELE A pouching or bulging of the wall of the rectum into the vaginal canal.

RECTUM Back passage where faeces is collected before being expelled through the anus.

RECURRENCE A condition or disease that reappears.

RETROFLEXED UTERUS A backward bend in the uterus at its junction with the cervix; a tipped uterus.

RETROVERTED UTERUS A backward tilt of the entire uterus towards the rectum; also known as a tipped uterus.

RHYTHM A method of birth control in which sexual intercourse is avoided during the fertile days.

RIPE CERVIX The cervix of a pregnant woman that has already thinned and partially dilated prior to the actual onset of labour.

SAFE PERIOD According to the rhythm method, the time during which ovulation is presumed not to occur, thus allowing sexual intercourse without risk of pregnancy.

SALPINGECTOMY Surgical removal of a Fallopian tube.

SALPINGITIS Inflammation and/or infection of the Fallopian tubes.

SALPINGO-OOPHORECTOMY Surgical removal of a Fallopian tube and an ovary.

SALPINX Another name for Fallopian tube.

SCROTUM Part of the male external genitalia; the saclike structure containing the testicles.

SEBACEOUS CYST Abnormal retention of sebaceous or oil material within a sebaceous gland.

SEBACEOUS GLAND A skin gland that opens into a hair follicle and excretes an oily substance; an oil gland.

SEBUM The oily substance excreted by sebaceous glands.

SECRETORY ENDOMETRIUM Normal endometrial tissue lining the uterine cavity following ovulation as a result of both oestrogen and progesterone stimulation.

SEMEN Thick, viscid, greyish fluid discharged by the male at the time of orgasm which contains sperm and secretions from the prostate and seminal vesicles; seminal fluid.

SEROLOGICAL STUDIES Blood studies that check for the presence of antibodies as the result of recent or past exposure to a specific virus, infectious agent, or foreign invader.

SEROLOGY   Term frequently used to mean specific serological studies to detect past or current infection with syphilis.

SERUM   The liquid portion of blood as distinguished from its formed elements, such as blood cells; that liquid portion of blood that remains after the blood elements have clotted.

SMEAR   Used to describe the smearing of cells, infected material, or discharge onto a glass slide for rapid microscopic identification of bacteria and/or abnormal cells.

SMEGMA   An accumulation of cellular debris and glandular secretions usually found under a skin fold.

SPECULUM   An instrument that enlarges a passageway for the purpose of inspecting the interior. Vaginal speculum – specifically used to see the interior of the vagina and cervix.

SPERM   The male germ seed produced by the testicles.

SPERMICIDAL   Destructive to sperm on contact.

SPERMICIDES   Vaginal creams, foams, jellies or suppositories that can immobilize or destroy sperm on contact.

STEIN-LEVINTHAL SYNDROME   See POLYCYSTIC OVARIAN SYNDROME.

STERILITY   Inability to conceive, usually on a permanent basis; infertility.

STERILIZATION   A procedure to render an individual permanently sterile or unable to reproduce.

SUPPOSITORY (also called PESSARY)   Medication, usually cone or bullet shaped, which is inserted into a body cavity such as the vagina urethra or rectum.

SYMPHYSIS PUBIS   That portion of the pubic bone that directly underlies the mons veneris in women.

SYMPTOM   A sign or indication of an infection, disease or other abnormal process which is experienced by the individual.

SYNDROME   A collection of signs and symptoms occurring together with sufficient frequency so as to constitute a specific medical condition.

SYNTHETIC DRUG   A man-made medication as opposed to a naturally occurring compound.

SYPHILIS   Venereal disease transmitted by the spirochete *Treponema pallidum*; 'the pox'.

SYSTEMIC   Involving the entire body; not localized.

TAMPON   A plug of cotton or other material worn in the vagina for the purpose of absorbing blood and cellular debris during menstruation.

TESTICLES (TESTES) Male gonads which produce sperm and testosterone.

TESTERONE The male sex hormone responsible for male sexual characteristics.

THERMOGRAPHY A diagnostic procedure to detect cancerous breast tumours by measuring temperature differences within the breast tissue.

THROMBOEMBOLIC DISEASE A condition in which blood clots or other undissolved material in the bloodstream travel to and partially or completely block distant blood vessels.

THROMBOPHLEBITIS A blood clot with associated inflammation of the vein in which it lodges.

THROMBUS A plug or blood clot that partially or completely blocks a blood vessel.

TIPPED UTERUS A uterus that is partially or completely tilted back toward the rectum. See RETROFLEXED and RETROVERTED UTERUS.

TRACT A long passageway; for example, the digestive, urinary and genital tracts.

TRAUMA Tissue injury, or wound from any cause.

TREPONEMA PALLIDUM The microorganism (spirochete) responsible for syphilis.

TRICHOMONAS VAGINALIS The protozoan organism responsible for the common vaginal infection trichomonas vaginitis (trich.)

TUBAL LIGATION A surgical method of female sterilization in which the Fallopian tubes are interrupted, thus preventing the egg and sperm from meeting.

TUBOPLASTY Plastic and reconstructive surgery of a Fallopian tube to restore normal function.

URETERS The two tubes that drain urine from the kidneys to the bladder.

URETHRA The passageway leading from the urinary bladder to the outside.

URETHRAL MEATUS The opening into the urethra; the opening through which one urinates.

URETHROCELE A prolapse of the urethra into the vagina; a bulging of the urethral wall into the vaginal canal.

UTERINE   Of the womb.

UTERUS   The womb; the hollow muscular organ of reproduction in which the fertilized egg implants and subsequently develops into a baby.

VACCINE   Any substance which, when injected into the body, will immunize or protect an individual against a specific disease or infection.

VAGINA   The birth canal; the genital canal in the female extending from the uterus to the outside.

VAGINAL HYSTERECTOMY   Removal of the uterus through the vagina. Sometimes done in conjunction with vaginal plastic surgery.

VAGINAL PLASTIC SURGERY   Any operation done in the vagina for the purpose of resuspending or resupporting dropped or prolapsed organs such as the urethra, bladder and rectum. Plastic surgery to improve the size and shape of the vagina itself.

VAGINISMUS   Strong involuntary and frequently painful contractions or spasms of the muscles surrounding the lower vagina whenever intercourse is attempted.

VAGINITIS   Any inflammation and/or infection of the vagina.

VAS DEFERENS   The male passageways (from the testicles to the prostatic portion of the urethra) through which sperm travel.

VASECTOMY   Surgical interruption of the vas deferens. Most commonly done as a method of sterilization in the male.

VASO-   Refers to blood vessels.

VASOCONGESTION   An engorgement of blood vessels with blood.

VASODILATION   A widening or dilation of blood vessels to permit more blood to flow through an area or body part.

VASOMOTOR SYMPTOM   A phenomenon occurring as the result of dilation and construction of tiny blood vessels in response to certain nervous impulses; for example, a hot flush is a vasomotor symptom.

VENEREAL DISEASE (VD)   Any infection that is transmitted predominantly by sexual intercourse.

VENEREAL WARTS   See GENITAL WARTS.

VENOUS STASIS   Poor venous circulation through a body part; inadequate or improper emptying of veins resulting in stagnation or pooling of the blood in that area or body part.

VESICLE   A small skin blister usually filled with clear fluid.

VESTIBULE   Portion of the vulva bounded by the labia minora (inner lips) that contains the vaginal and urethral openings.

VIABLE   Capable of surviving.

VIRGIN   A woman who has never had sexual intercourse. (Can also apply to a man who has never had sexual intercourse.)

VIRUS   An infectious agent capable of causing infection, disease or other pathological conditions.

VOLUNTARY MUSCLE   A muscle under conscious control, as opposed to an involuntary muscle, which functions below the level of conscious awareness (such as the heart muscle).

VULVA   The female external genitalia; that portion of the anatomy that lies between the legs.

VULVITIS   Inflammation of the vulva.

VULVOVAGINAL   Referring to the vulva and vagina.

WASSERMANN TEST   A blood test used for the detection of syphilis.

WEDGE RESECTION OF THE OVARIES   Removal of a wedge-shaped piece of tissue from both ovaries usually for the purpose of inducing ovulation.

XEROMAMMOGRAM   Xeroradiography of the breast. A special breast examination, similar to an X-ray, for the detection of abnormal tissue changes or tumours.

YEAST   Fungus-like organism. Sometimes used to describe an infection by the fungus *Candida albicans*.

Index

during sexual stimulation, 197–8, 201, 202, 212–13, 219

postmenopausal changes in, 328, 331

Clomiphene, 241–2; see also Fertility drugs

Coital positions

to enhance conception, 228–9

to increase clitoral stimulation, 199, 202

to minimize pain on deep penile penetration, 207

to snug up over-stretched vagina, 202

Coitus, see Sexual intercourse

Coitus interruptus, 226, 249, 269, 274

Colposcope, 46, 355

Conception; see also Fertility; Infertility

after tubal surgery, 239, 276–8

factors in, 225–40

Conception control, see Contraceptive methods

Condom, 131, 142, 207, 246

as a contraceptive method, 249, 263, 267–8, 274

as protection against cancer of the cervix, 353

as protection against infection, 142, 153, 268

Congenital abnormalities or infections, 157, 271

Congestion, see Pelvic congestion

Constipation, 89, 93, 186

Contact irritants in vulvitis, 131–2

Contraceptive methods, 247–75; see also Birth control; Sterilization

birth-control pills, 249–57; see also Birth-control

cap see diaphragm

coitus interruptus, 226, 249, 269, 274

condom, 131, 142, 153, 207, 246, 249, 263, 267–8, 274, 353

copper IUD, 262

diaphragm, 248–9, 263–7, 274

douching, 163–6, 249, 272–3

during the menopause, 321–2, 331

effectiveness of various, 249

in the future, 274–5, 366

intrauterine device (IUD), 248–9, 257–63, 274

minipill, 249, 256–7

morning after pill, 210, 273

oral contraceptives: see Birth-control pills

rhythm, 249, 269–71

selection of, 248, 274–5

slow release progesterone IUDs (T-shaped plastic device), 262–3

vaginal spermicides (foam, jelly), 131, 153, 247, 249, 265–6, 274

withdrawal, see Coitis interruptus

Corpus luteum, 64–6, 76, 80; see also Ovulation

Corpus luteum cyst of ovary, 66, 310

Crabs, 129–31

Cramps, see Dysmenorrhoea

Crash diets, effect on menstruation, 116

Culture, 45, 140, 151, 174–5, 209

in bladder infections, 174–5

definition of, 140

in gonorrhoea, 45, 151, 209

Cunnilingus, 135, 138, 144, 158, 215, 216

Cysts

of the Bartholin's gland, 43

of the breast, 337–9

of the cervix, 299, 301

of the ovary, 66, 299, 311–12

in endometriosis, 66, 299, 309–12

due to fertility drugs, 243

in polycystic ovarian syndrome, 112–13

sebaceous, 20

Tranquillizers, 94, 330
Transplants, *see* Organ transplants
    in the future
Treponema pallidum, *see* Syphilis
Trichomonas vaginalis, 134–7, 142–
    3, 164, 216; *see also* Vaginal
    infections
  mode of infection, 135–6, 216
  prevention of, 142, 164
  symptoms of, 134
  treatment of, 136–7, 143
T-shaped plastic device, 262–3
Tubal infection, 48, 147–9, 237; *see
    also* Gonorrhoea
Tubal ligation, 32–3, 276–8, 294;
    see also Sterilization
Tubal pregnancy, 48, 239
Tuberculosis of Fallopian tubes, 237
Tubes, *see* Fallopian tubes
Tuboplasty, 239–40, 281
Tumours, *see* Fibroid tumours of
    uterus; Labour and fibroid
    tumours; Menopause, effect
    on; Uterus, tumours of
Turner's syndrome, 82–4
Twins, 243
  fraternal, 81–2
  identical, 81

Urethra, 171
  and gonorrhoea, 146, 151
  location of, in self-examination,
    21–2
  and oestrogen deficiency, 174
  sagging of, 177, 179, 181–3; *see
    also* Pelvic organ relaxation
  suspension operations, 177
  trauma to, during intercourse,
    171, 173, 206, 328
Urethrocele, 177, 182–3
Urinalysis, in bladder infections,
    174–5
Urinary control, factors in, 176–7
Urinary infections, 170–76 *passim*,
    185, 218

Urination, painful
  after sexual intercourse, 173, 206,
    328
  due to bladder infection, 173, 183–
    4
  due to genital herpes, 159–60
  due to gonorrhoea, 146, 173
  due to oestrogen deficiency, 174
  due to vulvovaginal infections,
    137, 173
Urine
  blood in, 173
  culture, 174–5
  examination of, in bladder infec-
    tion, 175
  method of collecting specimen,
    175
  and stress incontinence, 176–7,
    183
    causes of, 177, 183
    corrective exercises in, 177–
    81
    corrective surgery in, 177, 184,
    188
    definition of, 176
  and urge incontinence, 184; *see
    also* Cystocele
Uterine cancer, *see* Cancer, of
    uterus
Uterine cavity; *see also* Uterus
  aspiration of, as screening test for
    cancer, 359
  curettage of, *see* Dilatation and
    curettage
  description of, 29–30
  infection of, 165
  polyps of, 123, 358
  X-ray examination of, *see* Hystero-
    salpingogram
Uterine lining, *see* Endometrial tis-
    sue; Endometrium
Uterus, 26–30; *see also* Uterine
    cavity
  adenomyosis of, 123–4
  anteflexed, definition of, 28

More about Penguins and Pelicans

MAN'S WORLD, WOMAN'S PLACE

Elizabeth Janeway

Taking the myth that 'a woman's place is in the home', Elizabeth
Janeway explores the historical, environmental and emotional influences
that have engendered this attitude. In doing so, she sounds a welcome note
of perceptive commonsense above the hubbub of 'women's lib'.

THE RIGHTS AND WRONGS OF WOMEN

Edited and Introduced by Juliet Mitchell and Ann Oakley

Are the rights of women any more recognized today than they ever were,
and are their wrongs any less? The authors of this book – historians,
sociologists, educationalists and literary critics – have, from many different
political positions, set out to answer the question. Their contributions
show that the world has changed but that the relative position of women
in it has not. They show that from the days of Mary Wollstonecraft's
struggles, through to the work of Harriet Martineau and Simone de
Beauvoir, little or nothing has happened. In education, work, even in the
clearly female province of childbearing, male attitudes, male controls and
male structures still rule the roost.

HOUSEWIFE

Ann Oakley

'In an interesting, carefully researched and well-written study, Ann Oakley
traces the historical development of the housewife role, examines the
present-day situation of women as housewives, not only in terms of how
society sees them, but more importantly, how they see themselves, an
analysis dramatically illustrated by four case histories' – *Hibernia*

THE EXPERIENCE OF CHILDBIRTH
Sheila Kitzinger

The Experience of Childbirth is written by a sociologist and ante-natal teacher – herself the mother of five children – as a complete manual of physical and emotional preparation for the expectant mother.

This fourth edition contains much new material. Mrs Kitzinger has expanded her section on sex during pregnancy, compiled a list of suggestions about what to take to hospital in your 'Labour kit' and explained modern obstetrical procedures and the drugs that go with them in more detail, with greater emphasis on the variations of rhythm in the second stage of labour.

NATUREBIRTH
Danaë Brook

A complete guide to pregnancy now, in which Danaë Brook shows parents how to use the benefits of modern medicine without losing the emotional depths of this natural miracle.

In part one, she looks at parents' rights; the difference between hospital and home deliveries; the use of drugs and machines; various kinds of natural birth; the role of men and women during pregnancy and labour; treatment of and attitudes to the newborn.

Part two is a lively practical guide which covers physiology and psychology, every aspect of preparation for birth, labour itself, the physical and mental wellbeing of the mother-to-be and newborn child.

BABYHOOD
Penelope Leach

This is not just another 'baby book'. Instead of handing out advice it gives facts – the hows and whys of infant development as far as they are understood; the pros and cons of different kinds of child-rearing as far as they have been studied.

Penelope Leach presents, not her own opinions, but an account of the best available information about how babies *are* handled and how they react. Discerning parents will find this compendium of fact invaluable in making their demanding job more interesting and satisfying. Concerned professionals too – student doctors, nurses, social workers and playgroup leaders – will welcome Dr Leach's unique and accessibly written distillation of the mountain of recent research which is expanding our understanding of small children.